HEART Restoration Project

OTHER TITLES BY BETH MERLIN AND DANIELLE MODAFFERI

The Last Phone Booth in Manhattan

Breakup Boot Camp

The Campfire Series

One S'more Summer

S'more to Lose

Love You S'more

Tell Me S'more

HEART
Restoration Project

BETH MERLIN
DANIELLE MODAFFERI

This is a work of fiction. Names, characters, organizations, places, events, and incidents are either products of the author's imagination or are used fictitiously. Otherwise, any resemblance to actual persons, living or dead, is purely coincidental.

Published by Montlake, Seattle

www.apub.com

ISBN-13: 9781662522239 (paperback)
ISBN-13: 9781662522246 (digital)

Cover design by Caroline Teagle Johnson
Cover image: © blossomstar / Shutterstock; © Atorri / Shutterstock;
© Yoko Design / Shutterstock

Printed in the United States of America

Les arbres tardifs sont ceux qui portent les meilleurs fruits.

The trees that are slow to grow bear the best fruit.

—*Molière*

Chapter One

The long-running and much-celebrated director of the reality show *Celebrity Ballroom*, Wes Duncan, poked his head around the dressing room door. "Plum, fifteen until showtime. How are you feeling? Pumped?"

I opened my mouth to answer (not exactly sure how to respond), but thankfully I didn't have to since Wes barreled on anyway. "Tonight, I need you to be bouncy, bubbly, effervescent—the girl America fell in love with on *EVERLYday*. Ready to give them that thousand-watt smile?"

No, I was not, in fact, ready. Far from it. My hair was still up in curlers while my stomach was tied up in knots. I could not, *would not*, vomit on live TV. If I'd somehow managed not to toss my cookies when I ate goat eyeballs as a contestant on *Guts or Glory Extreme Edition*, then there was absolutely no way I was letting a little two-step take me down. I focused on inhaling deeply and slowly through my nose and exhaling through my overlined and well-glossed lips.

Farrah Littman, the showrunner, squeezed past Wes, who was still lingering in the doorway, and gave a soft knock.

"Hey, girl," she called from behind her clipboard. "You look sensational. For tonight, I need you to really lean in to that sex appeal. We're planning on a lot of great close-up shots of you and Viktor, so it'd be good if you could pretend to actually like him."

"I *do* actually like him."

She looked up from her papers. "You do? Hmm . . . well, then let's make sure it's oozing out of you, okay? I want to see sensuality, passion, fire . . . like a deep carnal desire for one another . . ."

Wes cleared his throat. "I can't imagine it'll be too hard for you. For one, Viktor is gorgeous and is just dripping in sex appeal. And two . . . well"—he leaned in a little closer, as if everyone in the room wasn't already aware of the sex tape of me and my ex that was leaked out to the press a little over a year ago—"we all know how you can really make a splash when it comes to showcasing carnal desire on camera."

He'd meant it as a playful jab, but the remark packed a Mike Tyson–size wallop that practically knocked the wind out of me. It was one thing for the world to have been privy to what I believed was supposed to be a private and intimate moment between me and my ex-boyfriend Rhys, but quite another for that experience to now read as an actual credential on my résumé.

I wasn't sure if it was Wes mentioning that godforsaken tape, the mounting pressure of filming the show's biggest episode yet, or the thirty or so instructions that'd just been hurled at me in the last five minutes, but my head was racing just as fast as my heart was pounding. How the hell was I supposed to be bouncy and effervescent *aaaannn-nddd* sultry and seductive at the same time?!

Harley Quinn, the famed comic book antihero with red and blue pigtails and a maniacal grin, was the only image I could come up with, and I was almost certain that wasn't what they had in mind. I guess I had no choice but to figure it out. After all, that's what I was getting paid for, wasn't it? To be whoever the producers wanted me to be once the cameras started rolling.

I'd been doing it my whole life, jumping from one reality show to another: *EVERLYday*, *Guts and Glory Extreme Edition*, *Spelunking with the Stars*, *Love Lagoon*, *The Great Bake Off—Microwaves Only*, just to name a few from my hit list. This was simply another day, another persona, and I was ready to transform into whatever character they needed me to be.

Wes and Farrah left to make space for my glam squad, who were champing at the bit to finish getting me ready. Gabby, the makeup artist, came charging into the dressing room to mist setting spray on my face while Desi, the show's hairstylist, tugged out the last of the rollers from the top of my head. Thankfully, having been on TV from about the age of about eleven onward, this constant whirlwind of showrunners and glam squad members whizzing about felt normal. The chaos barely even fazed me anymore, the blurs zipping by sometimes barely registering as people at all. Just turbulence . . .

Desi spun me around in the chair as he began to tease the roots of my hair before pulling it up into a clever updo, meant to be easily unfastened in the middle of the number. "Are you nervous? Don't be. You've got it in the bag. What are you and Viktor dancing again?"

I sighed. "A paso doble."

He gasped.

The dreaded doble. A dance that required not only precise footwork but a rock-solid core and a commanding-enough presence to effectively convey the story and emotions of the music. Viktor and I completely botched it during week five of the competition.

Desi raised his eyebrows and slowly nodded. "Isn't that the same one that gave you two trouble earlier in the season?"

I mustered a forced smile. "Viktor and I thought it would be a good comeback story if we manage to nail it this time."

"Pucker your lips out like this," Gabby directed. "Perfect, a little goes a long way under the set lights. And close your eyes . . ." She raised the spray bottle in front of my face, and I quickly did as commanded. "One more coat," she said, then proceeded to spritz me with so much sealant, I was worried I might need a chisel to get the makeup off at the end of the night. For some reason, it seemed a bit excessive, but maybe Gabby could see how much more I was sweating this week than usual?

When she finished, I leaned toward the mirror to take in the whole look. The transformation, as always, was beyond impressive. The Regency-style updo, soft with wispy tendrils, paired so well with the stunning period costume. The rich, billowing scarlet fabric of its tufted bustle contrasted with the narrow curve of my waist and conveniently emphasized my ample chest. But for as gorgeous as it was and they made me look, I wasn't sure how I was supposed to dance, let alone kill it out there, when all I could focus on was the sharp poke of the bone corset digging firmly into my sides, causing me to wince.

"You need some help getting to the stage?" Desi asked, probably after catching me awkwardly adjusting the ribbing so that the hard edge wasn't causing me to lose my breath.

"I think I'm okay. I'll shuffle there if I have to," I joked, slapping on my game face. It was a move I had mastered over the years.

"How are you supposed to paso doble in that dress if you can't even walk in it?" Gabby asked.

"Our dance is an homage to *Bridgerton*. Viktor's playing the Duke of Hastings, and I'm playing Daphne. So really, I'm only in the dress for about fifteen seconds before he rips it off to reveal the much sexier costume underneath."

"How naughty," Desi purred.

"Right?" I answered with a curved brow.

"Knock, knock," said a singsongy voice at the door. Nancy, my longtime agent, joined us in the already way-too-crowded dressing room. "How are we *feeeeelinggggg*?"

The tornado of prep spiraled to a gentle gust as Desi tucked a few more bobby pins into my hair, gave me a good-luck kiss on the cheek, and ducked out of the dressing room, followed closely by Gabby, leaving only me and Nancy behind. I relished the momentary silence before I answered. Examining my reflection in the brightly lit mirror, I stared down at the girl now looking back at me and took in a deep lungful of air, the room a little less stifling now that everyone'd cleared out.

Nancy scooted closer and raised her voice, snapping me out of my momentary daze. "I saw your family seated in the audience. That'll be good for ratings." She waggled her eyebrows up and down and smirked. "No Rhys, though?" She pouted out her bottom lip in disappointment.

No matter how many times I told Nancy that Rhys and I were broken up, she still seemed surprised when he wasn't around, probably because he always had been. Rhys (back when he went by the name Brian Braunpheiffer) and I met as freshmen in high school. He was handsome but totally unaware of his good looks, funny, sweet, and best of all he was more into Dungeons & Dragons than TV and popularity. He didn't even watch *EVERLYday* and was pretty unfazed by me and my famous family.

We were initially paired up as lab partners during our freshman chemistry class, where our friendship began to blossom amid the bubbling beakers and humming Bunsen burners in the dimly lit classroom. Rhys and I didn't just share notes; we exchanged secrets, jokes, and our aspirations. In a world where everyone saw me on the screen, he was the only one genuinely interested in getting to know the real me. Our connection went beyond the spotlight, but eventually, it began to erode. Like everyone else in my life, he got entangled in the machinery of fame. He took on a recurring role on *EVERLYday*, portraying my loving boyfriend, rebranded as Rhys Braun from Brian Braunpheiffer, now a celebrity in his own right. That's when things started to unravel, culminating in a highly publicized breakup last year, caught, of course, by none other than TMZ.

Nancy continued, "So I just got off the phone with the folks at Lululemon, and if you win, they're prepared to do a full rollout of a Plum Everly athleisure wear line in the fall. Isn't that fantastic?"

It would be fantastic, especially considering my current financial situation, which I think anyone could safely call dire. It seemed no matter how many reality shows I landed, between my agent, manager, publicist, and lawyer's fees, I was still barely scraping by. "And if I don't win?"

Nancy tilted her head and sighed. "If you don't win, well, I'm not sure we can count on any of the endorsement deals coming through."

"No pressure or anything," I scoffed.

"Oh God, no! The last thing I wanted to do was come back here and stress you out. I was hoping to use this all as fuel to amp you up. But don't worry about any of that now. Just focus on that paso doble."

My head shot up. "How did *you* know we were doing a paso doble?"

Her overly fillered cheeks grew even tighter when she sassily pursed her lips. "Honey, after that disaster a few weeks ago, of course you and Viktor need to redeem yourselves."

Dammit, is this corset growing tighter? I'm not even dancing yet!

I could barely inhale a full breath, and small spots started to float like gnats in the beams of the vanity lights.

"Five minutes till showtime, five minutes till showtime," a voice bellowed over the stage's intercom.

I squinted my eyes, willing them like hell to adjust, as I hoisted myself up out of the chair. Wiggling fiercely against the bone ribbing, I tried everything I could to loosen the corset before I put on my brave face and sucked it up like the trained seal I was.

"I should really get going. Viktor likes to give me a pep talk before we perform."

"Well, darling, break a leg." Nancy gave me a quick kiss on each sweat-moistened cheek and a squeeze on the shoulder.

"Viktor told me dancers don't tell each other to 'break a leg,' it's bad luck. Instead, they say merde."

"Merde?" Her eyes darted back and forth as she tried to decipher the meaning. "I don't know that expression."

"It's French. I think it roughly translates to the word *shit*."

"Dancers wish each other *shit* before going out onstage?!" Nancy leaned in closer and wore the face of someone who was certain she'd grossly misheard something there.

"According to Viktor, back in the day, the patrons of the Paris Opera Ballet would arrive at the Palais Garnier in horse-drawn carriages. If there was a full house, there was sure to be a lot of horse manure in front of the theater. Saying merde became a way to tell your fellow dancers to have a good show for the packed audience."

"Well, merde right backatcha, then. See you after the show."

Chapter Two

I followed Nancy out of the dressing room, sauntering behind her with the swagger and confidence of a woman who wasn't currently being stabbed to death by her own costume. At the sound of the show's opening theme song echoing through the proscenium, Nancy hurried to join the rest of the studio audience, and I headed to the stage. Viktor was waiting for me in the reception area just off to the side of the cameras. He looked me up and down, nodding in enthusiastic approval, and gave me his usual greeting. "Moya vozlyublennaya." *My sweetheart*, in Russian. "You warmed up?"

I nodded and looked down to my feet. "My flamenco taps are still a quarter second off the beat."

Viktor grabbed me by the waist and pulled me closer, so we were eye to eye. He sucked in his core and straightened out his shoulders. "Plum, what have I told you about the paso doble? It is a sensual dance modeled after the drama of the Spanish bullfight," he breathed. "It is a theatrical dance of role-play. Forget about your flamenco taps. Tonight, I am the matador, the Duke of Hastings, and you are Daphne, the seductive cape. As long as you stay right here," he said, pointing at his face, "with me, right here, we will get through the dance. Merde?"

"Merde," I repeated. Shit was right! Now I was supposed to be not only bouncy and seductive but also Daphne *and* the matador? No, wait. Was I the bull or the cape?! Merde, merde, merde!

The studio lights dimmed, but I could still make them all out, the beautiful Everly girls—all distinctly different yet undeniably sisters with their iconic beach-blonde tresses, year-round sun-kissed skin, and effortless no-makeup makeup looks—seated second row center, directly in view of all the cameras. Lemon, my oldest sister, was on the aisle, followed by Kiwi, Pear, and Peach. Having just turned twenty-eight, I was the youngest Everly by about three years, and the only child not currently employed by our family's famous wellness-and-lifestyle brand. I wondered what kind of promotional placement *Celebrity Ballroom* had promised in order to get all my sisters to appear at the finale.

The sight of all of them perfectly coiffed and styled to the nines sent my heart into palpitations. I couldn't remember the last time they all showed up for any of my gigs, although in fairness, nobody besides the cast and crew was ever allowed in the *Star Spy House* houses, and *Celebrity Spelunking* required way too many waivers. Whatever the reason, my mind was racing, and I momentarily lost focus on the paso doble, Viktor, and the enormous stakes of the night.

After what may have been a solid fifteen seconds of Viktor frantically waving in my direction, he finally caught my eye and motioned for me to hurry into place for the start of the performance. I shifted my corset and froze in position. Suddenly, the haunting first notes of the song soared out from the orchestra, and just like that, we were off and running.

Viktor, embodying his role as the imposing matador, puffed out his chest wide and wrenched his shoulders back. Stepping into the spotlight in the center of the dance floor, he extended his right foot out ahead of the rest of his body and then popped onto the balls of his feet to shuffle forward in a frantic eight-step. He repeated a series of cape-like moves, tiptoeing in a tight, counterclockwise circle and finishing off the last beats with a few seductive strides in my direction to close the gap between us.

In the final rotation, he was *supposed* to rip the Regency-era gown from my body, revealing the sexy outfit underneath, but the snap that should've burst wide open barely budged. Terror shot through my body like a bolt. There was no way I could do the entire paso doble in a heavy taffeta ball gown.

Running through my mind was Wes's urging to be bouncy and effervescent, followed by Farrah's instruction to be sexy and sultry. I waved my arms around like a circus clown to highlight the obvious wardrobe malfunction before planting a smoldering look of lusty seduction on my face and ripping the dress from my body, tugging and tearing at every button, every seam, until it started to shed like a second skin. I must have looked absolutely ridiculous.

The breath held in by the tight corset finally released as the costume hit the ground, and I was left posing in the sexy skintight unitard the same wine color the dress had been—doing my best to act like the blunder had been planned all along. However, Viktor didn't sell the gaffe quite as well. He just stood there, horror-struck, his face twisting between panic and a somewhat futile attempt to stay in character, and waited for me to untangle my high heels from the discarded ball gown at my feet so I could rejoin the dance count. But it was too late, the damage was already done. We were so far off the beat, we couldn't possibly catch up. Viktor did his best to guide me, at one point even counting the steps out loud, but it was no use. I was completely lost, and so was he.

After a brutal round of judging, we were ushered to the post-dance interview where the show's host, famed ballroom dancer Vanessa Fairview, was waiting for us.

"Viktor? Plum? What happened out there?" she asked, pushing the microphone into both our faces.

Viktor grunted something in Russian that I was grateful I couldn't understand.

"We saw you struggling with the gown," Vanessa said sympathetically. "What was going through your mind at that exact moment?"

What was going through my mind? I was thinking about all the endorsement and promotional deals guaranteed to the winner of

Celebrity Ballroom going straight down the drain. I didn't just want to win—I needed to win the title and all that came with it.

"What was going through my mind?" I repeated. She nodded like one of those bobblehead dolls sold at novelty stores. "I knew I needed to get the dress off if we were going to have even a fighting chance."

"You and Viktor came into tonight as the front-runners. Now, it would take a miracle for you two to claim victory," she said.

Was there a question somewhere in there? Vanessa pushed the microphone closer to me. Question or not, she expected some sort of a response.

Viktor put his arm around me and offered a reassuring squeeze. "Plum did her best. Right, moya vozlyublennaya?"

Hot tears sprang to my eyes. This wasn't the first time I'd made a fool of myself on reality TV, but it *was* the first time I'd dragged someone else down with me.

Vanessa moistened her lips and asked her final question. "I couldn't help but notice your sisters in the audience. How did it feel to have them all here cheering you on tonight?"

At the mention of my family, another wave of mortification almost pummeled me off balance, and my stomach sank again. Another humiliating reminder I didn't inherit the Everly perfection gene. I forced a smile back on my face.

"Yes, it's wonderful to have their support, always," I answered.

Vanessa grinned and motioned to the cameraman that she got everything she needed and we could clear out. The grips were scurrying around us to reset the stage for the next pair of dancers. I glanced out into the audience to look for my sisters, but they were already gone.

Chapter Three

Nancy was on a call when I walked into her office about a week after the *Celebrity Ballroom* finale aired. She held up a finger and motioned for me to take a seat while she wrapped up her conversation. As she finished up, I slid my trench off my shoulders, draped it over the back of the chair, and took a seat across from her.

"Darling, it will be fabulous, and the ten weeks will fly by, trust me. Okay, call me when you're back from Sydney, love, and good luck." She hung up the phone, turned to me, and lowered her voice. "Hugh finally agreed to do *Star Spy House, Australia*. Can you believe it?"

I racked my brain. "Hugh? Hugh Jackman?"

She waved her hand in the air. "Doesn't matter. Anyway, how are you, darling? You look good, considering . . ."

"Considering what? That I'm a GIF now," I said, holding up my phone to show her a boomerang clip of me struggling to rip off the Regency ball gown. The video went viral mere minutes after the *Celebrity Ballroom* finale aired.

"Viral can be good—great, even. Viral gets you other gigs," Nancy said.

I slid back in my seat. "That's why I'm here. What's next? What've you got for me?"

She rolled her desk chair forward and lowered her voice. "I should have prefaced, viral gets you other gigs when you're a new sensation, and darling, you've been doing reality television longer than I've been an agent."

"*EVERLYday* doesn't count. I was eleven when the show started. So, c'mon, what's next? What fantastic opportunity to make a fool of myself on the national stage do you have waiting for me in your inbox?"

Nancy, completely oblivious to my sarcasm, swiveled her chair back around and popped open her laptop. "Like I told you before we got the offer for *Celebrity Ballroom*, the opportunities have been few and far between. That show was a gift." Leaning in to her computer and sliding her readers farther up on her nose with a rigid finger, she continued to read down her screen. "Let's see, there's that celebrity psychic show we talked about a few months back, but unless you've had a parent, sibling, spouse, or pet die recently, they're not interested. Hmm . . . what about the *Masked Painter* show? That sounded interesting. Nope, never mind, the network's decided not to move ahead with it." She looked up. "Can't imagine why. The Food Network's got to have something. They always have something. *Buuuut*, as we also discussed before, with Pear's new whole food, plant-based cooking show set to debut next month, they aren't interested in another Everly in the kitchen right now."

I shifted uncomfortably, mustering the bravado needed to tackle this next bit. Leaning in, I lowered my voice and struggled to keep it from breaking. "Nancy, the truth is, I don't want to compete for anything. I don't want to be the Real Housewife of anything. I don't want a makeover or a makeunder, and I'm pretty sure my joints can't take another *Wipeout*-style obstacle course. I cannot do another show where I'm the butt of the joke. I'm pathetic. I'm a twenty-eight-year-old washed-up reality star." I swallowed back my tears and managed to keep my face even, in spite of the humiliation I felt speaking those words aloud.

She sat back from her computer and folded her hands in her lap. Nancy was all business, and her discomfort with these kinds of emotional conversations was more than obvious. "Look, we were both banking on you winning *Celebrity Ballroom* and capitalizing on that for a while, so I didn't bother mentioning this one other project that was pitched to me a few weeks back. Have you ever heard of Tributary?"

"Um . . . they're that new streaming service, right?"

"They have that one show about zombies set in ancient Egypt with Jon Hamm, *Mummy Mayhem*, that's been getting some buzz. Anyway, their head of reality TV development, Kate Wembley, is incredibly hungry and apparently ready to make a name for herself after working for a number of seasons on that big *Top Designer* show. I just heard she got the green light for a passion project of hers about small villages in France that are selling dilapidated châteaus for one euro in the hope of infusing some new life into these old homes."

"Really?! What kind of property could you possibly get for one euro?" I was simultaneously shocked and intrigued. With my paltry bank account lately, I was actually curious. *What kind of property could I got for one euro?!*

Nancy turned the computer to face me. "Here, she included a few photos in the abstract. Voilà, Château Mirabelle," she said in an overly affected French accent.

I looked at the photos, realizing that while the estate was clearly impressive, it was in a *very* noticeable state of disrepair. This wasn't a little project, this was an overhaul. I thought of my last DIY project, when I attempted to wallpaper my bathroom. I forgot to account for the wall's electrical outlets. I ended up having to cut around them, resulting in horribly jagged and uneven edges that made it look like a kindergarten art project gone wrong. "Oh, it's very charming, but I don't know the first thing about home restoration or construction."

"Hmm . . ." Nancy scrolled through the abstract and shifted her readers again. "It says here they've hired a local contractor and small design team to assist the talent." She glanced up from the screen. "Kate's been pretty relentless. She seems very keen to get you attached to the project. But I won't lie to you. It's rather small potatoes, Plum. The production company will cover your expenses while filming—room, meals, blah, blah, blah—they can't actually *pay* you, which is another reason why I didn't mention it earlier. *Buuut,*" she said, skimming through the prospectus, "it does say that you would own the house outright at the end of the renovation. So I suppose you could keep the property or sell it."

"Where's it being filmed? What part of France?"

She adjusted her reading glasses again and inched closer to the screen. "Maubec, a small village in the Provence-Alpes-Côte d'Azur region in southeastern France, near Avignon. It says that filming runs from June through August."

"I don't know. This one sounds like too big of a stretch, even for me."

Nancy sighed, glimpsed the gold watch around her wrist for the time, and rose from her chair as if to suggest that this meeting had fizzled to its end, apparently much like my career. "Listen, hon, I'm gonna be frank with you, your options are limited. But c'mon, it's Paris in the springtime! That's gotta be a draw, no?" Nancy continued to bustle around her desk until she made her way behind me.

I craned my neck to look at her and asked, "I thought you said it was taping in Provence . . . in June?"

Nancy yanked my coat out from under my back, practically catapulting me out of the chair. She didn't miss a beat as she cooed, "Paris, Provence. Springtime, summer? Does it even matter?! I mean, it's all magnifique, no? At the very least, I think you should take a meeting with Kate. See what she has to say."

With a guiding hand crooked around my elbow, Nancy walked me out of her office and offered a supportive pat on the shoulder (or shove out to the elevator bank, I kinda couldn't tell).

"Nancy, I only know like five French words, and *merde* is one of them," I protested.

"Then, darling, you'll be just fine," she offered before turning on her heel and snapping the door closed behind her.

Chapter Four

When I left Nancy's office, I was so distracted by the racing thoughts fighting for my attention in my head that I almost ran a red light, the sound of a right-turning Range Rover blaring its horn startling me from my daze. I quickly wrenched my car into a gas station to pull myself together. With my heart still pounding and the car horn still echoing in my ears, I threw the gearshift into park and braced my arms on the steering wheel, my heaving chest still rising and falling in rapid succession.

France? There was no reason I technically couldn't go, but what did I know about *anything* over there? Aside from the being on TV part, I knew squat about France and even less about fixing anything. But . . . whether I wanted to admit it or not (or more like face it or not), maybe it was just the thing I needed to do in order to get myself off this path to nowhere.

My eyes flashed to the clock on my dashboard, and I sighed. If I didn't get back on the road, I was going to be late to meet Rhys. I backed out of my spot, pulled out of the gas station with a bit more focus on the road, and zoomed to the Ivy on North Robertson Boulevard, rolling up to the valet at precisely 12:30 p.m. Rhys had texted earlier in the week asking if he could take me to lunch, an attempt to cheer me up after the disastrous *Celebrity Ballroom* finale. I agreed. Though we were broken up and had been for almost a year, he was still a very important (and at times, though I'm embarrassed to admit it, influential) person in my life.

For as posh as the Ivy was, with its high-profile celebrity clientele and award-winning design and decor, I'd sorta wished that he'd asked me to meet him at Lucinda's, a stupid little hole-in-the-wall outside the LA city limits. Back when *EVERLYday* was airing and I was desperate to flee the barrage of cameras in the house, Brian (he went by his legal name back before the producers encouraged him to change it) and I would meet at Lucinda's Hacienda, away from the flashes of the paparazzi, away from the chaos of the Everly whirlwind, and just enjoy being a regular couple.

We'd snack on chips and salsa and greasy gorditas and talk about anything and everything that wasn't related to the show. And for just a little while . . . every so often . . . I felt normal again. I'd carry that feeling back to the house, and it would keep me grounded until the next time we could meet back up in our secret hideaway to recharge.

Brian and his nuclear family were just about the most ordinary people I'd ever met, which I know may not seem like such a feat, but living in Hollywood it was more than just a strange occurrence, it was like a goddamned alien sighting. And not gonna lie, back then I was ready for the Braunpheiffers to beam me the hell up and out of my house, which was becoming more of a circus with each passing year. *EVERLYday*, having started out as the smallest nugget of an idea, quickly spiraled into a cultural phenomenon none of us, especially my parents, could have ever seen coming.

Mom and Dad, self-proclaimed hippies, had dreamed of giving their five daughters a wholesome California upbringing, complete with farm-to-table meals and homemade beauty products long before either was particularly trendy. They started out selling their high-quality, homegrown organic products at farmers markets, specialty shops, and boutiques. Eventually, they opened a small store in downtown Santa Barbara called EVERLYthing and stocked it with Everly-brand recipe books, beauty and skin care products, candles, wine, home decor, and fabrics. The shop was popular with locals and the occasional tourist but didn't have much of a reach beyond Santa Barbara, that was until Oprah Winfrey decided to pay the store a visit.

Legend has it, on a recommendation from her aesthetician, Oprah stopped into EVERLYthing and fell in love with not just the unique products but also my unique parents. She invited our entire family to appear on a segment of "Oprah's Favorite Things," where she touted my parents' lifestyle brand and holistic approach to raising children. It wasn't long after that appearance that the E! network made an offer for our family to star in a brand-new reality television show.

It was the early days of reality TV, before anyone realized just how powerful a medium it would become. My parents reluctantly agreed, figuring the show would last a season (maybe two?) and, while it was on, would help drum up some publicity for their growing brand. Within the first few months of airing, *EVERLYday* became the number one show on cable television. People quickly became obsessed with Mom's natural aesthetic, clean living, vegetable garden, and tablescapes. They fell in love with Dad's sense of humor, knowledge of wine, and furniture making. Most of all, the audience became enraptured with me and my four sisters, our fruit-inspired names and teenage antics bringing viewers back week after week for over a decade.

"So, Plum," a hearty paparazzo called me back into the present, "when are we getting another sex tape? That first one was hot, but I think you've got more in you!"

"Or *could* have more in you, sweetheart!" an unidentified male voice added from the crowd of cameras. Sniggers and jeers tittered like the skittering of cockroaches.

My heart leaped into my throat, and it took everything in me to keep my pearly smile plastered to my face. The fat and slightly balding character known as "Brazen Brick" was always on the scene, equipped with vile one-liners and heart-stopping questions aimed to pull the usually composed celebs off their game and out of their stride.

"Oh, Brick, haven't you found a new bone to chase?"

"Haven't you?" he bit back. Another surge of laughter from the crowd.

I drew in a deep breath and turned back toward the sea of photographers. "Didn't your mother ever teach you that if you don't have anything nice to say, you should keep your big mouth shut?"

"My nickname's Brazen Brick, sweet cheeks, what do you think?" he replied, snapping one last flash in my face before I blindly ducked inside.

Upon recognizing me, the hostess motioned for me to follow her out to where I guessed she'd already seated Rhys on the patio. Seemingly straight out of a *Better Homes & Gardens* spread, the Ivy's expansive outdoor-seating area was lusciously decorated with peonies in full bloom, an ornate trellis covered with colorful spring buds, ivy. The earthy fragrance of Spanish moss paired perfectly with the aromas of bright citrus and farm-fresh vegetables wafting from the kitchen. Quaint mismatched tables rounded out the shabby-chic decor.

My eyes locked with Rhys's from across the room, causing my chest to tighten and my stomach to dip. I experienced that same dizzying sensation *every single time* I looked at him. Even after our many ups and downs, both in and out of the public eye, the sight of him threw me off balance just as much as when we first met. He had a knack for always looking impossibly perfect, yet so comfortably cool. Back in the day, back when he was still Brian Braunpheiffer, he was more unassuming about his appeal and the attention that came with it. Rhys Braun, however, was acutely aware of his undeniable good looks and relished every aspect of them.

That wasn't the reason we broke up, but it was certainly an indication of how much he'd transformed over the last couple of years. When we first met, he wanted nothing to do with the spotlight. But then the *EVERLYday* producers seized the opportunity to give me a bigger storyline and wooed Rhys onto the show with a contract large enough to cover his college tuition. They changed his name, his haircut, and his clothes, and by the time the team was through and the show had finally wrapped after its thirteenth season, he was almost unrecognizable to me.

For as much as he delighted in the limelight and attention, like Dr. Frankenstein, I couldn't help but feel a strange mixture of guilt and remorse at the monster I'd helped create. I'd never properly mourned Brian Braunpheiffer, his metamorphosis to Rhys Braun was just that fast. Though, some part of me still held out the smallest glimmer of hope that underneath all that pomade and Botox, the real him was still somewhere in there, and I couldn't help but wonder who he would have become had our paths never crossed.

With *EVERLYday* behind us, we both sought out new ventures, which resulted in spending less and less time together. And even though the relationship was already pretty frayed at that point, I wasn't ready to let it go. So when Rhys tossed out the idea of making a sex tape to reconnect and renew our intimacy, I'd initially been incredibly hesitant for obvious reasons. But then I thought about everything he and I had been through, and all we were at risk of losing, and how much I wanted to be who and what he wanted, and eventually I agreed.

And a few months later, when I'd almost completely forgotten about the tape, a hacker somehow cracked Rhys's files and data, including the private content intended for *his eyes only*, and leaked it out to the media. I fell apart, trying like hell to keep my head held high in spite of the shame and embarrassment I felt. My friends probably saw it. My family knew of it. And everyone in the country, if not the world, was a voyeur to a special moment that had been meant only for him. It took months for me to shake the feeling that everywhere I went, people were picturing me naked.

The irony, though, was that while the sex tape made me infamous, it made Rhys even more famous. He started to get bit parts in shows and movies while I became even more of a joke, a punch line, a cautionary tale. And even though it wasn't his fault, I couldn't help but start to resent the double standard. His star rose as mine began to flicker and fade. We drifted further and further apart until there was no reason to try to hold on any longer, and we broke up.

Standing up from his chair to kiss me on the cheek, he slipped his hand behind my neck and into the roots of my hair, sending sparks of electricity right down to my toes. If just looking at him took my breath away, then his touch completely robbed me of every oxygen molecule in my body.

"Hey, babe, you look fantastic." He pulled out my chair, escorted me to it, and slid it firmly beneath me.

"Do I? I feel like I was just ambushed by a firing squad."

I watched him circle the table to his seat, the crisp whiteness of his shirt sharp against the bright colors of the flowers and vibrant greenery around him.

"What do you mean? Brazen Brick? He's harmless," Rhys said as he unfurled a linen napkin onto his lap.

"Jesus, it's been over a year now. How is our sex tape still front-page news?"

He held up his phone and showed me the same GIF I'd shown Nancy, me frantically trying to essentially tear off my Regency gown on live TV. "I have a feeling this might have a little something to do with it," he answered with a shrug.

"Ugggghhh . . ." I hung my head in my hands.

He turned the phone back to himself and watched the GIF play through its loop a few more times, his face set in a look of approval. "It's really not that bad. You actually looked incredible. Then again, you always do," he offered as consolation, but the comment didn't make me feel any better. "But, if you ask me, you were robbed. It's not your fault the costume didn't come off in time."

"Unfortunately, you know that's not how it works on live TV. You don't get second chances. You get one shot, and I blew mine."

He reached across the table and covered my hand with his. "I still say you were robbed. You were the best damn dancer they had this season. Any season, for that matter."

And this was the side of Rhys I loved. He was firmly in my corner. Always.

"So what's next? What do you have lined up?"

Just as I was about to tell him about the show in France, our server came by to take our orders. I didn't even bother opening the menu; Rhys was already ordering for us both.

"Two Cobb salads and two iced teas. For her salad, no eggs or avocado, and if you could put the dressing on the side. Oh, and we'll take extra ice and lemon in both of the drinks." He looked up at me to confirm. I nodded. It was exactly right.

He handed the server back the menus and leaned in to the table. "So, tell me, what big and exciting project is Plum Everly headed off to next?"

"I met with Nancy this morning. To be honest with you, the well's starting to run a little dry."

"What do you mean?"

"I've been on ten different reality series. I've done *Karaoke Combat*, where I sang off-key renditions of pop classics while dodging foam projectiles being shot from the audience. I survived a competitive baking show where the microwave ovens spontaneously burst into flames. I even managed to come in second place on *Celebrity Zookeepers*."

"Wait, I don't remember that one."

My eyes grew wide. "It's because we don't talk about it. I don't think I will ever go back to a zoo so long as I live."

"I'm sure PETA will be glad to hear it," he joked.

"And you want to know the worst part?"

"Worse than being target practice while belting out 'Total Eclipse of the Heart'?" He laughed. "Sure, lay it on me."

"In not a single one of those shows was I actually able to be myself. I mean, not *really*. I'm always playing a character, a role, whatever version of Plum Everly best fit their narrative. Foam projectiles and flaming ovens aside, nothing about reality TV is real, least of all me."

"What are you even talking about?" He reached for my hands and gave them a squeeze. "You are Plum Everly—the same girl who walked into my freshman chemistry lab and took my breath away. You were real then, and you're real now. And it breaks my heart to think you don't see that."

"No, I'm not. I couldn't be that girl even if I tried. I've been too many other versions of her to even remember what she liked, what she wanted, who she was."

The server came by to deliver our teas. Rhys took a long sip and said, "Look at where you are. Why would you want to go backward? Life is about moving forward and embracing new and exciting opportunities."

"That's what I'm trying to say, Rhys. I'm not being offered new and exciting opportunities. Not anymore. I mean, there is this one thing filming in France that could maybe be—"

He cut me off. "Look, there are always ways to get yourself back into the spotlight, just ask Brazen Brick." His eyebrows bounced suggestively as he thumbed his attention to the entrance where Brick had been staked out earlier.

I blinked hard. "What? What did you just say?"

He rolled his eyes playfully. "What I'm saying is that maybe it's time for us to work on a sequel? You can even direct this one? We can spend a bit more time in editing . . ." His voice trailed off at the end of the sentence in consideration.

My heart plunged like a Marvel superhero in free fall. "So it wasn't a hacker at all? You put it out there, didn't you? You were the one who leaked the tape?" I could barely put the words together to form an actual question.

Rhys pushed his hand through his hair and sat up a little straighter. "I'm . . . I'm sorry, Plum. But really, I did it for you. For us. And let's be honest, whether it was a hacker or it was me, it doesn't change anything."

His words hurt, but his cavalier attitude was a knife in the gut. "Doesn't change *anything*? Rhys, it changes everything. You sold me out." I tried to keep my voice even and low, always aware of the watchful eyes.

"Don't you think you're overreacting a little bit here? How do you not realize I was doing it as a way to break both of us out of the box we'd been put in? You've got to see now how it was the right move for both of our careers."

Tears welled in the corners of my eyes, but I swiped at them before they could fall. "What career? I'm a joke."

He pulled his hands down off the table and tucked them in his lap. "Look, we can still flip the script here. The wardrobe malfunction you had on *Celebrity Ballroom*, well that . . . that can serve as the coming attraction for our little movie. C'mon, you can be Daphne again. I'll play the Duke. It'll be perfect."

I wanted to slap him. Punch him square in the throat. Or shove the tape so far up his ass, he'd be projecting the film out his eyeballs! He clearly had no remorse, and even worse, he was ready to double down. But instead of allowing my emotions to overtake me, I looked over at him . . . doleful and resigned. Who even was this man seated across from me? I didn't recognize him at all. We were a million miles and a thousand versions of ourselves apart since our days in freshman chemistry, and there was no going back. Not from this. Though I'd said goodbye to Brian Braunpheiffer years ago, now I knew without a shadow of a doubt that it was finally time to say goodbye to Rhys Braun for good.

"You can go to hell," I spat, tossing my cloth napkin from my lap onto the table in one fluid motion as I stood.

Rhys jumped up and called after me, but there was no looking back. I hurried out of the Ivy, flipping my ticket to the valet and jumping into my car as soon as it was pulled around. I had barely shifted into drive when I began jabbing at buttons on my steering wheel to activate the familiar ding of my car's automated Bluetooth system.

"Call Nancy on cell," I shouted, pulling out onto North Robertson without signaling and stepping on the gas. "Nancy, I'm in. Go ahead and set up that meeting with Tributary."

Chapter Five

I was grateful when Kate Wembley from Tributary agreed to take the hour-and-a-half drive from LA to Ojai to meet with me at one of my family's most illustrious properties. A little over six years ago, my parents opened the first of what would be many EVERLY Bed-and-Breakfasts, restoring a crumbling ten-thousand-square-foot, fourteen-room Queen Anne Victorian home into a luxurious B and B complete with the eclectic modern touches they were famous for, while also carefully preserving the home's original features. People came from far and wide to spend a weekend immersed in the Everly lifestyle, enjoying the farm-to-table food, wellness classes, and wine tastings.

I finished helping Mom set up the displays of Lemon's new EVERLYbody Matcha Green Tea Powder Enemas and hurried over to the dining room to meet Kate, who was already at a table in the back corner. She waved me over to where she was sitting and sprang out of her seat to greet me as soon as I got closer.

Kate could have easily been mistaken for one of my sisters, and it seemed more than a few people in the dining room thought she was, snapping pics of us on their iPhones. Like the rest of the Everly girls, she was sun-glossed with long blonde hair and big doe eyes. She seemed to embrace the effortless California vibe, wearing a crisp white tee and loose army-green trousers, a denim jacket hanging around her narrow shoulders.

"I have so been looking forward to meeting you," Kate gushed, settling back down into her chair.

A server came by to take our order. "I'll take a green tea," Kate said. "What about you? Same?"

I thought back to the mountain of matcha enemas I just unboxed in the boutique. "Water's great, thank you."

Kate leaned in to the table. "I cannot tell you how thrilled I was when my assistant told me you agreed to take this meeting. We've run through a litany of celebrity names to attach to this project, but I wanted you from the start. Your long-standing relationship with the television audience makes you the perfect lens. At Tributary, we want to elevate the reality TV genre beyond competitions and manufactured wedding proposals. We want to showcase the real you—the you the world hasn't met yet." Kate propped her elbows on the table and rested her chin on her hands. "To put it plainly, we want to give you a voice. Your voice. I mean, who is Plum Everly, anyway? Is she the baby of a wildly successful family? Is she Rhys Braun's ex-girlfriend? Is she a shallow fame whore? You want to know what I think? I think you are so much more than what this effed-up industry has allowed you to be. Let us help you tell your story the way you want to tell it."

Who is Plum Everly? Now, that was a question I wasn't even sure *I* could answer at the moment. Who the hell *was* Plum Everly? I certainly didn't know. But the fact that this was the first time I'd ever heard a show's production team mention any interest in getting to see the real me versus getting me to play the role they cast me in was already a welcomed breath of fresh air. Maybe this was *exactly* the opportunity I needed to put Rhys and the past behind me and figure out who I was and what the hell I wanted once and for all.

The server came by and set down our drinks and two menus on the table. "Can I get you ladies anything else?" he asked. "The carrot ginger soup with curried raisin relish is positively divine."

Kate wrinkled her nose. "I'm more of an In-N-Out Burger kind of gal, if you know what I mean."

"I know exactly what you mean." I motioned for the server to come a bit closer to the table. "Hey, can you ask Frank if he can whip up two Plum Specials?"

The server winked at me. "You got it."

"Plum Specials?" Kate asked.

I lowered my voice so no other patrons could hear me. "I'm not really a fan of the organic, whole grain, dairy-free, vegan fare around these parts. Frank, one of the chefs, keeps some real food on hand for me. I ordered us two burgers with crispy bacon and a side of fries."

"Bless you," she whispered back. "Oh, can we get a glass or two of your house white?" she called out to the waiter.

"Don't do the white," I instructed and turned to him. "We'll take the house red." He nodded and shuffled off. As soon as he was out of earshot, I leaned in to Kate and admitted, "Even though it seems like anything with the EVERLY logo slapped on it is an instant bestseller, the white wine's still a bit of a work in progress. Dad's been interviewing for a new vintner."

Kate and I talked for the next three hours. She told me about how she dreamed of a career in the entertainment industry since she was a little girl in Appleton, Wisconsin. She confessed to watching *EVERLYday* religiously as a kid, even telling her parents she wanted to change her name to Clementine and join our family.

Kate was a few years older than me, closer to Pear's age. After studying filmmaking at the University of Southern California and working her way up the ladder, she started out as Sofia Coppola's personal assistant and eventually stepped out on her own in the cutthroat world of TV and film development. She admitted that joining a no-name network like Tributary was a risky career move but that she was positively determined to make a go of it, knowing that if she did, the opportunities in the entertainment industry would be boundless.

I don't know what it was exactly, maybe her candor, the fact it felt like we had so much more than our similar looks in common, or the two bottles of EVERLY Cabernet we'd polished off, but I found myself opening up to her more than I planned.

"You've got to be shitting me! He leaked it?! So it wasn't a hacker after all . . ." Kate shook her head while tsking in disgust, poured the last of our bottle of Cabernet into my glass, and then nudged the glass closer supportively.

"He claims he did it for us. For both of us. To help ignite our careers and break us out of the perfect Everly mold."

"Well, if that isn't the biggest load of crap I've ever heard. Certainly didn't hurt *his* career, that's for damn sure."

I was surprised when hot tears flooded the corners of my eyes, and I sniffed them back before they could fall. "I . . . I just can't be another joke. This time it has to be different."

Kate reached across the table and covered my hands with her own. "I absolutely understand. Go to Maubec. Do *Heart Restoration Project.* Get away from the noise and the paparazzi flashes and let us capture who you truly are. And the best part of all, you get to write your own ending."

"*Heart Restoration Project*? Is that the name of the show?" I asked, genuinely intrigued.

Kate reached into her tote and placed a copy of the contract on the table. "It's a working title. We're still focus-grouping it. I'm sure it will change. Let me know if you have any ideas?"

For the first time in a long time, I didn't feel like I was being hired *just* for my notoriety or the Everly name. Kate seemed to see something in me beyond the spotlight and family expectations. She believed in my potential, and while there was something new and exciting about that belief, there was also something utterly terrifying about it. What if the "real me" wasn't enough?

I hesitated for a moment, my hand hovering over the contract. "Kate, I appreciate your offer more than I can express," I began, my voice filled with gratitude. "But I need some time to think about it. It's a big decision, and I need to be sure."

Kate smiled warmly. "Of course, take all the time you need. This is about your journey, and I want you to feel completely comfortable. But why don't you hold on to this copy of the contract, have your people look it over. I sent it through DocuSign just before I got here," she said, sliding the documents toward me. "Take as long as you need, we'll wait."

After Kate headed back to LA, I set out through the orchard for the whitewashed barn my father converted into a small winery about three years ago. While all my sisters had their own talent, brand, and passion, this little gem was *his*. Dad had always had an insatiable interest in wine and started to dabble in winemaking before really deciding to launch his little pet project.

He figured the property in Ojai, with its Mediterranean climate offering mild, wet winters and warm, dry summers, was conducive to growing a wide variety of grapes that could remain on the vines to ripen for the perfect amount of time because of the temperate seasons. The predictability of the weather and the overall seasonality of the region provided the necessary warmth and sunlight during the growing season and cooler temperatures in the evening, which, according to Dad, helped the grapes develop more complex flavors.

He was most proud of his EVERLY Cabernet, which was bold and complex, offering a rich blend of dark fruit flavors, like blackberry and cassis, combined with layers of complexity, including oak, earthy tones, and spices. The white wines, however, were still a bit of a work in progress, as Dad would say (and my taste buds agreed). Almost four years and many vintages later, sadly, the winery had yet to produce a white wine worth labeling.

Dad rounded the corner, and when he saw me, he called out, "Hey, Plumkin, wanna help me crate this Merlot shipment? I could really use the extra hand."

I had always loved the nickname my dad had for me, a perfectly charming term of affection. That was until the media took to calling me "Plum*p*kin" during a particularly rough time I had managing my weight during my teen years. My dad's version was sweet, but I couldn't help but internally cringe a little at the reminder of its harsher, less endearing denotation from my past.

I grabbed a few wooden boxes from the pile and carried them over to him. "I already had lunch, but feel free to put me to work."

He hoisted one of the crates onto the table. "What brings you to the inn?"

"Lemon asked if I could help her out with the collab event she and Kiwi are hosting this weekend."

"That's right, they're rolling out that line of Reiki-Charged Running Shoes. Clever idea they got there."

"Don't forget about the Aromatherapy-Infused Yoga Mats—'Get your own and you too can inhale serenity and exhale stress during your downward dog,'" I joked.

He grunted and rolled his eyes. "Don't remind me. Do you know how many test scents Lemon and Kiwi had us try before they found a winner? I will never get the smell of their Sweetened Sunflower and Sulfur Mat out of my nostrils. Don't tell your sisters, but I took that thing out back, and it has done wonders for keeping the foxes and other critters away from the chicken coop."

"Keep that little marketing nugget in your back pocket in case these don't fly off the shelves as expected. And for the record, consider yourself the lucky one. I had to test out the sample that smelled like their armpits. I guess after a candle that smells like your feet goes viral, you think everything should be body scented."

"Just goes to show that popularity doesn't necessarily equate to good taste," he smirked knowingly and continued to move the bottles of Merlot into the shipping crate.

Right behind him like a well-oiled machine, I stood where the bottles were lined in rows and started to pass them to Dad. "Seems to me you could slap an Everly label onto just about anything these days and it would sell." I looked up at him. "Except for me. I guess I'm the dud."

He stopped what he was doing, two bottles in his hands, and looked back around to meet my eye. "What's that supposed to mean?"

"C'mon, Dad. Don't tell me it hasn't crossed your mind. It sure as hell crosses mine . . . like every day. Lemon has EVERLYbody. Kiwi has the EVERLYfitness Pilates and yoga studios. Peach has EVERLYdesigns. Pear has EVERLYeats. What do I have?"

"Plumkin, you have opportunities. And support. And people who love you. And most of all, you have potential. You can have or be or do what*ever* you want. Do you know how many people only dream about that kind of freedom? You have the chance to start over to become the woman you want to be."

My eyes welled with tears, and it was hard to speak through my tightening throat. "But I'm . . . I'm scared. What if I never figure out who I am? Or worse, what if I do, and she doesn't measure up?" I moved a few of the bottles from the edge of the table and rested against it, almost deflating as the harsh truth spilled out of me. I swiped at the tears rolling down my cheeks and rubbed my wet fingertips down the smooth denim of my jeans. "All these years I've blamed the show, the fame, Rhys, even you and Mom for my failings. But what if it's not that at all? What if it's me? What if I'm just a lost cause?"

"Everyone . . . and I mean *everyone* feels lost at some point or another, Plum. It's human. But the thing is, you need to find what grounds you, what anchors you to the earth, to your authentic self, to your true purpose. For me, it's always been you girls, your mom. And maybe a little bit this winery," he smirked. "But once you find that *thing*, there'll be no stopping you."

I sniffed and pressed my knuckle to the corner of my lashes, catching another tear before it fell. "How do you know?"

"Because you're an Everly, my dear. It's in the family tree, and we've got good roots." He winked and started to reshuffle the bottles in the case, turning with open hands and motioning for me to pass the next set. I shifted my weight off the table and turned around to reach for the

Merlot. When I handed them to Dad, he paused as we held the bottles between us, his fingers laced with mine.

His bright-blue eyes looked more gray than usual, but the warmth behind them and the distinct crinkle in their corners were undeniably him. "But a tree can't thrive while shadowed under the canopy of a larger one, it needs to find its own sun. Maybe it's time for you to get away. Find that sun. There's a whole world of experiences out there for you to taste, to see, to live. You always have a home to return to, but you know as well as I do that you need to fly for a while before you decide where you want to nest."

His words felt like the permission I needed, or maybe the sign I'd been hoping for in regard to Kate's offer. "You know, the other reason I came to the inn today was to take a meeting with a producer who wants me for a home restoration show in a small town in Provence. Obviously, I know *nothing* about home restoration, but they assure me that isn't the focus, or well, it wouldn't be my focus anyway. Seems they want to give me a platform to show the world the real me, and so maybe . . . I don't know . . . maybe I'll find my sun in France?"

Dad's face lit up. "Talk about burying the lede! That's incredible, Plum." He set down the bottles we were holding and scooped me into his arms for a tight hug. The familiar smell of cedar and sawdust flooded my nose as my cheek hit the fibers of his flannel shirt. I closed my eyes and breathed it in for as long and as hard as I could.

He spoke softly next to my ear, still holding me tightly. "I think it's just the thing to give you the space and time you need to find yourself." He gave one last squeeze and then pulled away. "So tell me some details. Where exactly will you be filming?" Grabbing for the bottles he'd set down, he returned to stuffing them into the shipment crate.

I reached for two more and passed them over. "Maubec? Have you heard of it?"

He nodded. "Your mom and I visited there, gosh, it must have been around forty years ago. We ate the most delicious lavender ice cream from this tiny shop next to a gorgeous church I can't remember the name of now. Anyway, it was like nothing I'd ever tasted before. There was a small park right across the street where I decided I wanted . . . no, *had* to marry your mother. I got down on one knee and proposed right then and there. I tried to convince her to go back across the street to that gorgeous church and become my wife, but, of course, she turned me down. It took another three years for me to change her mind." Dad tapped his index finger against his lips. "Maybe I'll grab some lavender from the garden and ask Pear to give it a whirl."

I scrunched up my nose as I passed him the last of the wine. "Lavender ice cream?! Yeah, none for me, thanks."

"Don't knock it till you've tried it." He slid the big barn's stall door closed, snapping the metal clamp down to lock it, and brushed his hands off on his pants. "So when do you leave?"

"The show would film from June through August or so. If I agree, I'll be leaving in a few weeks, I guess?"

"France in the summertime"—he sighed and cast his eyes to me—"plenty of glorious sunshine." His face broke into a wide, supportive smile.

I threw my arms around him and planted a kiss on his cheek. "Then I better get going. It sounds like I have a contract to sign and a trip to pack for."

Chapter Six

I tapped my foot along to the beat of Dua Lipa drifting from my AirPods and waited in the airline's club lounge until the last possible second, sipping on a Bloody Mary and noshing on all the free bar snacks. They announced a final call over the loudspeaker for my flight, and I rose to gather my belongings. Slinging my purse and carry-on onto my shoulder and grabbing for my rolling suitcase with my other hand, I made my way to the counter, the sign over which blinked BOARDING. I flashed my phone screen at the gate agent to scan my ticket and walked down the Jetway into the next chapter of my life.

Three months away from LA, away from the peering paparazzi, away from the spotlight. I released a heavy sigh and thrust my bags in front of me, trying to wiggle them down the narrow path, bouncing off the sides of the aisle seats like a Ping-Pong ball. When I arrived at my cozy pod, I pushed my items onto my seat, trying to clear the way to let others pass.

I double-checked that I'd stashed my passport back in my purse's zippered pocket and confirmed my phone, which was tucked right next to it, was already powered to airplane mode. Moments later, a dapper flight attendant named Antoine, according to his winged name tag, bounced into my field of vision.

"Oh! Mademoiselle Everly, enchanté. Please make yourself com-fort-ableh, and as soon as we've reached ze cruizing altee-tude on our route to Marseille, I'll be over with ze in-flight champagne tout de suite," he said in a sort of Frenglish. His energy was infectious. I could already imagine myself sipping lattes at tiny cafés, soaking in the sights and smells of Provence.

"I just love your accent," I complimented.

Antoine leaned in closer to me. "They don't flat-out *ask us* to put on the accent, but the flight attendants who do, get the first pick of schedules," he said, completely abandoning his French inflections.

"Wait, so you're not French then?"

"Born and raised in Hoboken, New Jersey. Fake it till you make it, am I right? Let me know if I can get you anything else before we bid LA adieu!" He winked and hurried off before I could ask him for a hand getting my bags into the overhead compartment.

The Air France first-class cabin was spacious, and I couldn't help but smile with gratitude that Tributary was paying for the flight. When the coast was clear, I moved out of my seat and bent down to grab my carry-on to lift it into the bin, but as I went to hoist it above my head, the weight was too great, forcing my knees to buckle and sending me stumbling sideways into the neighboring seat, where a seated older woman shot me a nasty look.

"*Oops*, so sorry," I mumbled, momentarily confused by the fact that the bag that had been too heavy a second ago was magically much lighter and more manageable. It then dawned on me I was actually holding very little, if any, of the bag's weight at this point, and turned to face the mysterious force. The stranger, a bit too close to me, felt jarring until a smooth voice with a hint of a midwestern drawl wove its way up my neck.

"Easy there, let me help you," he said. As he heaved my bag into the bin, I noticed that the very tall stranger was boyishly good-looking, unassuming, with a bit of scruff that speckled his structured jawline. His awkward grip on the suitcase from behind me was clear from the grunts he tried hard to disguise. "My God, what did you pack in this thing? Lead weights? Gotta tell you, its size makes it a little deceiving."

"Says the guy who maybe could use a few more trips to the gym," I joked as I helped support the one side, and then together, we finally pushed it squarely into place.

"*Orrrrr* maybe you could learn the art of packing light? Ever hear of Marie Kondo? Or minimalism? I mean, they *do* have stores in France, you know."

"If life has taught me anything, it's to be ready for any possible fashion emergencies," I said—a nod to my *Celebrity Ballroom* catastrophe, which he apparently didn't get, resulting in an awkward silence between us. I cleared my throat and shifted my weight. "Anyway, thanks for your heroic efforts. You gotta name, Hercules?"

"Sorry, yeah, I'm Elliott."

I put my hand to my chest and responded, "Plum. Nice to meet you."

"Yeah . . . I know who you are. I'm actually here for—"

A loud ding cut him off, and he was quickly interrupted by Antoine's lilting voice (and faux accent) on the loudspeaker. "If everyone could please take z'air seats and fasten z'air seat belts, we are ready to push back from ze gate and begin our safe-tee dem-on-stra-see-on."

Elliott acknowledged the announcement with a quick nod. "We better take our seats. I have like a three-mile hike to get to mine all the way back in coach."

I reached over to snatch the green foil–wrapped pillow mint from my luxury pod's fold-out bed and waved it in the air. "Do you need any provisions for your journey? I think it's Godiva."

He rolled his eyes, lifted his tiny duffel farther up on his shoulder, and stalked through the flimsy curtain that separated the first-class cabin from economy.

As I watched him go, the grumpy, tight-lipped old lady that I'd bounced into earlier let out a not-so-subtle *ahem*, and when I looked over to her, she nodded in the direction of the attendant waiting for me to take my seat.

"Yep, got it. Sorry." I shoved my purse under the seat in front of me with my foot, plopped down into the plush leather chair, and expelled a deep sigh.

I was doing this. For real. No safety net of family close by. No backup plan. No Rhys. Even when we were broken up, Rhys was my barometer of normal. He was my biggest supporter. My rock. My touchstone. Now, he was another name to add to the long list of people whom I'd let use me for their own endgame. Whether he leaked the tape to break us out of our "box" like he claimed or to boost his own fame, what did it matter? In the end, the person I'd loved most in the world betrayed and lied to me, and in my heart I knew that shattered trust was the final blow ending us for good.

My heart started to quicken, and my rib cage seemed to squeeze the air out of my lungs. I looked straight ahead, and Antoine was gesturing with the seat belt and flotation devices. His arms moved fluidly, and his smile never faltered. But I couldn't hear a thing. My ears were filled with a thick, pulsing thrum that reverberated down to my toes.

Oh God. Am I having a stroke? What the hell's happening?

I bent in half to fumble for my purse, the one I'd kicked a bit too far under the seat in front of me, and the exertion and odd position squeezed out whatever small bit of air was left in my lungs. Dark speckles danced in my line of vision as I continued to blindly riffle about. Finally grabbing my clutch of toiletries, I fished around the bottom of the bag, desperate for my fingertips to find a few rogue Xanax pills that had spilled out on my last trip. *Aha! Success!* One lonely soldier ready to save the damn day! I pinched it between my fingernails and dropped it into my open palm before reaching for the bottle of water I'd bought at the kiosk right next to our gate. Swallowing the pill down, I sank back against my seat, the leather cooling my clammy neck, and focused on taking big, deep breaths.

And just as the cold liquid hit my stomach along with the pill, a heaviness settled like a fog between my ears as if a slow leak of carbon monoxide was streaming in through the little overhead vents instead of air. Out the small airplane window, I hazily watched the ground crew in their neon-orange vests waving their lighted wands as they directed the plane away from the gate and onto the runway.

As the Xanax took hold, the sharp edges of my consciousness softened into a calming blur and took me further and further away, though the plane's wheels were still on the asphalt. Rhys. The tape. I would never be able to find myself in France (or anywhere at all) if I continued to harp on his betrayal, and damn him, he didn't get to take that too. So, for as brief as the thought may have been before the medicine knocked me out for good, I was resolute and downright determined to leave Rhys behind in the US, and in my past.

My head lolled back against the headrest and I drifted off; the effect of the pill lifted me up, up, and away like the very plane I was on. My worrying and the nerves melted away, and the next thing I knew, Antoine was reaching over me to raise my window shade, holding a hot Styrofoam cup and asking me how I took my café.

I pulled out my cell phone, turned on the international data plan, and watched the tiny digital clock update to 8:00 a.m. I opened my Gmail and typed *Heart Restoration Project* into the search bar, and the email I was looking for popped up on the screen.

> Bienvenue en France! Once you land, head to the luggage carousel and look for a driver holding a sign with your name to take you to Maubec. We have sent some of the crew ahead—they will have your next week's itinerary as well as your lodging information. Please feel free to reach out with any questions or concerns. Have fun, and see you in a few weeks!
>
> —Kate

After tucking my phone back into my bag, I reapplied some lip gloss and made my way off the plane, through customs, and down to the luggage carousel. I inched up on my toes, and out of the far corner of my eye, over a sea of heads, I could just make out a driver holding up a sign that said P. EVERLY AND E. SCHAFFER. Dragging my heavy bag behind me, I wove through the crowd and over to where he was standing.

"Bonjour, I am P. Everly. Plum. Plum Everly."

"Bonjour, Mademoiselle, je m'appelle Gervais. Enchanté. Is this all your luggage?" he asked.

"Nice to meet you too, Gervais. I have a few more pieces coming off the plane."

"Allow me." He grabbed for my carry-on and roller bag, but I held on to my purse, which I kept slung across my body. "Are they labeled?" he asked.

"Yes, there'll be two large valises with my name on them."

Gervais poked around with something on his phone and then answered, "Very good. Do you mind waiting here for Monsieur Schaffer?"

I nodded, even though I had no idea if I was supposed to know who Mr. Schaffer was—because I didn't—and the driver stepped away to retrieve the rest of my luggage. Since I had a moment, I scanned the concourse, hoping to find an open kiosk or restaurant where I could get a drink for the car ride into Maubec, but the airport in Marseille was small, and it seemed I'd already passed most of the shops.

It certainly wasn't LAX with its bright lights, bustling crowds, and sea of retail chains. But I managed to spot a small patisserie in the corner, its bakery shelves lined with powdered-sugar- and almond-covered croissants and cloud-shaped, flaky brioche. Tufts of lavender sprigs tied together with rustic burlap ribbon were set out by the register, and an espresso machine hissed on the back counter.

Not seeing the driver returning just yet, I hurried to purchase a small latte, an Orangina for later, and a chocolate chip cookie in case Gervais needed a pick-me-up as well. Still not seeing him or any sign of a Mr. Schaffer, I returned to the spot where I'd been asked to wait and kneeled down to stuff the bottle of Orangina into the side of my purse for safekeeping.

"We meet again," a voice called from above me. I looked up and into the face of the tall gentleman who helped me lift my bag into the overhead bin back in LA. He offered me his hand, which I gratefully took as I climbed up off the ground.

"Was the flight any less turbulent in first class?" he snorted.

"I couldn't tell you either way. I took a Xanax before we even left LA and managed to knock myself out for most of it. I feel pretty great, actually."

"Must be nice. Besides the fact the plane was shaking like a cornstalk in a hurricane, I was stuck between a bickering married couple the entire flight and maybe slept for a couple of hours," he said through a yawn.

"Why didn't you offer to trade seats with one of them?"

"Oh, I did. Several times in fact. But neither wanted to swap. Instead, they used me as some sort of in-flight referee for almost the whole eleven-hour trip. The good news is Kathy and John have decided to give it one more chance, for the sake of the kids, of course. Even if he has been carrying on an affair with his assistant for the past nine years."

I put my hand in front of my mouth. "Nine years?!"

"Don't feel too bad for her, she's been working up a sweat with her personal trainer for the past five. This trip to France is their last-ditch effort to rekindle the flame."

"Well, if anywhere can do that, the Côte d'Azur can, right?" I noticed Gervais emerging from the crowd by baggage claim and looked back at Elliott. "Sorry to cut this short, but I can see my driver coming now. It was nice talking to you. Have a lovely holiday. Hope you enjoy Marseille."

"Oh, I'm not staying in Marseille, I'm actually heading to a small town called Maubec."

"What a coincidence, so am I."

"It's actually not a coincidence. I tried to introduce myself on the plane before they had us take our seats. I'm Elliott Schaffer, *Heart Restoration Project*'s production supervisor."

"Really? And they sat *you* in coach?" I teased.

"There are worse things in life, I can assure you," he scoffed.

Based on the look on his face, I couldn't tell if he was being serious about the coach joke, and worse, I was pretty sure he thought that I was.

Chapter Seven

Gervais escorted us outside the Marseille airport to a ridiculously small vehicle, which, by the looks of it, wasn't much larger than a Ringling Bros. clown car. I glanced over at Elliott, expecting an equal reaction of incredulity, but he showed no sign that he thought this to be anything strange or out of the ordinary.

"Excusez-moi, Monsieur, this car is to take *both* of us to Maubec?" I waggled a finger between me and Elliott, trying (unsuccessfully) to hide my confusion.

The driver shook his head. "Mais non, not exactly." He emphasized the *ee* sound at the end of *exactly* with an extra flourish.

I breathed a sigh of relief. "Oh, good, that's what I figured."

The driver pulled out his cell phone again and checked the messages. "Ouais, we are supposed to be waiting for un de plus."

"'Un de plus'? What's 'un de plus'?" I asked with a crooked brow.

He pointed a single digit in the air to answer.

"One more? Another whole person? Wait, *four* of us in this little roller skate?" I asked. Elliott shot me a look of distaste as I fidgeted uncomfortably. "No problem, I'm sure it'll be fine," I said, although I wasn't sure at all. I scanned my eyes up Elliott's humongous frame, at least six foot three if not taller, and was wondering if he'd spent time as a contortionist for as cool as he seemed about the situation.

Gervais continued to scroll through his phone and said, "Desolée, it seems there has been a change of plans. A member of your team was supposed to be in the car as well, but . . ." He tapped on his watch, as a way to explain their delay. "I will take you to the inn and return for her once her plane has arrivée."

"Oh, okay, great. Merci. I could really use a shower and catnap before I hit the ground running." I peeked around the back of the car, searching for a Harry Potter type of magical expanding trunk or more likely a trailer hitch. "Sir, where is my luggage going to go?"

"Oh no, everything is to remain here until all the production équipement arrives later. Then they'll load everything together in the van and deliver your luggage to the inn, n'est-ce pas?"

I sucked air through my teeth. "Hmm . . . I don't know if that's going to work. I have things in there that I may need. Is there any way—"

A *humph* escaped from Elliott's lips, and I shot a glance in his direction, spitting out, "Something to add?"

"Not at all." But his expression said otherwise, his face resembling a steaming kettle ready to pop. The tight, thin line of his mouth implied he was trying to remain silent, but clearly he could no longer hold his tongue. He patted the car's roof for emphasis. "Haven't you ever seen a smart car before? It is one of the most popular cars across Europe because it's practical. One, because of fuel costs; two, because of space; and three, because of price. But I can sense pragmatism isn't your strong suit."

Whoa, guess that little joke I made about him sitting in coach struck a nerve. I'd met him for less than ten whole minutes, and apparently he already felt some sort of contempt for me. Wait, no, that wasn't it at all, it was worse. Elliott didn't despise *me*; he despised the Plum Everly he'd seen on TV all these years. The one who sometimes played the villain, sometimes the flirt, sometimes the privileged princess—whoever and whatever the producers needed in order to sell their show.

Elliott confirmed my assumptions when he lifted his small duffel onto his shoulder and spat, "This isn't *EVERLYday* or *The Real Housewives of Maubec*. Extravagances like Escalades and your luggage 'essentials' are unnecessary. Are you sure this project's a good fit for you? It doesn't seem like you're accustomed to being inconvenienced."

I flushed with a mixture of embarrassment and annoyance. "I'm just being realistic. Seriously, tell me how *you* plan on fitting in this car?"

"I'm sure I'll manage. Can we just get on the road? I checked the GPS before we landed, and it will take about an hour to get to the inn from here. So we better get a move on."

The driver popped his head from around the open door and interrupted. "Allo, coucou, I may have une solution. I can squeeze one of the valises onto the passenger seat, if you two would be okay to"—he gestured with his hands in a narrowing, pinching motion until they met—"how you say, *smoosh*."

Our eyes shot to one another—a showdown without mercy until Elliott grunted in surrender. "Yeah, sure, fine. Can we just get going?"

"Bien sûr. Um . . . if you want to try to climb in the back and arrange yourself, I will return tout de suite." He rushed inside the airport, leaving me and Elliott to battle ourselves into the miniature back seat. A growl escaped his lips, and sweat dripped down my forehead.

"Whoa, watch your hands, buddy—" I cried.

"Ow! Careful there, will ya? God, is your bag really worth all this?" he asked.

"Move over a bit, would you?"

"Uh, *where* exactly would you like me to go?" he pressed.

Our voices continued to jump over one another, escalating in volume and growing in intensity.

Elliott's knees were practically up by his ears, and he was folded in half like an ironing board. The sound of slight panting puffed through the car, and out of the corner of my eye, I dared to look at him.

A smirk grew across my face. It reminded me of Chris Farley's infamous "Fat Man in a Little Coat" except as "Tall Man in a Baby Car," the mere thought of which sent me into an uncontrollable fit of giggles.

"Yes, hilarious. This should be a real hoot for an hour. Where is this guy with your bag? The sooner he gets back, the sooner we can leave, and the sooner I can unfold myself out of this ridiculous car," Elliott ranted.

"Oh, so *now* the car's ridiculous?!" I tried to peer through his arm and past his shoulder. "I see him now. Oh, thank God, he grabbed the right one," I said, noticing the pink luggage tag.

"Yes, thank God," Elliott mocked.

The driver lifted my suitcase into the front seat, slid behind the wheel, and adjusted the rearview mirror to try to see around Elliott's head. I leaned forward. "Sir, before we get going, can you turn off the child locks on the windows? I need to roll mine down, I get terribly carsick."

I didn't miss Elliott's eye roll. It was so exaggerated it was practically audible.

"Desolée, Mademoiselle. The window on that side is cassée." He blew a raspberry with his lips. "It does not descendre . . ." He pointed down with his index finger.

"Oh, no no no. That won't work." I glanced over at Elliott. "Any chance you'd be willing to switch sides with me? It's just that I—"

"No. How about you take another Xanax and get comfy, princess. We'll be there in an hour." With that, he rolled his head to the side, closed his eyes, and didn't open them again until about twenty minutes later, when I puked right into his lap.

Chapter Eight

Upon hearing me retch and Elliott shout in surprise, Gervais swerved off the road and into the pasture of a small farm. I leaped from the car, the smell of cow manure intensifying the wave of sickness, and I fought hard to keep my stomach from turning again. Once the nausea finally subsided, I folded myself into the back seat and offered to clean off Elliott's shirt with a few napkins from my pocket. He swatted my hand away, rolled down his window, and let Gervais know we should keep going, clearly anxious about us wasting any more time.

I realized that unless he had a change of clothes in that tiny duffel bag (which seemed unlikely given its size . . . and *his* size), he would have to wait until the luggage drop-off later to get a clean outfit. I slumped back against the seat, grateful for the abundant wind now whooshing through the car. The pinpricks of sweat on my forehead cooled, and I tried to keep my humiliation at bay as Elliott elbowed me square in the boob.

"Ow!" I cried and shot a glance in his direction.

"Sorry, but I mean, I'm kind of limited here. Can you give me a hand?" I realized he had been wearing a zip-up hoodie that bore the brunt of my digestive pyrotechnics and was struggling to take off his overshirt. "Pull this sleeve, would you? I can't maneuver around to yank it off myself."

"Oh, yeah, sure." I grabbed his sleeve and he leaned away, offering enough tension for me to be able to wrench it from behind his back. I rolled it in a ball, trying to arrange the vomit side of the shirt so it was concealed, and placed it by my feet. "I'll get that cleaned for you. Once again, I really am sorry. But in all fairness, I did try to warn you."

He didn't need to say anything. His expression said it all. He closed his eyes and returned to ignoring me until the melodic chimes of the Maubec village belfry woke him from a deep sleep.

I pulled myself up to the window, trying not to blink, afraid I'd miss even one moment. Scrambling in my pocket, I drew out my phone, pressed it up against the glass, hit record, and marveled as we passed the half-timbered houses with their thatched roofs and small stone bridges that led to pastel-colored shops covered with lush ivy that crawled up every surface. And off in the distance, lavender fields as far as the eye could see.

I zoomed the camera's lens in on certain items as we passed, allowing the background to defocus and fade into a Van Gogh–like impressionist haze behind the shot's new focal point. After so much time curating my accounts on Instagram and TikTok, I found I not only had a knack for creating engaging content, but the constant practice evoked an unexpected interest in taking and editing photos. Though I never really loved *being* the subject matter, in this day and age, social media was a necessary means to stay relevant. However, now I could do it my way, and how I was portrayed remained in my complete control.

As we zipped through the narrow passages and hair-thin alleyways, the flowers from the street vendors were so close I could practically touch the petals of the fragrant bouquets. The crowded streets bustling with merchants, their wares, and the patrons who were shopping seemed to be no match for our zippy driver, who zoomed through like we were in a live-action game of *Mario Kart*. I held my breath, certain we were going to clip someone or something, and was suddenly *very* grateful to be in our *very* tiny roller skate.

By the time we arrived at the inn, I was ready to call it a day. And it was only 11:00 a.m. Covered in dried vomit, completely windblown, and majorly dehydrated, I could only imagine what I looked like. God forbid there were any paparazzi in the vicinity. I slid my oversize sunglasses from my hair and onto my face, hoping to conceal at least a little of my bloodshot eyes and clumpy mascara.

Gervais managed to shimmy my valise out of the front seat and was getting ready to take it inside when I stepped up beside him and grabbed for the handle. "Thank you, but I've got it. I don't want to let this little baby out of my sight. I need a shower like *pronto*, and I don't want this getting lost with a bellhop somewhere. But merci."

As I struggled with my suitcase and toddled on my heels, I caught a glimpse of an old man across the street wiping down the café tables under a sweeping red awning. The man's triangular head seemed even more apparent as it contrasted his round belly. On his head, a few wisps of gray hair flopped about as they blew in the breeze. He was eyeing our car as we continued to unload it, and the spectacle we were making in the otherwise quiet square seemed to annoy him as he pushed in the café chairs more forcefully.

Although I knew I looked like a hot mess, I offered him a smile and a wave. But his face turned even more sour. He muttered something to himself, turned away without any acknowledgment, and returned inside.

"*Okaaayy*, nice to meet you too," I said to myself, before returning to my suitcase struggle.

Do I pull? Push? If I pull it, will it fall on me? Crush me? Should I—

"Jesus, please, for the love of God. I can't watch this anymore." Elliott grabbed the bag from me and effortlessly lifted it with one arm, forgoing the cobblestone entirely and carrying it inside.

"Oh, um . . . wait . . ." I chased behind him, my heels finding the cracks between the stones with every other step. Once inside the inn's lobby, he dropped it down on the smooth wood floor, where the wheels *finally* worked.

To my horror, the lobby was brimming with enthusiastic faces, a whole welcoming committee ready to greet us. I tried to smooth my hair down using the sweat from my palms, but it was no use. I was the definition of a disaster.

"Bonjour, Mademoiselle Everly. We are so delighted to have you staying with us for the duration of your project here," a delightful older woman with rosy cheeks and a silver bun exclaimed.

"Please, call me Plum." I extended my hand to meet hers.

"Ah, Prune, I am Agnès Sauveterre, and this is my husband, Pascal."

"Sorry, but my name is Plum," I repeated, exaggerating the pronunciation, "not Prune."

Pascal chuckled. "Ah oui, but *Prune* means *Plum* en français."

"Oh, um . . . okay. Well, when in Rome . . . uh, I mean, Maubec." I smiled, even though I wasn't sure I loved my new nickname.

"You don't speak French, then?" Agnès asked.

"No, no. Not really. Juste un peu." I pinched my fingers together to illustrate just how un peu I actually knew. "My dad gave me a French phrase book before I left, but all I've managed to master is merci, enchantée, où sont les toilettes, and je voudrais un verre de vin, s'il vous plait."

"Well, that last one is most necessary. Wine is the water of France!" Pascal joked.

"Speaking of, vous avez faim? Uh . . . hungry?" Agnès asked and directed our attention to a buffet of cheeses, breads, fruits, and coffee cups displayed in the small eating space adjacent to the lobby. It was decorated with white linen tablecloths and a bouquet of hand-tied lavender sprigs on every table—which was a little like the equivalent of putting lipstick on a pig. The structure of the inn was clearly struggling, apparent by the sway of the roof and the deep cracks in the ceiling. Sunlight flooded in from the big picture windows, and despite the shabby-chic vibe (emphasis on the *shabby*), it was still quite charming.

"Yes, I am hungry! Desperately! But more than food, I'm in even greater need of a shower," I confessed.

"Yes, of course. But there is only one shower. It is communal, for everyone, so as long as it is not occupied, it is all yours."

"Wait, I'm sorry. What? One shower? For everyone who's staying here?" I spoke out loud without even realizing how rude I must have sounded until Elliott elbowed me in the side. "Oh, um . . . I mean, how quaint." I forced a smile.

"I know it is not convenient, but we have been having some plumbing issues with the other two showers, so for the time being, we are down to only one. These pipes are hundreds of years old. It is a full-time job keeping these old buildings in working order," Pascal explained.

I turned to whisper to Elliott. "Just so you know, the second this conversation is over and I head upstairs, I am gunning it to the shower. But as a courtesy, since, you know, I barfed all over you, I'll give you a head start." I nodded up the stairs.

"Very generous of you. But I don't have anything to change into. Yours was the only bag that could fit in the clown car, if you recall."

A small pang of guilt struck me between the ribs but diminished when I considered his gruffness. I apologized. I'd given fair warning. I mean, what else did he want?! "Well, I'll ask Pascal if he has something. They probably won't fit you, though, since you're the size of a mountain troll, but they should cover all the necessary bits." I glanced down. "I'd assume."

Elliott snorted and swiped his key off the counter, blinked at me once, and then took off with a jolt. But surprisingly, before turning in his mad dash for the shower, he grabbed my suitcase, and without a word, carried it up the steep stairs for me.

Agnès, sensing the need for a change in topic, interjected, "I almost forgot. We have a little welcome gift for you." She turned and called down the corridor, "Odette, viens-ici. Ils sont arrivés!" She turned to me. "Our daughter, Odette, is home for the summer holiday in between her semesters at La Sorbonne, the Université de Paris. I know she was very much looking forward to meeting you."

"How nice," I said, and as soon as the words left my mouth, a young raven-haired goddess emerged from the back room. Her facial structure was impeccable, with defined cheekbones and a perfect slope to her nose. She was about my height, but her no-makeup, no-frills style was effortlessly Parisian chic. Looking at her made me acutely aware of my current state.

"Mademoiselle Everly, I am just so thrilled to meet you." She quickly kissed me on both cheeks, and I tried not to recoil in an effort to shield her from my inescapable odor.

"Enchantée," I echoed, grateful for having put that vocab word on my list to memorize.

"I am sorry to do this because I have been so looking forward to the opportunity to chat with you, but I have to run out to make a delivery for my parents, but we will catch up soon, n'est-ce pas? I will be serving breakfast in the morning. I hope to see you then. Oh, and this is for you." She offered me a small gift bag bursting with colorful tissue paper, gave me another squeeze, and rushed out the door.

"Wow, thank you," I called after her and then placed the bag on the counter to give myself the leverage to pull out the paper. Inside was a small handheld battery-operated fan, the kind you charge in a USB port. I pulled it out and looked over at Agnès and Pascal quizzically.

"We don't have air-conditioning at the inn. Well, in most places in France, anyway. And given that it is the summer, and you will be in the château without cool air, we just thought it may help to make you more comfortable during your stay here," Agnès explained.

No air-conditioning? Did I hear that right? I held the small fan in my hand, mustered every molecule of gratitude I could, and smiled. "This is incredibly thoughtful. Thank you. I'm sure I will be needing it." I tucked it back into the gift bag. "Before I head upstairs, Pascal, do you have a pair of pants and a T-shirt that Elliott can borrow? We had a little situation in the car on the way here from the airport, and unfortunately, his luggage won't arrive until later."

"Yes, I am sure I can find him something that will work."

"Wonderful. Merci." I grabbed my gift bag and my key and marched myself upstairs. My suitcase was resting right outside my door and, after battling with the old-fashioned brass knob and double lock, I wrestled the valise over the threshold to its final resting place.

All I want is to take a shower and a Xanax, and to sleep for like a day.

And as soon as I'd finished my thought, I heard the shower shut off, signaling it was my turn. I stripped off my crusty clothes, wrapped myself in a lavender-scented towel, and grabbed for my cache of toiletries. Cracking open my door, I made sure the coast was clear and then quickly tiptoed down the hall to the washroom.

I wrenched the water up to as hot as it could go (incidentally not very hot) and waited for the fog to billow up like a thick cumulus cloud. I rested my arm against the shower wall in front of me while the water streamed down my hair, and inhaled the steam.

But then, a sudden blast of ice-cold water knocked the wind from my lungs. "*Ahhh!* What the—" Hair still mid-lather, I shrieked and jiggled, unable to think logically while being blasted by the freezing jet. I finally managed to turn the dials (why were there so many dials?!) enough for the water to slow to a stop. Panting and still soapy, I tried to towel dry out the bubbles still left in my hair.

Forget it. Xanax and sleep. STAT. Do not pass go. Do not collect $200.

I wrapped my body back up in the now sopping-wet towel and shimmied down the hallway to my room. I heaved my bag open, threw on an oversize nightshirt, and dug around for the familiar bottle.

Oh no. A treacherous realization dawned on me: the Xanax prescription was in my *other* bag.

Merde.

Chapter Nine

The buttery, sweet aroma of fresh-baked baguettes and flaky croissants drizzled with lavender-infused honey floated up through the inn and under the door to my room, waking me from a deep and tranquil sleep. I don't know if it was the quiet of Maubec or the genuine feather mattress, but for the first time in years, I slept like a baby *without* the help of a sleep aid. I lifted my legs over the side of the bed while my stomach let out a deep growl.

I had been so exhausted when I arrived at the inn, I bypassed Agnès's welcome spread of meats and cheeses, opting for a handful of grapes and flaky croissant to go as I beelined to my room to shower and pass out for the night. Perhaps not my best decision to eat in bed since I woke to buttery crumbs embedded into my cheeks. I slipped on a clean T-shirt and jean shorts from the rest of my luggage that had been delivered late last night, washed my face extra well to ensure there were no remaining bits of pastry left behind, and raked my fingers through my hair as I studied my appearance in the cloudy antique mirror. After yanking my phone out of the charger, I shimmied it into my pocket before heading downstairs to the dining room.

A handful of guests were already seated at small tables, sipping frothy espressos and foam-topped café au laits while Agnès walked around with a basket offering a colorful assortment of homemade goodies. I spotted an empty chair by the window overlooking Maubec's belfry and made my way over to it.

"Bonjour, Prune. Sleep well?" Agnès asked in a cheerful tone.

"Very. It's so quiet here at night. Not at all like LA."

"Oui, nothing but les cigales."

"Les cigales?"

Agnès scrunched up her nose. "How you say . . . cicadas? Here . . ." She held up a linen napkin embroidered with the large-winged green insect and beamed proudly. "See?"

"Oh, um, a bug is stamped on your napkins? Well, that's an interesting little mascot," I said, hoping to sound genuine.

"Not just a mascot, Mademoiselle, la cigale has great significance in Provence. It is like your bald eagle. Similar to four-leaf clovers and rainbows, les cigales are thought to be signs of good luck and good fortune to come. In fact, that's how we came upon the name of our inn." She set the basket of treats down on the table and put a place mat and utensils in front of me, scarcely missing a beat of her story. "According to Provençal folklore, God sent the cicada to prevent peasants from becoming too lazy by keeping them from their afternoon naps. All that buzzing and chirping was thought to be a great nuisance. But the plan backfired. Rather than the people finding the cicada to be an annoyance, they found the singing relaxing, which in turn lulled them all into deep and tranquil sleeps. So the name of our inn, La Cigale Chantante, means the Singing Cicada, as we hope that our guests find their stay relaxing and full of peaceful rest."

"I love that story. My parents are always finding little details like that to celebrate in their properties too."

"Of course, happy to share. Mais faîtes-attention, les cigales have a reputation of stowing away into many a tourist's suitcases." Agnès laughed.

I wasn't sure if she was serious or not, but either way, I was very much considering encasing my luggage in Saran Wrap as soon as I returned to my room.

She flipped over the coffee cup in front of me and set it on its saucer. "Can I get you a coffee? Tea, perhaps?"

I set a napkin in my lap. "Espresso would be wonderful."

She nodded. "And Monsieur Schaffer? Where's he this morning?"

My head shot up. "Who? Oh, Elliott? I'm not sure? Still asleep, maybe?"

"Not asleep," Elliott said, coming up behind Agnès. "I've been awake for hours. I went for a run through the countryside before the sun was even up." He lifted up his T-shirt and used it to wipe the sweat pouring off his forehead, exposing the smallest hint of a washboard stomach I wasn't at all expecting.

Agnès clapped her hands together. "Pascal, une chaise, s'il te plaît," she shouted to her husband.

I shook my head. "He doesn't have to . . ."

"I don't have to sit here," Elliott said, finishing my sentence.

Pascal set a chair down across from my own. "Asseyez-vous," Agnès directed Elliott. "Sit."

Elliott nodded and slowly slid into the seat. He pushed his tousled hair out of his face and moistened his full lips. His eyes were really the most beautiful shade of baby blue. Was he this good-looking yesterday, or was I too distracted by his less-than-winning personality to even notice?

"Hope you don't mind the company?" he mumbled.

"What?" I said, quickly averting my eyes off his face. "Oh, it's fine," I answered.

"Coffee? Tea?" Agnès asked Elliott.

"Tea would be great," he answered.

Agnès called out to Odette, who scooted over with a steaming pot. "This is my daughter, Odette," Agnès said, introducing her to Elliott. "She is a grad student at La Sorbonne but comes home to work when she needs extra money."

"That's not the *only* reason, Maman." Odette flashed the most perfect pearly white smile in Elliott's direction.

"What are you studying?" Elliott asked her, clearly already smitten.

"Art history," she answered.

Elliott's eyebrows practically jumped up into his hairline. "Really? I minored in art history."

"Vraiment?! Quelle coïncidence! Where did you study? Have you visited Paris yet? All the museums there—oof, you would love it!" Her enthusiasm was palpable, and Odette inched closer to Elliott, their newfound connection seemingly ousting me out of their conversation.

"I grew up in Kansas City, but when I became interested in filmmaking and set my heart on UCLA, my single mom knew out-of-state tuition would be impossible. In-state was hard enough, even with loans and grants. So we moved to Fresno when I was in high school, I got accepted into UCLA's film school, and I put my nose to the grindstone to make it worth the sacrifice every day since. A professor I TA'ed for convinced me that an art history minor would help refine my eye as a filmmaker. Wise man." Elliott paused and set his napkin in his lap. "If I get to Paris, I may not have a ton of time to explore *all* the museums. So if you have any recommendations on your favorites or tips on how to see the best exhibits, I'd love to hear them."

I didn't quite catch her response as I was marveling at the ease of their conversation—like a friendly game of tennis, gently lobbing the ball back and forth with fluidity, when ours had been so . . . trying and difficult. Elliott hadn't said that many words in the full twenty-four hours I'd known him, let alone shown any kind of interest in me or my background like he was with Odette. I felt a pang of jealousy, and not because Odette was so beautiful and captivating (and she *was* undoubtedly both) but because I literally had nothing of substance to add to the conversation and felt a bit like an uninvited third wheel.

I didn't go to college. I'd thought about it, but in the end, I wasn't sure what I wanted to do with my life and didn't have the first clue as to what to major in. So when *Nude and Nervous, Celebrity Edition* came calling and offered me a big fat paycheck and the promise of a multi-season run, I gave up on the idea entirely. Now looking at the current state of things, I couldn't escape the nagging feeling I'd made all the wrong decisions.

Odette cracked open a small wooden box containing a variety of tea flavor options and showed the selection to Elliott.

"Which one do you recommend?" he asked.

"Le citrus is my favorite."

He offered her a smile and nodded. "I'll have that one, then."

Odette pulled the tea bag from the paper and placed it on the saucer. She surveyed the room quickly to check on the other patrons, and seeing no one needed her assistance, rested the teapot on the table and pulled up a seat in between me and Elliott.

"I am so pleased you are here, and I'm sorry I could not stay and chat with you yesterday. I must confess, I learned English from watching *EVERLYday*. I'm such a huge fan. Will your sisters be joining you in France?"

"No, it's just me on this project. I'm filming a new reality show here in Maubec."

"Vraiment? In Maubec? Nothing ever happens in Maubec."

Elliott raised his empty cup in the air, trying to get her attention without being rude.

"Oh, pardonnez-moi," Odette said, sliding the hot water over to him.

"Merci," he said, a big goofy grin plastered on his face.

"Will you be staying here the whole time while you film?" Odette asked.

"Until the château is habitable, I guess?" I answered, though I really had no clue.

Elliott pulled out his phone and scrolled through an email. "We're filming at Château Mirabelle? Do you know it?"

"Ah oui, Château Mirabelle. I know it well. I tried to convince Maman and Papa to purchase it a few years ago, since our inn has so many foundation issues. In fact, try to avoid slamming any doors, if you can?" she said with a joking tone, but her face implied some truth in her warning.

"I'm not sure what kind of shape Château Mirabelle is in, but I'll be renovating it, with the help of a local contractor," I said.

Elliott looked down at his watch. "Speaking of which, we're meeting Bastien at the château at eleven, so I should head upstairs soon to shower."

Odette's eyes widened. "Bastien Munier?"

Elliott glanced back down at his phone to verify and then looked up. "Yes, do you know him?"

"Everyone in Maubec knows Bastien . . . ," Odette said, her voice fading off. "The same way everyone in Maubec knows everyone," she quickly added. "That's why I moved to Paris."

Agnès returned to the table and set my espresso down in front of me. "Voilà. Can I offer you a pain au chocolat?"

I leaned closer and breathed in the rich scent of bittersweet chocolate paired with a hint of something I couldn't quite place. "The croissants smell divine."

"We bring them in each morning from the patisserie across the road," Agnès said, pointing out the picture window to the café across the street. "You may have even seen the proprietor, Monsieur Grenouille, out front. He is always bustling about."

"Oh yes, I think he grunted at me from afar yesterday."

Odette chuckled. "*Pfft.* Don't let his unpleasant expression fool you. He's a teddy bear at heart."

Agnès interjected, "And the very best pastry chef in all of Provence. Don't tell a soul, but I believe his secret ingredient is hazelnut extract."

"Hazelnut. That's it!" I covered the side of my face with my hand and whispered, "My sister Pear adds almond paste to hers."

Agnès smiled and pushed the basket toward Elliott. "One for the road?"

"Don't mind if I do," he said, grabbing a delicious-looking tarte aux pommes from the pile and ripping a huge chunk off with his teeth. "Will we see you again?" Elliott asked Odette once he'd swallowed.

"Oui, I'm home for . . . how do you say in America . . . summer break?"

"Good, maybe I'll catch you around, then. Plum, the van will be here at ten thirty. I'll meet you outside." He turned to leave before I even had the chance to respond.

"Is he your boyfriend?" Odette asked once Elliott was out of earshot.

"My boyfriend? God, no. He works on the production side of the show."

She moistened her lips, closed up the box of teas, and stood. "Why don't we all grab a drink later? Let me show you both around Avignon."

"Avignon? Not Maubec?"

"If you drove through the town square and passed the clock tower, then you have seen *all* of Maubec. Avignon, though, is a bit larger and feels much younger since it is where you'd find one of the bigger universities in Provence. Lots of music festivals, a cool art scene, fun nightlife. Much more exciting than Maubec."

I dabbed the corners of my mouth with the cloth napkin and set it down on the table. "Sure, sounds like fun."

"Magnifique!"

"Odette, dépêchez-vous," Agnès shouted from the next table.

She tilted her head to the right. "I should go."

"Me too," I said, standing from the table and pushing in my chair.

"See you later, n'est-ce pas?"

"Absolument."

Chapter Ten

At precisely 10:29 a.m., the Sprinter van sent from production rumbled up to the inn's entrance, kicking a thick cloud of dirt and gravel into the air. I waved my hand to clear away the swirling dust, but not before I managed to inhale a lungful. I coughed a few times, finally taking a large swig of water to stop the fit.

Elliott stepped outside the inn and raised his arms over his head to stretch. "Ah, smell that French country air. Just incredible."

I coughed a few more times as Gervais came around to slide the door open for us.

"After you," Elliott said, motioning to the van. "No first-class cabin in here, you'll have to make do in coach with the rest of us commoners."

Sheesh. Talk about not knowing how to let something go. He was holding on to the one stupid quip I made at the airport tighter than a squirrel hoarding acorns for the winter. "That's okay, you go ahead," I offered.

"No, you go. I have to get all the equipment loaded up in the back."

I nodded and climbed into the van. I yelled to Gervais and tapped on the window. "Can we open these? Remember, yesterday?" *Who could forget?* "I get motion sickness?" I lifted up my bag, pantomimed puking into it, and then pointed to the window again.

Gervais rolled his eyes and said, "Ah oui. Dégoûtant!" He reached over me and pushed open the window.

"Merci."

Elliott finished loading his equipment into the back and hopped into the captain's chair beside me in the van.

"Aren't we just meeting with the contractor? Why'd you bring all your camera equipment?" I asked.

"The network wants some exterior shots of the château for early promotional stuff. I figured I'd grab the footage while you meet with Bastien."

I scrolled through my phone to see if any new emails or texts came through from Kate or production. "So what do you know about him?"

"Know about who?" he asked with a grunt of impatience as he was scrolling through his own phone, clearly distracted.

"Bastien?" I asked, meeting his tone of agitation with one of my own.

Elliott reached into his backpack and pulled out a folder. He opened it on his lap and riffled through a bunch of papers before pulling one out of the stack. "Bastien Munier was born and raised in Maubec," he read off his résumé.

"I think it's pronounced *moo-nee-ay*, not *manure*."

"That's what I just said, Bastien Munier."

"You're still pronouncing it *manure*," I corrected.

Elliott huffed and passed me the paper. "Look at it yourself, then."

I scanned through Bastien's CV sprinkled with contracting experience and renovation projects throughout Provence and then flipped the page to find his professional headshot staring back at me. He was at least twenty years younger than I expected, with a classic square jaw, a tall forehead, strong and symmetrical features, and a slight scruff that gave him a bit more ruggedness than his broad shoulders did. There was no question he was gorgeous—sexy, mysterious, and undeniably French with a cool confidence conveyed through his smoldering stare.

Starting to feel a bit carsick from reading, I returned the folder to Elliott as the van slowed down. Gervais pulled up on the brake, and I looked out the window and squinted my eyes to see through the bars of a vine-covered wrought iron gate to the château, but I couldn't make out the house.

Gervais slid open the van door. "Voilà, Château Mirabelle," he said, tossing a half-smoked cigarette onto the ground. He tapped on his watch. "I will return precisely at two o'clock."

"Gervais, comment ça va?" an excited voice called out from behind us.

"Bastien!" Gervais said, throwing out his arms for a hug, and then launched into rapid-fire French that neither Elliott nor I could even attempt to follow. "Ça fait longtemps qu'on ne s'est pas vus. C'est bon de te voir."

Bastien patted Gervais on the back. "Toi aussi, mon ami!"

Bastien extended his hand in my direction. "Bonjour. Moi, c'est Bastien. You must be Plum and Elliott?"

"Yes. Oui. We are. I mean, I'm Plum, and this is Elliott," I said nervously. He was even better looking in person than his headshot, which in my experience was rarely *ever* the case. His eyes were warmer and more easygoing than the serious sex appeal of his photograph. Don't get me wrong, *there was still sex appeal*—and lots of it—but Bastien was even more enticing when he offered a wide grin and open arms in a genuinely enthusiastic welcome.

He scooped me into his arms, lifting me up off my feet in excitement, and pressed his lips to my right cheek and then my left. A school-girl-esque flutter flickered inside me like a live wire. He set me down, and as I tried to regain my balance, Bastien continued to make his introductions by extending an open hand out for Elliott's. Elliott didn't seem nearly as taken with him as I was. (Probably because Bastien was far more *my* type than Elliott's.) But like a professional, he shifted his camera to his other arm so that he could meet Bastien's hand with his own.

Bastien practically bounced out of his skin, unable to stand in one place for too long. "Lovely to meet you both, and bienvenue au Château Mirabelle. Did you know the word *mirabelle* roughly translates to mean *plum*, so it is . . . how do you say . . . sérendipité this home should be yours." He batted his eyes at me through thick lashes, and I'm pretty sure I melted a little. I don't know if it was the accent, the general air of charm and charisma, or the ambience of being flirted with in the middle of rolling lavender fields and grapevines, but he could have told me that I had bird poop in my hair, and I think I still would have swooned a bit.

"You've got to be kidding me," Elliott muttered under his breath.

"No, I am not kidding you," Bastien said, reeling around to answer Elliott, oblivious to his sarcasm. "The mirabelle, it is a very sweet, luscious fruit, but also quite rare. Because of the rich soil and abundant sunshine, however, they truly flourish in this part of France." Bastien motioned toward the château. "Ready to make our way? On y va!"

Bounding up the long, plum tree–lined drive toward the house, Elliott and I did our best to keep up with Bastien's quick stride and the amount of information he was dispensing about the property. All the while, I couldn't help but marvel at the expanse of the land, like a panoramic photograph that almost defied description. Rows of grapevines wound gracefully along the contours of the land, their young leaves vibrant with the promise of future bounty, and cypress trees, with their slender, dark-green silhouettes, punctuated the landscape, like tall sentinels standing watch over their flock.

We rounded the final bend, and there in front of us, perched atop a sloping hill, sat Château Mirabelle. The home must have been a breathtaking sight in its prime, but it wasn't hard to see that time and the elements had not been particularly kind. The once-majestic turrets were now leaning at odd angles, each looking as if it could collapse at any moment. The slate roof was covered in a plush green moss now threatening to overtake the uppermost sills. Thick, ropelike vines climbed up the stone walls, reaching into every crack and crevice. Most noticeable were the blown-out windows, doorways, and ramparts on the far end of the estate closest to the vineyard, almost as if a bomb had detonated somewhere deep within the belly of the house.

Despite all that, it wasn't hard to look past the decay and see all the wonderful potential of the place. The classic architecture and craftsmanship of a bygone era. From the marble fountains that still spouted fresh spring water, to the multicolored stained glass windows, to the menacing gargoyles carved in stone staring down at us from up above. I hadn't even set foot into the château, and already I loved everything about her.

I closed my eyes and inhaled the warm, sweet air, focusing on the symphony of lavender, the hints of earthy soil, and the delicate, fruity fragrance of ripening mirabelles, speckled like little globes of sunshine in fields of green. This place was truly magical, and though from the looks of the exterior we had our work cut out for us, I knew once it was all said and done, the finished result could be a masterpiece.

"Château Mirabelle . . . this house, well, maybe not *house,* more like *castle,* it's just amazing," I gushed.

"Wait until you step inside. It's in need of some love and attention, no doubt about that, but like all great and overlooked things," Bastien said, gazing into my eyes, "it is full of untapped potential." There was a sincerity in his voice that stopped me dead in my tracks. Rhys had been a lot of things, but earnest was not one of them.

"I have loved this château since I was a boy," he continued. "So when Kate Wembley and Tributary reached out about restoring the property, well, how could I say anything other than *oui.* You know, my grandfather used to work as the estate's vintner. His Chenin Blanc was the stuff of legends. We have just a few bottles left, one that was promised to me and my future bride to drink on our wedding night."

"Wow, that must be *some* wine." Elliott snorted.

"Oh, it is. It really is," Bastien said, oblivious to Elliott's swipe. "So shall we go inside?"

Elliott slung a camera onto his shoulder. "Not me, I have to take some exterior shots. You two go ahead. I'll find you in the house later."

Chapter Eleven

Bastien took my hand and helped me over the broken, cracked, dandelion-covered path that led up to the imposing front door.

"Le château has a long and complicated history in Maubec. Do you know much about it?" Bastien asked.

A little embarrassed, I shook my head. And I was grateful Elliott had left. I didn't need to endure his judgment for not having done my homework. But, to be fair, Kate didn't provide any materials about the house's history at all, only the projections for the film schedule and some notes back and forth about ways they planned to highlight a different side of Plum Everly. So technically, there really wasn't homework to do.

Ugh. Whatever. That's why we had Bastien. Plus, in all fairness, me *not* knowing much about the château (yet) made for a great opportunity to get a bit closer to our sexy lead contractor. Anyone worth their salt knew full well that chemistry and natural magnetism between costars was a crucial element to a show's success, so spending time together to fill in all the gaps of what I didn't know . . . would be time well spent.

"And yet you agreed to take on the project anyway? That was brave of you," he joked.

"Not brave. I was ready to get out of LA. I have a complicated history there. I hate to say it, but my agent could have offered me a gig on the moon, and I probably would have said yes."

"Well, it may not be the moon, but it is absolutely of a different time and place, like another world entirely."

"I'm beginning to see that."

Bastien laughed and stretched out his arm toward a crumbling rock wall in the courtyard. "Château Mirabelle started out as a fortress. That one barricade is all that is left of it. The house you see now was built in the late 1600s on the site of an older castle partially destroyed in 1580 during the Wars of Religion."

"Oh? But what happened between 1580 and now? Why was the house left abandoned?" I asked.

"In the summer of 1942, the mayor of Maubec received a telegram insisting he evacuate the château. The Third Reich wanted it as lodging for their officers. But what the German army didn't know was that beneath the house there's an elaborate web of caves built to store wine—but also useful for hiding things, like weapons, Resistance fighters, and Jewish families trying to make their way to Switzerland."

As he described what happened, I was spellbound by his storytelling and could immediately understand why, beyond his obvious good looks, Kate chose him to be on camera. "So what happened?"

"They blew it up," he said matter-of-factly.

My eyes were now as round as my mouth. When my brain caught up, I asked, "Who blew it up? The German army?"

"No, the town! Madame and Monsieur Adélaïse, the owners of Château Mirabelle, gathered all the Resistance fighters in Maubec, and together they destroyed as much of the house and as much evidence as they could. Their bravery likely saved hundreds of lives."

Goose bumps prickled up my arms, and suddenly the gorgeous, sun-soaked landscape darkened a bit under the shadow of such a tragic story of sacrifice and bravery. Afraid to know the answer, I continued in spite of myself, "And Madame and Monsieur Adélaïse, what happened to them?"

Bastien pressed his lips together and shook his head grimly. "They went into hiding, but eventually they were found, arrested for their disloyalty to the Third Reich, and never heard from again, I'm afraid. That is how the house came to be vacant all these years. The village did its best to maintain the property, but over time, it was simply too much, too hard." He glanced over at me. "Forgive me, I am talking on and on. I don't mean to bore you with all this history stuff."

"Bore me? Are you kidding? I'm riveted. But it's sad, isn't it? That more people don't know this story. About the bravery the town showed in the face of such adversity. Like, why weren't these the stories we'd hear about in school?"

Bastien's eyes turned more somber and soulful. "Sad? Perhaps? But we can give the story a happy ending, n'est-ce pas? We can rebuild what has been lost so that it may be found." A warmth radiated from the upturn of his lips, luring me into total agreement. He blushed and pushed open the front door with both of his hands. "Here," he said, handing me a hard hat. "Keep an eye out, quite a few of the floor planks are missing, and there is a low-hanging beam that could go at any time."

I followed Bastien through the entryway into the home's enormous three-story foyer adorned with a sweeping staircase embellished with ornate ironwork. Its sheer vastness took my breath away. Glancing up at the gold-leaf crown molding encircling the ceiling's entire perimeter, I pushed up on my toes for a better look.

Bastien grabbed me by the elbow. "*Attention!*" he shouted in French. "Watch out."

I was about two inches from completely wiping out on a knee-high cannon strewn in the middle of the foyer. Bastien touched my elbow lightly and helped me carefully step over it.

"What is that? It doesn't look big enough to be a weapon," I commented.

"Legend has it, the Adélaïse family would shoot the cannon off every time a male family member was born," he explained.

"Just the males? I wonder what my father would have to say about that tradition? He has five daughters."

"Of course, the beautiful and renowned Everly sisters."

Bastien's directness caught me off guard. Most people either feigned indifference to my fame or brought it up within seconds of meeting me. Bastien did neither, instead behaving in the most surprising way of all, like I was totally normal, nothing special.

"Let's go this way. I want to show you the rest of the rooms on this floor," he said excitedly.

Bastien led me through a maze of rooms, each in greater disarray than the one before it, with crumbling fireplaces, mushroom-covered beams, and walls stripped almost down to the studs. There was a huge hole in the floor of what Bastien told me was once the château's library. If you looked all the way down, you could see straight into the belly of the house. I shivered thinking about all the mice that likely made their way up from below every night looking for a warmer spot to nest.

"Are you cold?" Bastien asked.

"Yes. No. I'm fine," I said, my eyes now darting around at any small sound with the expectation of seeing a gopher-size rodent in every darkened nook.

When we finished exploring most of the primary space on the first floor, we arrived at the base of the very dilapidated grand staircase. "Do you want to see the upstairs now?"

I hesitated, not sure if the rotted wood and crumbling stone could handle the weight of the mice I'd mentioned earlier, let alone me and Bastien. I suddenly felt like the vast château was closing in on me, and the complete overhaul was a little more than I'd bargained for. I continued to meander down the corridor now, inspecting every detail more closely, the sheer scope of this project overwhelming. "When Kate said the château needed work, I didn't imagine *anything* of this magnitude. Are you sure I'm the right person for this?"

Now it was Bastien's turn to look surprised, his eyes doubled in size and his brows sky-high. "What do you mean? Of course you are." He grabbed my hand, laced his fingers with mine, and rubbed my skin with his thumb. "I'll be right here by your side through it all, and when it's finished, it will be magnifique." He twirled me around playfully, his hand still holding mine, the word *magnifique* like a firework of excitement . . . that fizzled to nothing but a fallen ember in the wake of my mounting doubt.

"But this whole house? We can't possibly renovate this *whole* house in three months."

Again, Bastien's enthusiasm swelled like another display of Fourth of July sparklers as he pulled me into the château's crumbling library. "Don't be ridiculous. We will renovate a few rooms, and the magic of television will make it appear as if we refurbished the entire château."

Wait, that can't be right. "But I thought—" I started, only to be interrupted by a deep male voice calling through the cavernous halls.

"Hello," Elliott shouted from the entranceway. "You guys in here?"

My hand fell away from Bastien's, and Bastien called back, "Oui, come around the staircase to the back room. Oh, and watch out for the low-hanging beam."

"Huh? What'd you say?" Elliott replied, quickly followed by a booming, "Damn it all to hell!"

"I don't think he heard what you said about the beam," I said to Bastien.

"Non. Nor do I."

Elliott came around the corner rubbing his forehead and joined us in the library. "I got all the footage I needed. Plum, it's almost two. The van will be outside soon. Are you ready to go?"

"We are finished here for today," Bastien answered, then turned to me, taking my hands again in his. "Can I ask you, though, are you doing anything this evening? I'd love to continue our talk about the renovation."

My eyes darted over to Elliott, who looked pained from both the conversation and the bump starting to protrude from his left temple.

"Tonight? Oh, well, I've been invited out to explore Avignon tonight."

"Parfait, I live in Avignon!" Bastien reached into my pocket for my phone. "Here, now you have my number," he said, typing it into the keypad. "Message me when you know where you are going to be."

The van honked its horn from outside.

"Plum, that's Gervais," Elliott urged.

I unbuckled the hard hat and passed it back to Bastien. "Thanks for the tour and the history lesson."

"Je vous en prie. See you tonight."

I climbed into the van and took out my phone to text Kate.

Me: The château is absolutely incredible.

Kate: Isn't it?! What'd you think of Bastien?

Me: Très charming.

Kate: LOL! That's one word for it. Don't you just want to devour him?!

Me: He's been wonderful. And this project—there's just so much potential! Thank you for championing me.

Kate: Thank YOU for saying yes. We couldn't do it without you! ☺

Me: À bientôt. That means "speak soon." Look at me, one day in and already my French is sooooooo much better!

Kate: C'est FANTASTIQUE! XO

Me: XO

I tucked my phone away, a soft smile on my lips. I was profoundly grateful for my new girlfriend and this chance to start anew, and this time, I wouldn't screw it up.

Chapter Twelve

Unsure of how the nightlife in Avignon compared to that of LA, I decided to wear a flouncy Balenciaga peasant dress paired with cute (but sturdy) Valentino Rockstud wedge boots to make the cobblestone streets not such a hazardous terrain. Avignon was one of the largest cities in the Luberon region, but even with that title, it was really more of a quaint and charming village. The stone buildings sat perched high over the sweeping views of Provence. And its ancient, paved streets boasted cozy chapels, open-air markets selling lavender-infused soaps and candles, and food stands peddling gamey boar sausages, yeasty breads, and pungent cheeses. The walls and buildings around the city were authentically eroded and cracked from wear over time, and many of the shops and restaurants were inset behind arched entryways made of carved limestone.

The noise, or lack thereof, was perhaps the most surprising of all. While I'd grown up used to the loud shouting of the LA hustle, the village seemed to whisper. Back home, the people were loud, the buildings were loud, and everyone seemed to be jockeying for their moment in the spotlight. But this town was so far removed from that pace of life that just standing in the square felt like taking a big, deep breath for the first time in a while.

"Elliott, nous sommes ici!" Odette waved, her voice interrupting my train of thought and bringing me back to the small entryway of the brasserie where we were all meeting up. Elliott strode over wearing dark-washed jeans paired with boots and a plain dark fitted T-shirt. And he looked *good.* I suppose when he was covered in camera equipment or when we were busy biting one another's heads off, I never really noticed the extent of his physique. Whereas Rhys had a spindly construction of lean muscle, Elliott was a hulking man whose size was made even more apparent as he stepped next to Odette, who greeted him warmly, kissing him on both cheeks.

"Elliott, Provence seems to agree with you," she gushed.

"I don't know if it's Provence as much as finally shaking off the jet lag."

"Well, I choose to believe it is l'air de Provence. It suits you well, I think." She slid her fingers from his chest and smoothed his T-shirt taut across his shoulder. It seemed like such an intimate gesture that I, in a fluster, turned to look away.

"I think I could use a drink," I announced and hightailed it in the direction of the bar.

"Don't do that," she called after me. "I have reserved us a table, and a server will come to take our order." Odette swept ahead of us, her brunette bob swinging as she maneuvered through the tight tables, and led us to a high top under a cozy chandelier made of vintage light bulbs and distressed iron spindles that looked like woven vines.

As soon as we took our seats and placed an order for a bottle of wine of Odette's choosing, she squealed with delight and said, "So tell me, I really have to know, why did you choose to set your show in Maubec?"

Elliott explained, "There are certain towns all over Italy and France selling properties on the cheap in order to bring money, attention, and new blood into struggling towns. Our show is kind of like travel porn meets HGTV. Two things we Americans just can't seem to get enough of."

She clapped her hands together with an enthusiasm that matched her bright eyes and big smile. "It really is wonderful. Maman and Papa tell stories about how this town used to be so vibrant, so full of life back when Château Mirabelle was a prominent winery in the region.

Did you know, it was widely regarded as one of the most notable vineyards, and its unique blends won numerous awards? That was until the war, anyway. Once it was destroyed, Maubec couldn't bounce back, and those who could afford to simply packed up and left. The region's fortunes have waned significantly over the past few decades, mostly because modern wine consumers prefer heavy, robust reds—the only style of wine the Luberon does not produce. So the people who stayed behind don't have much, but they have more backbone and heart than anyone else you're likely to know."

The waitress returned with a bottle of Sancerre and a few glasses for the table. Odette took a sip and dabbed at her mouth with her napkin. "So what is your plan? Are you looking to restore the château as a vineyard? I can't even imagine if you were to put the Everly name and popularity behind a winery in this region. It would certainly bolster our tourism and recognizability. Our little town would become a household name again. Our inn would be full, our restaurants would be brimming with new faces. Oh, Plum, I'm so excited you'll be staying."

I swallowed hard. "Well, yes, that all sounds wonderful, but I think you're misunderstanding just a *liiiiiittle* bit. I'm here to renovate the house and film a television show about that process, but I won't be staying in Maubec after we wrap. Once my commitment with the show ends, I'll put the house on the market and head back home to LA."

"Wait, what? You're just going to leave? But I don't understand." Odette's eyebrows wove together, and she leaned back in her seat, deflated.

"I have to go back to LA. That's where my life is, that's where my family is. I took this on as a job with every intention of heading back home once it's finished. I'm sorry if that's not what you want to hear, but I assure you, we will leave the château in such magnificent condition that people will be flooding here from all around to come visit."

"But couldn't this be your chance to make a new life? Just think about it, after all your bad press, I just assumed you were looking for a fresh start." Odette's comment caught me off guard, and it took me a minute to gather my thoughts in response.

Is this what people were always saying about the French and their brusqueness? Unlike us Americans who had a tendency to dance around sensitive topics, she went at this one full force without even realizing it might be a faux pas to do so. I could tell she was genuinely curious and in no way trying to be malicious, but her remark stung, a bitter reminder of not only the stupid tape, but the betrayal I swore I'd put out of my mind for the duration of this trip.

I glanced over at Elliott, trying to gauge his reaction, expecting harsh judgment—or worse, an indication he'd already seen the video the public aptly titled *Plum Everly: Ripe and Ready* (which was even worse than the film itself!) and incidentally probably seen me naked. *God, I hope not.* His expression remained blank, at least outwardly. Maybe he hadn't?

I cleared my throat. "Yeah, well, that whole situation was messy, but I hardly think it's a reason to abandon my life in LA full stop." I took a generous sip of wine to stop myself from saying something that would really tank the vibe of the evening.

Odette tucked a loose strand of dark hair behind her ear and propped her chin on her delicate hand. "Et toi, Elliott?" Her eyes seemed flirtier than before, sultrier, as she leaned in closer toward him. "And you? What's your story? How did you find yourself on a project like this? Do you have a lot of interest in home design and interior decor?" she teased. By his simple style and gruff manner, it seemed like a stretch.

He scoffed. "Not at all, but I've always been a history nerd. I just recently finished up an internship with Ken Burns's production company working on a three-part documentary series about the US and the Holocaust."

My ears perked up. "I saw that. On PBS, right? I didn't know you worked on that."

"Well, you didn't ask." His tone wasn't rude, simply matter of fact. And he was right. I hadn't asked. Come to think of it, I didn't really know anything about Elliott at all, aside from the fact that he traveled light and could efficiently fold himself into a smart car.

"From the sound of it, this reality show seems a far cry from a documentary. What made you think of taking this job?" Odette continued, missing entirely the layer of tension still present between me and Elliott.

He took a casual sip of his wine and said, "It isn't really my field of interest, but money was starting to get tight, and this is the kind of gig that actually pays the bills. I figured maybe I can find a passion project while I'm on this side of the Atlantic."

Nodding along enthusiastically as he spoke, I was fascinated to hear him articulating a lot of why I myself took the job in France. The thought of finding a passion project or something of interest to reignite my soul, something to maybe give me some insight on what the hell I was supposed to do for the rest of my life, felt especially poignant.

Lost in all the possibilities and opportunities that might await me in the rolling hills and rocky cliffsides of Provence, I didn't realize how fixated I'd become on Elliott until he looked over to me, interrupting himself midsentence, and asked, "What? Why are you nodding at me like you're a dashboard gnome in a dance battle? Something you want to add?"

I was still nodding when I realized he was speaking to me. His tone was surly, like he suspected perhaps that my over-the-top gesturing was mocking him instead of genuine. Stopping abruptly, I looked around the table to find Odette and Elliott staring at me, awaiting some kind of response. "Oh, no, it's just that I understand having to take gigs that pay the bills," I said.

"Yeah, I'm sure you do," Elliott scoffed, and Odette joined him in the laugh, both assuming (like everyone else did) I was rich just because of my family's empire. I didn't own my own lifestyle branch of the Everly brand. I didn't work for our family's multitude of properties. It was as clear to me as it was to everyone that my skill set was limited, but I was trying my best to figure out what I was good at so I too could find some stability and peace of mind just like everybody else.

"Coucou, mon chou!" Bastien announced as he made his way to the table, thankfully interrupting the painful awkwardness of the moment with his arrival. His expression was jovial and light as usual, which caused a refreshing shift in mood. After I texted him the address of the restaurant earlier, he said he planned on joining us but never specified exactly when. I was beginning to think he'd changed his mind and wasn't coming until I spotted him breezing through the tall doorway of the brasserie.

When he reached us, he immediately swept over to kiss me on both cheeks. My face flushed in response. Flipping a quick wave to Elliott, his smile dimmed almost imperceptibly as he simply nodded in Odette's direction. "Odette."

"Bastien." She nodded, equally as curt.

Wait, did they like *know each other* know each other? This morning Odette made it seem more like she knew *of* Bastien the same way apparently everyone in Maubec knew *of* everybody. But their awkward exchange suggested there was maybe more to it than that.

"Let's get you a drink," I offered, hoping to wash away the discomfort in the air. As I extended my arm up to wave to the waiter, Bastien grabbed the empty bottle I'd been mostly responsible for drinking while Odette and Elliott carried on in conversation.

"This bottle is finie, and perhaps instead of us getting another one, maybe we head somewhere else? Somewhere a little livelier, perhaps?" Bastien suggested.

"Oh? Well, where did you have in mind?" I asked.

A waitress made her way over, and before any of us could utter another word, Bastien scribbled in the air and interjected, "L'addition, s'il vous plait."

He stood up and grabbed my jean jacket from the back of my chair before I was even off my seat. "What kind of shoes are you wearing?" He eyed my feet.

"Huh?" I glanced down, not incredibly sure where he was going with this line of questioning.

"You should be fine. Allons-y!" And with that, he tossed a handful of euros on the table, grabbed me by the hand, and whisked me toward the door. I glanced back just in time to see Odette shrug in Elliott's direction as they grabbed their belongings and tried to keep up. By the time they met us on the street, Bastien had already hailed a taxi. Elliott jammed his Frankenstein frame into the front passenger side, while the rest of us piled into the small back seat.

"Bastien, do you mind cracking the window? I get motion sickness, and these winding roads aren't doing me any favors." I shuddered at the thought of ruining the night with a repeat of yesterday's performance.

"You should sit up front, then. Sortez! Allez! Allez!" He took my hand, led me around the side of the car to the front, and yanked open Elliott's door. "Changez, s'il vous plait!" he pleaded as he continued to gesture with a flap of his hands.

Elliott, startled, regarded Bastien like he'd lost his mind. But once he comprehended the ask, he begrudgingly squeezed himself out of the passenger seat and into the back.

"Bastien, where are we going?" Odette's expression was somewhere between annoyed and not surprised. I maneuvered the visor mirror, pretending to check my mascara, and glanced back and forth between the two of them. I searched their faces for some hint at the background of their past relationship. Were they ever an item? Nothing in their expressions indicated any kind of romantic history, even though the tension between them was certainly hard to miss.

Bastien leaned forward and poked his head between the two front seats. "Are you alright, Plum? Do you feel less sick?"

"Yes, thank you."

"Bien. I am glad."

A few turns later, the taxi pulled up under a streetlamp on a rather quiet side of town. We were dropped in front of a large, nondescript warehouse-type building not at all typical of the local architecture. And suddenly, I felt like I was back in West LA instead of Provence.

Chapter Thirteen

Did Bastien give the driver the correct address? This couldn't be right.

I glanced at Odette, who didn't seem the least bit nervous, which I took as a good sign. But still, I was worried that perhaps Bastien and I had some epic lost-in-translation moment. Maybe I somehow inferred that I wanted to tour a sketchy part of Avignon while slightly tipsy on a white blend?

"Bastien, where—"

But Bastien was already out of the car and knocking at the building's back door. "People usually use the front entrance around the corner," he explained, "but my friend works security most nights, and he said he'd just let us in through the back."

A clean-cut man in his midforties pulled the door open and, seeing Bastien, began bantering in fast French after exchanging the customary kiss on each cheek. The man let Bastien in and eyed us, holding the door open wide as we passed. "Bonsoir. This way."

I nodded in appreciation, and a tingle ran up my arm when I realized Bastien had doubled back to reach for my hand. He led the way with the confidence of someone who'd been there quite a few times. We wound through a maze of service entrances and employee-only areas finally to emerge into the depths of the building. With each step we took, a pounding, pulsing thump of powerful bass grew in intensity, rattling my bones until I had to set my jaw to keep my teeth from chattering.

Just as we reached the threshold of what I imagined was the entrance of the main dance club floor, based on the *thump thump thump* of the bass line, Bastien turned to us and said, "Don't worry, I know it is very noisy, and we may want something not so loud. I have another friend who works the door at the VIP, but the only way to get there is through the club—there is no shortcut."

By the looks on their faces, this seemed to assuage both Odette and Elliott. It was clear from everything I knew about him, plus the look of terrible discomfort plastered upon his face, this was definitely not Elliott's scene. Bastien opened the door, and the smell of sweat mixed with the heady, sweet aroma of the fog machine, tinted with the earthy scent of marijuana, wafted in our direction. Even more substantial than the smell was the heat. The temperature climbed at least fifteen degrees in an instant, and suddenly my clothes were clinging to me like a second skin.

We wriggled through the crowd of partygoers grinding and bouncing to the techno beats until we finally reached the VIP lounge entrance. I guessed by yet another warm reception of Bastien that this was his VIP buddy, and we were ushered in and took a seat at a small booth tucked into the corner. I wasn't sure how it was possible, but it was significantly quieter and more intimate in the small space.

"Drinks, yes?" Not waiting for an answer, Bastien was already on his feet heading to the bar. Elliott and Odette seemed to not even notice his departure. They were lost in conversation, looking super cozy as they spoke into one another's ears over the music.

"So, Odette," I spoke loudly, "have you ever been here before?"

My question seemed to catch her off guard, and she looked up at me, as if surprised by my presence. "Non. But I have had many friends who've organized hen parties here. It's très chic and bien sur, très populaire. I imagine your life in LA is full of VIP lounges and hot spots like this."

I wondered if she was alluding to my temporary reign as the Everly "wild child" during my later teen years. Yeah, I did go a little bananas back then, and even a few moments since when my role-of-the-moment called for it. It was as if I were trying to sow the oats I never could while the cameras were constantly rolling on *EVERLYday*. As Rhys's popularity grew and he was seeking more time in the spotlight, he and I went out most nights and partied hard. The barrage of tabloid pics and salacious headlines were a far cry from a flattering portrayal of me, and I guess they were also confirmation of my ultimate descent into the role of the black sheep.

While Lemon, Peach, Pear, and Kiwi were spending their time on high-powered phone calls with entrepreneurs working hard to get their businesses off the ground, I was usually nursing a hangover by day, and getting ready for my next alcohol-addled extravaganza by night. Maybe Bastien was under the impression that a place like this might impress me, but truth be told, it wasn't much my scene anymore, and thankfully hadn't been for some time. Just another phase, another stab at me trying to find myself.

"Not so much these days, but I have definitely seen a fair share of VIP lounges along the way."

Bastien, juggling two handfuls of drinks, chimed in, "My apologies if this place is not to your liking. I just figured that our small town is not so impressive as everything you are used to. I wanted to show you that we have some exciting things here too, no? It is not just sleepy, quaint villages full of old people and shriveling grapes. We can be fun, je te promet! I want you to love it here, Plum. Now take a big sip and let's go dance. C'mon, you two," Bastien said, looking at Odette and Elliott—who didn't look at all interested in going anywhere. "Everyone, let's dance!" he repeated.

I looked at them and tried to help Bastien's cause. "You guys sure you don't want to join us on the dance floor?" Maybe if I extended an olive branch, I could smooth out whatever weirdness had been brewing between all of us since the brasserie earlier.

Elliott opened his mouth to answer but was interrupted by Odette. "We're going to stay here and chat a bit. You two go ahead," she said and waved us on.

"Okay then. We'll be right over there if you guys change your minds." I pointed to the dance floor, and before I knew it, Bastien had taken my hand again and was pulling me in the direction of the music.

We moved to the corner of the floor and snaked into an open spot. Bastien pulled me close, the pressure of his body on mine like a weighted blanket. Suddenly, I forgot how to breathe, and my legs could no longer support me. I wrapped my arms around his neck, pressing my chest against him. I breathed him in; he smelled of cloves and well-worn leather. He held me close with an arm he wrapped around my waist. We swayed together with the song "We Found Love" by Rihanna, losing ourselves in the music, and the beat, and each other.

I glanced over Bastien's shoulder back to the table. It seemed that Elliott got up to grab some more drinks at the bar, while Odette sat alone, texting away on her cell. Just as Elliott approached with their next round, she tucked it back into her purse and smiled a little too graciously as she took her drink. He sat down next to her, so close their bodies touched, and I could not for the life of me figure out why I was worried about Elliott while in the arms of a very sexy Frenchman. I turned my attention away from their apparent canoodling to my drink and took a few hearty slugs, the cold and bitter liquid burning as it slid down to my stomach.

Shifting back to Bastien, I focused on the music, the feel of his hands on my hips, and relished in the freedom of the anonymity I was currently enjoying, unlike most of my nights in the US. Behind the DJ booth, beams of lights and lasers pulsed in time to the music, and sparks of bright colors zoomed across the dark space like a kaleidoscopic dream. Between the heaviness of my body and the hazy aura suspended around the lights, it was clear that the drinks had kicked in faster than I'd realized. I concentrated on standing upright as the blurred faces around me swirled like the stars of a Van Gogh painting. I glanced back over at Elliott and Odette again, squinting my eyes in their direction just in time to see the outlines of their bodies practically on top of one another.

"I think I need to sit for a minute," I announced in Bastien's ear.

"Parfait, I have to make a quick phone call, anyway, but will come right back," Bastien said.

I made a beeline to the table, and my sudden plop into the booth seemed to stir the little love birds from their nest. "So . . . whatcha guys talking about?" I raised my glass to take a sip out of a need to fill the awkward spaces between our conversation, but then placed it back down when I realized it'd already been drained.

"Here, have mine. I haven't touched it," Elliott said, sliding his full glass of wine across the table before continuing. "I was just telling Odette that I was thinking of calling it a night soon. It's almost one, and we have an early start tomorrow."

"No way!? It's one a.m.!"

Elliott's wide eyes and vigorously nodding head were like a silent *um YEAH* of incredulity. "I know this is probably your usual MO, to be out partyin' and frolicking about the night before filming starts, but it isn't really mine."

"It isn't mine either! I mean, not anymore . . . I mean, I can see how it might look that way seeing as we are in fact out at one a.m. the night before shooting *buuuut* in all fairness, I'm still on West Coast time. It's only like what? Four in the afternoon? Almost a whole day before shooting! I mean, for me, it's still yesterday."

Elliott stared at me for a solid ten seconds, probably trying to figure out if I was being serious or not. But after his rather long pause, he shook his head and barked, "I don't even know what the hell you just said. But for everyone else here, it's today . . . and it's really effin' late. So can we just go now?"

Bastien, now back from his call and having heard the tail end of the conversation, slid into the booth, wrapped his arm around my shoulders, pulled me in close, and said, "You cannot be serious? We need to live it up, especially if you will not be staying in Maubec for long, n'est-ce pas? Isn't that what you Americans say? *Leeeeve eeet* up!" he teased, all of his *i*'s sounding more like long *e*'s. "C'mon, ma chérie, let's go back and dance!" His hands reached for my waist, and the warmth of his fingertips sliding over my hips sent goose bumps across my skin.

I groaned, enticed by the insanely good-looking gent who kept sneaking in small touches and was begging me to rejoin him on the dance floor. "Can I take a rain check? I hate to say it, but I think Elliott's right and we should probably both get some sleep before we begin shooting tomorrow."

"Of course, of course. No problem." He grabbed for my jacket that had been folded on the booth's seat. He held it open for me, and I slung it over my shoulders before following in the wake Elliott was creating with his body through the sea of dancers. Once on the other side of the dance floor, Bastien took my hand and scooted ahead of Elliott. "Come this way, I know a different way out. Much quicker."

This time, Bastien led us through a few dark hallways to a back staircase that took us up and out to the street. But as Bastien opened the heavy door, flashes of cameras and shouts of my name startled the hell out of me and instinctively, I threw my hands up in front of my face.

"Plum! Plum! Over here!" a voice yelled.

Snap! Click! Snap!

"Is that your new boy toy?"

Flash! Flash!

"Can we expect a new tape from you two later this week? A foreign film with English subtitles perhaps?" another taunted.

Click! Flash! Snap!

"Or by tomorrow, by the looks of it."

Snap! Flash! Click!

In addition to the small pack of paps, an interested gaggle of club-goers hovered close with their phones raised in my direction, illuminating the night sky like a spotlight center stage. Sure, I was used to this to a certain degree, but not here. Not when so few people knew where I was. The paparazzi finding me without being tipped off was one in a million. Who could have told them? One of the servers? The taxi driver?

The bouncer? It could have been literally anyone. And it was so naive of me to have thought I could be anonymous for even a moment.

Bastien was still leading the way through the crowd as best as he could, frantically searching for a cab amid the chaos. From behind, Elliott shielded me from sight thanks to his mammoth frame and incredibly close proximity.

With his imposing body pinned against mine, my stomach did a little flip. His right arm was raised defensively between me and the photographers, while the other was warm, pressed against the small of my back. The gesture caught me somewhat off guard.

Between my family vying for sponsorships throughout our show's run and fighting to stay in the top spot on primetime TV, we were never ones to shy away from a photo op. Then as my sisters' brands began to grow, every flash of the camera meant more exposure for their products and their upcoming launches. Even Rhys. Even *my* Rhys, who'd been so removed from all of that in the beginning, suddenly was no longer immune to the allure of the attention and fame. By the end of our relationship, I grew almost used to Rhys reveling in the attention and sometimes even orchestrating run-ins with paparazzi and adoring fans. The idea of being protected from all of it struck me as so foreign, and so unbelievably appreciated.

Bastien ran to the street and frantically waved his arms to try to hail a taxi. One finally pulled over to the curb. He gestured to Elliott, who bulldozed through the gathering crowd, using his arms to force them to part like the Red Sea so that we could pass through safely.

"Plum, dépêchez-vous. Hurry. Please," Bastien cried as he motioned us to the waiting car where he flung open the door and waved us in.

Elliott, almost bearlike, shielded me with his body, positioning himself at the back of our party, allowing Odette to follow Bastien and keeping me closely tucked under his wing. As I held tight to Elliott's chest, I noticed he carried a robust scent of cedarwood, reminiscent of the dense forests and towering trees of a remote wilderness. I registered that smell as markedly different from the rich, exotic spices I had sensed from Bastien earlier in the evening.

My brain started to sound off like the bells on a slot machine, which paired with the continuous flashing of the cameras and made me teeter on my Valentino studded wedges. At the shifting of my weight, Elliott tightened his hold on me and continued pushing us in the direction of the car. Practically catapulting me and Odette inside with one final shove, he ran around to the other side and folded himself into the front seat before telling the driver to step on it, launching us back down the bumpy roads in the direction of Maubec.

Chapter Fourteen

My head was positively pounding, and the tannins from last night's wine were still thick on my tongue. I swallowed back a few Advil and chugged an entire bottle of Evian in practically one gulp. It sloshed around my empty stomach before threatening to come back up. Swallowing hard, I closed my eyes and prayed for the room to stop spinning. When I opened them, it took a second to refocus, but when they did, they fell to the television, which was inadvertently airing a rerun of *EVERLYday*.

It was odd to hear my own voice and those of my family dubbed in French voices that hardly matched their own. By the look of Lemon's bangs (which took her a full two years to grow out) it was one of the later seasons, maybe season eight or nine? I inched back on the bed, feeling for the remote, and flipped on the English subtitles just as Lemon was telling Mom she was going skiing with her boyfriend and wouldn't be home for Christmas that year. That's when Rhys, my "perfect" boyfriend, showed up, offering to spend the holidays with my family, winning everyone (including the audience) over with his thoughtful gesture and bold contrast to Lemon's lemon of a beau.

I couldn't help but wonder how much of it was real and how much of Rhys's performance was for the cameras at that point? Could I pinpoint the moment the switch had flipped for him? When the stardom became more important to him than I was? The lines between reality and performance blurred beyond recognition, and I was left to wonder if I truly knew the person I had once been unable to live a day without. I don't think I ever really did.

A bit hungover and very dehydrated, I begrudgingly fumbled around the room for something to wear until I found my jean shorts from the other day and a clean black tank top. I felt around in my bag for a pair of oversize sunglasses, slipped them on, and hurried downstairs to meet Bastien. Agnès and Pascal, already in the dining room setting up for breakfast, were turning chairs and setting the tables with utensils and sugar caddies.

"Bonjour, Prune, sleep well?" She glanced up, extending her usual greeting, and quickly returned to her laundry list of tasks. She unfolded a white linen tablecloth and spread it across the table, smoothing out any wrinkles with her hand. "Odette showed you a nice time in Avignon, I hope?"

"Yes, she did. We had a lovely time."

"Merveilleux, I am so pleased when visitors *really* get to experience Avignon *et* Maubec and the real experience de Provence," Agnès said with a flourish. When she was finally satisfied with the placement and wrinkle-free state of the tablecloth, she set down a small cup and saucer. "Croissant? Espresso?"

"Would it be possible to take them to go? I'm already running way behind."

She nodded. "Coming in une minute."

Agnès scooted off to fix the small order before I could even say thank you and brought a small paper cup and white wax paper bag back just as quickly. Tucking the pastry into my purse, I said, "Merci beaucoup."

Pascal said, "Prune, your French is already much improved."

I pushed my sunglasses onto my head. "Really?"

"No, I tease," he deadpanned. "But how about we work on it together. I can tutor you. Would you like that?"

I clapped my hands together enthusiastically. "Ooh yes! I am très excitée!"

He lifted an index finger in the air and waved it furiously. "Non, non, non!" He scooted closer, and I couldn't help but notice a rosy tint creeping up his face. "Mademoiselle, uh . . . excitée doesn't mean the same thing here as it does where you live, I think." The blush on his cheeks was even more pronounced as he fumbled through the explanation. "It has more of a connotation *sexual*, n'est-ce pas? Vous comprenez? Sex-u-al?" He lifted his brows and slowed the word, his embarrassment reaching a fever pitch.

"Oh . . . *Ohhhhhhh!*" I cupped my hand over my mouth, *finally at long last* understanding that *excited* in French means *excited*. "Oh my gosh, that's um . . . not what I meant . . . at all. I just meant I can't wait to start, but in a completely nonsexual and platonic type of way," I sputtered, already mortified and ready to cancel the lessons altogether.

He smiled warmly and nodded. "Ça va, ma belle. How could you have known? It is what we call a *faux-ami*, a false friend. It is a word that looks the same as your English one, but doesn't mean quite the same thing."

"Good to know. And I don't need any more of those, false friends that is," I joked. "But either way, I guess we've already gotten over me worrying about making a fool of myself, so nothing left to lose, right? Anyway, all that to say, I'm very interested, and I can pay you whatever the going rate is?"

"You can pay me nothing. Consider it a hotel amenity. We don't have a fancy spa or gym or swimming pool on property, so the least I can do is offer my services to teach you a few phrases to help you get around town."

"That is very generous. But I think you're ahead of the game. I mean, who needs a gym with all these steep hills everywhere anyway?" I craned my neck toward the door. "I should probably get going."

"À toute à l'heure! J'espère que tu as passé une merveilleuse journée!" Pascal called.

I froze in place trying to see if I recognized any of the *many* words he'd just thrown my way. Journée . . . journey? Ugh . . . I didn't know.

With that whole faux-amis thing, he could have been talking about the Academy Award nominees for all I knew. I just shrugged and smiled. "Yeah, not gonna lie, I didn't catch any of that. Maybe we can start our lessons tonight?"

"I am very much looking forward to it," he called after me with a wave.

I stepped outside into the cooler temperatures of the early June morning, surprised to find Bastien already waiting for me, fresh faced and wearing a crisp white T-shirt and dark jeans. He was holding a helmet and leaning up against his Vespa, seemingly unaware of the young Dylan McKay, 90210—or better even still, James Dean—vibes he was giving off.

"You look well." Bastien set the helmet down on the seat and kissed me hello. Smooch, smooch.

"Oh, well that's good because I feel a little bit like I was hit by a truck."

Monsieur Grenouille, the proprietor from across the way, was shooting daggers with his eyes. I wasn't sure what he disapproved of more: me, Bastien, Vespas, or the combination of all three so close to his patisserie. If looks could kill, there was no doubt in my mind I'd be a chalk outline in the middle of the town square by now.

"Bonjour, Monsieur Grenouille, top of the morning to you," I called out to him.

He made a sort of humph as he set his jaw, hugged his broom to his chest, and marched back into his shop.

Bastien's attention darted back and forth between us. "What was that all about?"

"I don't think he's particularly happy the circus has come to town. And by circus, I mean me." I took a huge swig of water and for just a second was worried it might come right back up. I put my hand over my mouth, closed my eyes, and swallowed again.

"If you want to do this another day, we can certainly reschedule," Bastien said.

"No, we cannot do this another day," Elliott said, walking out of the inn and interrupting our conversation. "The network wants to start reviewing footage this week."

I rolled my eyes. So much for compassion. "I'll be okay. Don't worry about me. A little more hydration, and I'll be right as rain in no time," I said, steadying myself against the stone wall outside the inn.

"So then, shall we?" Bastien pointed to his Vespa.

"Plum'll ride in the van with me," Elliott said, his eyes never leaving me.

For as *annoying* as it was to admit, Elliott was probably right. I was barely able to balance myself upright on solid ground, so my chances of staying on the scooter as it navigated curvy gravel roads were slim to none. I turned to Bastien. "Probably not a bad idea while my stomach settles down."

Bastien nodded, slipped his helmet on, and called out to Gervais, "Emmenez-les à l'église de Saint Orens. D'accord? À toute à l'heure!"

Elliott started to climb into the van, but then stopped himself and backed out, gesturing his arm into the vehicle instead. "No need for us to get all comfy, just in time for you to request a round of musical chairs. Better you just take the window seat and save us the shuffling."

It took me a moment to realize he wasn't kidding. "Oh, um . . . thanks. That was . . . thoughtful." I pushed my seat belt firmly into the buckle.

"Honestly, it was a little self-serving. I didn't bring a change of clothes," he said in almost stern admonishment, and a fresh round of mortification burbled up like the bile I was fighting like hell to keep down. His serious face remained stoic for an extra beat until he broke into a smirk. "I'm just messing with you. But truthfully, no one needs a repeat performance of our airport trip. Just better to set things off on the right foot straight out of the gate, am I right?" Elliott nodded as if affirming his own statement, reached into his backpack, and passed me the day's itinerary.

I looked over at his sheet and noticed our first stop was the church of Saint Orens. I looked up from the sheet. "Why are we going to this church instead of Château Mirabelle?"

"In these small villages, churches serve as the equivalent of a town hall. We should be able to find some of the original blueprints, maybe even some interior photographs of the house. All good fodder for the first episode. We're meeting with a Father . . ."—Elliott riffled through the papers—"ah, there it is, Father François. He oversees their archives. Apparently Château Mirabelle has quite a rich history in Maubec. Did you know that the house was actually used by the French Resist—"

I cut him off midsentence. "I know, Bastien told me all about it." Elliott's general know-it-all-iness was really starting to grate on me. Sure, he thought he was highfalutin when he interned for Ken Burns, and sure, he probably considered this gig to be a huge step down, but man, he really needed to take a chill pill. Between his condescension, Roy Kent–style gruffness, and overall attitude toward me, this was going to be a *looooong* three months.

Elliott pursed his lips together, satisfied, and folded the itinerary back into his bag. "Good. Well then, nothing more to talk about I guess." He pulled out his earbuds, popped them in, rolled his head to the side, and closed his eyes for the rest of the ride.

The van squeezed down a narrow alley, stopping in a picturesque town square with a large limestone fountain in the center of it. I pushed my face up against the window, my eyes trailing up a long cobblestone road lined with charming old white and honey-colored stone houses with blue wooden shutters.

Gervais threw the van into park and opened the door. "Sortez-ici. Out, out."

I looked around, confused. "What is happening? We're in the middle of the street in the middle of nowhere, and he wants us to get out of the van here?"

Elliott yanked his earbuds out and explained, "The van can't make it up the road to the church. It's too steep. We'll have to walk up the hill."

We both climbed out of the van and stepped onto the curb just as Bastien pulled up beside us in his Vespa. "Can I offer either of you a lift to the church?"

"I have to take up all the camera equipment, so I'll just meet you there," Elliott said.

"And Plum? Et toi?"

I glanced over at Elliott.

"Go ahead. There's no reason for both of us to sweat our asses off as we struggle up the hill," he said.

I turned to Bastien. "I don't have a helmet."

Bastien reached under the scooter's seat and pulled an extra from the small compartment. But instead of handing it to me, he gently plunked it down on my head and fastened the clip under my chin with a wide grin and a satisfying, "Voilà."

Elliott raised his arm. "Hold up a second. Can I have the two of you do that whole exchange again?"

"What exchange?" I asked.

"That whole bit with the helmet, that's the kind of thing Kate wants me to make sure I'm capturing. You two getting to know one another as the show kicks off."

A large lump formed in my throat. Yes, I knew perfectly well the reason I was in France was to film reality TV, but over the last couple of days that fact managed to slip further down in my consciousness. Elliott's request, though, brought it all right back to the surface. Like one of those trained seals, as soon as I saw the camera, boom I was standing up straighter and tracking the sun to figure out the most flattering light. Quippy one-liners that could be used as potential sound bites raced through my head.

"Are you serious?" Bastien asked.

I squeezed Bastien's forearm and looked up at him. "It's fine. Let's just give him what he needs so we can move on with our day."

Elliott repositioned me and Bastien so the steeple of Saint Orens was now our backdrop, held up five fingers, and started mouthing a countdown. When he got to one, he pointed to us, indicating it was time to start the scene, but Bastien just stood there in stunned silence.

"Bastien, say something," I whispered.

"Comme quoi?" He glanced at the camera and then at me, the panic clearly visible on his face.

I gripped his shoulders and stared into his dusky eyes. "Just pretend like nobody's watching us. It's just you and me and nobody else. I promise, after a while, you'll forget the camera's even there. Okay?"

Bastien nodded, moistened his lips, and exhaled. "D'accord."

Elliott stepped forward. "Let's do this. Bastien, you pull up on your Vespa, while Plum steps out of the van again. We'll pick up the conversation there. It'll read more naturally that way."

Elliott called out "Action" as Bastien revved up the Vespa's motor. He pulled up to the van, a curl of smoke trailing behind the engine. I hopped out of the van and turned my body slightly to accentuate my best angle to the camera and kept my face toward the light as I'd been taught from a young age.

"Bonjour, Mademoiselle Everly." Bastien flashed me his most dashing smile. "Are you ready for our adventure?"

I crooked my right eyebrow. "Adventure, did you say?"

"Ah oui. Provence is all about finding beautiful places to get lost in. Today, we'll get lost in the beauty of L'église de Saint Orens," he said, pointing up to the old church.

I tilted my head and turned up the flirt. "How will we get up there? The road looks far too steep for the van."

He patted the back of the Vespa.

I smiled coyly and looked from side to side. "But I don't have a helmet."

Elliott zoomed in for a close-up while Bastien reached under his seat, pulled one out, and placed it on my head. He leaned down to snap it closed, coming within inches of my face, and took my chin in his fingers once the clasp was fastened. His dark eyes were inviting, enticing me with every seductive flicker of his thick lashes. "Voilà, there you are."

His breath warmed my cheek, and I felt the undeniable and irresistible magnetic pull of us drawing closer and closer.

I chewed my bottom lip completely, forgetting about Elliott and the camera in front of us. "Merci," I whispered, eyeing his mouth and his eyes looking at mine as if we might—

"*Annnndddddd* cut!" Elliott yelled, shattering the moment in a blink.

"How was that? How was I?" Bastien stood upright. "Plum? What did you think?"

What did I think? I *thought* we were going to kiss, that's how real the moment felt. I expelled a breath that had been caught in my lungs in preparation for the smooch I thought was coming, but didn't. "You did great. It was all very, um, natural. Right?" I shifted from Bastien, stepping away to widen the space between us, and turned to Elliott. "So what did you think? Did you get what you need?"

"Yeah, it was great," Elliott replied flatly, in a tone that made me wonder if he was lying or simply over this job before it'd even really begun. He'd made no secret that he was here for the paycheck, nothing more. Hoisting the camera onto his shoulder, he wordlessly set up the steep road toward Saint Orens.

Bastien motioned for me to hop on the bike. I wrapped my arms around his waist, and off we went zipping up the hill, leaving Elliott in the dust.

Chapter Fifteen

Sitting high on a rocky outcrop overlooking Maubec, Saint Orens—with its white limestone ramparts, ancient rectangular walls, and bell towers—was even more spectacular up close.

"What's the church's denomination?" I asked Bastien as we approached the large and imposing front gate.

"Like most churches in this region, Catholique. You know, this chapel used to be a formidable Catholic defense site during the religious wars." He pointed up at the flared profile of the bells' bronze curves. "One of the two, I'm not sure which one, how do you say . . . commemorates? . . . the courage of the Maubec villagers who were massacred during the war." Bastien took my hand and led me to the church's arched entranceway. "In fact, symbolic characters and animals can be found carved into most of the limestone walls."

I glanced around the space. There were so many little details and flourishes. You could spend days here and not capture them all. "I love how people honor their history here. Back home, we're just flitting from one thing to the next. Me included. These days, I don't seem to stick anywhere for too long."

"Can I ask you a question? What happened last night with the paparazzi and you being ambushed like that, does that sort of thing happen to you a lot?"

I made my way around the perimeter of the church, admiring the old biblical scenes etched in colorful stained glass. "Not as much as it used to. But it still happens enough to make for a scary situation, especially when I'm not expecting that kind of attention."

"I cannot even imagine what it must feel like to be hunted like that," Bastien said sympathetically. "You are very brave, Plum."

Nobody had ever called me that before. Certainly not as it related to my public exploits. "To be fair, over the years, I've given the paparazzi plenty of reasons to chase me and seek me out for a salacious story. I'm not even sure I should step into this church, I might vanish into a pillar of salt," I joked.

"You know, anyone at all can seek sanctuary at a church, at any hour, day or night. That is the beautiful thing about churches. They never lock the doors. They're never closed to those who need them. I really love this one," he said, pointing to a stone carving of a lion surrounded by a pack of hyenas etched into the wall between two large arched windows. "Look at the fear and desperation in the lion's eyes. It is so realistic, non?" Bastien pulled a piece of paper and pencil out of his pocket. He kneeled down and placed the white sheet up against the carving. "If you rub the pencil over the image like this," he said, dragging the point back and forth over the deep lines in the stone, "the outline transfers onto the page."

He passed me the pencil, and I stooped down beside the image. Bastien put his hand over mine and moved the pencil forward and back, his warm breath making all the baby hairs on my arm stand up. I watched in amazement as the entire scene slowly appeared on the paper.

"There you are," he breathed. His fingers moved across the paper with a fluid grace, as if they possessed a language of their own, one that communicated desire and connection without words.

"There is an expression in French, 'les murs contiennent des souvenirs,' which roughly translates to 'walls have memories.' Now, ma chérie, you have a memento, of the church, and of our adventure." Bastien helped me off the ground just as Elliott came around the last bend in the road leading to the church's entrance, red faced, sweating profusely, and completely out of breath, which for a man who went running every morning was really something.

"Hey, are you doing okay over there?" I asked him.

"I'm fine," Elliott said, struggling to wipe the sweat that was pouring off his forehead as he was bent in half.

"Here, let me help you," Bastien offered. He reached into his pocket and pulled out a kerchief. Elliott grabbed the bandanna from Bastien's hand, sweeping it over his drenched face before attempting to hand it back to him.

Bastien's eyebrow lifted, and his lip curled. "Non merci, you can have it."

Elliott nodded and stuffed it into his back pocket. "Do we just go inside, or should we like knock first?"

"We can go inside," Bastien answered, never taking his eyes from my face as he pushed open the massive wooden double doors. "As I just explained to Plum, churches are never locked."

I broke away from his gaze and saw Elliott was already heading inside the chapel to find someone who could direct us around. After he spoke with a cloaked clergyman passing through the church's nave from the pulpit, Elliott walked back up the aisle to rejoin us at the front door.

"Bad news, Father François was called away to visit a sick parishioner earlier this morning and hasn't returned yet. We'll have to film this on a different day, although I'm not sure when we'll have time, the schedule is already pretty jam-packed," he explained.

Bastien held up his hand. "Give me une moment, *I'll* go and have a word with the clergyman." Then he whisked himself away with an enviable sense of confidence.

"He's wasting his time and ours," Elliott said once Bastien was out of earshot. "*Nobody's* allowed in the archives without Father François."

A few minutes later, Bastien clapped his hands together, the sound echoing off every wall of the chapel. He turned and gave us a big thumbs-up.

I elbowed Elliott. "Nobody, huh?"

"Maybe something I said earlier got lost in translation," he mumbled.

"Yeah, I'm sure that's exactly what happened."

Bastien hurried up the aisle. "Father Timothée agreed to chaperone us into the archives. We can poke around all we want, we just cannot take any of the items with us."

"Can we film?" Elliott asked.

Bastien pulled the release out of his pocket and waved it around proudly. "I got his Thomas Jefferson right here."

"Thomas Jefferson? Do you mean his John Hancock?" Elliott said.

Bastien shrugged. "Who's John Hancock?"

Elliott added the release to his clipboard. "You know what, it really doesn't matter just as long as it's signed."

We followed Father Timothée past the altar, down a long hallway, to a set of stairs leading up to a newly constructed addition to the church. Its modernity was in stark contrast to the ancient walls that otherwise surrounded us.

"This space has been a passion project of Père François for a long time," Father Timothée explained. "He wanted a place where the history of the region would be well preserved. It's taken most of his lifetime to collect enough money to build l'annexe, but here we are," he said, pushing open the heavy door.

We squeezed behind him into the archive room. A mahogany table sat in the middle of the room like an island surrounded by a sea of filing cabinets. Elliott turned on the camera's overhead light, which practically lit up the whole space.

Father Timothée jumped up and down, waving his arms in the air. "Non, non! The light can harm the artifacts."

Elliott turned it off and set down the camera. "I don't have the right equipment with me to shoot without proper lighting."

I interjected, "If you have a C100 you should be fine. Just switch out the 24-105 for the 18-135 lens."

"I guess that could work," he said, his voice tinged with disbelief at my knowledge of camera equipment.

But you didn't grow up on film sets and not pick up a few things. More than a few things. I used to spend every spare second I could with the *EVERLYday* crew, far more interested in what was happening behind the cameras than what was taking place in front of them. "It'll work. Trust me."

"This whole outing's been a bit of a bust. I'm hot and hungry and tired. What do you say we just wrap?"

"Wrap?" Bastien asked. "What do you mean *wrap*?"

"Call it a day. Go home," Elliott answered impassively.

Bastien's brows drew together. "Why would we do that? We can still learn about Château Mirabelle without the camera, n'est-ce pas?"

Elliott picked his bag up off the floor and turned to me. "I'm gonna start making my way down to the van. I have a bunch of calls to make back at the inn."

"You know what, I think I'll stay here with Bastien," I said. "I have my phone and can shoot some footage if we come across anything interesting."

Elliott scoffed. "It's not really the same thing. I wouldn't even bother."

"Between all my social media accounts I've actually gotten pretty good at it." I took out my phone and quickly showed Elliott a clip I took from when we first drove into Maubec captured with a dramatic time-lapse and overlaid with Édith Piaf singing "La Vie en Rose." The combination of stunning visuals and the iconic song created a compelling story, and Elliott's skepticism seemed to waver just a bit as he watched the enchanting scene unfold.

"Suit yourself, but I don't expect we'll be able to use much—if any of it," he said before turning on his heel to leave.

After he was gone, Bastien and I dove into the research, pulling out every last artifact related to Château Mirabelle from the cabinets and spreading them out across the table. One photograph in particular caught my attention: a handsome young man in a dark suit and a striking woman in a lace wedding gown standing arm in arm in the middle of the château's massive vineyard. I turned it over, and scribbled across the back were the words *Luc and Imène Adélaïse, 1931*.

I took out my phone and hit record. "Is this them? The last owners of Château Mirabelle? Luc and Imène Adélaïse?"

Bastien took the picture from my hand. "Oui, this must be their wedding day."

"It's strange, other than the clothes, and the fact it's in black and white, this picture could have been taken yesterday."

"Being young and in love is ageless, I suppose," Bastien said. A profound sense of recognition washed over me, as if Bastien had somehow tapped into an age-old truth, shining a spotlight on a truth many spent too much time forgetting.

I leaned in closer to the photo. "They really look like they were . . . in love, I mean?"

"Hard to know, but by all accounts, I believe so."

I turned off the recording. "Makes what happened to them all the more tragic." I picked up another photograph from the table, Luc and Imène standing arm in arm with two other couples in the château's grand foyer. On the back of the picture, I saw the letters *DP* in clear, distinct capital letters.

"DP? Do you know what that stands for?" I asked him.

Bastien took the picture from my hand. "I am not sure. A mystery, non?" He handed the photo back to me.

"Wait? Is that the same foyer we were standing in yesterday? And this room," I said, flipping to another picture, "with the lion clock on the mantel underneath the painting there? What room is that? It's so beautiful."

He glanced down. "I believe it is the grand salon. Trust me, it will be beautiful again if we have anything to do with it, ma belle. You see the staircase. We can take reclaimed wood from the region and re-create it in all its original splendor. Maybe even better than before." Bastien collected the photos from the table, carefully placing them back in their plastic storage bags. "Renovation not only restores the house, but the story of the home and the people who lived there. Trust me, you will see, we'll bring them all back to life. Are you hungry?"

"What?" I was so caught up in his beautiful words I lost my train of thought.

"Hungry? Are you hungry?" he repeated.

My stomach had been rumbling the better part of the last hour. "Maybe a little."

"There's an ice-cream shop down the hill that makes the most incredible lavender ice cream. I promise, you've never had anything quite like it."

I thought back to the conversation with my father by the barn the last time I was home. He'd mentioned a small ice-cream shop by a beautiful Provençal church, where he ate the most delicious lavender ice cream before getting down on one knee and asking for my mother's hand in marriage. Even though the idea of lavender ice cream still sounded kind of unappetizing, somehow, the way Bastien suggested the treat—with his sexy accent and unabashed enthusiasm—made it sound so much more tempting.

"So what do you say, Plum," Bastien repeated. "Want to give lavender ice cream a chance?"

"Yeah, you know what? I think I do."

Chapter Sixteen

We arrived at the ice-cream shop only to discover that the store was closed for the next two weeks while the owners were away on holiday in Nice. Hungry and disappointed, we hopped on Bastien's Vespa and took off for the town of Bonnieux, a walled village on a hilltop in the Luberon mountains. Bastien recently completed a château renovation there and wanted to show me the finished project.

We rode through beautiful countryside dotted with orchards of golden mirabelles and cool wooded hills of oak and pine. And towering above all, the giant of Provence, Mont Ventoux, appeared on the horizon with its white peak beckoning in the distance. We zoomed down the winding dirt road where, against the earthy browns and greens, popped the violets of lavender, crimson of poppy fields, and bright yellows of towering sunflowers. The stretch seemed to extend on for miles and miles until finally, we were met by a large wrought iron gate surrounding the enormous property.

Bastien hopped off the bike and unstrapped his helmet. "Bienvenue au Château du Val d'Été," he said. "The owners turned the house into a hotel, so we'll need to check in at the gate."

I followed him to the front of the estate where we were met by a brawny security guard who had at least a good five inches on Bastien. He may have even had a couple on Elliott. At first, the guard and Bastien swapped what sounded like formal pleasantries, but then the exchange ratcheted up a few notches into a full-blown argument complete with flying spittle and hand gestures.

With his hands on his hips, Bastien grumbled as he strode back to me.

"What's wrong? What's going on?" I asked.

"I spent close to three years renovating this house, and the clown over there won't let me past the front gate. He must be new, but even still, c'est répréhensible!"

"What about the owners? Can't you just call them?"

"This time of year they're on their yacht somewhere in the middle of the Med."

"Three years? Someone's bound to recognize you." I tilted my head toward the front gate. "Let's go back and ask around for someone else."

"I have a better idea. Come with me." He took me by the hand, flashing me his most devilish smile before leading me around the side of the gate and out of sight.

"Where are we going?"

"You'll see."

Bastien continued down to the estate's massive vineyard with rows of grapevines whose sprawl faded off into the horizon. We wove in and out through the meticulous rows until we made our way to the back of the estate. "If I am remembering right . . . yes, good, it's still there," he said, pointing to a large door that opened into what looked like a cellar. "That's the wine storage room. The servants' staircase connects through there into the lower level."

He started to advance toward the door, but I stayed in place, forcing Bastien to stop short when my hand, still connected with his, didn't move forward too. "No, we can't," I pleaded, pulling him back. I didn't need any scandals, any bad press, any additional attention. My palms started to prickle with sweat at the thought of doing any kind of stint in a federally mandated orange jumpsuit. "Wouldn't it be trespassing?"

He flashed a sexy grin. "Only in the most *literal* sense of the word. I don't know about you, but I'm not trying to steal any of the silver. I just want to show you around a bit, and then we'll go. No harm done."

Rhys and I used to pull crazy stunts like this together all the time. Skinny-dipping or staging elaborate pranks on the *EVERLYday* crew. He was always game for anything I suggested, and I loved him for it. We made a good team—that was until I realized he'd started *playing* the part of supportive boyfriend instead of actually *being* the supportive boyfriend he had always been. The more out of control I got, the more publicity he got, and with his recent admission about the tape, it was only now I realized he may have been fervently fanning the flames of my self-destruction all along.

Bastien took note of the uneasiness on my face and placed my hands in his. "Plum, turn around, you see these vineyards? They're characterized by their terroir."

I searched my limited French vocabulary and came up empty. "*Terroir?* I'm not sure I know that word."

"It loosely translates to mean 'a sense of place.' In a vineyard, *terroir* refers to the specific characteristics imparted to the wine itself. But it is no different with people or even houses. Everyone, really everything, has its own unique terroir or sense of place in this world. A restoration is about honoring such things. I did it here at Château du Val d'Été, and we will do it again at Le Château Mirabelle. Come inside with me. Let me show you what I mean," he said, gently cupping my chin in his palm. I looked up into his eyes, which were flickering with optimism. "What do you say, game for another adventure?" he whispered softly.

Realizing that this wasn't a publicity stunt but a genuine moment of spontaneity, I brushed aside my apprehension and allowed myself to be swept away. "Oui. Yes. Let's go inside," I answered.

Bastien set off into the cellar while I followed closely behind him. A few vineyard workers were inside packing up cases of wine for shipment. I took out my phone and filmed them. It was just the kind of slice-of-life moment I loved to capture. Over the last few days, I'd decided to keep my own video diary of my time in Provence. Maybe just for myself? Maybe I would use it for social media down the road? The truth was that I wasn't really sure what I was doing it for exactly, but with so much inspiration to be found here, I simply couldn't help myself.

I took a few steps closer to the table and zoomed in on the workers' rough hands, their weathered faces, and their mud-stained cuffs. I dragged the camera down the long rows of empty glass bottles that would soon be filled to the brim with crisp white wine.

Bastien leaned over as I continued to focus in on the tightly bound strips of the grainy French oak barrels. "Isn't it your job to host the show, not to film it?" he asked.

"There is something so beautiful about the simple things. You know, real life," I said, turning off the phone.

"Oui," he agreed, "there most certainly is."

We smiled and nodded at the workers as we continued past, but they barely batted an eye. They probably figured we were just guests of the château who lost their way. Climbing up the steep, cramped, winding servants' staircase, we emerged surreptitiously in a hallway between the kitchen and dining room.

"Château Mirabelle has a few things going for it that Château du Val d'Été did not," Bastien explained.

"Yeah? What are those?" I asked.

"Well, plumbing and running water for one. None of it's up to code, of course, but at least we have a better place to start from."

It was hard to believe that the gorgeous estate surrounding us didn't even have the bare basics when Bastien took it on as a restoration project. It sparked in me a renewed hope for the future of Château Mirabelle, and I could now envision those crumbling walls and dilapidated floorboards transforming into *this*. We continued down the dimly lit passageway and up another small flight of stairs into the château's sun-soaked entranceway with floor-to-ceiling windows. Carrara white and black marble tiles were laid out like a chessboard in front of us.

"Come," Bastien said, taking my hand. "I want to show you the salon."

Chapter Seventeen

We stepped into a cozy room with painted ceiling beams and a massive fireplace. Bastien pointed up at the rafters. "You see the lights? Chandeliers, girandoles, and candelabras were all redesigned to re-create the original feeling of . . . intimacy." We locked eyes for a moment before he continued his tour.

"The goal of this renovation was to restore the space to its original condition while being mindful of the decorative woodwork, paintings, gilding, and flooring." He drew my attention to the ground. "The paneling was entirely removed to allow for necessary structure and to hide the lighting and safety networks. We also worked on all the stone and brickwork, and the plastering, bien sûr. All but maybe a dozen walls in the château were compromised in some way or another when we started."

It was becoming increasingly clear why Bastien brought me here. He wanted to show me where a little vision and *a lot* of hard work could get you. He had every reason to be proud of Château du Val d'Été. It was more than a home, it was a painstakingly crafted work of art.

"So what do you say? Should we go get a drink in the garden? They have a lovely restaurant out there," he said.

We settled down at a table under a large black-and-white-striped umbrella. A server spotted us and came rushing over to take our order. I motioned for Bastien to take the lead. He picked up the wine list, rattling off a litany of wines and vintages.

Bastien handed the two menus to the server and crossed his legs at the ankle. "I hope you don't mind, I took the liberty of ordering a flight of their finest: Sancerre, Sauvignon Blanc, Melon de Bourgogne, Chenin Blanc, and one surprise. Although we're often overshadowed by France's more prestigious regions, most obviously Bordeaux, the Luberon Valley has played a vital role in French wine history for many centuries."

"You're so passionate about wine and winemaking. Did you ever consider becoming a vintner like your grandfather?"

"Pffi," he scoffed a bit sourly. "Considered it? Mais oui! Of course. It's all I wanted for as long as I could remember, but I don't come from a wealthy family, and these things, they are, how do you say . . . political. It's not like how it used to be, the trade being passed down through the generations. The newer châteaus and wineries want you to have all the formal accreditations, and I couldn't afford the tuition. A good vintner can make the difference between poverty and prosperity. I understand, though, these vineyards have become important businesses for this region."

"I guess that explains why Odette was so disappointed to hear I wouldn't be staying on to run Château Mirabelle," I said.

Bastien's lips flattened into a smooth line as he shifted in his seat. There was clearly something he wasn't telling me. "Hey, what's the real story with you and Odette?" I asked.

The server came over with our order and placed the two flights on the table, along with small plates of tangy olive tapenade, buttery foie gras, and creamy herb-infused fromage de chèvre paired with slices of crusty baguette. Bastien lifted the first glass and swallowed it down in one gulp. He set the empty glass back on the table. "What do you want to know?"

I shrugged. "I guess whatever you're comfortable sharing."

"Odette and I were childhood sweethearts. I thought I might even marry her one day."

I propped my elbows onto the table, my eyes wide in disbelief. "What happened?"

"So many things. But if I had to narrow it down to just one, I wasn't good enough for her."

"She actually *told* you that?"

"Not in so many words, but her actions made it clear enough. At one time I did think I would follow in my grandfather's footsteps. But when all those winery doors were slammed shut in my face, I wasn't sure how I would be able to support myself, let alone a wife and family. I promised Odette I would make something of myself, I just needed a bit of time to figure out how. Well, she couldn't wait. First chance she got, she hightailed it to Paris and started building a whole new life, one that didn't include *moi*."

I shook my head. "That's awful."

"No. She's always wanted more than this provincial life. I'm sure she would have come to that realization eventually, no matter what."

"But she seemed so committed to the idea that Château Mirabelle could help revitalize Maubec. She was talking like it was her own personal mission or something."

"I'm sure she wants what is best for Maubec. Her maman and papa have the inn there. But Odette won't be returning. She's very wrapped up in her new Parisian friends and their jet-set lifestyle. I'm certain that is why she attached herself to you so quickly, you represent everything she wants for herself—fame, fashion, status, followers."

How was it that even after all this time in the limelight, I was still such a poor judge of character? I hadn't gotten that impression of Odette at all. Maybe a bit flirtatious and somewhat direct for my taste, but nothing like what Bastien described.

Bastien shifted his weight in his chair as he simultaneously shifted the conversation away from Odette. "What do you think of that last wine?" he asked.

I was swimming in my own thoughts. "What?"

He motioned to my glass. "The last one you tried? It's best when you pair it with the fresh goat cheese. Brings out the nuttier notes."

He spread some of the goat cheese across the pillowy inside of the still-warm baguette and then extended it toward me, offering me a bite. My gaze was drawn to Bastien, his profile outlined by the soft amber light of the setting sun behind him. The flickering candle on our table mirrored the winking of the stars beginning to emerge in the dusky lavender sky. The scene was absolutely idyllic, storybook perfect. Good wine. Incredible views. Enchanting company.

With each sip of wine, his lips touched the glass with a sensuous elegance, and I found myself captivated by the way his strong yet graceful fingers cradled the stem. I leaned in and took a sip of the wine, the sweet crispness coating my mouth and tongue. I held up the glass. "This is far and away my favorite of the flight. It's delicious."

He set his glass down, sat back in his chair, and stretched his arms over his head, looking satisfied and proud. "Good, I'm glad you like it. It's my own creation—a special blend I've been working on for a few years."

I set down the goblet. "Wait? Really? You made this wine?!"

"I have a small vineyard I've managed to cobble together. Not as impressive as some, but the grapes are exquisite and the terroir is riche with vitamines. I share bottles with close friends, and the bartender, Guillaume, keeps one or two on hand for me when I want to impress future clients or very beautiful women. Who am I kidding, you are the first woman I've shared it with. Not only am I quite shy and too busy to really date much, but this wine is special . . . and it deserves to be shared with someone special, I think." He grinned.

My face flushed at his compliments, and I quickly changed the topic. "Can I ask, when you realized you couldn't become a vintner, how'd you find your way to doing home restoration? Seems like a big departure."

He exhaled and leaned forward. "A friend helped me get a job on a crew doing construction. It was a castle in Cavaillon being renovated by a wealthy couple from Perth. I was only supposed to work a couple of days. They had needed more diggers for the moat."

My eyebrows shot up in surprise. "The moat? Like a *real* moat?"

His lips turned upward. "Mais oui! A real moat. The project manager told the couple they should just fill it in. He imagined it would be too hard to repair, but they were adamant that their castle just would not be authentique without it. So I researched architecture from the period and figured out how we could solve the issues with the drainage and such. Not only were they able to keep their precious moat, but the house maintained its historical integrity. From that point on, I was, how do you say . . . hooked?"

I set my napkin down and wrapped my fingers around the stem of the wineglass. "I really love that story."

Bastien reached across the table and covered my hand with his own. I looked up and into his large, inviting eyes. He scooted a little closer to me and moved his face closer to my own. I recognized the intensity in his face.

My stomach tightened as I placed a hand to his chest, keeping the distance between us. "I'm not sure this is such a good idea. And if I gave you the wrong impression last night when we were dancing at the club or perhaps in being a bit too flirty today, I'm sorry. I've just never met anyone like you before, and it's been very easy to get swept away in your charm and the charm of this whole country."

He retreated quickly, pulling his hands back and into his lap. "No, I am the one who is désolée. It must be the wine and, of course, this place where I left so much of my soul. My heart. And I cannot deny there is something a bit magical about . . ." He pointed a finger back and forth between the two of us. "And I suppose, I just got swept up in how nice it has been to click with someone. It has been a while," he admitted, and his honesty and vulnerability made his genuineness even more apparent. This wasn't a performance for the cameras. This wasn't for the public. He was talking to me like a real human being about his real feelings without any showmanship or insincerity. No eyes watching, ears listening in, waiting to print it in tomorrow's tabloids.

I brought my hand up to my chest. "I just don't want to jump into anything too quickly. My heart's still on the mend from Rhys, for so many reasons, and to be honest, given how frequently it's been hurt, toyed with, and shattered, sometimes I'm amazed it's still functioning at all."

He nodded and reset his hand on top of my own, like a compromise. "Like Château Mirabelle, together, we will find a way to make it whole again," Bastien said in a firm tone that suggested this was a promise he intended to keep no matter what.

I choked back the tears starting to rise from the back of my throat and raised my wineglass high in the air. "Cheers to that."

Chapter Eighteen

The full production team from Tributary arrived over the weekend and set up their base camp in front of Château Mirabelle. Large hitched trailers and pop-up tents peppered almost the entirety of the front lawn. No wonder Monsieur Grenouille reacted like the circus had come to town; for a small, out-of-the-way village like Maubec, it probably felt that way.

The mere sight of the video village, the area of base camp where the show's producers and directors would sit huddled around small monitors watching dailies, sent my heart straight into my throat. Why was I so nervous? I'd spent most of my life surrounded by cameras and crews. Reality TV had always been my reality, so why did it feel so different this time?

Compared to some of the other shows I'd done, *Heart Restoration Project* was literally a paid vacation. There were no endorsement deals on the table, relationships on the line, or prize money to win, yet the stakes already felt just as high. *Spy House*, *Celebrity Ballroom*, *Love Lagoon*, those were all manufactured realities whereas Château Mirabelle was a real place with a real history. And it came with a real request from Kate herself for me to just be myself. Now, if there was a job I shouldn't be able to mess up, it *should* theoretically be this one!

"Come on," Elliott said, reaching around me. "Let's get you miked up." He finished tucking the wires into my pocket and looked at me with concern in his eyes. "Hey, you're shaking?"

"Just cold, I guess."

He backed away and eyed me up and down. "What's up? You look pale. Was it the car ride? Gervais *was* taking the turns a little hard this morning." His features hardened as he studied me, and he let out an annoyed huff. "You couldn't possibly still be hungover. Although, who knows what you and Bastien got up to the other day?" he muttered.

"I'm not hungover either," I spat back.

He tilted his head skeptically. "So then, what gives?"

"I don't know? I guess I'm a little nervous, maybe? First day jitters."

He snickered. "You? Nervous about being on TV? Isn't that like a fish being uncomfortable in water?"

"Ah, bonjour, Mademoiselle Everly et Monsieur Schaffer." Bastien walked toward us clutching a steaming cup of coffee, a broad grin across his face. "How are you both on this beautiful morning?"

I straightened out my shoulders and forced a smile on my lips. *Heart Restoration Project* might be a different type of show than I was accustomed to, but that didn't mean I didn't have to turn my enthusiasm up to a ten in order to earn my keep. "Good. Great. We're both doing very well," I answered in a voice so perky and upbeat, it caused Elliott to do a double take. I studied Bastien's face. Something about his appearance was different, but I couldn't quite put my finger on what it was? "You look . . ."

"Oh, I know, très ridicule. I spent the last hour in hair and makeup. They insisted."

Elliott shook his head disapprovingly at Bastien before throwing a camera over his shoulder. "I need to grab today's schedule from base camp. Service around here sucks, and I can't seem to pull anything up on my phone." He grunted as he stuffed his useless cell in his back pocket. "I'll see you both inside the house."

After Elliott walked away, I pointed to the trailers on the far side of the vineyard. "Was I supposed to go into hair and makeup? Nobody's said anything."

"If they didn't, it's only because you are such a natural beauty." Bastien reached over and pushed a stray hair out of my eyes. "Of course I'd seen photographs of you in magazines long before we met, but may I just say, none of them did you any justice," he said, his eyes lingering on my face.

"Plum? Plum Everly?" a voice called out from behind me. An older gentleman, probably close to my father's age, came around to join us. He tucked a walkie-talkie into his back pocket and extended his hand to me. "I am René Laroque, the project foreman."

Bastien slapped his forehead. "Where are my manners? Of course, Plum, this is Monsieur Laroque, one of my personal heroes. He just completed an unbelievable renovation of the Royal Chapel of Versailles. We should be very grateful he has agreed to join our crew. He is an absolute genius in the world of renovations."

René's forehead puckered as he rocked his weight from leg to leg. "Lovely to meet you, Mademoiselle Everly. I'm sure we'll be seeing quite a lot of each other." He tipped his hat forward and said, "Bastien," then quickly continued on his way.

Bastien leaned down to whisper to me, "René was on the shortlist for project manager, and he's been a bit irascible—um . . . how do you say . . . prickly? irritable?—since he learned Tributary offered him the foreman job instead of the top spot. I guess he figured after the Versailles job, he was a shoo-in. But none of that matters. Let's focus on what's really important, Château Mirabelle. She is the real star of the show, non? Today I thought we could take another tour of the house, this time for the benefit of the cameras, and then I can share some blueprints and a project plan with you for how we are going to get started."

"Plum Everly needed in hair and makeup. Repeat, Plum Everly needed in hair and makeup," a crackly voice coming through Bastien's walkie-talkie repeated.

I raised my eyebrows. "So much for the natural-beauty theory."

"Nah, it's la cerise sur la gâteau . . . just the cherry on the cake."

◆ ◆ ◆

Several hours later, Elliott had managed to film me and Bastien in almost every square inch of Château Mirabelle. We laughed, we exchanged light touches, and more than once, I managed to forget a small film crew was capturing every single one of our interactions. At Elliott's insistence, we even re-created some of our conversations from my first visit to the house, while also literally and figuratively covering new ground. This time, Bastien took me into Château Mirabelle's kitchen, bedrooms, and, most interestingly, the underground cellars—or what was left of them, anyway.

I followed Bastien down a dark, narrow tunnel to the exact spot where explosives had been set off over seventy-five years earlier and brushed my hand along the cracked walls, thinking about the courage of the men and women of Maubec who risked their lives to do what they believed was right. "Bastien, do you have a piece of paper and pencil I could borrow?"

He nodded and pulled a pencil out from behind his ear and a clean white sheet from his clipboard. He handed both to me, his hands lingering on mine. We broke apart, and I kneeled down in front of the damaged wall. Elliott motioned the boom operator to come in closer to us while he took two steps forward so that his camera was just a couple of inches from my face. I could practically feel the droplets of sweat beading down Elliott's forehead. He wiped it off with the same dark-blue handkerchief Bastien gifted him at the church.

I placed the paper over the deep fractures, dragging the pencil point back and forth until the spiderweb design appeared on the page, cracks zigzagging out from the epicenter in every direction. The metaphor wasn't lost on me. This one act, to blow up the house, had set into motion an expansive chain reaction from which Château Mirabelle was never able to recover. I held up the paper to show Bastien. "Walls *do* have memories."

"Yes, they do." He playfully wove his fingers into the belt loops of my jean shorts and inched me closer to him. He stroked my hair and slid his hands down my back to settle on my hips.

"Are you kidding me with this?" Elliott exclaimed, without realizing he'd committed the biggest reality TV gaffe of all: crossing the fourth wall. "Shit!" Elliott cried. "I just ruined the take. Plum, Bastien, can you two do that bit over again?"

I stood up from the ground and brushed off my knees. "What bit?"

Elliott waved his hand in the air. "You know, that bit where you pretend to be interested in the history of the house to get Bastien's attention?"

My jaw clenched. "I *am* interested in the history of the house."

"Yeah, and I took this gig because I thought we'd be making high art," Elliott barked sarcastically, before ripping the paper from my hand.

I thrust my hands on my hips. "What is your problem?"

"Nothing. Can we just finish the scene and get this wrapped up and in the can?"

I'd had just about enough of his passive-aggressive jabs and insults. "No, really? What did I do to offend your delicate sensibilities this time?"

Elliott set his camera down on the ground. "You see these tunnels? These passageways? I care about them. I care about the Resistance fighters who hid in them, and the brave people who helped them hide. I want to know their story, not yours—and certainly not Pepé Le Pew's over there. But nobody's about to pay me for that!"

"And what exactly makes you so sure that I don't?" I was going to let it go, but blood was pounding in my ears, and I was finding it difficult to stay calm. "You know what"—I reeled around on him and jabbed a finger into his chest—"you're just like the rest of them, aren't you? You think you know everything there is to know about me because you saw a few episodes of *EVERLYday* or some other show, because you read a few gossip sites? You haven't even bothered to get to know the real me. If you had, you'd see I am not *that* girl."

He lifted his camera to his shoulder, pointed it toward me, and gestured to the boom mic overhead. "Aren't you, though?"

I stared him down through the lens. How dare he? Judgmental, grumpy, pain in my—

"It is very warm down here, non?" Bastien—calm, cool, and collected as ever—stepped forward to break the tension. "Shall we head back upstairs, Plum?"

"What about the rest of the scene?" I asked.

"I am sure Elliott has more than enough without it," Bastien answered. "Besides, isn't that what editing is for?"

Elliott nodded and switched off the camera's light. "He's right, I've seen more than enough."

"Yeah, me too."

Chapter Nineteen

Bastien and I came out from the cellar and stopped by the craft service table. A spread of cured meats and crumbly blue cheeses; a crudité board of brightly colored bell peppers, carrots, and red cherry tomatoes; and loaves and loaves of French bread were set out for the cast and crew. We filled our plates and took them over to a dining hall–like area set up beside the vineyard. After we finished eating, Bastien arranged large-scale sketches of the restored château across the wooden table.

"It is important to me that the château retain all of its original detailing, including the hand-carved boiserie, limestone, tile, and parquet floors," Bastien said, pointing to what looked to be the home's original library.

I leaned in closer to him and the drawing. "What's that material in the tile inlay? It's gorgeous."

"Good eye. Silver. It was very fashionable during the reign of Louis XIV. You'll find it in all the great châteaus from this era." Bastien stood up. "I'm positively parched. Can I get you anything?"

I tapped on my water bottle. "I'm all set." I pushed my lunch to the side and picked up the rendering to get a closer look. The library, restored to all its original glory. I could almost imagine Luc and Imène Adélaïse curled up together reading novels beside the large fireplace.

"What have you got there?" René asked, approaching the table.

"A rendering of the finished library." I passed the drawing to him.

He slipped on his readers and studied the paper. "Who chose the floor inlay?"

"Bastien. He said silver was very fashionable in homes of this era."

"Did he? That's interesting, because beginning in 1689, Louis XIV issued a series of edicts that called for the confiscation of silver to pay for his armies and replenish a depleted treasury. He even ordered his eight-foot-high silver throne to be melted down and replaced by a more modest throne of gilded wood. Gilded wood, Mademoiselle Everly, that is what became fashionable in homes built during this era. Gilded wood, not silver!" René thrust the rendering back at me and continued on his way.

A few minutes later, Bastien reappeared at our table carrying two water bottles. "Production radioed me. They need us both over in video village after we finish our lunch. Hey, what was that all about?" he asked, glancing over at a still-fuming René. I wasn't sure if the cloud of smoke around him was coming from his cigarette or out of his ears.

"Nothing, he wanted to take a look at the renderings for the library, that's all. I see what you mean about being grumpy, though. I'm not sure the two of you share the same vision for the project."

Bastien agreed with a nod and took a swig of water. He wiped his mouth with the back of his hand and set the bottle down on the table. "Speaking of prickly, I hope I am not overstepping, but may I ask what happened between you and Elliott in the cellar earlier?"

"Elliott, all he sees is my TV persona. It's hard to understand unless you've experienced it, but once you let the fame monster out of the box, it's nearly impossible to put it back in. It taints everything, and most people can't see past it. Elliott's apparently one of those people."

Bastien's eyes softened. "You know there is a saying in home restoration. You can honor a home by restoring it to its original state, or you can honor it by restoring it to its original intention. I don't believe people are that different." Bastien took my hands in his. "Plum, you are thousands of miles from home. Think of Provence as your clean slate. It is high time you honor yourself, and be exactly who you intended to be."

Without thinking twice, I leaned over and kissed Bastien hard on the mouth. He was so caught off guard by my forcefulness that he had to steady himself before falling off the bench we shared. He pulled away first, his eyes darting around the vineyard to see if anyone spotted us.

"Whoa, Plum, I thought you didn't think this was a good idea?" Bastien said, repeating the concern I shared at Château du Val d'Été.

The irony of reality TV was that there was really *nothing* real about it. Storylines were fabricated, feelings exaggerated, and relationships coerced. For the first time in my life, I wanted to experience spontaneity and genuine human emotion. "I'm still not sure it is, but let's not decide all that right now? I like you. I think you like me. Let's live in the moment, whatever happens?" He reached over, cupped my chin in his hands, and guided my face so that we were centimeters apart. "Okay?" I asked.

"D'accord," he breathed, then kissed me again, this time with greater urgency. His hand moved from my chin and slid to cup the back of my head, his fingers gently playing with the small tendrils at the nape of my neck. The sensation of the kiss was familiar, yet wholly new. His body pressed close to mine. He smelled sweet like the ripe mirabelles all around Provence. I breathed him in, all of him, and allowed myself to be swept away by the fantasy of a fresh start.

I pulled back, my lips swollen and humming with electricity. He pushed a strand of hair from my face and tucked it behind my ear and then ran his thumb across my pulsing bottom lip.

"C'mon, we better go before someone spots us," I said.

We packed up the renderings and made our way to video village where the show's director, Claudine Renard, and producer, Jack Lyon, were crowded around a small monitor. I readied myself for the feedback and critique people in their positions usually had to offer. *Be funnier, no, be more serious. Act more engaged, no, act more aloof. Steal the scene, no, fade into the background.*

Instead, Claudine and Jack stood up to applaud us. I glanced over at Bastien, who also seemed taken aback. Claudine spoke first. "Bravo. The dailies are merveilleux. The sparks between you two are practically flying off the screen. Kate will be so pleased."

Yeah, I know, on and off screen. Sparks everywhere!

"They really are," Jack chimed in. "Plum, Bastien, your banter and playfulness are magical. You're both reading very natural and unscripted, exactly what we want at Tributary."

Elliott stepped into the tent, surprised to find me and Bastien standing there.

"Ah, Elliott, good timing," Claudine said. "We were just telling Plum and Bastien how pleased we are with the dailies."

Elliott's eyes gleamed. "Château Mirabelle is a real treasure trove of history, especially what I've learned about the role it played in the French Resistance. I think if I could interview some of the townspeople who knew Luc and Imène Adélaïse, we might be able to figure out who ratted them out to the Third Reich. It would add an entirely new angle to the show."

I turned to Bastien. "No, they were discovered by the Nazis, right? Isn't that what you told me?"

Elliott shook his head. "That doesn't make any sense. Somebody would have had to tell them exactly where to look. I was talking to Agnès and Pascal about it this morning, and they have some really interesting theories on what may have happened. I'd love to pick up some of those strands to see where they lead us, I mean, lead me."

Bastien interrupted, "We'll have quite enough material with just the house renovation. We don't want to overshadow the real star of the show with an unnecessary storyline."

Jack chimed in, his tone measured, "Elliott, if you're interested in exploring that further on your own time, we can evaluate its potential, but I wouldn't set high expectations. We already have an abundance of top-notch material right here in front of us, and we should be careful not to overextend ourselves." He brought his hands together with a soft clap, adding, "For now, let's stay the course. Keep up the excellent work, all of you. We'll keep our eyes on the path ahead."

As my mind raced, recalling my kiss with Bastien, I couldn't help but chime in, my voice filled with anticipation, "Absolutely, let's see where this journey takes us."

Chapter Twenty

Two weeks later and according to René, we'd already fallen at least a month behind on the renovation schedule, and I couldn't figure out where we'd gone wrong. Bastien blamed the incompetence and insubordination of the crew. He'd fired three workers so far, and we seemed to be growing in shorter and shorter supply of employees who met his high standards. The whole mess had slowed the project so greatly, I really started to worry about meeting the show's tight deadline.

If I knew one thing, it was that production delays equaled money. Lots of money. And money was not something that producers were happy about wasting, especially for avoidable issues. Maybe they'd blame me and toss me from the project? Or even worse, what if the whole operation folded because this small-bit company didn't have enough backing to extend production? My mind was reeling, and I could feel a migraine mounting at the base of my skull.

I rubbed my temples and sat on a stone retaining wall in front of the château. Bastien stormed out the front door and stood for a second under the entryway with his hands set firmly on his hips. After a few heated seconds of pacing and muttering to himself, he lifted his head, probably to see if anyone was watching, and caught sight of me. His stance softened, and the corners of his mouth curved up into a smile.

"What is that phrase you Americans say?" He sat down on the wall beside me. "A nickel for your thoughts?"

I laughed and leaned into him. "Penny. A penny for your thoughts."

"Okay, take all my money for your thoughts. Whatever you like, it is yours." His thick French accent made his silly banter even cuter. He lifted my hand and pressed my palm to his lips. "These workers don't know their col from their cul."

"Their *what* from their *what*?"

"They don't know their collar from ass! I know that you have been worried about the progress, but I promise, even if I have to be here morning, noon, and night. Tout ira bien, comme toujours, we will get it sorted."

He kissed my forehead and ran the tips of my hair between his fingers. When Bastien spoke to me in French, it was sexy as hell, but I rarely had any clue what he was saying. What did it even matter, though, when he was just so damn charming? "Don't work too hard. I was hoping we could grab some dinner later. Maybe Chez Noisette?"

"I don't know. I was thinking maybe more of a night *in*." He waggled his eyebrows to emphasize his suggestion.

"You're working that French-lover stereotype real hard now, aren't you?" I teased.

He gave his eyebrows one last definitive shimmy. "As if you mind," he said between brushing a few sweet kisses down the column of my neck before standing.

"Whoa, wait, Romeo, where are you going!?" I said, my skin still tingling in each spot where he'd pressed his soft lips.

"Ma belle, we are already behind schedule," he joked. "I cannot be responsible for any more delays. Plus, we are going to dinner later, non?"

"I thought we were staying *in* tonight?" I asked.

"Okay, well, if you insist." He winked and then headed back toward the house.

As soon as he was within earshot of any worker who would listen, Bastien was already starting back in with the shouting. "Non, non, non!" His voice grew louder with each iteration of the word.

All I could hear from where I was sitting was the worker speaking in rapid French, and Bastien meeting him with furious huffs and grunts. Out of my peripheral, I spotted Elliott coming my way from the house, but I didn't look up. The pressure in my head was increasing with every disagreement.

Elliott rested his camera equipment against the half wall and then sat next to me, wiping the dust from his sunglasses on his T-shirt. In the last two weeks, we'd settled into a cordial working relationship, realizing we both needed the other if we were to have any hope of success for this project.

"I can't film any of this. René and him are going at it like two cocks in a ring," Elliott grunted.

I tilted my head, picking up on the dig at his word choice. "What are they fighting about now?" I asked, not even sure I wanted to know.

"There are issues with the foundation, and the way Bastien wants the plumbing, and the electrical work is not up to code or something like that. I can't make out enough of the French to really be sure."

"I'm sure he just wants it all to be perfect. He cares so much about this project. Does Kate have any idea how behind schedule we are?" I asked.

"She says the dailies are testing so well that they'll find the money to make it work, so it seems we both still have a job, for now." He smirked and bent down to grab the camera at his feet. "Actually, I had an idea while I was waiting for something filmable in there. How about you and I go shoot a few clips off-site? We can grab some footage from around town and try to interview some locals? Beats sitting on our asses listening to this nonsense for the next few hours."

"Agreed. I'm sure by the time we return, Bastien will have it all sorted out, and we'll be back on schedule." My voice sounded hopeful as I tried to mask my skepticism.

"I doubt it."

"We'll see." I smiled at him, secretly grateful for the excuse of a temporary escape.

◆ ◆ ◆

We asked Gervais to drop us back in the town's center, where we plotted our route over garlicky mussels in a soupy, white-wine-and-herb-infused broth and extra-crispy frites. The small cliffside bistro had about ten small wrought iron tables with mosaic tops adorned with fanned white linen napkins that billowed gracefully in the afternoon breeze. When the server asked what we'd like to drink, we ordered two glasses of the Chenin Blanc he'd recommended to go with the meal.

A roving accordion player strolled past, and the melody of France's famous "La Vie En Rose" floated by on the back of a warm breeze. Elliott's foot grazed against mine as he inched closer to listen. As he scooted in, his eyes glanced at my cheek, and he moved his fingers toward my face. Confused and a little unnerved, I tried to lean back, but as I was pinned against the chair, his pointer finger and thumb reached out to brush my cheek. Considering the size of his mitt-like hands, his touch was surprisingly gentle.

"Uh . . . whatcha doing there, buddy?"

He pulled his fingers back, away from my face, and held out his thumb. "Eyelash. Make a wish." The sentence came out in one breath, like it was preprogrammed.

Out of the thousand things I saw Elliott do every day, nothing could have prepared me for *that* to have come out of his mouth. I squinted at him to check if he was joking, and then seeing that he wasn't, I looked to the tiny hair on the large pad of his thumb. I chuckled. "Make a wish!? I thought only eight-year-old girls did that?!"

Catching himself, he blushed, almost as if surprised he'd said it at all. "Eight-year-old girls and overly superstitious thirty-year-old men who grew up in a house full of little sisters. Some habits die hard, I guess." But in spite of his embarrassment, he extended his thumb out a bit closer, and, surrendering, I closed my eyes.

I inhaled deeply and considered my wish before opening my eyes, pursing my lips together, and expelling a whoosh of breath to send the eyelash into the warm summer air—and along with it, any traces of his previous embarrassment.

Elliott pulled back, awkwardly rubbing the back of his neck with one hand, while grabbing for a sip of his wine with the other. "So what'd you wish for?" he asked as soon as he swallowed.

"I can't tell you that! Or else it won't come true. Everybody knows that." I crossed my arms over my chest as if holding in my secret and grinned in mock defiance.

Maybe I was a little superstitious too. He smiled but he didn't speak, his eyes remaining focused on me. I wasn't sure if he was challenging me with his stare to tell him my wish, or just observing the fact that I wouldn't. Either way, usually, I would have ignored the attention, but from him, I held his gaze and studied his face, his relaxed posture, his lack of pretense.

When I finally pulled my eyes from his, I scanned the bistro as it twinkled under the string lights above. The warm, honeyed tones of the Provençal sky merged seamlessly with the landscape below, and the hills, dressed in a patchwork quilt of vibrant greens and soft purples, unfurled like a living tapestry tossed over the hills as if to keep it warm as the temperatures dipped at night.

I took out my phone, opened the video app, and zoomed in on the accordionist swaying to and fro in front of the whole picturesque view. The entire scene was so cinematic I couldn't help but be drawn to capturing it, even though I was certain the magnitude and true beauty could never adequately translate the same way as seeing it in person.

Elliott, spotting my camera, started waving his hands at me, his eyes growing wide in panic. "Ah, no! What are you doing!? That's just going to make him come over here!" He very inconspicuously tried to hide behind his menu, obviously unsuccessfully since his head alone could barely be concealed by the tiny paper flapping in the breeze.

The musician meandered closer as the final notes were played and peeked over his accordion to ask, "Excusez-moi, do you young lovers have any special requests?"

Elliott looked around, seeming to think the stranger was addressing someone else, and when the man stood there waiting for a response, Elliott finally sputtered, "Lo . . . lovers?! Us? No! We're not!"

"Jeez, relax. We're sharing a bowl of mussels and a bottle of wine and sitting like two feet away from one another. It's not completely unreasonable he might think we were on some sort of date. Doesn't make it true," I shot back. "And thank you for making it sound like a date with me is the most offensive idea on the planet. Real ego boost, thank you."

Elliott turned to the accordionist. "We're fine. This *isn't* a date and we . . . we're not . . . lovers. Um, here," he said, tossing some money into his porkpie hat, "take this, for the rose song."

The rose song, classic Elliott.

I continued filming him, zeroing in on his flushed face and him gulping down his glass of water, until the musician disappeared into the crowd to serenade some actual lovers, and then I tucked my phone back into my bag.

Elliott watched me as I put it away and said, "I know I was giving you a hard time about your little videos before, but I've seen some of the clips you've been posting to your TikTok account. And, I'm big enough to admit, they're not half bad. The one you posted a few days ago of Agnès shuffling around the inn in her housedress arranging sprigs of lavender was really very good. The editing was clever and original, and it showed her in a totally different light."

For a moment, I couldn't tell whether he was being serious or not, but the sincerity in his eyes left little doubt.

"No, really. Its simplicity captured her and the inn's essence perfectly. Have you ever considered a career behind the camera?"

I shook my head, considering the extent of my own creative potential. "What do you mean? To do what you do? I guess . . . I'm just not sure I have enough to say—to, you know, actually make people sit up and listen if I'm not the one shouting it from in front of the camera. Usually dressed in spandex. Or juggling something heavy or flaming."

"Well, for what it's worth," he began, his voice firm and supportive, "I stopped *and* watched *and* listened, and I think you have plenty to say."

I'd never been one to be short on getting compliments, usually on my looks, my perceived success, or some other nonsensical thing that had very little to do with *me*. But this compliment, coming from Elliott—who'd pulled no punches about how he felt about my past—struck me as not only more meaningful but also more genuine than any other I think I'd ever received.

"Well, I have been kind of obsessed with all the stuff we've been uncovering about the château, and I started to do a little digging on my own," I said, my words now flowing with a self-assuredness that had been previously absent. "I don't know how much of this you already know, but I've found some really interesting material about the wineries in this region and their significant role in the Resistance during the war. Remember what Odette said? The families who had money fled, and the ones who stayed either couldn't afford to leave, or simply refused to leave their homes behind. I think that's why we should speak to some of the families who've been here for centuries." With each word my conviction grew stronger. "Don't you want to know what really happened to the Adélaïses?"

Elliott's expression was one of pure surprise. "Wait, so you think someone sold them out too?"

I felt the same pit in my stomach I'd experienced the first day when I spotted all those cameras outside Château Mirabelle. From the moment I'd laid eyes on the photograph of Luc and Imène Adélaïse at Saint Orens, I knew this project meant more to me than just another credit on my IMDb page. For Elliott too. I could see it in his eyes. It was like the Adélaïses were calling out to the two of us to right the wrongs of the past and bring their beautiful home and community back to life.

I nodded and exhaled. "I know Jack and Claudine said this storyline was a waste of time, but I agree with you—it isn't. So where should we go first? Do you have a plan in mind?"

"I think we should talk to Elodie Archambeau. She owns Le Coquelicot, the floral shop up the road. Agnès told me her family's been in this town since the early 1700s. She may have some good stories for us to use as a jumping-off point. The only thing is, she's a bit of a drinker, so we may need to fact-check a bit after her interview."

I eyed Elliott up and down. "You've really done your homework, huh?"

"I have chronic insomnia. So does Agnès. She's spilled a lot of tea over late-night . . . *ummm* tea . . . and croissants."

"Sounds like either way, it'll be a good time. On y va!" I said as I rose out of my seat and pushed in the heavy iron bistro chair.

Elliott's eyebrows popped up, impressed. "Look at you, picking up some of the local lingo."

"While you've been busy spilling and sipping all the tea with Agnès, Pascal's been tutoring me in French, and as it turns out, I'm a quick study."

I grabbed my jacket from off my chair and went to place some cash on the table, but Elliott had beaten me to it and stepped aside to let me go by first.

Chapter Twenty-One

Elliott walked next to me as we made our way in the direction of Mme. Archambeau's shop. Though the town was small and there was really only one florist, Le Coquelicot was instantly recognizable by its abundantly colorful display of wildflowers that decorated the walkway in front of the store.

The bell chimed as we stepped inside the small but incredibly fragrant shop. The perfume of the various flowers pirouetted through the air, each note as distinct and delightful as the next. The peonies: bold and blousy. The eucalyptus: brisk and refreshing. The freesia: dainty and unassuming. That was one thing I still couldn't seem to get over (or get enough of)—the smells. The glorious aromas of potent cheeses in the markets and the fresh-baked bread never seemed to fade. In Disney World, it's rumored they piped in the scents of sweet treats to entice park goers to grab one more unnecessary confection, but in France, it was wholly organic.

Madame Archambeau was bustling about behind the counter, toying with sprigs of what looked like baby's breath and eucalyptus. Her graying auburn curls seemed to stand out among the greenery behind her and she moved with the grace and speed of someone half her age.

"Bonjour," she announced at the sound of the bell, like the Pavlov's dog of greetings: conditioned rather than truly welcoming. She never even looked up from the ornate display she was arranging.

"Bonjour, Madame." I walked toward the counter, trying not to be distracted by the exotic orchids, lilies, and dahlias of all different colors placed to contrast one another in the most artistic way. "We were wondering if you have a moment to speak with us."

"Ah oui, what kind of arrangement are you looking for? We are very busy preparing for a wedding on Sunday, so if it is anything compliqué, you will have to go to Avignon."

"No, we're not here for flowers," Elliott said.

Madame Archambeau set down her shears and furrowed her brows. "Not here for flowers?"

"We understand your family has been an integral part of this community for centuries. We would love to share that sort of personalized history with viewers for a show we're filming here in town. Would you be willing to talk with us?" he asked.

She pinched her face into a prune-like expression. "Are you part of the film crew I've seen over at Château Mirabelle?"

"Yes, we are," I answered. "We're restoring the house, but also trying to learn more about the people who lived there. Your family's name has come up quite a few times."

She had been distracted as she finished wrapping the floral arrangement on the counter in front of her, but at the mention of her family's prominence in the historical fabric of the town, she lifted her head and beamed with pride. "Oui, oh well, in that case, I think I can find some time to speak with you," she said, conveniently forgetting about the Sunday wedding excuse. "Let's go across the street and sit. Maybe Monsieur Grenouille will be able to join us for a little while. He owns the patisserie, and his family has been here for a very long time as well. Not as long as mine, but still, he may be able to offer *some* insight. Just give me dix minutes." She held up both of her hands in *five* gestures.

"Very good. Merci!" I led the way out the door and across the street. I slowed my pace to allow Elliott, saddled with his camera bag, to catch up. When he did, we paused at the corner and stared in the direction of the bakery. Monsieur Grenouille was clearing a few plates from the outside tables and wiping them down with a rag. "Doesn't 'grenouille' mean *frog* in French?" I asked.

Elliott shrugged. "I'm not sure. Why?"

"It just suits him and his weirdly wide, sinking jawline. I think you should do the talking on this one, though, I've gotten the impression he doesn't like me all that much," I said.

"You've met him before?"

"We've crossed paths a few times. I don't think he's overjoyed that a film crew's taken over his town."

"Well then, you'll just have to change his mind. I have a feeling you're good at that," Elliott said in such an assured tone that I wasn't sure if he meant it as a biting insult or the highest possible compliment.

"Why don't you secure that larger table in the back, and I'll order something so Monsieur Grenouille stops staring at us," Elliott offered and headed to the back of the line.

A few minutes later he came back balancing two pains au chocolat and two cafés au lait. Monsieur Grenouille's eyes were still locked on me like a laser, forcing me to wonder what was really behind his intense gaze. Could he really be this upset that we were filming a TV show about Château Mirabelle? Didn't he realize it would bring tourism and attention to Maubec? Something they desperately needed by the looks of the quiet and crumbling streets. No, Monsieur Grenouille's disdain felt more personal somehow. There had to be something I was missing.

When Madame Archambeau shuffled in a few minutes later, she hurried to the counter speaking in lightning-speed French to Monsieur Grenouille, who after a few seconds of her chatter started to wave his hands at her to stress his "Non! Non! Non!"s.

The two of them began to bicker back and forth until their tittering came to a sudden halt and they turned to look at Elliott and me sitting at the table. At the abrupt silence, time seemed to pause for a moment while the four of us just looked at one another in a painfully tense will he / won't he limbo. We readjusted our attention back to our cafés au lait, unsure if we'd be joined by Madame and Monsieur, or only Madame, or if we'd all be tossed out on our asses and charged for the foot out the door.

But after we took a few more sips of our coffees—pretending not to listen to Madame Archambeau coerce Monsieur Grenouille to join us—he finally relented and plopped down at the farthest end of the table, as if he was going to try to make a run for it as soon as he was out of Madame Archambeau's arm's reach. She shuffled behind Monsieur Grenouille, and when he was finally settled into a seat, she scurried quickly behind the bakery counter, our eyes trailing her as she returned with a half-full bottle of wine.

"You don't mind, I'm sure, Remy, non?" she asked as she was already uncorking and pouring the golden liquid into a glass she'd grabbed from the counter.

Elliott looked at me as if to say, *Take it away, cowboy*, but all of a sudden I felt the weight of all the words I didn't know how to say in French and realized I couldn't even offer pleasantries. How embarrassing. Every time I opened my mouth to start to say something, I paused, wondering if he would understand me or even care what I had to say. But thankfully, Madame Archambeau saved the day, delighted to hold court and lead our conversation, so long as her wine was kept full to the brim. Thank goodness, because Monsieur Grenouille remained locked up tighter than Fort Knox.

"Mais oui, you see, there wasn't much of anything left of Maubec after the war," she explained. "Once the winery had been destroyed, it was just a matter of time . . . the Bordeaux region would take care of the last of what little the Nazis left behind." She accentuated her sentences with her wineglass, sending golden droplets sloshing about. "My family managed to remain here during the Huguenots' mass exodus from France during the 17e siècle, and then we had to fight like mad to stay yet again during the Second World War. But what can I say? We are a resilient lot."

Madame Archambeau lifted the glass to her lips once again, and I noticed that she'd almost polished off the rest of the bottle. Aside from a tinge of rosiness in her cheeks, she barely missed a beat and didn't stumble over any words. She scooped the bottle off the table and waggled it in our direction as a sign of offering, but at our refusal, she went on to pour herself what was left of the wine.

"What exactly are you looking for, Mademoiselle Everly? Because these walls have a lot of history and a lot of dark secrets hidden behind them. If you were looking for a nice fluffy story to tell your friends, I am afraid this will be a short conversation." She cast her eyes out the window dismissively, as if she knew she'd already intrigued us enough that we'd ask her to continue.

"I'm not sure I understand," I admitted as a way to coax her to keep talking. I eyed Elliott to see if he was any more in the know, but he shook his head, affirming that he too had no idea what she was talking about. And lastly I looked over to Monsieur Grenouille, who was seeming to ignore us entirely as he mindlessly continued to use a spoon far too tiny for his large hands to stir sugar into his espresso.

Madame Archambeau took another sip and leaned in a little closer. "The history of this town is one of resilience and integrity, but it is not a pretty story. It's full of betrayal, and I'm *not* just talking about the Nazis. I'm not sure your superficiel little television program is the right platform to tell it."

"With all due respect, Madame," Elliott interrupted before I could respond, "that is precisely why we feel it is such an important story to tell."

Madame Archambeau bit her bottom lip and gnawed on it as she thought. I took the opportunity to glance over at Monsieur Grenouille to gauge his thoughts, but his face was as blank as it had been when we first began.

I had one last trick up my sleeve to try to get her to talk. I set my mug down, slung my purse over my shoulder, and pushed up from the table. “C’mon, Elliott, we’ve overstayed our welcome as it is. Maybe it’s time to get going.”

“You know, that is the first intelligent thing you’ve said all day,” Monsieur Grenouille mumbled.

I whipped my head around at him. “Excuse me?”

Elliott tugged on the arm of my shirt. “Leave it, Plum.”

“No! He doesn’t get to just insult me like that.” I turned to face Monsieur Grenouille. “Sir, you don’t even know me.”

Monsieur Grenouille *humphed* with annoyance, clearly devoid of any remorse. “I’ve seen the things you’re willing to put your name on, Mademoiselle Everly. And if our little town’s going to be dragged through the mud, I’d rather it not be on one of your sleazy television programs. We have been through enough.”

Elliott zeroed in on his last sentence. “What do you mean by that?”

Monsieur Grenouille folded his arms over his chest. “Why don’t you ask Monsieur Munier?”

“Bastien? What could he possibly have to do with *any* of this?” I asked.

Madame Archambeau touched Monsieur Grenouille gently on the forearm. “Remy, leave it. The boy’s not to blame for the sins of the past.”

Monsieur Grenouille pounded his fists into the table. “They are all to blame! Monsieur Munier most of all.” He reached for his cane. “C’est ridicule. Pourquoi remuer le passé? Ces Americains . . . *pfft*,” he mumbled and spat as he ambled back behind the counter.

Elliott looked up at me. “Care to translate?”

“My French isn’t that good yet, but I am going to take a guess and say he more or less just told us where we could stick it?”

Elliott agreed. “My French isn’t good at all, and he definitely told us where we could stick it.”

Madame Archambeau rose from her seat. “I should get back to the shop. The bride and her maman are coming by very soon to look at centerpieces.”

Chapter Twenty-Two

After Madame Archambeau left the patisserie, we gathered our belongings and followed her out to the street to head back to the inn. As soon as we stepped outside, Monsieur Grenouille slammed the door closed behind us and flipped the sign on the window to read FERMÉ. CLOSED.

"Well, that was a colossal waste of time," I said, glancing back.

"Was it?" Elliott snapped. "We learned your little boy toy is somehow entangled in all of this."

I shot him a dirty look. "Don't call him that. Besides, Bastien already told me his grandfather worked for the Adélaïses."

"There's more to *that* story," Elliott said, pacing in circles.

"Admit it, you just don't like him."

He stopped dead in his tracks. "Okay, fine, I admit it, I don't like Bastien. I think he's a pretty face devoid of any real substance. I'm sure half of the things that I say would sound sexy and charming if they were said in a French accent too."

"I sincerely doubt that."

"Whatever, either way, I just think he's vapid. Shallow. Get real, Plum, nobody is *that* perfect."

"Well, I do like him. Unlike you, he hasn't given me any reason not to."

"Yet," Elliott smirked. "I have no doubt that it's just a matter of time before one or both of you does something to blow this whole project up in the name of good television drama."

"Why do I still feel like even though you are insulting Bastien, the person you're really annoyed with, for God knows what reason, is me. I don't know what I ever did to piss you off so badly, but I can't figure out where I stand with you. We had a nice day, some actual *nice* moments between us, and then poof, the switch flips and I'm back to being Plum Everly, the diva you can't stand."

He rolled his eyes like I just didn't understand, as if I was misunderstanding the entire situation. "You think a whole lot of yourself, *Ms. Everly*," he said, turning my name into some sort of insult. "I have news for you, not everything in this world *is* actually about you. But you can't stand that. You can't stand for anyone else to take center stage. You know what they say, don't you? People who shine from within don't actually crave the spotlight."

My anger was replaced by hurt and deep sadness. How many people out there hated me or had such a wrong idea of the real me because of my public persona? Did everyone think I was nothing better than an attention whore putting myself on show after show because I needed the constant validation, when in truth I was so lost I was just grasping at anything to stay afloat? "You've got it so wrong, you know. That person you keep referencing, she isn't me. This isn't the life I want. Not really."

"Which life are you talking about here, Plum? It's hard to keep track—you've pretended to have so many."

Just as I went to fire back, the almost comical *meep meep* of Bastien's small Peugeot tooted up the drive.

"Plum! Elliott! Venez, come, I have something I want to show you both," Bastien called, pulling up beside us. "I know we have not been able to film much these past few days with all the troubles with the construction, but I think this is something you will both want to see."

I glanced at Elliott and, without a word, jumped into the front seat of the car. He stood unmoving, as if weighing how badly he needed the footage against how badly he didn't want to spend time with me and Bastien one-on-one.

I leaned out of the passenger side and said, "Kate's gonna be pissed if you don't have enough content for the dailies and testing audience, so get the lead out of your shoes and just get in the damn car. Stop being so obstinate."

Muttering to himself about "wasting time" and "this damn shoot," Elliott begrudgingly climbed into the back seat to wedge himself between Bastien's large soccer duffel and the camera and boom, which we had to stick the top of out the window—again, Elliott the Grouch was less than pleased.

Bastien eased off the clutch and shifted into first gear to set off toward Château Mirabelle just as the pastel sunset began to settle across the rolling vineyards. Small pulses of light flickered across the horizon as a scattering of fireflies floated in the slight breeze, and I rolled the window down to breathe in the warm evening air. Bastien zipped up the long drive and threw the car into park right beside the stone staircase leading to the wooden front door of the château.

"Bastien, where are we going? What are you up to?" I eyed him and smirked, and my stomach fluttered at the sight of his wink.

"Elliott, you'll want to start filming, non?"

Elliott half-heartedly lifted the camera to his shoulder and turned his back to the entryway so that the camera was focused on me and Bastien making our way up the front stairs.

"Come with me, Plum, I have a little surprise for you," Bastien said, as if scripted, and led me by the hand inside. I tried to ignore Elliott, and the camera, and the fact that Bastien was probably doing this all for the TV show and not necessarily as a personal romantic gesture.

He led me through the main floor, which, while still in ruins, was in better shape than before. Bastien began to speak as we tunneled through the halls. "I know that you have been très stressée with this project, and I know it has been difficult these past few weeks with the construction. But I am a perfectionist, what can I say?"

Elliott snorted from behind his camera.

"Are you alright?" Bastien asked.

"Just dusty in here," he fibbed.

"Ah, oui. Dust is very common in an old house. Come, follow me this way, ma cherie."

Bastien smiled, and a flush warmed my cheeks. He paused at the doorway to a large, windowed solarium, letting Elliott go past us so that he could capture our arrival on film. He pulled back the rich, heavy dark-green velvet drapes, using the decorative tassel tieback to secure one at each side. Almost instantly, the sherbety oranges and pinks of the sunset flooded the room with a warm wash of color. It was like stepping into a fever dream, the setting immersive and vibrant, positively magnificent.

"Oh wow, Bastien. This view is just . . . wow." My eyes could hardly take in the surreal panorama.

"Is it, how do you say, 'awesome'?" he teased and pulled me close. His hands wrapped around my waist, and he drew me back against his chest in a reverse hug. He rested his chin on my shoulder as we both watched out the window as the sun slipped away to the hypnotizing hum of the cicadas singing in the distance.

"I must say, this was a wonderful surprise. And a much needed one," I said, hoping Elliott would catch the implication. I turned into Bastien's arms and drew my lips to his, softly weaving my hands up through the soft curls at the nape of his neck.

After kissing me back (and turning my legs to Jell-O), he laughed and said, "This isn't even the half of it. Oh, I have more."

"You do, do you?" I purred seductively.

"Yes, I do!" he exclaimed and pulled me across the room to a small corner under the biggest picture window.

Silhouettes of hundreds of twisted grapevines cast against the periwinkle night sky. "Just . . . wow," I breathed.

Bastien entwined his fingers in mine and kissed the back of my hand. "Though it took a bit longer and caused more than a few headaches, today, Plum, we finally finished the foundation. We should be able to move much more quickly now that the main structural issues are meilleures. Now you will be able to be much more hands-on, and we can start filming your contributions to the renovation."

"So it's all fixed? We can move forward? That's incredible news. I know how hard you've been working to try to get this all straightened out." I kissed him again and hoped he could feel my gratitude.

I was used to intimate moments like this one being captured on film, but somehow it felt completely different with Elliott behind the camera. I glanced over and caught his eye before we both quickly looked away.

"Yes, because I want it all to be perfect. It will be so great for both of us when this show is a hit, right?" He pressed his lips to the top of my head. "Okay so, now look down. On the ground. By your feet. I wanted you to see this before we laid down the wood flooring."

Confused, I stepped back, and with just the littlest light left from the descending sun, I could make out the faint outline of something in the floor's layer of concrete. "What is—"

I squatted down to inspect, and there in the floor's foundation, etched in for the rest of time, were my initials, PE, encased in a heart. Bastien continued, "This way no matter when you return home to Hollywood or wherever you jet off to next, you will be a part of this house here in Maubec so long as this house stays standing. And hopefully, it will be a part of you too."

I traced my fingers over the letters and stood up to face him. "Always, Bastien. No matter where I go, this"—I gestured to the floor—"and you"—I took his hands in mine—"will always have a special place in my heart. This was just so thoughtful." I stretched up on my toes and pulled him in for a long, deep kiss, taking the time to run my hands from his waist up his torso to settle on the tight muscles in his back. He passionately returned the gesture, his hands grabbing my hips and drawing me in close. He trailed sweet kisses down my neck, and breathless, I tugged lightly on fistfuls of his hair.

Elliott cleared his throat forcefully. "That's enough for tonight. I've seen everything I need to." He switched off the camera light and covered the lens.

I took my phone out of my pocket and snapped a photo of my initials in the concrete, quickly shooting it off to Kate in a text. Within seconds she responded.

Kate: Let me guess, Bastien? That's quite the romantic gesture.

Me: I don't know about that . . . but he said he wants me to always be a part of the château which was very sweet.

Kate: Sweet my ass. Flowers are sweet. Chocolates are sweet. That my friend was a gesture.

Me: LOL! See you in a few days.

Kate: Packing my bags as we speak. What's the weather like?

Me: HOT and aircon is not a given.

Kate: Noted.

Me: À bientôt!

Kate: Can't wait. XO

I shimmied my phone back into my pocket.

"I have another surprise for Plum, but let me drive you back to the inn first," Bastien offered.

"That's okay, I texted Odette. She's already on her way to pick me up."

Here I was feeling, I don't know, guilty? . . . uncomfortable? . . . at Elliott having to play audience to Bastien's and my PDA, but why? There was clearly something sparking between Odette and him. I mean, he had her on speed dial for god's sake! And it's not like he gave two figs about me in general, so why should he care who I was kissing? I'm sure he didn't, and I was making something out of a big fat nothing.

We didn't owe each other anything, let alone explanations, and I sure as hell had no right or reason to feel the small twinge of what I could only call jealousy needling somewhere deep under my skin. Especially not when I had a gorgeous, sexy, and attentive Frenchman *literally* in my arms. What the hell was wrong with me?! Why did I have to remind myself to stop paying attention to Elliott while Bastien was giving me all the attention I needed?!

Bastien took my hand to lead me toward the back door. "Parfait!" he said to the back of Elliott's head as he headed out the front.

"Have a good night," Elliott said.

"Yeah, you too." I glanced back over at him, his hulking shadow moving out the door, pausing for one second to glance back at me too.

Outside, Bastien had set a small picnic, and though the vineyards were overgrown and untended, the expanse was still breathtaking—a world away from LA. He had cleverly strung a few bistro lights from some branches and a dilapidated trellis so that we were haloed in a soft glow as the sun continued to set behind the Provençal hills.

"Come, assieds-toi." Bastien gestured to the fleece plaid blanket he'd laid out on a grassy stretch, which was adorned with a few fluffy, colorful throw pillows for us to sit on.

"Bastien, this is so sweet."

We kicked off our shoes and got comfy on the blanket. Bastien reached over to a very stereotypical brown wicker picnic basket—it almost looked like a set prop—and took out a container of olive tapenade, a few small brown-paper-wrapped cheeses, a jar of lavender honey, a small bowl of bright-red strawberries and purple grapes, a slice of quiche lorraine, and two halves of a crusty baguette. Finally, the pièce de résistance: he fished around at the bottom to reach for a bottle of wine, a rosé from what I could tell in the dim light.

I didn't realize just how hungry I was until Bastien popped a piece of gooey brie drizzled with the lavender honey in my mouth to try.

He licked the remaining honey off his finger and asked, "What do you think?"

"Of you? Of this? Or of the brie? All of it is very sweet."

"You are the one who is very sweet. Speaking of, I brought a mirabelle for you to try," he said, pulling two speckled, bright-yellow ripe plums from inside his pocket, along with a Swiss Army knife. He carved out a succulent slice and held it in his palm, the golden juice starting to trickle down his forearm. "Here, taste," he offered, bringing the fruit to my lips.

With a gentle bite my teeth sank down into the tender flesh, releasing a burst of sweetness different from the dark-purple plums I was used to at home. The flavor was more complex, more nuanced, the subtle earthy notes of lavender and other aromatic flowers from the region deeply infused in the skin. It was like tasting Provence itself.

"So what do you think?" Bastien asked.

"I think it's delicious."

He pressed his lips to mine, sweeping his tongue with sweet kisses down my chin to lap up the sticky nectar. "I quite agree, delicious."

Once we'd had our fill, sated with wine, bread, and cheese, we tossed everything back into the basket, clearing the blanket to make room for us to stretch out across the fleece. Bastien rolled over on his side and slid his hand onto my stomach, pulling me to him, his fingers finding the skin under my shirt. I sucked in a gasp as his cold touch moved up my warm skin, and his eyes found mine before drawing me in for an enveloping kiss. His hands in my hair and his breath mingling with mine were intoxicating, and yet I still felt so in my head, unable to let go and enjoy the moment.

"Let's take this back to my appartement," he whispered against my neck, every few words interrupted with a peck to the soft spot behind my ear.

Goose bumps trailed over my skin and down my legs. I wanted *this*. I wanted *him*. What was with my apprehension? I pulled away from Bastien and slowly shook my head. "I don't think that's a good idea. Not yet, Bastien. I just . . ."

"I do not understand." His pained face registered as hurt more than upset. He tilted my chin up toward his face to look him in the eye.

"It's just . . . this is all so new for me—this town, you, this relationship. I was with my ex, Rhys, for years. He was so intrinsically tied to my life and my happiness—it was like I didn't know how to breathe without him. I'm just trying to figure out who I am on my own, and

I'm not sure if it's smart to get involved, especially with the distance and the short duration of the project . . ."

I wasn't sure if it was the language barrier or if I was starting to ramble senselessly, but Bastien looked more confused than when I had pulled away. "I still . . . I don't . . ." He struggled to find the right words. "What you are saying is that you do not want me, n'est-ce pas? That you are still in love with Rhys?"

"God, no! That's not what I'm saying at all. I just don't want to rush into anything. I don't want to feel pressured by our limited time together, or by what we feel like we need to squeeze in before I leave. I just want it to feel right, you know? And at this moment, it doesn't. I'm sorry." I searched his eyes for any indication of his emotion. "Is that okay?"

Though he looked hurt and still confused, his shoulders softened, and he wrapped me in a hug. "Of course it is okay. I just want to be with you in whatever way I can be. I do not wish to pressure you to do anything you feel you are not ready for. We can just stay here and enjoy the night together like this, yes?" He quickly popped up from the blanket, and I sat up too, wondering where on earth he was going and at such a strange moment. But before I knew it, the glow of the garden lights disappeared, leaving us in complete darkness. Bastien pulled his phone from his pocket and used the flashlight to make his way back to me on the blanket.

"Now we can see the stars. There is little light for kilometers and kilometers, you will be amazed at everything you can see." He lowered himself down to snuggle close to me, pulling me in and tucking me into his chest where his heart beat steadily like a clock. "We can lay here, together, and just be. I don't want you to do anything you do not feel is right for you. In my culture, we are très expressifs with our affection." He kissed me softly, pulling the breath from my lungs. I could see he was trying to lighten the situation and conceal his hurt.

I moistened my lips. "In my culture, if we are too expressifs, we risk getting hurt."

He caressed the side of my face. "I will not hurt you, Plum."

I wanted so badly to believe him. To let him take me in his arms and back to his apartment and help me forget about the tape, about Rhys, about all of it. But I wasn't ready, not yet anyway. "Can we just take things slow?"

"You are right," he said, his tone gentle and reassuring, "there is no reason to rush something you want to last."

"Merci." And as I melted into his embrace, I couldn't help but wonder two things. One: How did Bastien always seem to know just the right thing to say? And two: When would the weight of my past begin to feel just a little bit lighter?

Chapter Twenty-Three

Ever since arriving in France, I'd been looking forward to Kate's visit to the set. She'd become a lifeline for me, taking early-morning calls, answering late-night texts, and basically reassuring me every chance she could that even though Château Mirabelle was far behind its renovation schedule, *Heart Restoration Project* would still be a success.

Since the crew would be continuing to work full steam ahead to get things ready before we could restart filming, Kate suggested we meet in Paris for a quick weekend jaunt before joining up with the rest of the production team in Provence. I jumped at the offer, desperately needing a change of scenery, some breathing room from whatever was starting to develop between me and Bastien, and a chance to escape to the City of Lights. There was one downside, though: Kate wanted Elliott to come along to film a bit of me in the bustling metropolis, a stark contrast from the sleepy vibe of Maubec. She thought our little foray to Paris might even serve as a good midpoint or lighthearted transition episode for the series.

It was a three-hour-plus train ride from Avignon to Paris, and for most of it, Elliott sat curled up in his seat, engrossed in a book. Some nonfiction, boring-looking behemoth with a plain cover and a thick spine. Every so often he'd yank out an earbud and ask me to scoot my knees over so he could pass to get to les toilettes or the café car. But for the most part we kept to our separate corners. Since our heated argument that afternoon we'd spent in town, he and I had barely spoken more than a few necessary words to one another. Still, with so much of the show left to shoot, I knew I needed to keep it civil between us if we were going to have any hope of making it through to the end.

We met Kate at George V, one of the swankiest hotels in the city with oversize suites and Eiffel Tower views right off the Champs-Élysées. She was waiting for me in the lobby, looking chic as ever, pin-straight blonde extensions framing her perfectly made-up face. You would never have guessed she just stepped off an almost twelve-hour flight.

"Plum, darling," she said, springing over to me. "You look fabulous!" She eyed Elliott up and down. "Hello, you must be Elliott Schaffer?"

"Nice to finally meet you in person, Ms. Wembley," Elliott said with a nod. He hoisted his camera onto his shoulder and switched it on, its bright light practically blinding us both.

Kate looked into the camera, seemingly startled that it was focused on her. The footage was supposed to be of me, not necessarily *us*, in Paris, but Elliott would need to film as much material as possible in order to ensure we'd get great edits.

"Best to think of him as a piece of furniture or a plant, something in the background nobody pays much attention to. Better yet, pretend like he's not even here." I waved a hand at him dismissively, only half joking.

Kate eyed him up and down and whispered, "Looking like *that*, easier said than done, am I right?" She brought her voice back up to a normal level. "Anyway, I dropped my bags in my room and came straight downstairs to meet you." She jumped up and down, clapping her hands like an overexcited schoolgirl. "I planned the *most* fabulous day for us. The first dailies are testing so well with our focus groups that Tributary has almost quadrupled our budget and my expense account," Kate said with a mischievous grin. "We'll start with coffee and a macaron at Ladurée and then hurry over to Le Bon Marché, where two personal shoppers will be waiting to assist us through the store. Then, I arranged for a private tour of Coco Chanel's Paris apartment followed by spa treatments here at the hotel and finally, dinner at Café de Flore. You've been working so hard, I wanted to treat you to a special day."

"That all sounds wonderful," I gushed. And it did. After lots of long hours sweeping and disposing of construction debris, attaching and mudding drywall panels, and spackling every godforsaken hole I could find, I was in dire need of some good R & R. And I had a feeling Parisien R & R was going to be just what the doctor ordered.

Kate lifted her tote over her shoulder and pushed her oversize sunglasses down off her head onto her face. "Good, let's go, all of Paris awaits."

We left the hotel, turned onto the Champs-Élysées, and headed straight to Ladurée, a gorgeous old French tearoom famous for its brightly colored macarons and people watching. As we approached the front door of the restaurant, Kate turned to Elliott and said, "Why don't you let me and Plum have a private girls-only catch-up? We'll meet you in front of Le Bon Marché at eleven to start filming for real."

"You're the boss," Elliott grumbled, and without being told twice, he turned and headed in the opposite direction.

"Is he always like that?" Kate asked once Elliott had left.

"Yes, always."

"Noted."

Kate gave our name to the maître d', who seated us at a small banquette right off the main dining room. After browsing through the menu, we settled on a few pastries: un plaisir sucré, un millefeuille, and a selection of colorful macarons. The sweet scent of powdered sugar swirled with the bitter aroma of fresh-brewing espresso, and I inhaled it as deeply as I could.

"Did you know that until the late 1800s, women weren't allowed in cafés without their husbands?" Kate said, passing the two menus back to the server. "Ladurée was one of the first restaurants in Paris that allowed women to dine on their own."

I folded a mint-green linen napkin onto my lap. "I have to say, I love it here even more now."

"There's a Ladurée in Beverly Hills over on Wilshire, but it's not the same. For a start, you'd never see people in LA shoving their faces full of pastries," she teased. The server came over, balancing a tray with two coffees and our assortment of sweets. He carefully set them on our table, along with a small metal pitcher of warm milk. "I have to be honest with you," Kate said, stirring a heaping spoonful of sugar into her mug, "I have slightly ulterior motives for asking you to join me in Paris."

I took a bite of my macaron, the crisp outside melting into a soft, delicate texture. The pistachio flavor was perfectly balanced, and my mouth flooded with nutty sweetness. "Oh yeah?" I asked midchew, catching a crumb on the corner of my lips with my pinkie.

"I'm hearing different things about the construction delays at Château Mirabelle. What's really going on?"

"Well, I guess that depends on who you ask."

"I'm asking you," she said pointedly.

"Bastien and the crew haven't exactly been seeing eye to eye."

She took a nibble of her macaron and batted her lash extensions. "What do you think the problem is?"

"Bastien has a clear vision for Château Mirabelle, one not everyone's on board with. He's an artist, really. Maybe a bit of a perfectionist too, which is of course slowing down the train, but he just wants it all to be right. I don't know if it's that he sees it to be a personal reflection of him? Or the work he's capable of? Maybe he is using the renovation of the house as an opportunity to prove himself a bit? He's so talented and so passionate, I can see how much he is putting his whole self into this thing."

Kate rested her chin on her hands. "You're one smitten kitten, aren't you?"

I shifted uncomfortably. "What? No. I'm not. I mean, I like him. He's an easy person to like."

"It's okay, Plum, you can tell me. I've seen the dailies, the sexual tension between the two of you is as thick as ganache," she said, leaning back in her chair.

A deep flush crept up my face. "It's the language barrier. Most of the time, I can't understand even half of what he's talking about."

A smile erupted across her face. "You understand everything he says perfectly. Look, I don't blame you for falling for Monsieur Munier. And all the women in our focus groups, they don't blame you either. He's pretty easy on the eyes and charming to boot? He's practically Prince Charming! I mean, you have the castle and everything." She threw her head back with a laugh and took a sip of her Earl Grey from the bone china teacup.

Bastien was easy on the eyes, no question, but it was more than that. He was thoughtful, kind, and sensitive. He was frank and unaffected. But there wasn't anything serious happening between us. Not really. So far, my entire courtship with Bastien consisted of some heavy flirtation and a few light make-out sessions. And though the other night he was angling for us to take the next step, he understood I wasn't ready. I'd already had my share of showmances, most of them ending as soon as the director yelled *cut*. I was determined not to go down that road again, unless there was something and someone real waiting for me at the end of it.

"What about Elliott? Personality aside, he's one tall drink of water, no doubt about that," Kate purred.

I looked up from my plate. "Elliott?"

"Production has discussed extensively ways to get him on film, but he's remained pretty adamant he wants to stay behind the camera. Can you imagine someone *not* wanting to be famous?"

I set down my fork. "Actually, I think he's become a little more interested in being part of the show in a different way. You know, Elliott and I have uncovered a lot of interesting history about Château Mirabelle that he wants to try to include in the show somehow. I mean, it's called *Heart Restoration Project*, right? The house is the heart of the village, or will be once we finish the renovation. We could put such a meaningful and profound twist on its significance to the town."

"Yes and no, *Heart Restoration Project* can mean lots of different things. It's why we ended up sticking with it," she said matter-of-factly. "Shoot, look at the time, Elliott doesn't seem like the type who'd be happy to be kept waiting." Kate waved her hand in the air to flag down the server. "L'addition, s'il vous plait."

"I didn't know you spoke French?"

"Un peu. I studied in Paris for a semester during my junior year. I use the term *studied* loosely. Ran around like a silly American drinking far too much wine and having baguette sword fights in the streets with mes amis." She laughed at the recollection and threw some euros down on the table before adding, "Shall we?"

We sped over to the sixth arrondissement and spent the rest of the morning being pampered by the personal shoppers at Le Bon Marché. They brought us champagne, canapés, and the best of French fashion. Elliott looked bored out of his mind, but he diligently captured every moment on film as directed.

Kate refilled her flute and collapsed onto the round cotton candy–pink chaise longue in the center of the dressing room while I finished zipping up a body-conscious Balmain ribbed dress with metallic braid detail up the front.

Kate sat upright. "Shut the front door! You look hot in that dress. You have to get it."

In the mirror, I caught a quick glimpse of Elliott, whose mouth was dropped open, his eyes locked on mine. He immediately shifted his gaze away and tucked himself back behind the camera. I glanced down at the price tag dangling off the bottom of the dress: €3,950. "I can't afford it."

Kate shot me the same look of astonishment almost everyone did when they heard I wasn't rolling in the Everly millions.

"How's that even possible? You got paid for *EVERLYday*, right?"

"I was young and stupid and had a lot of people in my ear giving me all the wrong advice," I admitted.

"What about your parents? Where were they during that time?"

"Believe me, they tried to tame my wild ways, but back then, I didn't listen to anyone besides Rhys, and look at where that got me."

I glanced over at Elliott. For the first time all day he seemed to be invested in our conversation, not just recording it.

"You weren't stupid, you were in love. We've all been guilty of making poor decisions in the name of love." Kate refilled my champagne flute, and I downed the glass in one gulp before stepping back into the dressing room. I slipped out of the Balmain number and handed it to one of the personal shoppers.

"We should wrap things up. Our guide's meeting us at Coco Chanel's apartment in about an hour for our tour. Let me close out here," Kate said, holding up her small pile of purchases. "Can you flag down the driver, and I'll meet you both outside?"

I spotted our driver, who was parked on the other side of the street, and Elliott and I crossed over the Rue de Sèvres to meet him. The driver opened the door to let me inside, and Elliott jumped into the front seat, probably so he didn't have to make awkward chitchat while we waited. A few minutes later, Kate approached juggling a handful of shopping and garment bags, putting all but one in the trunk.

"31 Rue Cambon, s'il vous plaît," Kate told the driver as she slid into the car. "Here," she said, passing me the garment bag. "This is for you."

"For me?" I slowly unzipped the garment bag, revealing the incredible Balmain dress inside. "Kate! It's too much, I can't accept this."

"Of course you can. *Heart Restoration Project*'s shaping up to be a hit, and we have you to thank for that. You and Bastien."

"This is way too generous."

"Generous nothing, it's called friendship." Kate rolled down the window. "Is that the apartment building?"

"Non, Mademoiselle, c'est le Musée de la Résistance nationale, the museum of the French Resistance," the driver translated.

"Excusez-moi, excusez-moi, can we pull over here, s'il vous plaît?" Elliott asked the driver excitedly.

"Here?" Kate questioned and looked at her phone for the time. With urgency in her voice, she said, "Well, we don't really have time to stop if we're going to make our tour at Chanel."

"What if I just make a quick pit stop and meet the two of you over there?" Elliott asked.

I turned to face Kate and said, "Actually, I'd love to go too. Is there any way to squeeze it into our day?"

Kate hesitated before responding, "I mean, I guess if you really want to visit a museum more than Coco Chanel's apartment? You know her home's not normally open to the public. I set the tour up as something special for us," Kate said, a tinge of disappointment in her voice.

"We'll be a half hour at the most, an hour, tops. I think we might be able to find some useful nuggets for the show. I promise to make it quick," I pleaded.

She pressed her lips together into a smile. "Yes, of course, go. This is your day. I'll try to hold off going to the *exclusive* Chanel boutique without you, but no promises," she teased before turning more serious. "As much fun as this trip has been, I still need all this footage for the show, so Elliott, you stay close to Plum, and be sure to film the rest of the day. Can you both be back at the hotel by five for our spa appointment? We need to be sure to check in promptly, or else they double charge. Or I suppose I could cancel the spa too, if that's what you really want?"

"No, I don't want that. Don't cancel. I'll be there, and I promise Elliott will film every mundane moment," I said, crossing my heart.

"Go, have fun. I'll see you back at the hotel—five sharp. Pardonnez-moi, Monsieur, arrêtez-ici, s'il vous plait," Kate called to the driver.

The car pulled in front of the museum's entranceway, and the driver opened the door to let me out. Elliott had already hopped out and hustled up the front steps. I followed him, hurrying to catch up, but stopped halfway. He looked over his shoulder and then, puzzled, came down four stairs to meet me.

"What's wrong?" he asked.

I held out my palm. "What do you say, temporary truce in the name of Château Mirabelle?"

"Deal," he said, shaking my hand and sending a warm tingle up my arm. Our eyes met for a second before letting go. "Actually"—he stepped a bit closer, and I craned my neck up to look at him—"I'm . . . I'm surprised and dare I say impressed that you'd sacrifice your trip to Chanel to come here. Maybe I was wrong, and you do care about this thing?"

"And *I* am excited to hear you admit you're wrong. I promise to cherish that nugget in the deepest recesses of my heart until the day I die. I do care about Château Mirabelle—and these people. I know my résumé. And I know the kind of person I must've seemed like. I almost can't even blame you—if all I had to go on was what was shown on the screen and in the papers, I'd have a pretty poor opinion of me too."

"Plum . . ."

"No, really. I get it. Maybe I even was that girl when I made the crack about sitting in coach when we left LA. But being here and experiencing the world this way . . . it's like I'm seeing it, really seeing it, for the first time. I've probably been to more countries and cities than I can count, but did I ever get to know them? The people? What makes a place unique and special? Never. But Maubec is different. I've come to care about it. About Agnès and Pascal. Even crotchety Monsieur Grenouille. Is that crazy?"

He nodded and scratched at his chin. "No. Not crazy. Strangely . . . I feel the very same way. Look, I had my mind made up about you from the start, and that wasn't fair. I see that now. So truce accepted. Now, let's go and see what else we can uncover to solve this mystery of ours and do our best to get you back to Kate on time. Don't want to piss off the boss."

Though over the past few weeks, I'd grown to find Elliott's gruff demeanor weirdly comforting, the sight of the smallest smirk that crossed his lips was a reassuring sign that we were finally starting to find some middle ground.

"Yeah, hurry your ass up, I didn't blow off Chanel for nuthin," I poked back and hurried up the stairs, leaving him in my wake to catch up.

Without hesitation, Elliott lifted his camera to his shoulder and tracked me as we hurried into the Resistance Museum and over to the ticket window. Grabbing a handful of brochures off the counter, I skimmed through them, landing on a pamphlet about a newer exhibit called *Vines and Victory, the Role Provence Played in the Resistance*. I held it up to the plexiglass information window. "This? Où? Where?"

"Ah oui, follow the signs that way and turn right. You cannot miss it," the volunteer instructed.

"Merci," we both called, speed walking as respectfully as we could to the exhibit.

Following her instructions down the narrow hallway into the retrospective, I was immediately drawn in by the photos, testimonials, and maps detailing the Provence region's involvement in the French Resistance. Elliott and I wandered over to an exhibit about Camp des Milles, an internment camp in Aix-en-Provence for political dissidents, artists, intellectuals, and people to be deported to Auschwitz.

According to a quick Google search, the camp was about an hour from Maubec, so it was pretty likely Luc and Imène Adélaïse had been taken there following their arrest. We might be able to find out what happened to them if we were able to visit. We separated to cover more ground, and I jotted down as much information as I could on the scraps of paper and pamphlets I had on hand before noticing the time. We'd blown well past the one-hour mark, and it was almost five o'clock.

"Why are you still filming!? Move your ass—Kate's going to kill me!" I cried as we scurried down the steps out of the museum. "Here," I said, thrusting my pile of notes at him once we climbed in a taxi. "We should try to go to Camp des Milles. I think it may be where the Adélaïses were taken."

Elliott looked impressed with my discoveries. He glanced over my notes and tucked them deep into his jacket pocket as the taxi pulled up in front of George V. We quickly hopped out, and Elliott paused to anchor his camera atop his shoulder, pointing it in my direction.

"Seriously?!" I gawked at him with the camera still on me. "I know Kate said to film *everything*, but we're so late and I doubt anything significant is going to happen between us getting out of this cab and me making it by the skin of my teeth to our spa appointment."

But Elliott, already filming, was still hot on my tail and wasn't missing a beat. He probably just didn't want to be caught without his camera in hand when we met up with Kate. I rushed over to the concierge desk to ask for directions to the spa, and that's when I spotted *him*, my heart practically exploding in a single beat. His arms were wrapped around the tiny waist of one of the most beautiful women I'd ever seen.

Rhys was standing in the middle of George V.

Chapter Twenty-Four

I leaned against the concierge desk at the entranceway of George V, hoping it would help support my trembling frame. What the hell was Rhys doing in Paris, and who was the leggy redhead on his arm? God, he looked good, though. The sleeves of his tight-fitting, white button-down were rolled just past his muscular forearms, showing off a new tan—no doubt fresh from Saint-Tropez or some other exotic destination on the Côte d'Azur. He pushed his fingers through his tousled hair, revealing sun-kissed strands that glistened under the lobby's swanky lights.

The redhead kissed him softly on the cheek, and a sweet smile swelled from Rhys's lips. He pushed a pair of mirrored aviator sunglasses off his face, and for just a moment, our eyes locked. His face split into a wide grin as if I were an old college buddy instead of his ex-girlfriend of half a lifetime. As excited as he looked to see me, I was pummeled with a sense of dread that almost knocked me off my feet. I had exactly three seconds to decide whether to turn and run, or face him and his new arm candy head-on. Too late, they were already striding over, his swagger and magnetism cutting through the crowd like a hot knife through butter. I moistened my lips, shook out my shoulders, and smoothed my hair down behind my ears.

"Plum, what are you doing here?" he offered casually, as if we were stumbling into each other at a supermarket in West Hollywood.

I blinked hard. "Rhys? Wha . . . What are *you* doing here?" I scanned the room, and my face grew hot as I noticed all the hotel guests who now had their phones and cameras pointed in our direction. Flashes snapped and the familiar red lights of video recording illuminated through the space, and a spell of dizziness rolled from my stomach to my head.

Rhys looked over his shoulder toward them and then back at me. "I'm here with Anya," he answered, like I was supposed to know exactly who she was.

"Sorry, and who are you?" I asked, my voice going up at least three octaves.

He reached over and massaged my left shoulder. "Anya, my fiancée. I wanted to tell you, but, you know, you've been here . . ."

My eyebrows practically jumped off my face. "Your fiancée? Rhys, I saw you right before I left, and I've only been in France for like a month. You met someone you want to spend the rest of your life with in the last four weeks?!" I spoke like she *wasn't* standing in front of me.

He tightened his grip around her. "When you know you know, and as soon as I saw her on TikTok, I knew."

"You met her on TikTok? He met you on TikTok?" I bounced my gaze back and forth between them, unable to digest what he was saying.

"Anya's a huge influencer. She has like over eight million followers."

"It's actually ten, sweetie," she said, correcting him as she puckered her lips into her compact and slathered on a fresh coat of gloss.

My head was spinning. Engaged? Engaged to be married? Rhys had been categorically clear that he wanted to focus his energies on his burgeoning acting career and felt anything that distracted him from that pursuit was now a waste of time. So how did marriage fare in that equation?

"I thought you didn't want to get married. I thought you were all about your career right now?"

"I guess I changed my mind. I mean, when you meet the one, I guess you *do* just know," he said while gazing at Anya, oblivious to how it would hit me . . . throwing it out there as if he were talking about switching deodorant brands or the type of milk he preferred in his latte. "Anyway, what's new with you? In Paris for work? Can't say I've seen your name in the trade papers lately."

"Um no, just here for a few days on holiday," I offered.

He pushed his sunglasses down to the bridge of his nose. "Well, whatever it is . . . you look good, P."

P?! Don't you "P" me!

"Rhys, we were together forever. You didn't think I maybe deserved a phone call or even a text to tell me that you're engaged to be married?"

"I figured you'd heard about it on one site or another. It was reported in *Us Weekly*, *People*, the *Daily Mail*, TMZ, *Page Six*," he said, rattling off the usual list of suspects. "I mean, you'd have to have been living under a rock *not* to know."

Maubec wasn't a rock, exactly, but he was right, I'd more or less tuned out the outside world these last couple of weeks. And it's not that I wanted him back, but was I that easy to get over? So easy that he found a fiancée in thirty days? Even those folks on *90 Day Fiancé* took a full ninety days!

"Well," I said, choking back the tears forming, "I guess congratulations are in order, then."

I swallowed the lump now lodged in my throat, and my hands trembled as my eyes finally peeled themselves from Rhys and scanned the room to still see a flurry of hotel guests, workers, and worst of all Elliott filming the entire, god-awful, humiliating exchange.

"Aww, Plumster, that means a lot. Are you here through the weekend? We just flew in from Venice. The new Tarantino film I'm in premiered at the festival, so the hotel's throwing a little soirée to celebrate the movie and our engagement. You should come."

If he wasn't careful, I was gonna toss his ass in a Plumster. And his big film at the festival? He had like three lines in the movie!

"Yes, please do come," Anya added.

"I can't, I have dinner plans with a friend."

"Well, if you change your mind," he said, "the party's at L'Orangerie, and it starts at nine."

"L'Orangerie? The Michelin-starred restaurant?"

"Grey Goose L'Orange is sponsoring the party, so . . . ," Anya chimed in.

"Your party has a corporate sponsor?"

"Quite a few, actually. Caudalie, Air France, Evian. Grey Goose's the main one, though. The swag's gonna be *insaaaaanne*." He tilted his head toward the elevator banks. "We should get going, Anya's glam squad's waiting for us upstairs. Think about coming to the party, you and your friend, if you want," he said with a nod toward Elliott. "Just text me beforehand, so I can make sure your names are on the list. It's going to be pretty exclusive." Rhys leaned in and gave me a European kiss, one on each cheek. "It was good to see you, P."

Exclusive?! You were Brian Braunpheiffer before you met me!

"Yeah, you too," I muttered as the man I never thought would be such a stranger walked away. A few seconds later, Elliott approached me from behind.

"Hey, you okay? You look white as a sheet. Who was that guy?" he asked.

I gave him a once-over, the skin in my face pulsing with a mixture of anger and adrenaline. "Did you film that?"

He looked up. "What?"

"That whole exchange? Me and Rhys? Did you film us? Our conversation? Isn't that just the kind of *gotcha* moment you people dream about?!"

"You people? Yeah, I filmed it. I've been filming everything all day. What's your problem?!" He set his camera on the ground and stood up straight, his enormous frame towering over me.

I narrowed my eyes on him. "Who knew I was coming to Paris?"

"What are you talking about? Everyone who works on the show knew we were coming to Paris. What does that have to do with anything?"

"So you're telling me I'm supposed to just *believe* it's one big coincidence—that my ex-boyfriend's staying at the exact same hotel on the exact same weekend as I am in Paris out of the blue?"

"I don't know? You tell me," Elliott said. "I'm half expecting a swarm of paparazzi to jump out of those potted plants across the room any minute now."

I reeled back like I'd been slapped. "Wait, you think *I* staged this?" I couldn't even process the lunacy of his accusation. "You know what, Elliott, screw you!" I turned and ran down the hall to the elevators.

"Oh, that's *real* mature, Plum," Elliott called after me.

I frantically pressed the down button over and over until the bell finally chimed, and I threw myself inside. When the double doors slid open again, I was immediately hit with the overwhelming floral fragrance of creams, serums, and aromatherapy candles wafting in from the spa. The smell, combined with my pounding heart, made me feel like I could pass out at any moment. I stumbled out of the elevator and onto the cream-colored tufted sofa in the middle of the spa's waiting area.

"Mademoiselle, Mademoiselle," one of the spa employees called as she came rushing over. "Tout va bien?"

I nodded. "I'm okay. I just got a little dizzy, that's all."

The spa employee clapped her hands together. "Nadine, un verre d'eau, tout de suite!"

A younger woman came speeding over with a glass of cucumber water and a cold towel.

She placed the towel on my forehead, then urged me to take a few slow sips of the water and lie down.

"Oh my God, Plum, what happened?" Kate exclaimed. She sprinted toward me, barely noticing her robe flapping open in the wind.

"I just ran into Rhys in the hotel lobby," I panted.

She tightened the tie on her robe. "Rhys? Rhys Braun? What the hell is he doing here?"

I propped up on my elbows. "Celebrating his engagement. Did you know he was engaged?"

"The gossip rags have not stopped talking about him and that influencer fiancée of his and their engagement world tour." Kate pantomimed sticking her finger down her throat and gagging. "She's been posting about their itinerary nonstop. They were just in Venice for the film festival, and then after Paris they're heading to Saint-Tropez, I think. Rhys has become a bit of a media whore, but you know that." She studied my face. "Wait, you really hadn't heard the news?"

I shrugged. "No, not a peep. I guess I've been off the grid these last few weeks."

"I'm so sorry, Plum. If I knew, I would've said something earlier when his name came up. I assumed you were fine with it and had moved on with Bastien. Look, from the little I know, Rhys was a toxic figure in your life." She continued, "I'm not trying to diminish what the two of you had together, but sometimes when the past comes calling, it's best not to answer, especially if it has nothing new to say."

"Or sold your sex tape."

She put her arm around me and squeezed the top of my shoulder. "Yeah, that too."

I couldn't help but smile. "You're right, it's the same old Rhys *new* Rhys who cares more about the red carpet outside the party than the reason for the party itself." My head shot up. "Oh my God, I just realized, the hotel's going to be swarming with paparazzi later, if it isn't already? How can I face them?" I looked around the spa. "I suppose I could be happy making a life and home down here. The towel closet looks cozy, and the cucumber water's *really* good."

"I'll tell you what you're going to do. You're going to go inside and enjoy the Signature Serum Hydro Glow Facial, followed by the Hot Basalt Stone Massage, and then we'll emerge ready to face whatever awaits *us* upstairs."

"Us?"

"Didn't you know? I'm ride or die, baby."

Chapter Twenty-Five

The engagement party hadn't even started yet, and already George V was positively swarming with paparazzi. The last thing I wanted was to drag Kate into the mud with me, so after the spa, I returned to my room and packed up my things. I left a note for Elliott and Kate with the front desk, letting them know I decided to return to Maubec earlier than planned, and headed straight to the station to catch the next train to Provence, which unfortunately wasn't leaving anytime soon.

A little over five hours later, I stepped out onto the train platform in Avignon, the closest stop to Maubec, and still almost forty-five minutes away by car from the inn. I hadn't thought my plan through very well. It was almost 1:00 a.m., and the station was practically deserted. I wouldn't dare text or call Gervais. This was my mess, and I wasn't waking the poor man before a long day of work. The small line of eager taxis usually circling the busy train station early in the morning was nowhere to be found, and my Uber app was showing zero drivers available within a fifty-kilometer radius. My hands shook as all the saliva drained from my mouth.

Just as the realization of my situation (and subsequent panic) was settling in, the bright beam of a Vespa's headlight lit up the tracks and everything around them. I squinted into the light and heard my name being called out from the bike.

"Bastien?" I called back.

"Ouais, are you alright?"

I hurried down the platform steps toward the light. "I'm fine. I'm relieved to see you, but I'm fine. What are you doing here? How did you even know I was coming in?"

Bastien turned off the bike's engine and removed his helmet. "You should not be here so late on your own. It isn't safe. What made you do such a foolish thing?"

He answered my questions with more questions, but honestly, I didn't care. I guessed Kate called him or texted him. The main thing was that he was here and I wasn't stranded. My knight in worn leather. "Long story, but Rhys showed up at our hotel apparently to promote a new film or something, and as you can imagine, a horde of paparazzi followed. I . . . I just had to get out of Paris."

"Rhys, your ex-boyfriend? What was he doing at your hotel?"

"I know, it's too much of a coincidence to be a coincidence, right?"

"A coincidence, maybe, but not if he was promoting a film, which is what you said he was doing?"

I went to answer, but the words got caught in a soft sob. "It . . . it . . . the whole thing just made me look like such a fool." Mortified, I swiped at my lashes and blew out my lips to get myself together.

He took my chin in his hand and swiped his thumb across my cheek to catch a falling tear. "Please don't cry." He pressed a sweet kiss to my forehead and then returned to cupping my cheek. "Our show will make him look like the fool, you'll see. You and I will be shining stars, and this show is going to be . . . how do you say . . . a big hit." With his fingers in my hair, he pulled me in for a kiss, and I drank in the security of his embrace.

He drew back and said, "This show is going to be something incroyable. Because of you and me together. I can feel it deep inside my bones. I just need you to trust me, trust in us, d'accord?" He squeezed my hands in his and waited with a held breath.

"Yes, okay. D'accord," I said, pressing one more peck to his lips before a soft, low growl rumbled from my very empty stomach. My hand flew to it, surprised at how loud it'd been. "Sorry, I haven't eaten anything since this morning."

"Oh, we can fix that. I make a life-changing croque Monsieur. The secret is to mix a little honey in with the Dijon mustard. Hop on." He patted the back of his bike and handed me the spare helmet. His ability to turn such a shit night into something somewhat promising was more than appreciated, it was needed.

"At this point, I'm so delirious, I'd settle for a can of SpaghettiOs."

"Excusez-moi?" He quickly snatched the helmet away as I went to take it and offered me a mischievous grin instead. "SpaghettiOs?! Quel blasphme!" He tsked his tongue disapprovingly and re-offered me the helmet with a playful grin. "Mademoiselle, I would be happy to take you on this bike back to my house so long as you never say the word *SpaghettiOs* in my presence again."

"Deal," I said as we locked eyes over me taking the helmet from him.

It was nearing 2:00 a.m. when we pulled into a spot in front of Bastien's building. A starry night awash in a moonlit glow spilled over the horizon. With the exception of the crescendo of buzzing cicadas characteristic of midsummer, the stillness of Avignon made it even more magical. Bastien led me up three flights of stairs until we reached his front door. Before inserting the key, he pulled me up the last few steps to the platform and turned me so my back pressed against the door. He gently swept the hair from my shoulders, his fingers grazing my skin with meticulous attention, and kissed the side of my neck. A soft nibble of my earlobe made the stairwell spin, but I stayed upright, supported by his weight against me.

He pulled back and cupped my face in his hands, leaving me breathless. "I missed you," he breathed.

"I was only gone for a day."

"Well, whatever it has been, all I know is I have very much been enjoying my time with you. I feel like we are really building something here, ma cherie, non?"

This time I reached for him, placing my hands on his chest. "I just can't believe you're real. You're thoughtful and considerate. You're always one step ahead, and you always know just what to say. I mean, you came to pick me up at the train station. At one a.m.! I was stranded and alone, and you appeared out of nowhere. I . . . I can't tell you what that means to me. Rhys would never have done that unless there was a photo op at the other end." My eyes shifted away from his, tears brimming and threatening to spill over. I kissed him sweetly before taking the key from his fingers and slipping it into the lock. I reached for his hand and pulled him inside.

His apartment was spacious, but I couldn't make out much more than outlines of furniture in the darkness while we fumbled toward Bastien's bedroom. As we bounced off one wall of the corridor and then the other, he kissed me deeply, the pressure of his hard body against mine pushing me farther into the living room as he tugged off my shirt in one fluid motion. I spun him around so that I was now walking forward and him backward toward the bedroom, unbuckling his belt along the way. Between urgent kisses and clothing confetti, we stumbled our way down the hallway until we tumbled onto his bed.

Bastien lay on top of me, his eyes never breaking contact. "Are you sure, ma cherie? Is this really what you want? I heard what you said the other day, and we can wait. I will wait." He caressed the side of my face with a gentle touch. I smiled widely and rolled him over, now straddling his hips and hovering over his devilishly sexy face. I tossed my hair over my shoulder, and then I kissed him hard and scooted down his body to press my lips along the column of his throat. I turned my cheek and rested my head against his chest. His heart beat hard against his rib cage, each thump like the pendulum of a grandfather clock.

My mind drifted first to Rhys and how the shock of seeing him just a few hours earlier hadn't quite worn off yet. Then to Elliott. Despite all our misunderstandings, all our fiery debates, there was something about our exchanges that felt more honest and real than any other relationship I could remember. And there was Bastien. If you typed *holiday fling* into the Google search bar, I was pretty certain his image would pop up. Handsome, fun, charming, with a sexy accent to boot. He was exactly the type of man you'd want to *get under* in an effort to *get over* somebody else. But maybe what we had could be more? One thing, though, I knew for sure: sleeping together before I fully figured that out would be the quickest route to never really knowing.

Bastien ran a hand through my hair, snapping me into the present. I trailed kisses back up his neck until we were eye to eye. "Is it okay if we just *sleep* together, with you just holding me tonight? Would that be okay?"

He kissed my forehead, and I pressed my eyes closed at the sensation of his warm lips on my skin. "But of course, ma cherie. I would love nothing more than to be your biggest spoon." Grinning, he took me in his arms and we rolled onto our sides, so that I was safely curled against his chest. Together, our breaths fell into a deep relaxation and a steady rhythm of soft snores.

Chapter Twenty-Six

After a few hours of sleep tucked in the crook of Bastien's arm, the rich scent of freshly brewed coffee floating through the apartment woke me before I'd even opened my eyes. I squinted against the light streaming through the large bedroom window and reached for Bastien, whose side of the bed was empty. I sat up just in time to see him enter the room holding two steaming mugs and wearing nothing but a smile.

He handed me a cup and climbed back into bed, nuzzling in close and giving me a kiss on the cheek before taking a sip of his coffee.

I moaned against his kisses and nudged against him playfully. "As much as I'd love to stay in bed with you all day, we'd better get going. This château is nowhere near ready, and if we—"

"Non, non, non," he interrupted. "We have a common phrase here in Provence, 'Il ne fait pas bon de travailler quand la cigale chante.' Meaning, 'It's not good to work when the cicada is singing.'" He took my cup from me and set them both on the nightstand before rolling over to snuggle me close. His dark hair smelled like rosemary shampoo and rich, bright notes of citrusy bodywash. He smelled good enough to taste. As if reading my mind, he tucked his head in the crook of my neck and slid his hand across my stomach until it curved to cup my hips, pulling me close to kiss me again.

I sighed against his mouth. "It's hard to believe that yesterday I was in Paris with Rhys, and now, as if by magic or time machine, I'm here with you."

He propped himself up on his elbow. "You didn't tell me much about what happened. Actually, we didn't talk much at all last night." He smirked. "Do you want to tell me about it now?"

I stared at the ceiling, not sure if I wanted to get into it. "Yes and no. Long story short, *somehow* Rhys showed up at the same hotel where we were staying, which I know in my bones was no coincidence. We had a very public and very awkward encounter with his new fiancée, and Elliott captured it all on camera." I didn't want to allow it to work me up, but by the anxiety building in my chest, I knew it was already too late. My throat tightened, and I felt the threat of tears.

Bastien stayed quiet for a moment. I looked over at him to make sure he didn't doze off during my rant. He was awake, just thinking. "Honestly, Plum, I know you're upset, but if you take your emotion out of it, I don't think Elliott did anything wrong. He did his job. It's what he's paid to do. To film you, non? I don't think it was personal."

I sprang up onto my elbow and said, "I'm sorry. You're *defending* him?"

"Well, yes, I think I am. He was asked to go to Paris for work to capture candid moments of you around town as promo for the show. It's exactly what he did. I don't really see the problem." He pursed his lips together and shrugged. "Maybe give Elliott a break. At least he cared enough to text me to make sure you got home safely in the middle of the night. That has to count for something. Really, if anything, you should thank him. I shudder to think what could have happened to you at an abandoned train station all alone at that hour."

"Elliott? Elliott was the one who texted you?"

"He was genuinely concerned for your well-being. Asked me to let him know once I had you safely in my possession."

I wanted to be angry at Bastien's honesty, grow defensive at his assertions, but instead, I marveled at his frankness. Few people in my life had been so forthright, and though my instinct was to fight back, maybe this was the perspective I needed. Didn't I come to France to get a new outlook along with this new opportunity? My mind drifted to Rhys, who would have riled me up, fanning the fires of the drama to see how it could be used as a headline. He didn't care about me and my best interests. And truth be told, he hadn't for a long, long time.

But this honesty from Bastien was refreshing and real. It was an adult conversation, a genuine back and forth, with no ulterior motives. I could either meet the challenge or shy away from this test of growth. I took a deep breath to settle the adrenaline coursing through me.

"You know what? You're right," I said. "Though your direct approach is a bit hard to swallow at times, I should thank Elliott for reaching out to you last night."

"And you know, if it were not for him, maybe you would not be here with me right now, n'est-ce pas?" Bastien smiled and pushed me gently back against the pillows as he positioned himself over me. He kissed me sweetly, and I sank farther into the cocoon of covers. He slid his hand behind my neck, drawing me closer with each affectionate brush of his lips. I wrapped my arms around him and traced my fingernails gently down his spine.

Bastien leaned close to my ear and whispered, "L'amour fait les plus grandes douceurs et les plus sensibles infortunes de la vie."

"Hmm . . . ," I moaned against his neck. "What . . . what does that mean?" I asked between kisses. Breathless.

"It means, 'Love makes life's sweetest pleasures and worst misfortunes.' When we are falling in love, we lose all sense of reason, non? It is fun, and wild, and unpredictable." He pulled back to look me in the eyes. "Just like in the song, 'La Vie En Rose,' I like looking at the world through rose-colored glasses with you, Plum."

At the mention of the song, my mind flashed to the street musician playing "La Vie En Rose" on his accordion as I sat across from Elliott in Maubec's town square—and to Elliott's gentle hand delicately swiping the eyelash from my cheek. The sudden intrusion of the memory momentarily disoriented me. Bastien nuzzled his nose close to my neck, his pillowy lips resting by my ear. He whispered my name, the timbre of his breathy voice snapping me back to the present.

I rolled Bastien over, pinning him down. Seductively, I pushed his hands above his head with one arm, my other trailing down his side until it settled on the smallest part of his waist. And then I gave it a playful squeeze, and he let out a laugh-filled yelp. "*Aie!* No, Plum, I am ticklish there!"

I continued to squeeze and nip at his sides, now with both hands, as he folded in genuine laughter. He reached for my legs and waist and anything he could grab and mimicked the squeezes. "Careful! Ah! The coffee!" Our laughter continued to bounce off the apartment walls. It was the most delightful sound I'd heard in a long time.

When we settled back on the bed, breathless and eyes tearing, he pressed a final peck to the tip of my nose, before catching sight of the bedside clock.

"Merde. We have played too long, and it is getting late. We better get on-site before René changes any more of my blueprints." He climbed out of bed and headed toward the bathroom. He turned back, a mischievous grin on his face. "I am going to take a quick shower. Care to join?"

His infectious smile was all the invitation I needed.

Chapter Twenty-Seven

Kate's visit a few days later when she was finished with her affairs in Paris had everyone at Château Mirabelle on edge. We were still behind schedule, and with each day that passed, it seemed less likely we'd be restoring Château Mirabelle to its original glory, let alone even ensuring there'd be working toilets in the house.

Despite the uphill climb, the crew—back from their weekend hiatus—was hard at work finishing the flooring, plumbing updates, and drywall while René watched closely from the sidelines, barking out orders like a seasoned drill sergeant.

I tapped him lightly on the shoulder. "Bonjour, René, où est Bastien? I didn't see him at craft services this morning."

"I'm not sure. As soon as I arrived, Mademoiselle Wembley presented me with a long list of items she wanted to see completed on the château before the week is out."

"And Elliott?"

He shrugged and turned his attention back to the team of welders restoring a section of original copper piping. A few moments later, Kate came hurrying up to us. "Good, I found you," she said, slightly out of breath. "Where's Bastien?"

"I was about to ask you the same thing."

Since I wasn't needed on set until today, the last time I'd seen Bastien was when he dropped me off at the inn after our night together. Agnès, Pascal, and Odette were turning chairs over, getting the dining room ready for the early breakfast crowd. I tiptoed up the stairs and back into my room before anyone spotted me in my state of disarray and pretended like I'd been there sleeping all along.

"I'm sure he's around here somewhere. Anyway, how are you holding up?" Kate asked.

I held up my phone. "Aside from these, just dandy." Over the last forty-eight hours, my sisters, parents, Nancy, and almost every person on my contact list had forwarded one article or another about my Paris run-in with Rhys. Some of my favorite headlines were City of Fights, Plum Everly and Rhys Braun Showdown at the George V and Ménage à Trois—Plum Everly Confronts Rhys Braun and New Fiancée Anya Vanhulle.

"What's that thing people say? No press is bad press?" Kate reasoned.

"I can tell you for a fact that's not true. Especially where my family's concerned. They don't love seeing my name in *Page Six*. Especially after that tape."

"I find that hard to believe. The Everly empire didn't exactly build itself in a vacuum," she said, tossing her blonde hair behind her shoulders.

Normally I appreciated when someone recognized my family's little bit of hypocrisy, but the tone in her voice was just a *little* too familiar with people she'd never actually met. For some reason it rubbed me the wrong way.

"So today's going to be a blast. Have you ever heard of Simone Allard?" Kate said, shifting the subject.

The name didn't ring any bells. "I don't think so."

"Me either," she joked, "but she's supposed to be one of the best interior designers in Provence, specializing in château restorations. She'll be here filming the next couple of days."

"Interior design? Shouldn't we be worried about the *state* of the estate first? The château's a mess. Half the rooms are missing walls and the other half, floors."

"Don't worry about that. I made it clear to René that he needs to make sure the facades of the library, kitchen, drawing room, two bedrooms, and the grand salon are complete by the end of this month. The magic of television will take care of the rest."

The magic of television. I'd heard that phrase before. Bastien said the very same thing to me the first day he showed me around the house. "Filming wraps in what, eight weeks? There's no way the house is going to be anywhere near habitable by then."

"Either way, the publicity Château Mirabelle generates from the show should help it sell in no time, and then you can use that money toward a down payment on a house in the Valley complete with walls, floors, *and* flushing toilets." Kate glanced down at her phone. "Simone's here. Want to walk to the front of the house with me to meet her?"

"Sure, let me grab a cup of coffee first, and then I'll be right there."

I set off for craft services hoping I'd spot Bastien somewhere along the route, but he was nowhere to be found. I took a paper cup from a large stack on the edge of the table and filled it all the way to the top. Just as I put the steaming brim to my mouth, Bastien came up behind me, his lips settling firmly at the base of my neck.

"Bonjour, ma chérie," he purred.

I turned around to face him. "Hey, I've been looking everywhere for you."

"I asked Madame Archambeau if she would open her shop early for me." He pulled a gorgeous bouquet of red poppies, white peonies, lavender wisteria, and bright-yellow sunflowers out from behind his back and pushed a stray hair behind my ear. "You know, the other morning when you were asleep in my arms, you looked like an absolute angel. If Kate wasn't in town, I would have tried to convince you to play hockey with me."

"Hockey? You wanted to play hockey? *Ohhhhh*, do you mean *hooky*?" I giggled.

His cheeks streaked an adorable beet red. "Ah yes, hooky," he said, giving an especially cute *ooh* sound when he pronounced *hooky*.

I pushed up on my toes and kissed him softly on the mouth.

Bastien's name came crackling through his walkie-talkie. He unclipped it from his belt and answered the page in rapid, unintelligible French. "Les poutres en bois ne supporteront pas le poids. Nous avons besoin des poutres en acier." He lowered the walkie-talkie to his side. "I have to go, duty calls."

"Maybe I can convince you to stay, just a little while longer?" I pleaded.

"There's no *maybe* about it, you could convince me with the tiniest crook of a finger," he said, kissing each of mine. "But I really should get going. I have a big, beautiful house to finish building for you. I'll find you later, I promise."

I set out for the front of the château and found Kate and a woman I assumed was Simone Allard standing in the foyer, deep in conversation. Kate spotted me and waved me over to them. Simone was the epitome of boho chic, pairing a multicolored peasant skirt with a high-end denim crop top I was pretty sure I'd spotted hanging in the Dior section of Le Bon Marché. She jutted a perfectly manicured hand forward, her bouncy beach waves landing softly on her delicate shoulders.

"I'm Simone. Lovely to meet you," she said in a surprising British accent.

"You're not . . ."

"French? I am but spent most of my childhood in England at Mayfield, a boarding school in Sussex. I only came home on holidays, and sometimes not even then, depending on whether or not my parents could afford the train fare after paying for tuition that semester."

"So where's home, then?"

"Cabrières-d'Avignon, about five kilometers from here. It's not perched on a hill like many of the other towns in Provence. It has no real natural beauty to speak of. I think that's why I fell in love with all the other villages and their grand châteaus." She looked up at the incredible arched entranceway. "And Château Mirabelle, she is one of my favorites."

I smiled. "Mine too."

"Great, so let's talk about what we can do to spruce the old girl up a bit. I have some ideas."

For the next several hours, Simone and I walked through each and every room of the château discussing the interior design and decor, finally landing back in the grand salon where we started the house tour.

"And finally for this room," she said, spinning around on her heels. "You see those dark spots on the walls? That's where the crystal girandoles once hung. I know we're repairing all the electricity in the home, but I think there's just something about these cavernous rooms that calls out for candlelight, don't you? Here, let me show you what I did on another project."

Simone zipped open an oversize leather portfolio and carefully slid out a large photograph affixed to a Styrofoam backing. She carried it over to the side of the room and leaned it up against the wall so we could take it all in. "This is from a home I worked on not too far from here that's been converted to a luxury hotel. Perhaps you've heard of it, Château du Val d'Été?"

"Yes! I actually spent an afternoon there not too long ago. It's absolutely gorgeous. You worked on that renovation? Then you must know Bastien Munier?"

She looked up. "I'm sorry, who?"

I grew self-conscious about my pronunciation and gave a bit more flourish to the vowel sounds as Pascal had been teaching me. "Bastien Mun-i-er? He worked on the renovation there. For a few years, I think."

She packed the photograph back into the portfolio. "I don't really recall, but to be fair, it was a while ago now. All these restoration projects start to blend together after a while."

"Well, I'll try to find him later, that way the two of you can catch up."

"I'd like that."

Elliott poked his head into the salon. "Kate said I'd find you both here."

"We're just wrapping up for the day," Simone said.

He handed each of us the filming schedule. I scanned it and looked up from the paper. "We're not filming at the château tomorrow?"

"René wants everyone out of the château the next couple of days. He needs to deal with some mold removal on the second floor. It's pretty toxic stuff."

"And Bastien?"

Elliott snapped his notebook closed. "I'm not sure what he's working on?"

"Well, lucky us, we get to spend the day at Brocante de Beaucaire," Simone said, clapping her hands together with a wide grin.

"What's that?" I asked.

"My favorite antiques market in all of France. You will absolutely love it. Where shall we meet?" Simone asked.

I looked over at Elliott. "The van will be at the inn at five a.m.," he answered.

I did a double take. "Five a.m.?"

"Trust me, you want to get to the market bright and early, that's how you find the very best stuff," Simone said with a nod.

"We're staying at the La Cigale Chantante," Elliott added.

She nodded, tucked the itinerary into the side pocket of her portfolio, and said, "I know it well. See you both tomorrow morning."

After Simone left, Elliott stepped a little farther into the room to examine the crumbling fireplace. He reached up and grabbed hold of a small paint curl dangling above the mantel and dragged it down the wall, peeling it away to reveal the faint outline of an image underneath. He reached up again, tugging at an even larger paint curl, and like a streamer, this time, exposed a huge section of the picture.

"From here, it looks like it could maybe be the top half of a lion. That's right, I remember seeing a painting over the mantel in one of the photos at Saint Orens," I said.

Elliott backed away from the fireplace. "I noticed a lion was part of the Adélaïse family crest. I bet if we kept peeling away the paint, we'd find the whole thing intact. You should make sure to point it out to your designer friend. It'd be a shame to see it covered up again. Maybe they can restore it? Feature it in the design?" Elliott wiped the paint dust from his hands off onto his pants.

"Hey, Elliott?"

He faced me. "Yeah?"

"I wanted to say thank you for letting Bastien know I'd be coming into Avignon so late the other night. That was really . . . um . . . thoughtful."

He shrugged his broad shoulders. "It's fine, Plum. Don't mention it, it's no big deal."

"It was a big deal. I don't know if you could ever understand, but when the paparazzi closes in on me like that, I feel like one of those animals with their legs caught in a trap. Like a lion being chased by hyenas. Completely helpless. I needed to get out of there, and I wasn't thinking clearly, so I'm grateful that you were."

"I swear, I didn't know who it was you were talking to in the hotel lobby, on my life, I didn't. Or I wouldn't have filmed you and Rhys. All that *gotcha* stuff, that isn't me. That isn't who I am as a person or filmmaker." He took a few steps closer so we were just inches apart. "I'd never do anything to hurt or embarrass you."

"I know," I whispered.

We stood there, so close our breaths were practically touching.

"Plum, good, there you are," Bastien called from the doorway. "I have a busy next couple of days, so I wanted to see if you were free to grab some dinner?"

"Sounds good. Just give me one minute to finish up," I called out to him. I turned back to Elliott. "Are you finished for the day too?"

"I think I'll stick around and explore a little more before heading out." Elliott fixed his light-blue eyes on me. "I feel like there might still be something here I'm missing. Sometimes the most special things are right there in front of us, just waiting to be discovered," he said softly, his words hanging delicately in the air between us.

Chapter Twenty-Eight

Framed by castle walls and the Rhône River, the port town of Beaucaire was bustling with activity. The sun was barely up, but already hundreds of people were streaming into the Brocante de Beaucaire looking for everything from household items, furniture, silver, and copperware to decorative accessories like vintage photos and jewelry.

"Every town in Provence has its own unique market. Some specialize in fresh fruits and vegetables. Some in seafood, some in furniture, and some in flowers," Simone explained as Gervais circled around for a spot to drop us off. "A brocante is a simple market with goods offered mostly by dealers, while a Marché des Antiquités tends to have high-quality antiques. Brocante de Beaucaire has a bit of both, which is why it's my favorite in the area."

"Gervais, laissez-nous au bas de la colline," Simone instructed, before continuing on. "I asked Gervais to drop us off at the bottom of the hill. We can meet the van back up top in a few hours. Usually, you can negotiate for delivery for any larger pieces of furniture, so don't worry about that."

We climbed out of the van, followed closely by Elliott and his small film crew. As we stepped into the warm summer heat, I inhaled and closed my eyes, trying to place some of the unique smells of the market. "I will never get tired of that smell. I wish we could bottle it.

It's just so distinct." I stretched my arms over my head and sucked in another lungful.

"Funny you should say that. It's called garrigue. It is the signature scent of the south of France. It comes from the combination of the vegetation and herbs that grow in the region, along with the terroir—the soil—the sea air, and the limestone on the coast. What you smell is the essence of juniper, thyme, rosemary, and lavender. Garrigue enhances the food of Provence, the culture, the wine, and even the people—those born here and even those just visiting for a while," she said with a wink and a smile.

Simone slung a messenger bag across her body and led the way through the different stalls, pointing out interesting pieces along the way.

"These would be divine by the fireplace in the grand salon," she said, pointing to two large cream chairs with rose stitching. "What do you think, Plum?"

"They're gorgeous. Do you know anything about them?" I asked the seller.

He shook his head. "Désolée, je ne parle pas anglais."

Simone stepped forward. "Pardon, pouvez-vous me parler de ces chaises."

The seller nodded before providing us with the chairs' history in rapid-fire French. Unfortunately, I was only able to make out a few words. I looked to Simone for some assistance.

"He found the chairs in the thirteenth-century monastery village of Fanjeaux, about two hours away. Based on their quality, he thinks they may have belonged to the mother superior of the abbey. He wanted one hundred eighty euros a chair, but I talked him down to three hundred euros for the pair," Simone said, passing the seller the bills.

"The left leg on that one looks broken," I said.

Simone glanced down. "No problem, that is an easy repair."

Elliott had Simone reenact the exchange two more times and directed her to ask a few more pointed questions about the chairs in English for the benefit of *Heart Restoration Project*'s American audience.

She caught on quickly, able to extract the information without it seeming directed or forced.

Elliott addressed his small crew. "I think we got what we need here. Why don't you guys grab some shots of the eager crowds coming into the market. I think it'll really up the stakes of the negotiation scenes." He looked over at me. "So much for the reality aspect of reality TV, right? But I guess I don't need to tell *you* that."

"You know it's funny, but in the early days of *EVERLYday*, everything we put out there *was* real. It was only when the show started to take off that things began to change. We weren't the Everly family anymore, we were the Everly brand." I glanced up from the ground and into Elliott's sympathetic eyes. "What? What'd I say?"

"I guess I never thought about what that must've been like for you. You always seemed so, I don't know, happy? The perfect nuclear family? Two parents who loved their kids *and* liked each other. Pretty novel stuff."

"Is it?"

"I wouldn't know, my dad walked out on us when I was a baby, and my mom's tablescapes, well, they were made up of paper plates and red Solo cups," he snickered.

His rigid posture and balled fists clued me in to the fact we were treading on uncomfortable territory. I arched my right eyebrow and tried to lighten the mood. "Elliott Schaffer, did you watch *EVERLYday*?"

"Gimme a break, *everyone* watched *EVERLYday*. It was on so many damn channels you couldn't avoid it even if you wanted to. But only the early seasons—before I got a PlayStation."

"So who was your favorite?"

"Favorite what?"

"Sister?"

He pursed his lips and jutted out his chin. "Do you really want to know?"

Simone rushed over, stealing the moment his answer was supposed to fill. "Okay, so good news, I got the seller to agree to transport the chairs free of charge. Turns out he always wanted to be an actor and was pretty jazzed about his five minutes of fame. He asked if he might get a chance to be on camera again when he delivers them to the château? Since he has another even better booth at the top of the hill, I told him we *might* be able to work something out." Simone fanned her face with a map of the market. "Goodness, it's hot today. What do you say we divide and conquer? That way we can cover as much ground as possible before the temperature becomes unbearable?"

The sun was starting to come up over the market and already the summer heat felt sweltering. Even the breeze off the river was doing little to help cool down the air. "I'm fine with that. Although, I'm not sure how it will affect the filming schedule?" I looked at Elliott.

"I'll go with Plum, and radio the guys to meet up with you, Simone. We should have more than enough footage already, but this way we're definitely covered."

Elliott and I set off deeper into the market, while Simone headed up the hill to check out the professional antique booths. Brocante de Beaucaire was a feast for the senses, with vibrant textiles, unique art, and local food vendors. Rows of vendor stalls were set up to display some of the region's most desirable goods: fleur-de-lis-adorned linens and needlework, antiques and bric-a-brac like weather-worn tins and handblown glassware, artisan-crafted ceramics, and household furniture of varying sizes from all periods of history.

In the center of the market, the most beautiful antique carousel spun in the sunlight. It featured candy-colored horses, bejeweled carriages, and classic storybook characters. The scene was so overwhelmingly animated it was hard to know what to focus on first. But then, out of the corner of my eye, I spotted a large mantel clock decorated with a black onyx lion sitting on a table in a nondescript booth full of knickknacks and small trinkets. I crossed over and wiggled through some foot traffic for a closer look.

"Pardon, Monsieur. What can you tell me about this clock?" I asked the seller.

"Ah, it is a French specimen-marble, four-glass clock by the renowned maker Japy Frères. As you can see, the pretty dial is porcelain enamel on copper with floral swags between the hours and fretted gilt-brass hands. The lion is one hundred percent polished black onyx dipped in gold leaf. She is a beauty, non?"

"Oui." Elliott came up behind me, and I picked up the clock to show it to him. "What do you think? For the mantel in the salon? It looks just like the one I saw in a photograph of Château Mirabelle back at Saint Orens."

Elliott studied the clock. "Who knows? It could very well be the same one? When the Germans occupied Château Mirabelle, it is more than likely they looted and traded whatever they could."

A wave of sadness washed over me. What if the clock had been a wedding gift for Luc and Imène, or maybe it was an Adélaïse family heirloom? And while I knew it was highly unlikely this was the very same one, even the remote possibility it could be had my heart beating just a little bit faster. "Can you tell me the price?" I asked the seller.

"Three hundred fifty euros. But for you, ma cherie, three hundred euros."

Elliott picked up his camera to film our exchange.

"Merci," I said and set it back down on the table.

Elliott lowered his camera. "What happened? You're not gonna get it?"

"Simone was pretty strict with her orders, furniture only today. Besides, we can't know for sure if this was the same one, and it's a bit pricey and out of budget for something not entirely practical."

"Does it matter?"

"Bastien says you can honor a home by restoring it to its original state, or you can honor it by restoring it to its original intention, so maybe it doesn't matter?"

His expression couldn't mask his surprise. "Bastien said that?"

"He probably read it off a fortune cookie or something," I teased.

Elliott looked up from the ground. "I don't hate him, you know? Bastien."

I tilted my head and side-eyed him. "Could've fooled me."

"I don't," he confirmed. "When I messaged him to pick you up from the station in the middle of the night, he didn't hesitate for even a second. I told you, I can admit when I'm wrong."

The stall was quiet with the exception of one other patron who was being helped by the slightly balding seller behind the tables. Elliott rested his camera by his feet, then shoved his hands in his pockets. "Luckily, first impressions aren't always the most accurate," he smirked, a playful glint in his eye. Thinking of the *awkwardly painful* car ride that first day, I broke into a grin as I remembered hurling all over him in the back of a car the size of a toy truck.

My smile quickly evolved into a fit of giggles. "I will never forget, for the rest of my life, how you looked folded into the back of that car. It was a bit like how I imagine Houdini looked inside a safe." And just saying the words out loud launched me into an outbreak of uncontrollable laughter.

"Well, at least I kept my breakfast *in* my stomach and not launched all over the colleague I'd just met," Elliott fired back. And to my surprise, he started to laugh too. Loudly. And the sound was delightful. Always so serious and focused, he rarely, if ever, let his hair down, so to speak. Since we'd been working together, this was the first time I'd really heard him let loose. The sound stirred something within me, and a twinkle I'd never quite noticed before flickered from behind his smile.

"Hey," I said, sobering a little with the realization, "you have a great laugh. You should do it more often." I swatted at him playfully, and catching his eye as my hand landed on his forearm, I felt a current of electricity rocket straight through me. Our shared giggles dissolved with that one glance and melted into a sweet moment that lingered between us like a haze. He stepped toward me, and his body brushed against mine so closely that the soft hairs on his arms tickled my skin.

I shifted uncomfortably, lowering my eyes to break the spell. "Come on, we should keep moving if we want to meet Simone on time." A flash of disappointment registered on his face, but he didn't say anything. He just nodded and hoisted his camera on his shoulder again, and we continued on our way meandering through the stalls.

I glanced around the market, noticing scores of pottery and antiques of different shapes, colors, and countries of origin, and instinctively reached for my phone to capture the distinct pieces as we passed. Tapping the record button, I zoomed in on an older couple strolling hand in hand down the wide aisles of the market who paused to examine a lemon-colored lace tablecloth displayed on a rustic and oddly shaped wooden table. They'd probably been married for at least forty years and had their children and their grandchildren over every Sunday for roast chicken dinner on their little garden patio. From behind the camera, it was easy to get lost in endless possibilities. Lately, I was finding the same to be true of France itself.

I stopped filming and turned to Elliott. "Being here, sometimes I feel like I'm not just on a different continent but a completely different planet. The sights, the smells, the freedom I have to walk around a place like this in complete anonymity. I know people call Paris the City of Love, but it feels like there's a magical spell cast over the whole damn country. I like Bastien, I do, but sometimes I can't help but wonder if it's him I'm falling for or if it's Provence?" I looked up. "Do you ever feel that way about Odette?"

"Odette? No, there's nothing going on between me and Odette."

I squinted at him, unsure if he'd feel a need to lie. I wasn't sure why he would, but I was almost certain that I'd noticed them getting more and more chummy over the weeks we'd been here, ever since that first night in Avignon. "There isn't?" I urged, "But that night at the club, she seemed so into you? And all those afternoons I spied the two of you sharing a bottle of wine out in the garden at the inn, it sure looked like there was."

He paused before answering, maybe catching how much I must have been paying attention to have noted so much of their interactions. "She was going through a difficult breakup, and I was a shoulder to cry on—a *convenient* shoulder. She isn't interested in me like that."

"It sure seemed like it was more than that," I said and then realized that, again, I was showing him my hand.

He tilted his head and said, "Maybe, in the beginning, there was a little playful flirtation between us, but that fizzled out quickly. She wasn't a formidable enough sparring partner . . ."

He lowered his gaze to mine, and at the intensity, my stomach bottomed out, and suddenly my breath caught in my chest. Locked in an unspoken conversation laden with undeniable tension and respectful hesitation, it was as though the bustling market around us had momentarily ceased to exist, leaving only the gravitational pull that kept us focused on one another. For a fleeting heartbeat, it seemed as though we might surrender to the magnetism between us, but as quickly as the moment arose, it passed, leaving us standing there, hearts pounding.

I cleared my throat and took a step back. "Wow, I am positively melting," I announced as I fanned myself with my hand and shifted my eyes from his.

"What do you say we get out of the sun for a few minutes?" Elliott asked.

I looked around the market. There wasn't an umbrella or awning anywhere in sight. "What do you have in mind?"

Elliott took my hand. "Follow me."

I trailed him through the crowded market to the antique carousel. He knocked lightly on the ticket window and held up two fingers before handing over five euros in exchange for our tickets.

I stopped him in his tracks. "Elliott, you know I get motion sickness."

"Still better than sunstroke, right? We won't ride anything that goes up and down, promise." He held up his fingers in a scout's honor salute and winked.

Elliott passed the tickets to the barker, and we stepped onto the ride. I popped up on my toes, looking for a free space. "Over there," I called, and we squeezed into a weathered enamel carriage that looked like the half-transformed pumpkin from *Cinderella*. Moments later, the lively sounds of an organ piped out of the center as the platform started to spin beneath us. Round and round we went, taking in the sights from every possible vantage point—children gripping bright balloons, friends sipping coffees, and couples strolling hand in hand through the long aisles of the marketplace.

Elliott glanced over at me. "You okay? The spinning and everything?"

I nodded. "Actually, I'm great."

Elliott smiled and stretched his arm up and over the top of our tiny carriage normally intended for children—or at least an adult shorter than six foot four. We were sitting so close I could smell his aftershave, clean and crisp against the muggy warmth of the air.

"You know, I don't think I've ridden a carousel, maybe ever?" I said to distract me from the closeness of his body next to mine.

"Really? Isn't that a childhood rite of passage?"

"I didn't have the most typical childhood, remember? Don't misunderstand, I've lived a wonderful life, and my parents are good people. They didn't know what *EVERLYday* would become, nobody did. But being here in Provence, I've grown to appreciate the slower pace of life. People here don't just sip their coffee or wine, they immerse themselves in it. It's a whole goddamn experience for them." I shook my head. "No, I can't go back to the way my life was before. Flitting from place to place and thing to thing, existing but not really living. I won't do it. I can't." Just saying the words out loud made my throat squeeze tight—a desperate desire to convince myself that my future would be different.

"So then, what is it you *do* want?"

"You know, nobody's ever asked me that before. I guess, deep down, I want you." I almost choked on my blunder before fumbling to correct myself. "Um . . . *to be you* . . . I mean."

Elliott pretended not to hear the error, but by the sweep of blush that rosied his cheeks, it was evident he did. "You want to be me?"

"Well, a less grumpy version, maybe," I teased. "Seriously, though, I'm starting to wonder if maybe I've spent my whole life on the wrong side of the camera."

"So turn it around—the camera, the narrative, your life. It's up to you, you know?"

I nudged him playfully and said, "Easy as that, huh?"

"You know, you keep surprising me . . . and I don't usually like surprises," he said, his voice almost a whisper.

"Oh, I do?" I breathed back and adjusted myself to face him. "And you don't?" I pressed.

He closed the few inches between us, pressing his full lips against mine, igniting the fibers of my body like a wildfire. But I'd been burned by fire before, and I wanted to believe that after all the scars and ash, I'd learned my lesson. I pulled away from his embrace—my lips still tingling, my heart pounding so hard against my chest I was sure it was going to break a rib.

"Elliott, I can't do this," I said, placing my hand to his chest to put as much distance between us as I could in the carousel car. "Maybe I shouldn't feel this way, and we haven't put a label on things yet, but I know how I'd feel if I found out Bastien kissed somebody else."

"Of course. You're right," he said, his voice breaking. The ride began to slow, and Elliott rose from the metal carriage seat. "This is our stop."

"Hey, wait . . . Can we talk about this?" I pleaded.

"There's nothing to talk about. I . . . I really shouldn't have done that. You're right—I must have just gotten swept up in the moment, that's all. Chalk it up to the heat. Maybe I do have sunstroke after all," he joked before glancing down at his phone. "I have like half a dozen missed calls from the crew. I should really check in with them. Don't bother waiting for me, I'll catch up with you back at the château, okay?"

"Oh, yeah. Sure. Okay."

I watched Elliott hop off the still-rotating platform and disappear into the crowd. The ride's turntable finally ground to a halt, but I couldn't move. In Cinderella's tiny fairy-tale carriage, I was left paralyzed—my body buzzing and my head still spinning.

Chapter Twenty-Nine

Simone was running late to another appointment, so Gervais dropped her off at the inn before driving me and Elliott over to Château Mirabelle. According to Simone, the market trip was a rousing success. In addition to the chairs, she negotiated for an antique white rococo headboard, a small settee upholstered in a lavender Schumacher linen, and two English chinoiserie mirrors from the 1880s she thought would be perfect in the bright entranceway, all of which would be delivered over the next few days.

Gervais stopped the van at the front gate and let me out. The château seemed eerily deserted. I glanced down at my watch: 3:00 p.m. The hottest point of the day. The crew was probably taking a break. When Elliott climbed out of the van, he mumbled something about having some paperwork to do and stalked off in the direction of video village. Now, left pretty much alone, I decided to go in search of Kate and Bastien by making my way through the vineyard to craft services, where René and a few of his guys were sitting at one of the long picnic tables drinking beer.

He took a long swig and set the bottle down on the table. "Bonjour, Mademoiselle Everly, come, have a drink with us."

I sat down beside him as an invitation to pass me one.

He chuckled and said, "We really should not be drinking on a worksite, but when it is this hot, you sweat it out anyway, n'est-ce pas?"

"'N'est-ce pas' means 'do you not,' right?" I guessed.

His eyes beamed. "Bien joué, your French is much improved, Plum."

"Pascal Sauveterre has been tutoring me a bit in the evenings," I shared.

"Ah, Pascal Sauveterre. I did some work on La Cigale Chantante not too long ago." He shook his head, fishing around in the cooler for a beer from the very bottom, deep in the ice. "They have some very serious foundation problems. The inn on top of the hill will be the inn at the bottom of the hill in not too long if they cannot get it properly fixed." He popped the top off with his hand effortlessly and passed me the frosty bottle with an easy smile.

"Merci," I said and clinked my bottle to his before taking a long sip. The hoppy tang was surprisingly refreshing, and I relished in the cold chill working its way down my chest and into my stomach. "Have you seen Bastien or Kate at all?"

"Oui, they were in le château earlier."

"Oh, it's been deemed safe to go inside now?"

"Almost, so long as you stay on the rez-de-chaussée . . . um, ground floor. The last of the mold was removed earlier today, and the second floor should be secured by tomorrow evening so filming inside can safely resume."

I nodded, and we sat for a few moments enjoying the cold beers as the sun continued to beat down from high in the blue sky. The condensation from the bottle dripping down the skin on my fingers mirrored the beads of sweat rolling down the small of my back, and I enjoyed another long pull of the crisp but mildly bitter beer, cooling me from the inside as it snaked its way down to my stomach. I finished my beer as we sat in comfortable silence, and after swigging back the very last frothy sip, I thanked him, clinking my empty bottle once more to his, and set off to look for Kate and Bastien for an update.

I stepped into the grand foyer and called into the house. No answer. I inched a little farther into the hallway, but still no answer. There was a light knock on the front door.

"Hello?" I called.

"Bonjour, y a-t-il quelqu'un ici?" a cheerful voice sang out.

I recognized the seller from the booth where we bought the antique cream-colored chairs with rose stitching and went to greet him at the entranceway. "Je ne parle pas beaucoup le français, Simone n'est . . . Simone n'est . . . I'm afraid Simone's not here."

"Voilà, the chairs. For you," he said, carrying them into the house, one wedged under each of his arms. His eyes darted around the space. "Où?"

"Où? Oh right, where? Follow me," I said, motioning him toward the salon.

"Où sont les caméras?" he asked as we made our way down the long hall.

"Where are the cameras?" I translated and repeated back to him. "Not today," I responded and held up two fingers. "Deux jours. Two days." His face fell in disappointment. "Maybe you can come back then, and we can reenact the chair delivery? Sorry, I don't know how to say *reenact* in French."

The seller plopped the two chairs down in the middle of the room with a resounding humph.

"Um . . . if you can wait a few minutes, I can try to find someone who can speak better French who can explain," I offered.

"Non, non, non, Simone m'a promis!" With that, he turned on his heel and marched out the front door, muttering a handful of what I imagined to be French expletives along the way.

"I'll have her call you," I yelled after him, but he was already halfway to his truck. Once he was gone, I turned my attention to the beautiful chairs now strewn in the middle of the room. They were heavier than they looked, and it took almost all the upper body strength I had to drag them across the floor to the front of the fireplace, but Simone was right, they made the most perfect addition to the space.

Exhausted from the early wake-up call, I plunked down in one of them and stretched my feet out in front of me. Even though it was close to ninety degrees in the house, it was easy to imagine a family gathered around the massive hearth playing card games and telling stories. I glanced up, and there above the fireplace was the fully excavated Adélaïse family coat of arms. The workers must have finished it while we were at the market. I don't know how I'd overlooked it earlier, maybe it was all the commotion with the yelling chair vendor, but as soon as I spotted it, I sprang out of the seat to take a closer look.

Most of the color on the crest that had been faded from the layers of paint that had to be scraped to unearth it were renewed, now clearly detailing the heralding trumpets, fleur-de-lis, and rampant lions on its shield. The proud name Adélaïse, now clearly visible in a stylized Old English–looking font stamped across the middle, added to its regality and prominence. With the colors restored to a distinctly vibrant crimson, green, and gold, the crest looked dynamic and powerful, a true symbol of what this house and this family stood for—and seeing it displayed front and center in the space made me feel a sense of pride I hadn't felt while working on any project . . . or maybe ever.

What sounded like a man's and a woman's voice cascaded down the hallway. I poked my head out of the salon doorway and spied Bastien and Kate locked in an intimate conversation, Bastien's hand on the small of Kate's back as they walked. I couldn't make out what they were saying, but every couple of words were interspersed by laughter. They stopped at the stairway, huddling closer together. Kate placed her palm on Bastien's chest, nodding along to whatever it was he was saying before he pulled her in for a long hug. She broke away and threw him one last smile before turning on her heel and walking out of the house.

I waited a few seconds, cleared my throat, and called out, "Bastien? Bastien, is that you?"

He strode into the salon. "Plum, there you are! How are you, ma chérie? You were at Brocante de Beaucaire, non? How was it? A rousing success?"

"Honestly, it was hot. But we did manage to find these two beauties," I said, pointing to the chairs.

He stood back to admire them. "Elles sont magnifiques."

"Where've you been? I've been looking everywhere for you."

"Oh, I have been up with the cicadas since this morning . . . busy, busy. First, I did a walk-through of the house to make sure we cleared all the mold. Believe me, mold is not something you want to play around with, very serious if any at all is left behind. I think the fans and dehumidifiers need just one more day to run to make sure everything is dried out before we secure the floors, and *then* we can resume filming."

"That is very good news."

He cupped my chin in his hands. "Why do you look like that when you say, 'that is very good news'?"

"Why do I look like what?"

"Like the very good news is actually very bad news."

I stepped back and away from him. "No, it's nothing. Just a long, hot, exhausting day is all. And it *is* very good news. I'm sure Kate was delighted."

"Maybe? I am sure René has already provided her with an update."

"René? Not you? You're not the one who's been updating her?" So if Bastien wasn't giving her the lowdown on the mold situation, then what were they so cozied up about?

"Oui, I asked René to take the lead on this part of the renovation. There are just too many things to tend to, and I needed to, um, how do you say . . . give some jobs away?"

"Um . . . delegate?"

"Oui, yes, delegate. He will update Kate on his part."

"I see."

Bastien took two long steps past me toward the fireplace. "Hmm, what is this?"

I spun around to look at where he was now pointing. "Oh, isn't it incredible?! It's the Adélaïse family crest. Elliott uncovered it from beneath like a dozen layers of paint."

"Oui, I saw the crest already. I meant this," he said, pointing to a clock sitting on the mantel.

I was so enamored by the coat of arms earlier, I completely overlooked it sitting right there in front of me. I carefully lifted the base up off the shelf. "Wow, it's the clock that we . . . me and Elliott . . . came across at the market this morning. It reminded me so much of the one I saw in that original photograph we found at Saint Orens. I even joked with Elliott that it just might be the very same clock. I wanted to get it, but it was a little too expensive. I guess he must've gone back to the booth to buy it after we split up."

"Well, it fits perfectly, non? Like it was made for this exact spot?"

"Oui, it really does."

He put his arm around me. "C'mon, you must be hungry. Can I interest you in that life-changing croque Monsieur now?"

"Can I take a rain check? I'm tired and sweaty and could use a cold shower and a full night's rest. Besides, I have a tutoring session with Pascal tonight."

"Pascal? Should I be jealous?" he teased.

"I don't know, should I be jealous of Kate?" I said before I could stop the words from tumbling out of my mouth.

His eyes went round. "Kate? Don't be ridicule. She is only my colleague, the same way Elliott is your colleague, non?"

At the mention of Elliott's name, I felt my body stiffen, remembering the feel of his soft lips on mine and the jolt of electricity that almost knocked me off my espadrilles. "Yes. Of course, you're right, I am being ridicule."

He gently stroked the side of my face. "Le cœur a ses raisons que la raison ne connaît point."

My brain tried to catch what it could of his French, running through my limited vocab with Pascal. I came up woefully short. "The only thing I got was cœur . . . heart, right? So what does the rest mean?"

"The heart has reasons for which reason knows nothing."

"Tell me, why does the expression 'you're being ridiculous' sound so much better when it's said in French? It's almost infuriating."

The corners of his mouth turned up to a flirty grin. "I don't know, why don't you ask Pascal?"

Mon dieu, he was charming. And seemed to be very into me. Maybe I *was* jumping to the entirely wrong conclusion about him and Kate. Maybe I was just still in my head after the whole Rhys encounter? I didn't have anything to worry about . . . Colleagues talked, right? Colleagues even occasionally touched. Sure. Colleagues sometimes even kissed on romantic antique carousels, and that didn't mean there was necessarily anything more to the story.

But there was just something about the look in Kate's eyes and the way she and Bastien were overly familiar with one another. As hard as I tried, I couldn't shake the sinking feeling that in this case, there really did seem to be more to their story.

Chapter Thirty

With filming shut down on *Heart Restoration Project* for one more day because of the mold issue, Elliott and I decided it was the perfect opportunity to visit Aix-en-Provence and the Camp des Milles Memorial. I was relieved when he knocked on my door late last night suggesting the trip, not even the slightest trace of awkwardness still lingering from our kiss and his subsequent quick exodus from the carousel.

The camp was about an hour south of Maubec, so we set out early, wanting to take full advantage of our day off. Unfortunately, Jack and Claudine didn't seem any keener on our pursuit of the true story behind Château Mirabelle as a facet for the show, but it no longer mattered to either one of us. Elliott and I were on a mission to unveil the reasons behind the town's collective silence about what had truly transpired there.

Gervais parked the van in front of a dark-red, run-down brick building resembling an old factory, and we stepped out onto an empty dirt road. Elliott lifted his backpack and camera onto his shoulder and said, "I called ahead and arranged for a tour guide to meet us at the entrance at eight thirty."

It was probably around eighty-five degrees, yet goose bumps trailed up and down my arms. There was something wholly unsettling about this place. If Provence was impressionist art with its color and light, this landscape was the complete opposite—dull, monochrome, and lifeless.

I didn't need a tour guide to tell me this was somewhere you didn't want to stay for very long.

A few minutes later, an older woman with a nameplate that read *Hélène* approached us. "Bonjour, you must be Elliott?" she said, glancing down at her clipboard and then back up at us.

"I'm Elliott Schaffer, and this is Plum Everly," he answered.

"Pleased to meet you both. I have your tickets right here," she said, patting her right breast pocket. "But they know me so well, they won't be necessary. Come, we can go inside this way." She motioned for us to follow her around the side of the building to a small gatehouse. The security guard glanced at Hélène's credentials and waved her inside while we followed closely behind.

"So," Hélène asked us over her shoulder as she led the way, "what is your interest in Camp des Milles? Perhaps that will help to better structure our day?"

"We are working on the restoration of a château in Maubec for a television show, and we understand the former owners played a role in the French Resistance. We're trying to learn a bit more about what may have happened to them," I answered. "I was wondering if it would be okay if we film a bit of our tour and conversations here for the project?"

"Actually, that would be wonderful. Very few people know France even had internment camps during World War II. What a great platform to be able to educate them. Please, film away, but perhaps we should start at the beginning then, non?"

Over the next several hours, Hélène walked us through Camp des Milles, from the main building, once a fully operational tile factory before it was converted to a prison, to the guards' dining room, now known as the Room of Murals.

Hélène motioned to the wall. "This mural is called 'The Last Supper,' one prisoner's very dark take on the Leonardo da Vinci masterpiece," she explained. "Camp des Milles imprisoned many artists believed to be political dissidents. You will see that they left their mark all over the grounds."

"That's just incredible. Elliott, can you bring the camera up close to it, get tight shots of each and every painted face? Be sure to give special attention to the detail work when you zoom in. If we can show the actual brushstrokes on the wall, it would be a way to subtly acknowledge the people who made them," I directed.

Elliott, not missing a beat, took my cue and moved about the space filming the sequence as I requested. "This looks great. Nice touch, Plum." He stroked my arm affirmingly and moved to follow after Hélène, who continued her guided tour of the room.

"Camp des Milles was used to house various 'undesirables'—emigrants awaiting exit visas, political enemies, escapees from Germany and Austria, and, as I said, an exceptionally high proportion of artists. The painters, sculptors, writers, actors, and musicians had to be endlessly inventive in devising ways to ward off boredom and lift their spirits," Hélène explained. "Over three hundred paintings and drawings are thought to have originated here."

I thought back to the exhibit at the French Resistance Museum in Paris and the black-and-white photographs of the cattle cars standing outside Camp des Milles's front gates. "When did things change? When did it become more of a deportation camp?"

"Between 1941 and 1942, Camp des Milles became one of the centres de rassemblement before deportation. About two thousand of the inmates were shipped off to the Drancy internment camp, and then, for many, eventually they were brought to Auschwitz," Hélène answered solemnly, not needing to fill in the rest.

"Are there records on-site? Lists of prisoners? The former owners of Château Mirabelle, the Adélaïses, we believe that they may have been brought here. They were arrested sometime in 1942, so the timelines sync up," I said.

"Yes, there is an archive in the main building we can check. I think they should be amenable to letting you both visit given the nature of your project." Hélène glanced down at her watch and tsked. "Oof, but we should go now. The archive is only open a few hours every day, and that's assuming Madame Razat even came in at all." Hélène turned to me. "She watches her grandson every other Tuesday, and I cannot remember if she worked last week?"

We hurried across the sparse yard back to the main factory building. Hélène flashed her credentials for a second time at the guard standing outside the entrance, and he ushered us inside. We scurried down two flights of stairs to a dank basement, white fluorescent lights flickering overhead.

Hélène knocked gently on a door that was slightly ajar, and a heavy-set woman with high cheekbones and snow-white hair shuffled over to answer it.

"Bonjour, Hélène, tellement content de vous voir," Madame Razat said, pushing the door completely open to greet us. They spoke in conversational French, clearly not meant for us. Though I picked up a bit, I wasn't confident enough to join in, and so instead, we just waited politely beside Hélène for further instruction.

"Bonjour, Marjorie, vous ne gardez pas Mathieu aujourd'hui?" Hélène asked.

Madame Razat nodded. "Mathieu est malade. Sa maman l'emmène chez le médecin. Allez, viens-ici."

Hélène waved the three of us inside the room and lowered her voice to translate. "We are in luck, Madame Razat was *supposed* to babysit Mathieu today, but he has a cold so his maman is going to take him to the doctor."

"Please, come inside," Madame Razat said, coaxing us farther into the room. "What can I help you with?"

"This is Elliott Schaffer and Plum Everly. They are working on a film project," Hélène answered.

Madame Razat eyed me up and down. "Plum Everly? From *EVERLYday*?" She peeked around us, expecting to see a large film crew trailing behind.

"Yes, I'm that Plum, but this isn't for *EVERLYday*."

Elliott chimed in. "We're working on a new television show documenting the restoration of a château in Maubec that we've come to understand may have played a role in the Resistance. We were hoping to learn a bit more about the couple who owned the château. We know they were arrested by the Third Reich in 1942, but we don't know what happened to them after that."

Madame Razat strummed her stubby fingers against her chin. "If they were arrested in the Provence region in 1942, it is more than likely they were sent here. Do you know the couple's name?"

"Luc and Imène Adélaïse," I replied.

Madame Razat nodded and sat down at a small wooden desk in the corner of the room. She popped open a laptop and began furiously typing away on the keyboard. After a few clicks of the mouse, she pushed the computer closed and sprang up from the seat. She motioned for the three of us to follow her down another hallway to a room crammed full of filing cabinets and shelving units full of plain-looking storage containers.

Madame Razat inched up on her toes to reach for the highest shelf of one of the cabinets. "The Nazis were nothing if not meticulous. They kept records of absolutely everything. Every arrest. Every prisoner. Every single transport in and out of the camp." She eyed Elliott up and down. "You, you're very tall, aren't you?"

"Yes, ma'am, I am," he replied.

"I could go retrieve the stepladder, but why bother with you here? Can you reach far into the back and pull out the files labeled ANNECY?"

Elliott stretched his arms up, not even needing to stand on his tiptoes, hefted a box marked ANNECY from its spot, and effortlessly placed it down on the counter in front of Madame Razat.

"I'm sorry, but . . . what is Annecy? Is it another camp?" I asked.

"It is a French town about forty kilometers south of Geneva, Switzerland," Madame Razat answered. "So actually I need you to grab the folders behind this," she instructed with a rigid finger pointing back up to the top shelf.

Elliott, now on his toes to see what he was missing, reached far back into the cabinet and pried out two large files, which he handed to Madame Razat, their weight practically knocking her over. She left the box on the counter but carried the folders into a room adjacent to the one we were in and set them down with a thud. Loose papers, photographs, and maps spilled out onto the table, covering more than half of the top of it.

Madame Razat passed around latex gloves, and I picked up one of the photographs of a small, unremarkable-looking farm sitting on a remote hilltop. I flipped it over, and scribbled on the back were the words *Beliveau, Bauernhof.* I held the picture up. "Beliveau, Bauernhof? What does that mean?"

"Bauernhof means *farm* in German. So that is the Beliveau farm," Hélène answered confidently.

"May we film in here? Is it alright?" I asked.

"Oui, go right ahead." Madame Razat gestured, and Elliott stood up to capture our exchange. Though I knew he would shoot most of the footage with his professional camera, I couldn't help but take out my iPhone, adjust some of my settings, and film close-ups of the splayed pictures and documents, the inky scrawls of signatures of those long forgotten and photographs in black and white. The cinematography practically took its own shape, telling its own story, as Madame Razat shuffled through the images and narrated along the way.

I took another look at the tattered photograph of the Beliveau farm. "I'm still trying to piece this all together. What's the connection between *this* farm and the Adélaïses?"

"Have you ever heard of the Dutch-Paris network?" Madame Razat asked.

I looked up at Elliott, who was shaking his head. "No, no I don't think so."

"It was a small but quite successful Resistance network instrumental in saving many, many lives. Their main mission was to rescue people from the Nazis by hiding them or taking them to neutral countries using falsified documents. Annecy was the town where the Dutch-Paris network brought the refugees to cross the border from France into Switzerland." Madame Razat lifted the photograph off the table. "Beliveau, Bauernhof was one of the safe houses used to shelter people on their way to Switzerland." She shuffled through a handful of papers until she finally landed on the one she was in search of. "Ah, here it is. A list of all those who were captured at Beliveau, Bauernhof on November 16, 1942."

She slid the paper across the table over to me, and there in block type were the names Luc and Imène Adélaïse, Marthe and Grégoire Archambeau, and Ginette and Alain Grenouille listed among half a dozen others. I almost fell off my chair. I handed the sheet to Elliott, whose mouth dropped wide open. "All of them, every name on this list, were arrested and brought to Camp des Milles?" I asked.

"Oui." Madame Razat shuffled to another paper and pushed her reading glasses farther down the bridge of her nose. "They were processed into Camp des Milles on November 28, 1942, and remained here until December 23, when they were transported to Drancy internment camp."

"And from there?" I asked.

"Transported to another camp, most likely Auschwitz, but unfortunately, this is where our paper trail ends. It is possible that there could be more records in Geneva or Poland."

I pulled my phone from my pocket, snapped a shot of the list of names and the photograph of the farm, and tucked my phone back into my pocket.

"It is well past my lunch hour," Madame Razat said, pushing up from the table. "Is there anything else I can help you with?"

Elliott switched off the camera. "Thank you, you've been more than generous with your time."

"Yes, merci," I echoed.

Hélène escorted us out of the dark basement and back into the light, back to the front gate where Gervais was waiting with the van.

"It was lovely spending the morning with you both," she said.

"Thank you again. This was incredibly eye opening," Elliott answered.

"Is that . . . ?" I asked and motioned into the distance.

Elliott and Hélène turned to look where I was pointing.

"Ah oui, it is one of the cattle cars that was used for transport, now a permanent fixture at our memorial," Hélène confirmed.

My chest tightened as hot tears flooded my eyes. I wiped them with the back of my hand and cleared my throat. "Elliott, we should grab a few exterior and interior shots of the car before we go." Before I'd even finished my sentence, he was already moving toward the train car with his camera mounted on his shoulder.

"Thank you again," he called over to Hélène with a wave.

After shooting the footage and expressing one more round of gratitude to our lovely guide, we climbed back into the van, dripping with sweat and emotionally drained.

"Gervais, would you be able to turn up the air-conditioning? Plum gets motion sickness," Elliott mentioned, without one hint of sarcasm or irony.

Gervais nodded into the rearview mirror and blasted cold air from all the vents. It was the coolest I'd felt in France since we arrived.

"Gervais, La Cigale Chantante, s'il vous plaît," Elliott directed with an exhausted sigh.

I leaned forward, between the two front seats. "Actually, if neither of you are in a hurry, I have a small detour I'd like to make."

Chapter Thirty-One

After a long trek up the cobblestone road, Elliott and I were finally once again standing at the grand entrance of Saint Orens. I wiped at my forehead with the back of my arm and brushed a few hairs from my eyes. It was close to two o'clock, the sun was still burning brightly upon the rolling hills of Provence, and its warmth felt wonderful on my skin. Elliott pushed open the church's large front door, and a cool breeze greeted us from inside, the old marble building helping to retain some of the cooler morning air. We stepped into the chapel and navigated our way to the rectory, familiar with the route from the last time we'd come.

I peeked my head past the open door and saw an older, portly gentleman dressed in ordinary but formal clothes. He was peering over his readers at some handwritten notes and marking edits as he went.

"Bonjour, we are looking for Father François. Do you know if he is in today?" I asked.

"Oui, Mademoiselle." He gestured at himself and said, "Moi, c'est Père François." He rose to greet us and extended a hand. "Are you here for a certificat de mariage?" He shook a finger between me and Elliott. "Vous faites un couple adorable."

"Un couple adorable? Certificat de mariage?" I repeated back slowly in my painfully American accent. I looked over at Elliott, who had turned an endearing shade of pink. "Oh no, Monsieur. We aren't here for a marriage license. Um. I mean, he and I aren't together. We're just . . ." *Are just what?* I shook the question from my head and focused on the real purpose of the visit. "We were hoping you could allow us back into the church's archives?"

"Back in?" he repeated, trying to work out the meaning of the expression. "Oh, are you Mademoiselle Everly?"

"Yes. I am Plum Everly."

"Ah, my apologies that I was not here to meet you on your last visit. I have some time to take you there now before afternoon Mass, if you are available?"

We followed Father François past the altar and down a long hallway to the set of stairs leading up to the annex.

"Remind me," Father François said, "what it is you are looking for?"

"Any information you have on Château Mirabelle or Maubec?"

"Or the Adélaïses?" Elliott added.

Father François pulled a ring of keys from his pocket, searched for just the right one, and used it to crack open the door. Then he went around the room unearthing files and placing them in neat stacks on the table.

"Every artifact on Château Mirabelle is here," he said, pointing to the two largest mounds.

Elliott placed his camera on his shoulder and turned it on. "I brought the right one this time—no light. May I?"

Father François nodded and sat down at the table beside us.

I reached for one of the piles. "Somewhere in here there's a photograph of the Adélaïses with two other couples I saw the last time."

Father François held up a picture he managed to wedge out of his thick stack. "Is this the one?"

I snatched it from his fingertips. "Yes! Look at the back." I turned the photo over to show Elliott what I was talking about.

He lowered his camera and shrugged. "DP? I don't get it. Who are those other people in the photo?"

"Don't you see? DP? Dutch-Paris network? Those other couples *have* to be Marthe and Grégoire Archambeau and Ginette and Alain Grenouille. They all must've been a part of the Dutch-Paris network."

Father François's head shot up. "Oui, the Dutch-Paris network had a small operation out of Château Mirabelle." He reached across the table for one of the accordion folders. "You will find whatever information we have here."

Over the next two hours, Father François, Elliott, and I sorted through mountains of documents that helped (along with Google) piece together the history of the Dutch-Paris network in Maubec and the role that the Adélaïses played in it. We learned that in 1942, Jean Weidner, a Dutchman living in France, began helping smuggle those targeted by the Nazis into the south of France, via Paris, and then eventually to Switzerland. He recruited help along the way, eventually growing his Resistance efforts to include over three hundred people.

Based on a letter we found among the files, in early 1942, Jean Weidner was introduced to the Adélaïses, and by that spring, Château Mirabelle was being used as a safe house along the route to Geneva, its winery serving as cover and its underground cellars excellent hiding space. It was unclear exactly when Marthe and Grégoire Archambeau and Ginette and Alain Grenouille joined forces with the Adélaïses, but their names began to appear on falsified winery invoices by late August.

Father François set the documents out on the table in a line. "Here, look at the names of the towns of the wine deliveries: Privas, Valence, Grenoble, Chambéry. It's a straight shot to Annecy. This must have been the route they followed." He stood up from the table and stretched. "I am so sorry to do this, but I must get downstairs to get ready for Mass. You are welcome to stay here a bit longer, if you would like."

"I think we have everything we need. Plum, what do you think?" Elliott asked.

"Actually, would you mind if I snapped a picture of the photograph?" I asked, holding up the black-and-white shot of the group. "And Elliott, can you be sure to get a close-up of it also?"

"You may borrow the picture, if you would like," Father François said.

"Are you sure?"

"Please, if it helps in your efforts, I am happy to let you hold on to it a bit longer."

I tucked the photograph safely into my bag.

"Are you finished? Would you both like to stay for Mass?" Father François asked.

"Thank you, but it's been a long day. We should probably start heading back to the inn," Elliott replied.

"Actually, I'd like to stay, if that's okay?" I said.

Elliott did a double take. "You would?"

"I'm not a particularly religious person, but after everything we learned today, it feels only right to pay our respects."

He nodded, and we followed Father François down to the chapel where, together, we lit seven candles: one each for Luc and Imène Adélaïse, Marthe and Grégoire Archambeau, and Ginette and Alain Grenouille, and one extra for all the other brave men and women we would never know the names of.

After Mass, Elliott and I took a seat on a stone wall outside the church that overlooked lush lavender fields outlined by rows of tall cypress. Elliott was pitching small pebbles into the road, and my eyes trailed them as they tumbled down the steep hill.

"How are you holding up?" he asked.

I was swimming in my own thoughts. "Sorry, what?"

"I asked how you're holding up?"

"They were around our age, right? The Adélaïses, the Grenouilles, the Archambeaus."

"I think so. They looked to be, anyway."

"They could've easily stayed under the radar through the end of the war and gone on to lead full and happy lives."

He considered this for a moment before responding. "I think *could've* is a relative term. They literally *could have* looked the other way and stayed safe, sure, but maybe they couldn't have lived with themselves if they had an opportunity to do something and didn't. They did what they felt was right, even knowing what could happen to them. It's remarkably courageous."

"I know. It's incredible. So selfless and brave. When I think back to the girl I was, the girl who fretted about her luggage not fitting into the car, I'm ashamed." I looked up and into Elliott's warm eyes.

"You're a good person, Plum. I've really gotten to know you, and you're a good person." Elliott's eyes crinkled in the corners as he hopped down from the wall. "Hungry?"

"Actually, I am."

He craned his neck toward the bottom of the hill. "C'mon, there's a little ice-cream shop in town Agnès told me about that supposedly serves legendary lavender ice cream. Not normally my kind of thing, but I'm feeling inspired to open myself up to a world of new possibilities."

I smiled and nodded. "You know what, so am I."

And for possibly the first time since we met, we found ourselves in absolute and total agreement.

Chapter Thirty-Two

The bell chimed on the door of the ice-cream shop, and we were greeted by a middle-aged couple who could have passed for siblings. With similar wavy brown hair and rail-thin physiques, they looked a bit like a cartoon duo. "Bienvenue!" they announced simultaneously.

"Bonjour," we echoed back. I stepped up to the counter and leaned over to Elliott. "Allow me," I said and gestured playfully with my hand to my chest. "Nous voudrions deux boules de glace à la lavande, dans deux cornets, s'il vous plaît." The phrase came out painfully slow, but I guess I said it well enough that the woman nodded and bustled away behind the counter to grab our order.

Casting Elliott an *aren't you impressed* face for my stellar (enough) French, to which he slow-clapped, I jokingly took a bow.

"Seriously, Plum, you really are getting so much better. I mean, when we first met you knew like four words, and one of them was *shit*."

"Funnily enough, I think that one's gotten the most mileage, actually. But thank you for saying that. I've really begun to enjoy my lessons with Pascal once I started to see them as more than just a means to an end, but actually something I wanted to learn, just for me."

The woman handed us the ice creams piled high with two perfect scoops perched atop toasted cones.

"Let's taste. On three?" Elliott suggested.

"Un, deux, trois," I assented.

And at the first lick of the creamy, cold confection, my eyes practically rolled back in my head. The soft flavors of lavender and sweet cream, mixed with a citrusy brightness I couldn't quite place, kicked my taste buds into overdrive.

Though the recipe was a deeply held family secret, Henri and Nadine Chapdelaine, the store's owners, did let us in on a few of the ingredients, like cold-pressed orange zest and black currants. Really, it was the locally grown lavender that was the star of the show. They didn't need to worry about thievery, though; there would be no way to re-create that unique flavor profile outside Provence.

"Let's take this outside and find a bench or something," I suggested.

We made our way across the street to a tiny park and sat in a garden of fully bloomed hydrangeas in pastel shades of pink and periwinkle. Elliott and I squeezed close, watching people pass by with their little dogs or boisterous children while we enjoyed the last of our treat.

Anyone walking by would've thought we were on a romantic date, enjoying ice cream on a beautiful day. If I didn't know better, I could have easily believed it myself. I stood up to throw away a pile of sticky napkins and glanced over at Elliott, who was shifting uncomfortably on the bench.

"Everything okay?" I asked.

His face contorted, and he ran a hand through his hair. "Listen, can I say something? I just . . . I don't know when else I'll have the guts, and I think I just need to say it."

My breath quickened, unsure what kind of confession Elliott was about to unleash. Hopefully not a romantic one. "Elliott, please don't, we've already talked about this. I just don't think—"

"No, it's not that. It's about Bastien."

I sat back down. "Bastien?"

"I tried to keep an open mind." He looked at me and waited, but as I was processing his words, he continued instead. "And I need you to know, I'm not saying this as a jealous guy. But the other day, when

I was putting the clock from the market on the mantel in the salon, I saw Bastien and Kate huddled together in a dark corner of the château. They were laughing and talking like old friends, more than friends."

"Sure, but I mean look at *us* now. If someone spotted us sitting here like this, who knows what conclusion they'd draw. Or on the carousel. Lines can get blurry sometimes. I've worked on enough shows to know how easily it can happen."

He shook his head. "There's something else. I didn't think much of this when I saw it pop up on the master production schedule a few weeks ago, but did you know Kate was in Avignon a week or so before the trip to Paris?"

"No, that can't be right. She told me she flew into Paris from LA that morning. We even texted a few days before her trip, and she asked me what the weather was like in France because she was packing." My stomach knotted as I thought back to our meetup in the lobby of the George V where I remembered thinking she *did* look impossibly fresh for someone who'd just stepped off a twelve-hour flight.

He scrolled through his phone. "I'm pretty sure she was in France that whole week leading up to our weekend away. Yes, here it is, look." He turned his phone to show me the schedule, and there it was on line three, Kate Wembley—Air France flight 1628, arriving in Avignon about eleven days before I'd met her in Paris.

"But why would she lie about that? And why would she go to Avignon, not Maubec?"

"Do you really want me to have to be the one to say it?" he asked.

I wanted to jump to Bastien's defense—to tell Elliott that he's wrong and to keep his unwanted opinions to himself. That he was the pot calling the kettle black since *he* had kissed me and maybe *he* should be the one not to be trusted, not Bastien. That Kate's secret trip to Avignon was obviously to meet about the show and its production and nothing else. But something in my gut was telling me I needed to give this more thought. I'd never been the best judge of character when it came to people or love, and maybe I did need an outsider's perspective, even if the outsider wasn't entirely unbiased.

I sucked in a deep breath and said, "I appreciate you wanting to protect me, I do, but Bastien's been good to me, and I want to believe his intentions are genuine. There has to be another reason."

"Well, that's the thing, Plum. Do you want to believe it, or do you *actually* believe it?"

I stood up to gather my thoughts, but instead my eyes darted up to Saint Orens and down to the ice-cream shop and back up to the church again. I blinked hard. Wait, was this the same place where my dad proposed to my mom!? I did a full circle in my spot and muttered, "I think this *is* it."

"You think this is what?"

"I think this is the exact spot my dad proposed to my mom forty years ago."

"Wait, really?"

"Before I left for France, he told me about a trip he and my mom took to Provence. He talked about a gorgeous church on a hill, delicious lavender ice cream, and a small park where he got down on one knee to ask her to be his forever. This has to be it."

He chuckled. "I have news for you, Provence is practically made up of gorgeous churches and quaint little ice-cream shops."

"No, I know this is it," I said resolutely.

"So what happened? I guess she accepted, right?"

"No, she didn't actually. The timing wasn't right. They needed to live a little more, learn a lot more, and let some things go before they were ready to settle down to make a life together."

"There's a good lesson there. Do me a favor, Plum, just don't rush into anything with Bastien. You deserve better."

"And by 'better,' do you mean . . . ?" I lifted my brows, expecting him to understand my implication without me having to say it.

"I mean, better." Elliott shifted his bag onto his shoulder. "I can't believe how late it is. I need to check in at the château to see if we're on schedule to resume filming tomorrow. Want the van to drop you back at the inn?"

With the seeds of doubt I already had about Bastien and Kate now having been watered by Elliott, I said, "Actually, I think I'll go with you."

To say that the château was in a state of chaos when we arrived was a gross understatement. René had walked off the job about an hour earlier, and the general mood of panic and stress among everyone who was left on-site was almost palpable.

"Bastien, what on earth is going on here?" I asked, trying not to allow my horror to overtake my voice. "Where's Kate?"

He ranted in French, of which I could understand nothing. He railed and hollered, and I couldn't believe my eyes when he grabbed one of the samples of decorative stone we were looking at for the fireplace and hurled it across the room to put a hole in the already damaged Sheetrock.

"Okay, we're leaving," Elliott announced, stepping next to me. "You need to calm down and get your shit together, man. What the hell is wrong with you?"

Bastien stepped toward Elliott, their size difference ever apparent, and he stuck a finger to Elliott's chest. "Stay out of it. You don't know anything about anything!"

For as escalated as Bastien's blood pressure was growing, Elliott's face and voice remained even and clear. "As production director, actually, I kind of do. And I think you're acting like an asshole right now. Unprofessional. Hostile. And a little unhinged."

"Va te faire foutre!" Bastien spat back. I wasn't exactly sure what that translated to, but if the vein popping out of his neck was any indication, I had a feeling I knew the meaning.

Elliott grabbed for my hand and started pulling me toward the door. "C'mon, Plum, Gervais is waiting out front. Let's head back to the inn, and we can sort this out with Kate tomorrow."

I was pinned, trapped between the two of them, and the metaphor of the whole situation was not lost on me. Who the hell was this guy throwing rocks through walls and screeching like a banshee? This wasn't the Bastien I had come to know and fall for over these past several weeks. I stood there suspended in indecision and saddled with confusion over the utter mess in front of me. The château was in disarray. My beau was acting like a horse's ass *while also* possibly carrying out a torrid love affair behind my back.

And all I knew for certain was that my sanity was hanging on by one very rapidly fraying thread.

Chapter Thirty-Three

Gervais had barely pulled the van in to park in front of the inn when Elliott, still fuming from his fight back at the château with Bastien, threw the door open and beelined inside, his heavy footfall as he stomped up the stairs practically shaking the inn's already unsteady foundation. Odette's head snapped up from some papers she was holding behind the front desk, her eyebrows slumped with concern as her gaze trailed Elliott up the steps. Agnès, startled by the sound, hurried into the salon from the dining room clutching a pot of tea with the edge of her apron to see what all the noise was about.

"Ah, Prune, it is you," she sighed with relief as she eyed the now-empty staircase. "I thought perhaps a stampede of truffle hogs had broken loose and made their way into the inn," she joked.

"Not so much a hog . . . more like a bull in a china shop. But it was just Monsieur Schaffer. He's um . . . not in a great mood."

"Really? But M. Schaffer is usually so bubbly and full of smiles," Agnès teased again. "Not to worry, he just needs a bit of tea and some cookies, I believe. That always seems to do the trick."

I nodded and moved to make my way up the stairs as well, but Agnès placed the teapot on the desk and said, "I wasn't expecting you until later tonight. I haven't quite fixed anything for our dinner yet."

"Oh, no, don't worry about us. Elliott and I can fend for ourselves."

"But I am just about to rustle something up. If you can wait for a bit, we'd love for you to join us."

"Yes, please do. It will be so much more lively that way," Odette said, coming out from behind the reception desk.

"Oui, go shower and clean up and come back down in fifteen minutes. I will have at least a petit amuse-bouche for you both," Agnès said. "Pascal was hoping you might be home a bit early tonight for your lesson. He found some of Odette's old books from l'école primaire, or how you say in the States . . . elementary school? He thought they might be useful."

"I know Pascal has refused, but you must let me start paying for my lessons. He has already given up so much of his time."

She leaned in close to me. "He would never admit this, but I think he is enjoying playing the role of teacher. There is so much around here that he cannot improve—the foundation, the roof, the pipes. But your French? With that, he can make much improvement."

Agnès and Odette shooed me upstairs to wash up while they shuffled off to the kitchen to prepare some light snacks. I couldn't hear the shower running anymore, so I figured Elliott had finished and I could hop in for a quick rinse. I quickly shimmied out of my clothes, wrapped a fresh towel from the stack on the bed around me, grabbed my toiletry caddy, and headed down the hall to the bathroom.

The door had been left ajar, and grabbing for the handle, I burst in—and straight into a still soaking, half-naked Elliott who was shaving in the mirror. His back muscles were impressive, and my mouth fell open as my eyes trailed all the way down to his—

"Excuse me! What are you doing?!" he yelped.

I picked my mouth up off the floor and swallowed. "Um . . . what are you doing? The door was half open! Seems reasonable to have thought you'd finished." I shrugged with a bit of sass, but the motion caused the towel to start to slip and my edge quickly gave way to mounting embarrassment.

He held up his razor and continued to eye me through the still mostly fogged-up vanity. "I had to let some of the steam out so the mirror would defog and I could see what I was doing. The light in here is bad enough as it is, I didn't want to cut my face to shreds . . . again."

I put a hand up in retreat. "Okay. Okay. Finish up. I'll wait."

He grimaced at me from the mirror and said, "Well, actually, I think you'd need to wait anyway. There's um . . . no hot water. Sorry about that."

Throwing my head back, I groaned. "Ugh!" I turned on my heel, making an effort to nudge Elliott with my caddy as I left and *not* ogle the broadness of his shoulders . . . again. Returning to my room to change back into some clothes, I resigned to just shower before bed, once the hot water was restored.

When I came back downstairs to the dining room only about ten minutes later, Agnès and Pascal were busy setting up a small buffet of assorted cheeses and canapés paired with pieces of warm crusty baguette while Odette set a round table in the back of the dining room. Along with the cheeses, Agnès set out a small plate of pâté and a bowl of fat green olives rolling around in their golden oil, which was flecked with herbes de Provence.

"Hmm . . . these look incredible. What are they?" I asked, my mouth watering at the different scents of thyme, rosemary, and citrus as I scanned the savory dishes.

Agnès slid a few more items around the table to make sure they were evenly spaced and nodded with satisfaction at her work. "Oh, you must try. This here is salmon rillettes, a creamy dip made of smoked salmon, cream cheese, lemon juice, and dill served with slices of cucumber. It is very fresh, the fish. I just bought everything at the market this morning."

I plucked a cucumber slice from the serving platter, used the small knife to plop a dollop onto the round base, and took a crunchy bite. She was right. Not only was the fish bright with flavor, the lemon a prominent contrast to the salty salmon, but the cucumber—which was equally fresh—brought a clean crunch to the whole profile. If I wasn't careful, I was certain I could eat the whole plate! A few minutes (and a handful of cucumber slices) later, Elliott clomped down the stairs, freshly showered, shaved, and looking (and smelling) like a million francs.

Pascal grabbed a bottle of wine with a nondescript label and five glasses and said, "Let us first feast and then immerse ourselves in study, for no one can truly learn on an empty stomach."

We eagerly heaped our plates with delectable morsels and settled into our seats at an intimate table tucked away at the room's far end, removed from the lone remaining guest who was leisurely sipping an after-dinner cup of tea. Pascal, with an inviting smile, poured us each a generous glass of the wine, urging both Elliott and me to taste.

"What do you think?" he asked.

"It's really delicious. I don't think I've ever tasted anything quite like it."

"Prune, en français s'il vous plaît."

"Le vin est délicieux."

Pascal clapped his hands together. "Très bien."

I arched my right eyebrow and teased, "Hey, I thought we were eating, then learning?"

"We can do both, non?"

"Agnès, you didn't have to go to all this trouble. But I'm not gonna lie, this is awesome," Elliott confirmed as he took another sip between bites of his baguette and pâté.

"Oh, I love that word *awesome*!" Pascal squealed with delight as he clapped his hands together. "It is just so *American*, is it not?"

"Papa, Parisians say *awesome* all the time. In fact, they have adopted many American words and phrases into everyday speech. Walking around you would almost think you are in Californie," Odette said, a wistful longing in her voice. It was clear she missed her life in Paris.

I turned to Odette. "Will you be going back to La Sorbonne soon?"

"Unfortunately, non. I have decided to . . . how do you say . . . postpone my studies next semester to help Maman and Papa with the inn."

Odette kept her face bright as she explained, but I could see, as someone who fiercely understood what it was like to put on a brave face, that there was something not quite settled behind her eyes. I'm sure she didn't want to make her parents feel guilty about her decision, but I could tell, from all the conversations we had before and now from the look in her eyes, that half her heart was in Paris, even though the other half remained here.

I felt foolish for unintentionally bringing up such a sore subject and tried to steer the conversation back to the incredible wine. "So"—I held the wineglass up high as if to inspect it—"what is this we're drinking? It's delightful! I want to send my father the name of the vineyard so that maybe we can carry it at our B and B? My father's been on the hunt for a prize-winning white for forever. Even though it's not *his*, he might jump at the chance to have something this delicious as a nice substitute."

Agnès held up the wine bottle and proudly displayed it around the table. "If you can believe it? The wine, it is from Château Mirabelle."

"Château Mirabelle? But how?" I asked.

"Only a few crates remained after the cellars were bombed. The Muniers gifted one to us at our wedding. We only drink it at the most special of occasions," she explained, her smile reaching all the way up to her twinkling blue eyes.

I glanced down at my shirt, still stained with a faded purple splotch from my failed attempt to hoover my melty mess of lavender ice cream earlier, and my very wrinkled shorts. I cringed. "If I had known I would've . . . made more of an effort to clean up. You see, Elliott used up all the hot water so . . ."

He rolled his eyes, barely looking up from the plate of food he hadn't stopped eating.

"If my English is not clear, forgive me. Tonight is special because you and Elliott are special. You have come to Maubec, and you have shared with us your stories and a little bit of your lives . . . for us here in this small town, this has been a whole new adventure. It is nice to have new blood surge through this place. More than nice . . . it has been . . . what is the word . . . *nécessaire*?"

"C'est le même . . . necessary," I replied. "Holy merde! Did I just say that in French? Like correctly?"

Pascal clapped his hands enthusiastically, "Oui, mon chou! You did! 'C'est le même,' means 'it is the same.' Félicitations! By this time next week, you will be teaching me French, non?" he joked.

I lifted my glass of wine off the table. "Well, this whole experience has been necessary for me too. I know my life may have looked perfect from the outside—everybody assumes it is, that I am, that my family is—but we are far from it, especially me. Your hospitality . . . your inn . . . your town . . . that is what's special. I know people believe Maubec lost some of its vitality when Château Mirabelle was destroyed, but it's still here, in every single person I've been lucky enough to meet, well maybe except for Monsieur Grenouille . . . he and I still have a ways to go. Anyway, I am so grateful I was given the opportunity to come here and meet all of you."

I glanced around the table to meet each of their gazes, my paltry attempt at expressing an iota of the gratitude that was filling me up to the brim. Pascal—his hazel eyes filled with patience and kindness, his cheeks rosy and flecked with a distinct and oh-so-French beauty mark right under his left eye, and his dark hair messy on his head as he animated his stories with wild hand gestures. Agnès, so maternal and so commanding; I was incredibly impressed by how much of the inn and property she ran compared to Pascal, whose arthritis wouldn't allow it. This was her show, and she was not afraid or ashamed to wear the proverbial pants in order to get things done. I loved that about her. And Odette, who loved her parents so much she was willing to put her own dreams on pause to try to help them hold on to theirs. Together they reminded me that families, though sometimes messy and often complicated, make up the very best parts of who we are, keeping us forever rooted to home no matter how far we may stray.

Finally, I took in Elliott with his brooding physique and floppy boy-band hairstyle. Like a more rugged Beckham in his '90s glory days, Elliott was remarkably more handsome than I remembered him being this morning when I had been surprisingly taken with his empathy and interest in our research at Camp des Milles. I couldn't keep myself from staring at him across the table as I remembered how closely we stood lighting candles at Saint Orens, how he guided my trembling hand with his own to make sure the match touched each wick. We'd shared something unspoken in that moment, and I knew that despite our past, something had irrevocably shifted between us.

I sucked in a breath, bolstering up the courage to say this next bit in only French to show my deep gratitude and appreciation for all they had given to me. "Je veux avoir un préservatif pour mon cœur toujours!"

Odette started to choke and practically spit her wine back into her glass. "Um, Plum, what is it exactly that you were just trying to say?"

"That I want to preserve . . . you know, capture . . . hold on to . . . this moment in my heart, always." I thought back to the gaffe with Pascal a few weeks ago when I said to him that I was *très excitée* about starting French lessons with no idea of the phrase's sexual connotation. "Why? Oh God, what did I actually just say?"

The table erupted into giggles—except for Elliott, who seemed just as lost as I was.

Odette did her best to stifle her laughter. "Préservatif . . . it does not mean . . . it loosely translates to . . . a word in English that is more like—"

"Condom," Agnès finished, causing the table to burst into uncontrollable fits again, including Elliott, who finally understood the meaning.

Odette, still rife with giggles, managed, "What you said was, 'I want to always have a condom for my heart!'"

"Well, that's one way to express your gratitude," Elliott teased, his smile so genuine and heartwarming as it reached all the way to his eyes.

My face flushed with heat, and I pressed my palm, cold from holding my wine, to my feverish cheek.

Pascal, still chuckling, said, "My dear, now you really do look like a mirabelle!"

And the table again erupted into giggles, and at the sheer silliness of my error, I too couldn't keep the tears from leaking out of my eyes through my uncontrollable fit of laughter.

Pascal, wiping the corners of his eyes with a napkin, stood up from the table and extended his arm out to me. "Come, it seems there is no better time for us to get back to our lessons. It appears we still have much work to do."

Chapter Thirty-Four

The next morning, at least a dozen flatbed trucks and Vespas lined the driveway leading to the front gates of Château Mirabelle. Since Gervais couldn't squeeze the van through, he had to stop halfway up the road to let me and Elliott out so we could walk the rest of the way. Construction crews I'd never seen before were making trips back and forth to the trucks, carrying scaffolding and other equipment into the house.

"Oh, good, Plum, you're here," Kate said, catching her breath as she jogged up to meet us outside the front gates.

I looked around. "What's happening? Who are all these people?"

"No surprise, between Bastien's perfectionism and the mold and foundation issues, we're massively behind schedule on the château. The network decided it was time to bring in reinforcements."

No wonder Bastien had become unhinged. Reinforcements meant he was no longer in absolute control of every aspect of the project.

"We've assembled construction crews from all across France, and they've assured us we will have a finished project ready for the big reveal," she added.

"Hey, have you heard from Bastien since yesterday?" I asked her.

"Not a word. You?"

Since he stormed off the project, I'd left him a bunch of messages and shot off a handful of texts. No answer. I assumed he was laying low and cooling off, but the truth was, even after these last few weeks, I didn't *really* know him well enough to be sure. "No, I haven't heard a peep."

Kate's eyes softened. "I'm sure he's just blowing off some steam." Her eyebrows furrowed with concern. "You two are okay, right? You and Bastien?"

Even though Elliott was scribbling away on his clipboard pretending not to listen, his forehead puckered at the mention of Bastien's name.

I examined Kate's face at her question, but she wasn't giving one iota or even a morsel of a hint that there was anything more between them. "Yeah, sure. We're good," I answered quickly, but honestly, I didn't know. My mind replayed the day before: Elliott's revelation about Kate's mystery trip to Avignon, the stone crashing through the Sheetrock, the unrecognizable look on Bastien's face—a face *I* thought I'd grown to know pretty well. But the realization now hit me that it might be the face of a man I really didn't know at all. And maybe all this time, I'd just been spellbound by this town and the romance of it all.

Kate sneezed through a cloud of dust kicked up by a passing flatbed truck full of lumber, startling me back to the conversation. She coughed, waving a hand in front of her face, and said, "I'm glad to hear it. The social media team will be especially glad to hear it."

I covered my nose and mouth with the collar of my T-shirt as the dust settled. "Social media team?"

Kate grabbed for her cell phone but continued talking as she scrolled. "We have to start getting the word out about the show. I mean, of course, *you* know how that goes. Okay," she said, sliding her phone back into her pocket and clapping her hands together, "since we can't have you go into the house today with all the crew activity, we had a mobile recording studio brought in from Paris. We thought it would be the perfect opportunity for you to start recording the show's voiceovers. You've done those before, right?"

I thought back to the confessional moments and voiceover work I'd done over the years. *Love Lagoon*'s Grotto Gab. *Celebrity Spy*'s Squawk Box. "Lots of times," I answered.

Kate's face lit up. "Wonderful." She craned her neck to look into the distance. "If you follow Elliott, the trailer is *riiiigght* past video village on the edge of the vineyard. They'll have your sides waiting for you."

I made a quick stop at craft services, where I filled up a mug with steaming hot tea to take into the session. If past experience was any indication, I was in for a long morning of repeating the same word or phrase until the sound engineer felt I projected just the right amount of emotion. I knocked on the trailer door and entered the soundproof mobile recording studio complete with a small but fully equipped control room.

"Entrez," a male voice called out through a mic.

I stepped fully into the trailer. A man and a woman were sitting behind a soundboard and glass partition. The woman leaned in to her microphone. "Plum, nice to meet you, I'm Jess," she said in an American accent. "This is Cédric. You'll find your sides and headphones on the music stand. Let me know if you need any water. We have a small fridge on this side of the glass."

I held up my mug of tea. "Thanks, I'm all set." Jess pointed to my microphone, and I slipped on the headphones and repeated, "Thanks, I'm all set." I picked up the first page of the script with the word *intro* bolded on top and scanned it quickly.

Jess tapped the glass and spoke into her microphone. "Whenever you're ready, Plum. Let's use this take as a sound check."

I set my phone down on the stand and began to read. "Nestled against the northern slope of the Petit Luberon sits an old hilltop village, Maubec, surrounded by a sea of vineyards with long and slim cypresses stretching up to the sky. Beautiful stone houses with blue shutters line the small, steep cobblestone lanes. Nearby sits a small Baroque church, Saint Orens, built with the noble materials from the immediate vicinity. And then, there is Château Mirabelle. Once upon a time a thirteenth-century fortress, a fifteenth-century castle, and then an eighteenth-century palatial estate, Château Mirabelle was left abandoned and in ruins . . . until now." I looked up from the page. "How was that?"

"Très bien. Perhaps when you say it again you can put just a little more feeling into the descriptions. Also, just a touch slower." Cédric circled his finger in an *again* gesture. "Encore, s'il vous plait . . ."

As I recited the lines again, a warmth radiated through me. I loved the vibe they were going for, the audience instantly transported away to Provence—the sights, smells, and colors practically soaring off the page. The show was going to be everything I hoped it would. Everything Kate promised.

Cédric gave a big thumbs-up. "Parfait!"

Jess put her hand over the mic while she and Cédric huddled closely to discuss the take. Finally, she said, "You nailed it, so I think we are ready to move on. You can go ahead and flip to the next page."

I turned the page over and picked up the next sheet from the pile. The heading said, *first impressions*.

"Whenever you're ready, Plum," Jess said.

I took a sip of tea and started to read. "The château, with its lack of indoor heating, may have been freezing, but the contractor, Bastien Munier, was HOT HOT HOT." I blinked, waiting for my thoughts to catch up to my mouth. I looked up from the paper. "Excuse me, is this right?"

Jess glanced down at her script. "Spot on, but when you say, 'HOT HOT HOT,' I need you to really punctuate each HOT."

I paused for a moment, unsure of how to proceed. *"Okaaaay?"* I moistened my lips and repeated the take, this time focusing on the script and its implications. "The château, with its lack of indoor heating, may have been freezing, but the contractor, Bastien Munier, was HOT HOT HOT. Bastien showed me around the house, but I was distracted by his eyes, his lips, and the faint outline of stomach muscles I could just make out under his tight shirt." The hairs on the back of my neck started to rise, but in spite of myself, I continued reading. "Rhys Braun didn't hold a candle to this incredibly sexy . . ." I threw the paper down on the ground. "What the hell is this? Are you kidding me! Who wrote this copy?"

Jess's expression grew uneasy at my outburst. "Um . . . it came from the network," she answered as she eyed Cédric for backup.

"Has Kate seen it?" I pressed.

"Of course, she greenlit it this morning," Cédric confirmed.

My stomach dropped as my legs practically gave way. I threw off my headphones and picked up the stack of sides, reading through them as quickly as my eyes would let me. Scattered across almost every page, every scene intro, was narration about a budding passionate relationship with Bastien. My feelings about him. His feelings about me. Our feelings about each other. There was hardly anything I could find about Maubec, Château Mirabelle, or even the renovation itself.

Kate greenlit this? No way. Not possible.

Without another word, I snatched the rest of the papers off the stand and stormed out of the trailer to find her. I didn't have to look far; she and Bastien were cozied up by the coffee machine at craft services.

Kate spotted me and glanced down at her watch. "You can't be finished already? Although you're such a pro, I guess anything's possible."

I eyed Bastien, fighting to keep my face expressionless. I'd deal with him later. *This* was more important. I stared straight at Kate and pulled myself up to full height. "Can I talk to you for a minute?"

Bastien stood to join us, but I put up my hand to stop him. "No. Just Kate."

Kate looked between the two of us and nodded sympathetically. She set her frothy cappuccino down on the picnic table. "Sure, let's step over there. Bastien, be a dear and go let Jess and Cédric know that Plum just needs a moment and we'll be back on schedule in ten? Thank you so much," she instructed, not waiting for him to respond, and then motioned me over to a more remote spot where we could speak away from the rest of the crew. "What's going on, Plum? What's the matter?"

"What the hell are these pages?" I asked, tossing them at her feet.

She looked genuinely surprised by my harsh tone and open hostility, not to mention the flurry of paper now scattered across the ground. "What do you mean?"

"'The château, with its lack of indoor heating, may have been freezing, but the contractor, Bastien Munier, was HOT HOT HOT,'" I said, parroting back the lines from the script. "This is not what I signed up for."

A pouty smile appeared to warm Kate's face, but her expression was more indignant than sympathetic. "Sweetie, that's exactly what you signed up for. The show's called *Heart Restoration Project*, what'd you think it was going to be about?"

I threw my hands up. "The town. The house. THE RESTORATION! The things you *said* it would be about!"

"Sure, those are all important background components and a great parallel, but you had to know it was never the main storyline."

My mouth turned sour, and a lump of pressure solidified in my throat. I closed my eyes and mustered the courage to ask the question I was afraid I already knew the answer to. "So then, what *is* the main storyline?"

Kate set her face into a mock-pitying expression. "Oh, sweetie, hasn't it been obvious from the very beginning? You are."

Chapter Thirty-Five

My vision turned cloudy, and my breath fell out of me in quick and ragged huffs of panic. The feeling of pins and needles pricked my hands and feet, and an overwhelming dizziness threatened to topple me right over.

I misheard her. I'm misunderstanding. This has to be a mistake.

But my internal assurances fell short as a mounting panic attack began to pull me under. My thoughts urged me to get out of there as quickly as my feet could move. But they stayed planted firmly to the ground as if I were rooted to it.

With my tongue thick and dry in my mouth, I managed a meek, "What did you just say?"

Cocking her head to the side, she wore a neutral, if not disappointed, expression. "Oh, c'mon, Plum. You really had no idea? You didn't see that *you* were the real project all along? Clever, right?" she chirped, proud of herself and not exuding one fleeting moment of remorse or regret for her cunning duplicity.

My worst nightmare had come true, another betrayal *even worse* than the tape, and I couldn't do anything but stand there and face it. There was nowhere to run and no one to run to, and the loneliness of it hit me almost harder than Kate's confession. My thoughts raced, trying to put the pieces together, desperately trying to remember all of the moments that were likely played up for the show. The easy flirtations. The special moments in the house like when he showed me the cellars, spinning stories about walls having memories. My initials forever sealed in the concrete? Jesus, had I really been that naive? Blind? Stupid?

The tea and scone I'd eaten for breakfast were now fighting their way back up as waves of nausea rolled through me and the speckles that dotted my vision grew into disorienting, warbling blobs.

With tears already pooling in the corners of my eyes, another realization hit me like a punch to the gut. "Wait . . . Bastien?" I breathed. "Was Bastien a part of this? Was he hired as an *actor*? Oh my God. Oh my God." I needed to sit down or else I was going to end up on my ass, in the dirt, in the middle of this hectic driveway.

Kate, noticing me unsteady on my feet, took me by the elbow and led me to sit on the edge of an open truck bed and handed me a half-full bottle of Evian from inside her tote. "Yes, of course, Bastien was in on it from the start. But if it makes you feel any better, though he came on initially to play the role of paramour, I don't think *all* your interactions were fabricated. I mean, I saw the dailies. You can't fake that kind of chemistry." Her face registered no remorse, no guilt for blindsiding me, and no shame for setting me up. I wanted to punch her square in the nose and tell her to shove the show right up her ass.

How many of them knew? How many of them did I let in as they willingly tricked me to sell the show? With every bomb Kate dropped in my lap, the past few weeks of my life exploded into shards and debris that floated down past my eyes one piece at a time, snatching my attention with each memory.

The paparazzi who appeared out of nowhere at the club in Avignon. It was Bastien who'd alerted them! The over-the-top girls' weekend in Paris. It was all a ploy for Kate to further gain my trust. Rhys oh-so-coincidentally showing up at George V . . . Kate orchestrated it all, down to the well-timed spa appointment to lure me back to the hotel at just the right moment. And then of course, the cherry on top, having Elliott capture it all on camera.

Elliott? Oh God, not him too.

I *had* to know. And since she was dishing the details, I figured I'd already hit rock bottom, so what's one more shovelful of dirt? "Elliott too?" The words caught, and I almost couldn't finish the question. "Was Elliott in on it the whole time??"

Her expression folded, and she seemed to survey her memory. "No, Elliott, like most everyone actually, was kept in the dark intentionally so that the reveal had more *pow* when it was finally executed. He just filmed what he filmed, and it was up to me to piece together your love story with Bastien with what he provided. But lucky for me, he always managed to focus his attention on you and Bastien, perhaps because there wasn't much house to film since the reno went sideways. Maybe because the notes we gave him on how great the content was kept him filming much of the same? Or maybe it was because he was smitten with you and just followed you about like a lost puppy? Who knows? Either way, he sent us his material, and I put together the footage to portray a fire brewing between you and Bastien, the way I always knew we could sell your romance as our main storyline. Honestly, I mean, it's how I designed the whole show from the start. Like I told you when we first met, I was always such a fan of *EVERLYday*, and I watched like everyone else in America the back and forth between you and Rhys. I felt it along with you. It was great TV drama."

"No! That was my life, this *is* my life, Kate," I bit back.

"C'mon, Plum. You and I both know that when you're famous, your life is never really your own. It's the public's. That's what you get paid for. So after the release of that sex tape and your breakup, you just fell into one mess after the next, and as a fan of yours and as someone who was ready to make her way as a producer, this story idea was like gold! *Heart Restoration Project*, get it?" Kate smirked, clearly impressed with the cleverness of her twist, a proud mastermind who'd managed to arrange all the pawns and pieces in order to take down the king. Checkmate.

She continued, in spite of the look of devastation firmly registered on my face, "This has been my baby from the beginning. Even Jack and Claudine have been completely in the dark about the reveal. They believe all the romance between you two is one hundred percent genuine, born out of working so closely together on this project. And let me just say, they have been eating. It. Up!" She clapped her hands on each word, startling me out of the tornado of spiraling thoughts swirling through my head. Barely coming up for breath, Kate continued, "Our test audiences have been eating it up too, and girlfriend, get ready, because we are, without a doubt, going to have a serious hit on our hands."

I still couldn't speak. Though it seemed no one else in production had been in on Kate's twist (at least no one who'd been working directly with me), there were too many pieces for me to try to make sense of.

Kate drew in a breath and then kept on going, as if she was so excited and overcome by her ability to have pulled it off that she was bursting at the seams to share. "Whew!" she exclaimed, "I gotta be honest, a few moments got a *liiiiiiiittle* dicey, like in Paris when you and Elliott decided to go rogue and take that detour to the museum instead of Coco Chanel's house. But thankfully, you two made it just in time for the lobby run-in I worked my ass off to orchestrate. Ugh . . . you can't even imagine what that took. But, whew, so worth it when we got that shot of your face . . . seeing Rhys . . . with Anya. Now *that* is an episode cliffhanger if ever I saw one!"

The tears that had pooled now fell freely, and I didn't even bother wiping them away. "I just don't understand. How could you do this to me? To anyone?" As angry as I felt, and as much as I wanted to scream, my questions came out as a weak whisper.

Kate cocked her head to the side and mock-pouted, as if *she* was the one hurt by my implication. "Plum, I like you a lot. You're a nice girl. But this isn't personal. It's showbiz. We figured if anyone could understand that, it's you," Kate offered casually.

I turned to face her, wanting her to see my anguish, my cheeks wet with hot tears. "Not personal? Not personal? Okay then, why did you pick me?"

"Well, when you put it like that, I mean yes, Plum, we did *personally* slate you for this role because of your family history with television, but mostly because of your very public relationship with Rhys. It's a media frenzy whenever you two are at odds—especially ever since that sex tape went viral. And when you confessed to me that day at your family's bed-and-breakfast that Rhys had been the one who'd sold it to the media?! God, you can't *pay* for a nugget of drama that good. We knew we had an opportunity to build an incredibly compelling show around your heartbreak with Rhys and set you up on a course to a mended heart with a sexy Frenchy for a bit. I mean, what's to be mad about? You had a little fling with a hot guy, and at the end of it all, you get a château in Provence." She crossed her arms and scoffed, as if offended by my clear misinterpretation of such a fantastic opportunity. "I really don't see the problem."

"You don't see the problem with manipulating the people in my life and deceiving me in the worst possible way, all for television ratings?"

"But isn't that *exactly* what reality TV is? What it's *always* been? You can't tell me that your romances on *Love Lagoon* were any more real or less scripted than what we're doing here. Or that your chemistry with Viktor on *Celebrity Ballroom* was one hundred percent genuine. That's the game, Plum, and I am really shocked that you're reacting this way, quite frankly. On the long list of reasons why we picked you was the fact that you are a reality TV pro, an institution. The girl who can plaster a smile on her face or manufacture a river of tears as soon as the director calls *action*. We figured you'd get it more than anyone."

"Don't gaslight me like this is my misunderstanding or like this is my fault for not being cool with it. I don't care how you qualify or justify it, it's betrayal plain and simple. I thought I was hosting a home improvement show—*that's* what I signed on for. The fact that I happened to fall for Bastien along the way, I thought, was an organic by-product of all our time together. Our romance was the cherry on top of this project, never *the* project!"

"You can't tell me it never crossed your mind that he was quite possibly a little too good to be true? A cherry indeed—we 'cherry-picked' him specifically to play the role we needed, someone who could mend your broken heart, even if we knew he could never mend the broken house in the time we gave him."

"So you asked Bastien to seduce me? Romance me? Screw with me just enough to get me to fall for him? How much did he know?"

Kate crossed her arms and thought for a moment. "He knew the real premise of the show, but I may have told him you were in on it as well. He was told to play up the romance, both on and off camera, to really develop an authentic chemistry for on-screen, and not worry so much about the renovation. That's why we hired René, who we can all agree knows a hell of a lot more about construction, but isn't as easy on the eyes. We figured you'd be more smitten with a Bastien type, and I guess we were right."

I shook my head, the realization of her words hitting in real time as she spoke them aloud. I hopped off the truck bed and stepped in close to Kate. "I'm done. I'm out. Good luck filming your finale without me." I turned on my heel and started to make my way toward the cobblestone driveway where Gervais was waiting.

"Not so fast, Ms. Everly." Kate's voice was stiffer, more authoritative than her previously amused banter. "You're still under contract. If you walk away, you get absolutely nothing. No house, no pay, nada. Or should I say 'rien.'" She drew her pointer finger and thumb together to make a perfectly round O.

I froze in my spot, still facing away from Kate, my back firmly turned on the house, Bastien, and everything that went with it. New thoughts bombarded my consciousness. I quickly tried to weigh my options: the house and the money I'd earn once it sold (which I *desperately* needed), versus my pride, my ego, my sanity? Additionally, the weight of leaving the Adélaïses' house abandoned and unfinished after everything we'd learned struck me almost harder than anything else.

I wasn't prepared to make a decision I was going to regret. I needed some time to think and process all of it. I finally turned to face her. "You know what, Kate, you're right. Since I am bound by contract to fulfill my obligations in order for me to get the château, I am going to need some time to think about this. I'm going back to the inn, and I'll give you my answer tomorrow."

Spinning around to leave, I called back to her in a biting tone, "If you're having any trouble with the rest of the reno, you know where I'll be, since we're ride or die and all. Your words, not mine."

Bleary-eyed through tears I couldn't keep from falling down my cheeks, I continued to amble down the dirt path to where the van was parked. I took one more glance at the house from over my shoulder as the sun blazed behind it, wondering if it would be the last time I would ever see Château Mirabelle.

Chapter Thirty-Six

Though I felt a little bad for giving Gervais the silent treatment in the van, it was either that or I was going to unleash the fire of a thousand suns upon someone, and he would be the lucky, yet undeserving, recipient. So instead, I stayed quiet and stewed in my anger and hurt for the entire twenty-minute ride back into town.

Gervais stopped the van and let me out in front of the inn. I managed to squeak out a *merci* before closing the door behind me. Dropping my bag down on the ground, I knelt beside it to fish around for my phone to call my agent, Nancy. While deep down I knew she'd never intentionally set me up, at this moment, I needed a sanity check. I dumped the bag over, shook the contents onto the ground, and sifted through the pile. No phone. I patted my pockets, my hips, my bra. Still nothing. *Dammit.*

Maybe I left it by the production trailer when I picked up my walkie? Or by the electric kettle when I made the cup of tea? Or on the music stand next to my mic in the recording studio?

"Merde! Merde! Merde!"

Kneeling on all fours, I swept the contents of my tote back inside the bag. I stood up and made direct eye contact with Monsieur Grenouille. He shook his head and mouthed the word "incroyable" before heading back inside his shop.

Seriously? Today was not the day, and I was *not* the one. What the hell was his problem anyway? He didn't even know me, didn't know anything about me. I didn't care how delicious his hazelnut croissants were, it was time to give Mr. Frogface a piece of my mind.

Adrenaline coursing through me, I slung my bag over my shoulder and stalked toward the patisserie. I pushed open the shop's double door with all my might, only I overestimated the amount of effort needed and slipped on the freshly mopped floor, taking a nosedive onto the tiled ground and sliding to land just inches from the pastry case.

Monsieur Grenouille rushed over to me, maneuvering around the sign marked ATTENTION: SOL GLISSANT (CAUTION: WET FLOOR). "Mon dieu! Are you okay, Mademoiselle?" he cried.

I sat upright and looked around, embarrassed and confused, and immediately burst into tears.

"Zut! Mademoiselle! Are you hurt? Should I call le médecin?" Monsieur Grenouille's usual gruff demeanor was quickly replaced by concern that seemed to grow with each gasp of my sobs.

"No, I'm fine. I'm . . . I'm—" I blubbered.

"If you're not hurt, then let me help you up? Come sit." He pulled out a chair and then extended his hand to me, which I gratefully accepted. I examined my elbow and bent down again to retrieve some of the contents of my purse, now scattered across the floor of the shop.

"Here," Monsieur Grenouille said, handing me my phone, which had somehow flown over one of the glass cases to land somewhere behind the counter.

"Are you kidding me?! It was in the bag this whole time?" I said, shoving the phone back into my tote and bursting into a fresh round of tears.

Moments later, Monsieur Grenouille returned with a bag of ice, a glass of water, and a warm pain au chocolat. "Something sweet always helps to calm the nerves. And the ice is for your elbow," he said, handing both to me and then placing the drink on the table. "I'll leave you to it."

"Monsieur Grenouille?"

"Oui."

"Merci." I nodded, tears still in my eyes.

"Ce n'est rien. It is nothing."

I held the ice to my throbbing elbow and sipped on the cool water while customers came in and out of the shop ordering fresh baguettes and other meticulously artful treats. Monsieur Grenouille served each of them with a wide smile and some friendly banter, so different from the encounters I'd grown used to with him.

When the shop finally cleared out, Monsieur Grenouille came back over to check on me. I handed him back the now almost completely melted bag of ice and a soggy handful of napkins from the bag's condensation, and let him know my elbow was feeling better. He cleared away the items as I dabbed the corners of my eyes with the cloth napkin and set it down. "You've been more than gracious. I'll get out of your way soon. In fact, you'll be happy to know I'm probably leaving Maubec as early as I can get on a flight."

"You've finished your little project, then?" he asked, his condescension clear from the slight upturn of his nose.

"No, not quite. I got taken for a fool, and now all I want to do is go home."

He squinted, confused. "Taken for a fool? I don't understand . . ."

"Oh, taken for a fool means when you're kinda—"

"Non, Mademoiselle, that I understand. I just don't know what you mean. How were you deceived?"

"It's a long, complicated story. I'm not sure you would understand. You might even think I had it coming."

"Had it coming?" he said slowly, trying to work out the right translation. "Now that phrase I am unsure of?"

"It means you'd probably think I deserve what I got."

"I guess that all depends? What did you get?" he asked plainly.

"Kicked in the teeth, that's what," I said, not even sure where I'd start if I were to explain. "Can I ask you something?" I didn't know exactly why I'd chosen Monsieur Grenouille to be my sounding board but figured he wouldn't have any problem being painfully frank, something I desperately needed at this moment.

"Go ahead." He pulled out a chair and dropped into it, seemingly grateful for the chance to get off his tired feet.

"Did you ever trust someone? I mean, really trust them. Believe they had your best interest at heart only to find out they betrayed you in the worst possible way?"

"What is that expression? Let me think if I can do it justice in English." He focused his eyes, trying to work out just the right words to use so I would understand his meaning, and finally said, "The hardest thing about betrayal is that it never comes from your enemies."

"Exactly. I loved Rhys. I trusted Rhys. And I was wrong about him. And now, all this time, I thought Kate had been my friend, but it turns out, I was very wrong about that too. Seems I'm either an incredibly terrible judge of character, or there's something about *me* that gives people the impression I'm dispensable."

"I don't know this Rhys you speak of or this Kate, but if she hurt you, you should let her know. It does no good to hold on to the pain of the past. I can assure you of that."

I thought back to his outburst that day with Madame Archambeau and Elliott at the corner table in his shop when he pounded his fist and said the town had been through enough, heartbreak seeping through his every pore. I thought I now had an inkling about the pain he was referring to. Reaching into my bag, I unzipped the small inside pocket and pulled out the picture Father François had let me hold on to at Saint Orens. I set it down on the table and slid it over to Monsieur Grenouille. He picked up the photograph, his eyes growing larger and larger.

"Where did you get this?" he exclaimed.

"It was in the archives at Saint Orens."

His face lit up with recognition. "Those are my parents, Ginette and Alain Grenouille."

I got up and stood behind him. "I know," I said, using a rigid finger to point to the other two couples. "And that's Luc and Imène Adélaïse, and Marthe and Grégoire Archambeau beside them."

He turned the picture over and looked back at me. "What's that? What's DP mean?"

"It stands for Dutch-Paris. Your parents. The Adélaïses. The Archambeaus. They were all part of a Resistance network that helped people escape France during World War II."

"I was only two years old when they disappeared. My brother was just a few months. My grandparents were Nazi sympathizers, and I was forbidden to even speak their names. The little I know about what happened to them, I've spent my life trying to piece together."

"Monsieur Grenouille, what I've been trying to piece together is that day in your shop, you said Bastien was somehow to blame for what happened. How would that even be possible?"

"Not Bastien. I misspoke. His grandfather and namesake, Sébastien Munier."

"Château Mirabelle's vintner?"

"So Bastien *did* tell you?"

I shook my head in disbelief. "Apparently not everything."

Monsieur Grenouille went behind the counter and pulled out two small glasses and a bottle that, based on its brownish color, I guessed to be whiskey. He uncorked the top and poured us each a shot's worth before sitting back down. He lifted the glass in the air and threw back the entire thing in a single gulp. I followed suit, but being unaccustomed to a drink that strong, I launched into a coughing fit of epic proportions. He chuckled and encouraged me to chase the shot with some water, which finally stopped the outburst.

"You are wrong, you know," Monsieur Grenouille said. "Sébastien Munier wasn't Château Mirabelle's vintner, he was the vigneron."

"I'm not sure I know the difference."

"A vintner makes the wine but does not have involvement in farming the grapes, whereas a vigneron cultivates the grapes and also makes the resulting wine. From what I understand, Sébastien Munier was the very best vigneron in the Provence region, personally selecting every vine at Château Mirabelle. His Chenin Blanc became the stuff of legends and put the winery on the map." He refilled his glass and continued, "Of course, the Adélaïses enjoyed having a profitable vineyard, but wine was not a particular passion of theirs, and they left most of the day-to-day operations to Monsieur Munier. That is, until 1942."

"Right, of course. That's when the Adélaïses joined the Resistance?"

"Oui, that's when they started to use the winery as a cover. As far as I know, Sébastien Munier wasn't political. I don't think he cared for anything really beyond his precious vineyard and mostly turned a blind eye to what the Adélaïses were doing. But I have to imagine that at some point, their covert operations started to get in the way of his winemaking. From what I have been told, he tried to buy the winery from them, but because they were using it as a means to transport weapons and even people, they refused to separate it from the estate."

I was on the edge of my seat, transfixed by his every word and gesture. "So what happened?" I whispered.

"He gave them one last opportunity to sell or else he would go to the Nazis and tell them everything. But rather than turn the house over and risk the lives of everyone involved, the Adélaïses decided to blow it up, erase all evidence of the Resistance, protect the other networks, and go into hiding."

I slumped back in my chair. "And Monsieur Munier knew exactly what route they would take, the same route they had been using to get people out of France and into Switzerland."

"Précisément."

"He sold them out? He sold all of them out? Over wine!?" The magnitude of his treachery washed over me like a wave.

"Perhaps he thought he could give enough information that he would be rewarded for his loyalty and be able to hold on to the vineyard, but as you know the Nazis weren't ones to let things go. I know my parents were somehow caught up in it, but that is all the information I have. It is like one day they just disappeared off the face of the earth." He refilled his glass one last time and drank it down.

My throat constricted, and I grew anxious to finish his story. "I know what happened to them."

His head shot up like a bolt. "You do?"

"The six of them, Luc and Imène Adélaïse, and Marthe and Grégoire Archambeau, and your parents were captured at the Beliveau farm in Annecy, about forty kilometers south of Geneva, on November 16, 1942. From there, they were processed into Camp des Milles and remained there until December 23, when they were transported to another camp called Drancy."

"And after that?"

"They were most likely transported to Auschwitz. Camp des Milles didn't have records, but they think they could be found in Poland."

Tears streamed down Monsieur Grenouille's face, and he remained quiet for a few minutes before speaking. "I always wondered . . ."

"Thank you, Monsieur, for your honesty and for sharing all of this with me. Your parents were incredibly brave. Very selfless and very brave. They saved hundreds of innocent people." I took his soft hand in mine and gave it a supportive squeeze.

His expression softened, and he smiled, his eyes crinkling in the corners. "Thank you for helping to heal an old man's heart. You may call me Remy. I am sorry I misjudged you, Mademoiselle Everly. I see now you care more deeply for Maubec than I originally imagined."

Laying out a spread of the other photographs and notes I'd taken at the camp and the church archives and sharing the pictures and videos I'd taken on my phone, I recounted every bit of information Elliott and I learned throughout our investigation to Monsieur Grenouille as we sipped on whiskey. And while our findings wouldn't bring any of them back, or erase the wrongdoings of the past, I was grateful to have given Monsieur Grenouille the missing pieces to his puzzle and even more so the closure he hadn't realized he needed until now.

We filled our cups one last time. Monsieur Grenouille lifted his and said, "L'amour est un sacrifice, et l'amour se sacrifie pour son prochain, which means: Love is sacrifice, and love sacrifices itself for its neighbor."

I lifted my glass to meet his. "Well, then, to love."

Chapter Thirty-Seven

While I was speaking with Monsieur Grenouille, the sky had turned dark and opened up to an unexpected steady roll of afternoon showers. I threw my cardigan up over my head to scurry across the street back to the inn. My mind was reeling over the information Monsieur Grenouille had revealed, and I wasn't sure how many more surprises I could handle. I had so much to try to sort out and less than twenty-four hours to make a decision about airing the show.

Truth be told, I already knew what I was going to do. I had to walk away. It was my dignity on the line, my reputation. Not to mention, that leaked sex tape became such a rift between me and my family, I knew another embarrassment of that caliber would firmly cement in their minds that I was hopeless—bound forever to exist as the permanent blemish that tarnished the family name.

The rain was warm and fell in rhythmic patterns across the square, fat drops plopping into the fountain in the center. I lowered the cardigan down off my head and allowed myself to close my eyes, tilt my face up, and take it all in. Raindrops slid down my forehead, into the creases of my lids and lashes, and sloped down my cheeks and neck. My clothes soaked up the moisture, the layers growing heavier with the passing time. I inhaled a deep breath and looked out into the distance:

the lush fields of green and violet, the cypress trees, and Saint Orens in the distance on the hill.

I'd learned so much since arriving in Provence—not all lessons I'd volunteered to learn, necessarily, but they came nonetheless. I learned about the Adélaïses, and the Resistance, and the brave people who fought back in spite of the repercussions they knew they'd face if caught. I learned about the heartbreak of betrayal (*intimately*), a lesson it seemed the universe was insistent I hadn't mastered quite yet.

I wiped my hand across my face, picked up my bag, and went inside to take a hot shower and give careful consideration to a decision I'd already subconsciously made.

The silver bell chimed above the inn door, a sound I'd miss once I was back at home, and I noticed Odette hustling around the dining room, moving small buckets around the floor and up onto tables to catch the drops of water leaking through the roof. As soon as she placed them, it seemed another leak opened somewhere else across the room. It was like watching a much less humorous game of Whac-A-Mole.

"Do you need some help?" I asked, instinctively grabbing a bucket and moving it to a stream of water that started to pour out harder than before.

Odette didn't even lift her head to see who was speaking. She was too busy trying to balance three buckets in her arms to dump some of the caught water into the side sink. "Yeah, I do, actually. Any chance you have a new inn on you? In a pocket somewhere or in your luggage? Or a new roof at least?" she joked.

"Actually, funny you should ask . . . ," I joked back.

Odette lifted her head at the response. "Oh, Plum, hello. Yes, I guess you *do* have a château . . ." Odette laughed. "Sorry, that comment wasn't meant for you, I was just making a general joke. But, as you can see, we need a bit of renovation work ourselves if we hope to stay open for much longer." She repositioned the newly emptied buckets back under the leaks and grabbed a dish towel to mop up any puddles left behind. "It's one of the many reasons why I cannot return to Paris. It feels so selfish. Clearly, my parents need me here. With the state of the inn as it is, it's all too much."

"I can understand that," I said and nodded.

"And I couldn't think to move them to Paris. This is their home—Maubec, our neighbors, every piece of this town. I could never do that to them, no matter how much my dreams and future may live outside Provence." She took a deep breath and continued, "Actually, since it's just the two of us down here, I do have something I wanted to broach with you."

She used the dishcloth to wipe off the chairs once more to ensure no wetness was left and then gestured for me to take a seat. She plopped herself across from me and fidgeted with the rag in her hands. "I've been giving it some thought, and though I know I was initially upset that you wouldn't be staying in Maubec, I've come to realize that maybe it is the opportunity we've all been waiting for."

Her eyes burned with anticipation and optimism. "Not that I wouldn't love for you to stay," she clarified and continued, "it's just that, if you're *not*, then I have a proposition for you. I was wondering if you would consider selling the château to us once it's finished. We never could afford the renovations that property needed, and the project, quite frankly, was just too big and overwhelming for my parents to take on before. I know you'll probably have your share of offers for it, many of them way over asking, but I just would like to throw our hat in the ring, and though our offer may not be as tempting, I was hoping that now that you've gotten to know us and the town, you'd see it as a sound investment. You see, if my parents were able to run a property that didn't need quite so much upkeep, then perhaps I might be able to return to Paris and finish my studies with greater peace of mind."

The idea tumbled out of her mouth like she was afraid if she didn't get it all out in one breath, she'd lose her nerve. Once finished, she drew in a long breath and set her hands on top of the table, wringing her fingers with anxiety. "What do you think?"

How was I supposed to answer Odette with the future of the property and the show so up in the air? Where did I even begin to explain?

"Odette, I love the idea of Château Mirabelle being run by your family, but . . ." My chin began to quiver, and I was afraid I wouldn't be able to get the words out before completely breaking down. "The house. It's not . . . It won't . . . It's just a *mess*."

She reached across the table and squeezed my forearm jovially. "Oh, Plum, I know. It's okay. I mean, once it's finished," she laughed, clearly misunderstanding.

"No, I mean, it won't *ever* be finished. I'm leaving the show. It was all a setup, and the renovations were all staged, just a backdrop for a love-story gotcha moment they dreamed up to embarrass me on a national stage . . . all for TV ratings." Fresh tears sprang to my eyes, the hurt still a raw ache.

"Wait, what? No. That can't be true. How cruel!" Odette swung her chair around the table to scoot closer to me and slung an arm around my sunken shoulders.

"It's true. And I feel like such an idiot. Now even more so in learning the project had gotten your hopes up about a possible future for you and your family." The tears started to spill in steady streams, and I hid my face in my hands in embarrassment.

Odette was maybe the last person I thought I'd be crying to, but alas, here we were, and I couldn't keep the floodgates from opening again. "What's worse is that the house," I continued, "at least aesthetically, is in just as poor a condition as when it started. They fixed the foundation and the mold problem and the plumbing. But those things pushed the schedule so far off course it never found its way back. There are no floors or walls, no decor. No charm or flavor. It is a blank and chaotic canvas, and after everything they put me through, I may need to walk away from the project to preserve what little dignity I have left."

"Oh my God, Plum. I had no idea. I am sorry to have even asked." She lowered her head, unsure of what else to say and how to proceed. "Are . . . are you okay?"

I looked up at her and into her brown eyes. Before I answered, I surveyed the dining room again. Amid the buckets rapidly filling with water from dozens of leaks actively pouring from the roof, Odette was asking about *me*. About my troubles. About my mental health. Her selflessness was jarring, yet incredibly appreciated, and I felt a hollowness of regret for not warming to her sooner. Perhaps it was jealousy in seeing how Elliott behaved around her? I didn't know. All I knew was that I suddenly felt a deep remorse for the time we'd lost. It'd been a long time since I'd had a real and genuine friendship, and if I hadn't been so caught up in myself, I could've been building one with Odette.

"Actually, I don't know how I am, quite honestly. I feel pretty lost right now, and I'm trying not to act rashly and make a decision I may live to regret. But I feel like I'm hanging upside down. The world is present, as I've always known it, but it's all wrong. It's inverted and confusing and out of balance. I feel like I'm looking at a Jackson Pollock painting that someone is telling me is a Renoir."

She squeezed my fingers supportively and did not let go. She stayed quiet, not trying to dispense advice or empty encouragement like so many would; she just stayed by my side and listened.

I continued, "So now I'm left at a crossroads. Do I allow Tributary to air this fabricated season, complete with the mortifying gotcha moment in Paris with Rhys they are sure to include, or do I back out of my contract, chalk it all up to a very arduous learning experience, return to LA, and never look back?"

"You know I can't answer that for you," she said, her eyebrows woven together in sympathy.

"You sure? At this point, I'm thinking of flipping a coin. At least *you* are a bit more qualified." I cracked a smile. "Thank you, though. For listening. For understanding. And for giving me the benefit of the doubt."

"I had a feeling that once Elliott and I started to become a little closer, you pulled away. But nothing is going on or has ever gone on with us. Actually, I think he is quite taken with someone else." She lifted her eyebrows at me, an obvious hint at who she meant.

"No," I said and shook my head. "I mean, maybe? But I can't even think about all of that right now. I need to close this Bastien chapter first, figure out what I'm doing with Château Mirabelle, and then maybe I can sort out whatever is going on or not going on between me and Elliott."

"Ouais, I understand, but don't take too long. Don't throw away this entire experience because it ended up not being what you expected. Sometimes life's greatest treasures are the ones we don't expect."

I smiled and nodded. "I'll try to keep that in mind. Can I ask you something?"

"Anything," she replied.

"Can you tell me more about Bastien? I just feel so blindsided, like I never knew him at all. You tried to warn me, didn't you?"

An expression of guilt washed over her face. "Listen, Bastien and I have a long history—un peu compliqué. We grew up together. We were young and in love as high school sweethearts, but he had a difficult time growing up in this town, and it has haunted him, dictating his actions and forcing him to live in survival mode ever since he was a little boy with the last name Munier."

I pressed my lips together and nodded in contemplation. "I've been trying to put this puzzle together, and Monsieur Grenouille just slid the proverbial last piece into place by telling me about Bastien's grandfather. I can't tell you how shocked I was to learn that he was the one who turned in the Adélaïses and the rest of the townspeople involved in the Resistance."

"Ouais," Odette consented, "can you imagine living in the shadow of such a treacherous betrayal? Bastien had nothing to do with it but was forced to pay for the sins of his family's past. It was one of the biggest wedges that existed in our relationship early on. He wanted to run away from Maubec and start a new life, somewhere the story couldn't follow him. It had always been his dream to be a vintner like his grandfather, but no one would give him the chance to apprentice in this region, a necessary step."

"It doesn't excuse what Bastien did," I responded coldly.

"Non, of course, it doesn't. But perhaps it may justify it a little. He tried to hitch his wagon to your star, or maybe tried to right the wrongs of the past through rebuilding what his grandfather was responsible for destroying—which isn't right, but is maybe at least a bit more understandable given the circumstances."

"You are undeservingly gracious with him. He said it was you who wanted more, who needed to get out of Maubec, who left everyone behind—ruthlessly and selfishly. When given the chance, he threw you right under the bus. So, why, after all that happened, do you still defend him?"

"Because he is a genuinely good man. He is just a product of his family and his history. Like you. Like me. Like we all are. And he is a hell of a vintner to boot. It's a shame no one ever gave him a real shot. He is actually quite talented."

Odette stood from the table and pushed in the chair. "Whatever it is you decide, Plum, don't let it be because of what Bastien or Rhys did or Kate . . . or anyone else in your past. Let it be your decision, wholly and completely. It's the only way it will ever be the right one."

Chapter Thirty-Eight

Before I could change my mind, I sent a text to Bastien asking him to meet me at Château Mirabelle in an hour. In the meantime, I needed to take a walk to clear my mind. The landslide of the past several hours was almost too much to believe, let alone bear. Between the show turning out to be a prank, the revelation about Bastien and his grandfather, the heartache of learning about the Adélaïses, and my complicated feelings for Elliott, I was hitting my limit on things I could handle.

It was still raining, but significantly less. And what was a little rain? I was already soaked from when I'd left Monsieur Grenouille's shop and helped Odette in the dining room. In fact, the warm summer shower felt cathartic, like a baptism washing away my troubles and sending them in rivulets down the cobblestone road. I walked past Monsieur Grenouille's shop and waved with a smile when I caught his eye through the window. He returned the gesture, and I immediately felt lighter.

I continued my stroll, passing Le Coquelicot floral shop and a few other storefronts that lined the town's main street. The stores weren't busy; in fact, they looked a bit like they were taking a siesta in this afternoon rainstorm. For the almost six weeks I'd been in Maubec, I'd walked down this road before, many times, but I'd never really surveyed the town as a whole. It was quiet and insular. It looked like a movie set built on a film stage in LA, but one that had been constructed years ago and then left to wither away, unattended and overlooked.

It had all the makings of a beautiful, luscious tourist destination, one that would bring along with it the money and the attention that could reinvigorate Maubec back to its original glory. The potential was there. The story was just waiting to be written. I sighed, heavy with the weight of my impending decision about airing the show. It would change so much for this town and these people, but greenlighting its broadcast also would force me to take a hit from which I wasn't sure I could recover.

After a quick shower and a change of clothes, I met Gervais out in front of the inn. For the entire twenty-minute drive, I mentally rehearsed my speech. And every time I did, it took on a new inflection. Anger turned to hurt, hurt turned to sadness, and then sadness turned back around to rage. I wasn't sure if, once I was actually face-to-face with Bastien, I'd lose all sense of the self-control I was mustering and instead, go simply ballistic. I guess once the time came, I would be just as surprised at what would come out of my mouth as he would.

Gervais was able to pull up the full length of the driveway this time, as almost all the trucks and crew had left for the day. There was only one work vehicle left, the workers marching in and out loading up the back with their tools and excess materials, and one small car that I recognized as Simone's. Most of the rain had cleared since my walk in town, and the clouds were finally breaking just in time for sunset.

I walked in the front entrance and gasped, clasping my hands over my mouth in awe. The space was stunning: intricate area rugs and lush Queen Anne furniture, golden fixtures and rich tapestry drapes that hung the length of the full picture windows. The light from the descending sun streamed in, casting everything in a warm, hazy hue. I caught a glimpse of Simone walking gingerly around the space, adjusting the floral arrangements that adorned all the tabletops—tall yellow sunflowers paired with lavender sprigs and clusters of hyacinths.

"Simone, I can't even believe this. How? How did this all get finished? This house was a disaster just this morning!" I exclaimed, still marveling at the amazing art on the walls and the meticulous details—like the fully staged dining room complete with place settings of bone china.

Simone shook her head and skirted around an area rug on the floor as she made her way over to me. "Yes, it does *look* incredible. But don't be fooled, not everything is as finished as it seems. In fact, this is all just for show. Look . . ." She lifted the area rug she'd just stepped over to reveal a large hole in the wood floor. My eyes widened. "Yeah, don't step there, or over there." She pointed to another small rug across the room. "But don't worry, they'll mark the places where it isn't safe to walk when you film the finale."

"Wait, it's staying like this? *This* is the finished product? This is how I'd get the house?" I asked.

"Pretty much. They just need it to be staged adequately to where they can shoot around the space and make it appear like the renovation is complete. Just enough to get the necessary footage."

"I see," I said, disappointed that there was *one more thing* I had either misunderstood or been duped by in this agreement.

"Good luck with the show, Ms. Everly. It has been nice working with you." Simone extended her hand, seemingly oblivious to the mental short-circuit I was currently experiencing inside my head.

"Oh, yeah. Same, Simone, thank you," I responded and then watched her walk out the front door.

I drew in a long, deep breath and stood enjoying the stillness. In spite of the phony decor and staging, I could finally see Château Mirabelle's true potential.

I heard the soft growl of Bastien's Vespa putting its way up the drive. My heart started to race, and I was afraid I'd lose the nerve to stand up for myself when it came down to it. The snap of the front door opening caused my palms to sweat, and I raked them down my jeans before he saw me. Finally, he walked into the foyer and our eyes met.

I expected to feel the familiar sensation of butterflies fluttering in my stomach, but it seemed they'd migrated north, fuzzying my head with too many thoughts at once.

"Plum, ma cherie," Bastien started.

I expected to erupt with anger, but instead, all I could manage was, "Please, don't do that."

He stepped closer. "Kate told me about your conversation earlier. She told me how upset you were."

"Upset is an understatement, Bastien. You lied. You both lied to me. And then filmed it to make a fool out of me." My voice was escalating along with my blood pressure.

I paused to take a breath and recalibrate. This was not the way I wanted this conversation to go. I shook my head and looked him in the eye. "You can't imagine what that feels like, to be betrayed by someone who I thought cared about me. It's happened to me more times than I can count, and I just . . . I didn't expect it from you."

"I never meant to hurt you, Plum. I thought we were having fun and, though I was asked to be flirtatious with you and make bigger my affections, I did not know their true intention for the show. I didn't know it was te tromper . . . um, to trick you. They just told me that they loved the scenes with us being séduisant and charmant together, and when Kate came to see me a few weeks ago, she told me that the test groups couldn't get enough and asked me to keep it up, keep it going, keep you interested. I asked about the renovation, I did. They said it was secondary to la magie happening between you and me on-screen. Nous étions comme des feux d'artifice." He gestured, his hands pantomiming fireworks in the sky. "So I gave them more of what they asked for. And I thought you were doing the same. But I'm not a bad guy, Plum. I promise, I did not set out to hurt you."

"Bastien, I am just so confused. How am I supposed to know what was true and what wasn't? What was for the show and what was authentically you? It feels like every interaction we've had has been a lie, and I don't know how to parse out what was real. I genuinely thought I liked you. And after everything I'd been through with Rhys, it was nice to be thought of, to be considered, to be romanced. But now, I . . . feel like the butt of a sick joke."

Bastien grabbed my hand and held it in his. "I never meant for that to happen." He led me to the salon, the couches and chairs arranged around a rustic coffee table and set in front of the majestic fireplace adorned with the Adélaïses' coat of arms. I went to sit in the cream-colored chair with rose stitching, across from him, but he grabbed for me before I could drop my weight into the seat.

"Pas là! Don't sit on that one. The left back leg is attached with a zip tie. You'll end up right on your cul. Asseyez-vous ici." He stepped over a loose floorboard and gestured for me to take a seat in the other rose-stitched chair instead. I eyed it warily before gently testing its limit. Seemed fine, for now. I sat back and watched Bastien perch on the arm of the Queen Anne couch on the other side of the coffee table.

We sat in silence for a moment, either waiting for the other to speak or just trying to decide what problem to tackle first.

I finally started, "I had a pretty enlightening conversation with Odette today."

Bastien lifted his eyes to meet mine, and his self-assuredness gave way to a flash of dread. "Oh? I'm afraid to ask . . ."

"She actually defended you."

His posture stiffened, and his brows jumped in surprise. "She . . . she did? But why? I mean, uh . . . what did she say?"

"She explained to me how much your family's past mistakes have haunted you, following you around like a ghost. If anyone understands having to bear the weight of their family's decisions, it's me."

His eyes filled with tears. "I don't deserve your sympathie, but I do appreciate your empathie. It takes a person qui est très spéciale, someone who can see beyond themselves, to put aside their own hurt to recognize someone else's. I wish I had been more honest with you from the start. It's just I have been plagued by my past for so long, it's affected the way people treat me, the opportunities I've had, and the chances I've never gotten. I was ashamed, and I wanted you to get to know me without being tainted by the stain of my family's mistake."

How could I fault him for wanting me to get to know him apart from the story his family's legacy told? It was the exact problem I'd been facing my whole life, six thousand miles away on the other side of the world. It didn't excuse it, but damn if I didn't understand him and his motives in a new way. I nodded. "But now that everything's out in the open, I need to ask you a few things. And I need you to be one hundred percent honest."

"Of course. You deserve that. Et maintenant, what else is there to lose?"

"Did you ever really work on Château du Val d'Été? Or was that a lie too? Was our date just part of the fantasy you were trying to sell me?"

"Non! I did work there. Je jure devant Dieu." He gestured with a quick cross marked over his heart. "But I was just one of the members of the construction crew, not the foreman or the lead designer or anything like that. But, as I'd told you on that tour, all the research I did on the moat, and the seventeenth-century detailing, all of that was true. I took you to Val d'Été not to trick you, but for you to see the potential Château Mirabelle had as a similar project to Château du Val d'Été."

My brain was catching up one piece at a time. "That's why the security guard there didn't recognize you . . . why you'd gotten into the heated argument . . . huh . . ." I nodded and continued to sort through my memory of that day. "And that's why we had to sneak around the back to access the salon." I mentally sorted through my time in Maubec, starting back at the beginning, and my gut clenched at the recollection of our first night out together. "Bastien, please don't tell me—it . . . it was you who called the paparazzi that night at the club in Avignon, wasn't it?"

He cast his eyes toward the floor. It was all the answer I needed. Jesus, I had it all wrong from the very start—about him, about the show, all of it. I blew out a breath.

"I know, I know," he started, "that was reprehensible. But . . . I was just so excited that it was all happening. I could see the show becoming a big success and me finally getting my chance to make amends for good. I didn't really know you then, and what I did know and had been told about you by Kate led me to believe you'd be on board. I thought I was doing us all a favor—hyping up the show, creating buzz. I thought you'd be used to it and that it wouldn't be a problème."

He stood up, his nervous energy fighting for an outlet. He started to pace behind the couch. "Honestly, Plum, I knew I was never qualified for a project like this. Not by a long shot. When they'd advertised the casting in town I felt like maybe, just maybe, that by renovating Château Mirabelle I could atone for my grandfather's sins—set history as right as I could from this side of it. I wanted to do right by the Adélaïses. I wanted to do right by all the people he wronged. I thought if I could make the house perfect again, maybe Maubec would finally see that the fruit *can* fall far from the tree."

He continued, "When I met with Kate, she loved my look, and though she appreciated my passion for the project because of my personal connection, she was certainly more interested in how I appeared on camera and how much I could amplifier my charm. She assured me we'd have professionals on-site to help with the construction. And when I saw René Laroque, I believed Kate lived up to her end of the agreement. She never told me that she'd sold you a completely different bill of goods. I thought we'd both signed on for the same project, and I see now that wasn't the case."

Finally, he stopped pacing, placed his hands on the back of the couch, and looked me straight in the eye. "Kate didn't *ever* explain that the show was a setup. She told me it was a love story framed in a home renovation show but made me believe you were game too. She said we'd work perfectly together, and as soon as I met you, I knew she was right. We had an instant spark. I know you felt it too. That night in my apartment. That was all real. I swear it. I would never have—"

I was glad to hear him say it, even if I still wasn't sure what to believe. But there was something in the tone of his voice and the sincerity of his stance that convinced me he was telling the truth.

"I did . . . I do care for you, but I was led astray . . . by fame . . . by Kate. All I could think was how much the world was going to love us and our show, and even though some of it was smoke and mirrors, I'd finally get my chance at redemption. But I ended up making un tas de merde, more than I could've imagined. Plum, I am so profoundly sorry."

"Thank you for saying that. I appreciate your apology, and I do believe you did not set out to hurt me, but nothing about this is easy. Your confession. Kate's manipulation. This decision. It all feels like a ticking time bomb, and I know the only one who can contain the detonation is me."

The silence that fell between us was punctuated by his heavy sigh. "Will . . . will you do the finale?" he asked.

I looked up at the mantel and saw the clock Elliott and I found together at the Brocante de Beaucaire—the clock that may have belonged to the Adélaïses—and wondered if it was the one and only authentic thing in the entire room? The entire château? My entire life?

"I think all the smoke and mirrors are making it hard to see and breathe. I need to go and clear my head," I said.

Bastien nodded, his understanding evident in the gentle dip of his head. "Whatever you decide, I'll understand."

Chapter Thirty-Nine

Like a siren song, Saint Orens called out to me. I remembered what Bastien said the first time we visited, that anyone could seek sanctuary at a church, at any hour, day or night. Hours after our conversation at Château Mirabelle, I found myself alone, walking up the cobblestone road lined with charming old houses with blue wooden shutters toward the baroque cathedral. I wasn't sure what I was in search of—sympathy, understanding, or the ability to forgive—but I figured Saint Orens was as good a place as any to look.

I pushed lightly on the large oak doors and stepped into the empty chapel. To my surprise, Father François was still inside cleaning up from the evening Mass. He spotted me from the dais and came hurrying down from the altar to greet me.

"Plum, what are you doing here? Unfortunately, we just concluded our evening prayer service," he said.

"I'm so sorry. I don't want to disturb you, I just . . . I don't know . . . I needed a quiet place to think, and this was the first one that came to mind."

"Oui, of course, our doors are never closed to those in need. Take as long as you wish."

"Merci."

Taking a seat in a pew at the back of the church, the bench squeaking loudly as if welcoming me in, I rested my back against the unforgiving wood and took comfort in its refuge. Even though I'd been here before, I hadn't really stopped to appreciate how beautiful it was inside. The large stained-glass windows reflected colored light from long, tapered candles placed all along the chapel walls, so that almost everything shimmered with a golden hue. Like all of Provence, it too was magical.

Father François made his way up the aisle and sat down beside me. "I was going to retire for the evening shortly, but before I do, is there anything I can help with, mon enfant?"

"I wish, but unfortunately, I'm not Catholic."

"Ça va, this isn't confession. Just an old priest here to offer a sympathetic ear."

Before I even realized what was happening, the entire sordid tale came tumbling out. When I finished, Father François pursed his lips, nodded solemnly, and simply said, "Je comprends," like it was a story he'd heard a thousand times before.

"So you see, I can't win," I continued to explain, certain there was no way he could really comprendre. "No matter what I do, someone will be disappointed."

Father François turned to face me. "There is a saying: a truly strong person does not need the approval of others any more than a lion needs the approval of sheep. Now, if you'll excuse me, I should take my leave, but please, stay as long as you need."

His words hung in the air like a prayer. What *did* I want? For myself? For Château Mirabelle? Before I came to Provence, I wasn't living, I was floating. From project to project and one mistake to the next. Blaming everyone—my parents, my sisters, the tape, Rhys, even the paparazzi—for the person I'd become. Now, if I wanted to, I could easily add Kate and Bastien to that ever-growing list. But maybe it was high time I acknowledged that I was the constant, the common denominator threading my own story together.

The sound of footsteps echoed off the walls of the chapel. I looked back and saw Elliott ambling down the aisle. Our eyes met, and a soft smile tiptoed across his lips. "I knew this is where you'd be," he said, easing into the pew.

"You did?"

"It's hard to explain, but it was as if, when I heard the church bells resounding through the town, the church was trying to call out for me to come find you. I'm sure that sounds completely bonkers."

"It doesn't, actually."

Elliott's eyes flitted around the room. "It's really different being here at night, isn't it? With the candlelight and everything, it's so ethereal." He turned so that his body faced mine, our knees practically touching in the narrow row. "I heard about what happened between you and Kate, and I need you to know I was in the dark too. I promise you, Plum, I would never have signed on for this project if I knew what it was really about."

Kate had already confirmed Elliott was just an innocent bystander, unknowingly capturing moments on film that would be twisted and distorted to fit her secret narrative. If anything, he'd also been duped. It was clear now, Tributary probably also never had any intention of using the additional material we'd been gathering on Château Mirabelle's history.

"I know. Kate told me. I'm sorry you got entangled in this whole mess when all you thought you were doing was your job."

He took my hand in his. "I'm not sorry."

I looked up. "You're not?"

"I've never felt more engaged or alive than when you and I were working together, uncovering all the history about the château. I want us to tell the world about the Dutch-Paris network and the Adélaïses and their bravery, and if Tributary doesn't want it, we'll find someone who does. We have to give them all the ending they deserve."

"You don't understand, if I don't do the finale, I'm in breach of contract and don't get the house. There is no happy ending."

"So what happens then? It falls back into disarray and disrepair? Their legacy gets buried in the blown-out cellars of Château Mirabelle?"

"You don't know what you're asking. If I agree, I play right into *everyone's* worst perceptions of me—the Everly sister with no direction, no real passion, just in it for the good time and easy money. My family's businesses will suffer, I'll be another joke . . . I just—" I couldn't finish the sentence. It got caught in the back of my throat.

"Not everyone thinks that of you. Come, I want to show you something," he said, squeezing my hand a little tighter and pulling me out of our pew and down an aisle toward the side door. I followed him out of the church, where he led me over to the arched stained glass windows carved with the symbolic scenes and characters that Bastien had pointed out to me the first day we visited Saint Orens. "You see this etching? The one you were so taken with? The lion surrounded by the pack of hyenas?" Elliott shone the flashlight from his phone on the archway. "Here, take this and follow it all the way around," he said, passing me his cell.

I aimed the bright light at the wall and trailed the image up and over the arch to the other side. I bent down, and there, carved into the stone, was the second half of the narrative, the pack of hyenas that'd been relentlessly hunting the lion were now scattered to the wind, chased off by his mighty roar.

I stood up and found myself inches from Elliott's face, the light from the phone glowing between us.

"The dominance of a lion has nothing to do with its size, right? I mean, it's far from the largest animal in the jungle," Elliott said, the metaphor sinking in as he spoke it aloud. "The lion's real power is in its strength and fearlessness." His voice lowered to a whisper, and his body was so close I could feel the heat radiating off his chest. "Plum, I know you. You're a lion. So *be* the lion."

I edged up onto my toes and planted a sweet kiss on his lips. At my touch, he grinned against my mouth. I pulled back, worried I'd gotten too swept up in the moment, but I was met with a boyish smirk and a mischievous twinkle in Elliott's gaze. He leaned in, cupping my face in his warm hands, and *really* kissed me. My knees buckled under my weight, and I caught myself by holding on to his broad shoulders. Breathless, I touched a hand to my lips and stared at him, relishing in the sensation still buzzing through me.

For the weeks where I felt uncertain about him, and Bastien, and Rhys, and France, and the show, I realized Elliott had been the only constant who'd been nothing but his true and authentic self since the minute I'd met him. While I tried to navigate all of the newness and figure out what I really wanted after so much time being told who I was and what was expected of me, it had been Elliott who remained a steadfast voice of reason and clarity, even if what he said was at times hard to hear.

Now, at long last, despite our relentless efforts to deny the connection that had been brewing between us from the very moment the accordionist serenaded us with "La Vie En Rose" in the middle of the town, to our errant kiss on the carousel when my feelings about everything still seemed so hazy, to the onyx clock replaced on the Adélaïses' mantel after he'd returned to the vendor to purchase it at the Brocante de Beaucaire . . . the realization hit me hard. It'd always been Elliott. I knew it the way I knew the sky was blue or that the sun would rise each morning. I knew it the way a river knows its course, unwavering and unyielding. And I knew it the same way I finally knew exactly what I was going to do.

I glanced down at the etching of the lion one last time, its expression stoic and triumphant. "I've made my decision," I declared before resting my hands upon Elliott's chest. "I'm done being swayed by the opinions of sheep—I'm ready to be the goddamned lion."

Chapter Forty

After my heart-to-heart with Elliott the night before at Saint Orens, I called Bastien to come and meet us at the inn to strategize a game plan about how best to regain control of the finale's narrative from Kate's clutches. A little after 8:00 a.m., seated in the small breakfast nook of La Cigale Chantante, Elliott and I sipped on a fresh pot of English Breakfast tea while reviewing all the photos, notes, video clips, and articles we'd been gathering on Château Mirabelle over the past almost six weeks. Since it'd been done piecemeal, I hadn't realized how many artifacts and tidbits we'd found on our quest at all the stops we'd made along the way. As I examined the images and collected materials, the small blonde hairs on my forearms stood on end. *This* was the story that needed to be told. I'd never been more certain of anything in my life.

Bastien slowly made his way into the dining room a little after eight fifteen, his eyes sweeping the space like he was about to be ambushed by a firing squad. Maybe he was. Though Elliott had promised to be on his best behavior and theoretically understood that Bastien's understanding of the show had also been deluded, I couldn't be certain that one ill-timed or overly flirtatious joke from Bastien might result in Elliott knocking him flat on his ass.

Odette greeted him at the doorway and guided him over to where we were sitting. She offered him tea or coffee, but he politely declined both. He pulled out the empty chair and eased into it, sighing as he sat. "Bonjour," he mumbled, a bit reticent.

"Thank you for coming," I said.

"Why would I not come? You two are my friends, are you or non?"

"Yeah, non," Elliott jabbed.

I shot him a disapproving look, rested my forearms on the table's edge, and folded my clasped hands on the paper place mat in front of me. I sat up a bit straighter and decided to just jump in. "I have given this a lot of thought since my talk with Kate. Between my contractual obligation to the show and the ultimatum Kate posed during our argument, I'm not left with many options. But if you are sorry—sincerely sorry—for your role in deceiving me and truly interested in making amends for your family's past, then I believe I have come up with a way we can all get what we want. Well, all of us besides Kate."

Bastien rubbed at his chin and squinted at me dubiously. "Yes, of course, I am truly and sincerely désolée—"

"Désolée, my ass," Elliott muttered under his breath.

Bastien, oblivious to Elliott's jibes, continued, "But I don't quite understand what you need from me?"

"Here's the thing: I could walk away, but Kate would still figure out how to finish her narrative by omitting me from the finale and just shooting you. Restructuring the story to paint me as the villain who broke your heart and trampled on your dreams of us living happily ever after in Château Mirabelle. I won't lie to you, Bastien, you would come out looking great. You'd be the big hero—the one who restored the house even if you couldn't restore me, and the audience would love you all the more for trying."

Elliott looked up from his cup and directly at Bastien. I could tell he was trying to suss out if Bastien seemed allured by this version, but Bastien remained impassive—perhaps waiting to hear what was stashed behind door number two.

"*Or* we both threaten to walk away. No, we'd need to do both—not threaten—we'd need to actually leave, unless they play this our way. Sure, there's a good possibility they then just scrap the whole thing altogether, which would mean everything you staked on this project as a way to redeem your reputation and family name might be for naught.

But it has to be both of us in this together for there to be any chance for this attempt at collective bargaining to work."

Now I was the one staring at Bastien, trying to make out if anything I was saying was registering. If he even cared? I believed him yesterday when he told me he'd been just as manipulated by Kate as I was, but with so much at stake for him, that didn't necessarily mean he was willing to throw it all away.

For Bastien, *Heart Restoration Project*—where he played the handsome hero—was his chance to change *everything*. His life. His finances. His stability. And for me, on the outside looking in, this disaster was just par for the course. It wouldn't help or hurt my reputation any more than every other fake ridiculous show I'd done before.

But for me, *for real*, telling the true story of Château Mirabelle and its history was the one chance I had to show the world who I was and what I had to offer, beyond my famous name and pretty face.

When his face remained unchanged, I continued, "Right now, they believe the heart of the show is our fabricated relationship because we haven't given them anything else. They don't know about all of this"—I gestured to the materials covering the table—"the Adélaïses, Dutch-Paris, the occupation. They don't know about your grandfather and how his one reckless decision changed the whole course of history for this region. They don't know anything about how you've struggled to become a vintner and how every door's been slammed in your face. Or how much it would mean to the people of Maubec if we could somehow bring the winery back to life again. They don't know . . . and if we can bring all the things they don't know about to them as a beautifully touching narrative wrapped in a big, shiny, inspirational bow, then *maybe* we can finish this project by telling the story we want, the story the Adélaïses deserve to have told, and the one Maubec can finally be proud of."

Bastien nodded along as I spoke, taking in every word carefully. He sat silently for a few moments in deep contemplation before finally responding. "Plum, Kate has manipulated us at every turn to get what she wants for the show, and now that she has and managed to convince Claudine and Jack and everyone, what makes you so sure that they would ever trade a sure hit for a possible flop? What if no one cares about the history? About our story? About Château Mirabelle? Then what?"

"I know that is a very real possibility. But I really think we can make them see it, make them understand what all *this* is." I gestured again to the photos and artifacts spread around us and then looked him in the eye. "But it has to be both of us. Throughout these past months, I placed my trust in you, and now, I need you to do the same for me. Can you trust me?" Now it was my turn to wait with a held breath.

He tilted his head and set his lips together before responding. "Do you remember that day in the garden at Château du Val d'Été when I told you that you can honor a home by restoring it to its original state or you can honor it by restoring it to its original intention? You are right, if we let Kate win, Château Mirabelle will become nothing more than a cheap spectacle. If we stand together, we can make sure *Heart Restoration Project* is everything we intended for it to be."

"You're saying you'll walk away from the show—with me?"

"Yes, ma cherie. Okay. D'accord," he assented.

Even Elliott looked impressed with Bastien's sincerity. I nudged Elliott playfully and whispered, "Can you see now how a girl could get a little swept away when a guy talks like *that*?"

"Yeah, yeah, that and the full lips that look like doughy pillows, I get it." Elliott rolled his eyes.

"Sorry, what did you say about pillows?" Bastien asked, oblivious as ever.

"Don't worry about it," Elliott replied. "What you do need to worry about is how the two of you are going to convince Claudine and Jack to get on board with this new direction."

"Oh, I'll convince them," I stated. "I just need you to help arrange the meeting without Kate finding out. And it *has* to be in the house. In the cellars preferably. For this to work, we need to take them straight into the heart of Château Mirabelle."

Chapter Forty-One

As Bastien and I stood shoulder to shoulder in the dimly lit, bombed-out cellars of Château Mirabelle, the gravity of the moment weighed upon us like the thick, musty air pinned between the dirt floors and the impressive oak beams up above. We awaited the arrival of Claudine, Jack, and Elliott, well aware of the immense stakes at play. Convincing Jack and Claudine to embrace an alternative vision for *Heart Restoration Project*—one centered not on a manufactured romance storyline but on the profound sacrifices made by the Adélaïses and others—would be an uphill battle.

But if I could make them see that the château *wasn't* just a star vehicle, but the true star of the show—a place where the very walls whispered stories of courage and strength—we might have a fighting chance. No, there was no "if." I *had* to make them see. And not because I wanted to stick it to Kate, and believe me I did. This was about something far more significant. It was about honoring the legacy of those who had given so much and ensuring that Château Mirabelle's true story would finally be told.

"Hello? Is anyone down here?" Jack called into the tunnel, his voice echoing off the cavernous walls.

"Oui, come down a few more steps, we are here," Bastien called back.

Seconds later, Claudine, trailed by Jack and Elliott, emerged in the old wine cellar, a labyrinth of stone passages littered with piles of splintered wood from broken wine barrels and glass bottles, all blanketed in thick cobwebs. Crates were strewn about, and metal cogs and other gears that had once belonged to the enormous grape press were scattered in broken and bent pieces across the ground. The walls bore the scars of time, adorned with sparse patches of moss and crumbling plaster, and the low, vaulted ceilings added to the sense of confinement the deeper one descended.

Claudine ducked her head as her eyes darted around the room. "Is it even safe to be down here?"

"Do not worry, we reinforced the structural supports when we repaired the foundation. You will be perfectly safe," Bastien confirmed.

Claudine breathed a sigh of relief as all three of them shuffled a little farther into the space.

Jack turned to Elliott. "So, Mr. Schaffer, what's this big surprise you have to show us?"

Elliott motioned for me to step forward and said, "Floor's yours, Plum." Then he leaned in close, his warm breath brushing my ear as he whispered, "Remember, *be* the lion. You've got this."

He stepped to the side, leaving me center stage. Though I should've grown accustomed to the spotlight's glare by now, the white-hot intensity of this moment felt strikingly different. I steadied my voice and began. "I'm sure you're wondering what you're doing here? And, more to the point, where *here* even is? Look around; you are in the place where Château Mirabelle's story began and ended. Let me explain . . ."

And as I unraveled the long, winding, complicated, and tragic history of Château Mirabelle, Jack and Claudine became increasingly enthralled, their unwavering attention revealing that they had never heard any of this before—because they hadn't. As showrunner, Kate had been curating the material based on her vision, prioritizing falsehoods over the far more compelling and profound truth, most of which, according to Elliott, had ended up on the cutting-room floor.

The scene of me and Bastien examining the cracks on the cellar walls—cut! The footage of the crew working painstakingly to preserve the Adélaïse family crest—cut! The sequences of René walking me through the vineyard, explaining how the soil was still rich and fertile and how it might be brought back to life—cut! Anything that couldn't be used to trick the audience into believing Bastien and I were entwined in a messy, passionate, and intense love affair—cut! Everything that might suggest I wasn't the Plum Everly people had come to expect on TV—chaotic, reckless, aimless—cut! *Cut! Cut! Cut!* Until *Heart Restoration Project* was nothing more than another cliché reality TV show where genuine moments were thrown away to make room for the manufactured drama.

But it didn't have to be that way. *Heart Restoration Project* could be so much more—a show where humanity took center stage. It *could* be that, assuming I could get Jack and Claudine on board, and by the contemplative looks on their faces, that was far from a sure thing.

"I don't understand. Why wasn't any of this backstory included? Elliott, where's all that footage?" Jack demanded.

Elliott did a double take. Apparently Jack had completely forgotten the conversation in video village where he told Elliott that researching the house's history was a complete waste of time.

"Sir, as I recall, you weren't particularly interested in including anything in the show other than Plum and Bastien's romance," Elliott retorted as politely as his gruff nature would allow.

I stepped forward. "About that . . . I think it's only right that you know that Kate manufactured that relationship. She lied to me, and she lied to Bastien. She edited the storyline to make it seem as though we were a real couple."

"But you were a *real* couple. We all saw you off camera together. Nobody forced you to spend time with one another," Claudine fired back, her eyes now darting between the two of us.

Bastien cleared his throat. "I am not proud of my role in any of this. What I did, I did because I believed by being a part of this show, by helping to restore le château, I would somehow make amends for my grandfather's misdeeds. Kate cast me as her leading man, and I played along because I thought it was what the show needed to be a success. I believed Plum was in on it too. But as I recently discovered, she was not."

"Is that true?" Jack asked.

"Yes."

Claudine narrowed in on Bastien and me. "So you two? You're not? You never were—"

With an open palm, I gestured to explain. "The lines may have been blurry. They may have even been crossed once or twice. But the fantasy Kate was crafting was complete fiction, one I never signed on for. So what I want to do is take the narrative back and give it to the rightful storyteller, Château Mirabelle."

Claudine took two steps closer to me. "So, Mademoiselle Everly, what exactly did you have in mind?"

Over the next hour, I walked Jack and Claudine through my revamped version of the show. Elliott shared the clips we captured around Maubec, at Camp des Milles, and in the archives of Saint Orens. We showed them the interviews we'd conducted over our stay and the dozens of artifacts we'd painstakingly collected during any downtime we could find away from the show.

"This is a tale that has remained lost for more than eighty years. If you're looking for a hit, why not go with the unexpected? Plum Everly getting humiliated on a grand stage? Well, it's been done. More than once, in fact. And if I'm being candid, more than I care to remember. But what if all the intrigue, heartbreak, drama, and tension, what if it didn't need to be manufactured the way it is in so many reality shows? What if it didn't have to be staged, because it's already all here," I said, pointing to the stack of materials and research, which was more than enough to prove my point. "This history, although certainly devastating, is compelling and honest and is one that I know will affect an audience in a way that a cheesy, made-up love story never could. It's the difference between making entertainment and making art, making something fleeting versus making something that will remain a part of this town's story and could be part of Tributary's story long after it's aired." I surrendered a silent exhale and said, "Well, what do you think?"

Claudine eyed Jack, who stood with his arms crossed, as they both deeply considered my pitch.

Jack scrubbed at his chin and nodded his head. "This is going to require a bit more discussion and consideration on our part before we can say one way or the other what we'll decide to do. You've certainly given us a lot to consider, and in light of this new information, let's take a few days while they are putting the finishing touches on the house for filming, and we'll get back to you with a decision."

Less than forty-eight hours later, I received a text from the production team to meet them at Château Mirabelle so they could render their final decision. Though confident the idea to change the focus of the show from me to the château was a solid one, I was still plagued by doubt, knowing that salacious gotcha-style reality TV might, at least on its face, seem like more of a surefire hit. But when I spotted Kate carrying an armful of items and rolling her suitcase behind her as she made her way out of her trailer and through video village, my heart leaped at the notion she was leaving and hopefully taking her fake show and her even faker friendship with her.

With where I was positioned, concealed out of sight, I considered letting Kate disappear off into the sunset fairly confident (and content) our paths wouldn't cross again anytime soon. The timid lion I used to be would have stayed safely tucked away behind the large mirabelle tree until she was gone, but the brave lion I'd become needed to face her head-on and demand closure.

I stepped out onto the path, heading Kate off before she made it to the car that was waiting for her at the gate. Not sure what to say or how to even start, I just opened my mouth and hoped the right words would follow, but instead I uttered a simple, "We need to talk."

Kate rolled her suitcase in front of herself on the dusty road, the wheels kicking dirt onto her black pumps and up to the hem of her pencil skirt, and then set her belongings on top. "You must be pretty pleased with yourself. Hijacking my show *and* getting me fired, I really didn't think you had it in you." She slowly clapped her hands together, the pace more sardonic than celebratory. "Congratulations, they loved your pitch and decided to take the show in a whole new direction and scrapped everything I worked on, the entire brilliant concept. Such a shame, their shortsightedness. But hey, that's showbiz, right?" She smiled smugly, her attitude still oozing with poor-me energy.

"You really still think what you did was okay, don't you? You still believe that it was perfectly fine to tear me down in order to build yourself up?"

Her face looked hardened and unflappable as she held her ground. "I'll repeat what I said back at the château. You know how this game is played, Plum. You and your family practically invented how it works, and *you* continued playing long after everyone else had grown tired of it. So don't stand there on your soapbox and act like I did anything different than the rest of them. Christ, your own boyfriend sold you out with a sex tape. What exactly did you expect from me?"

As she continued to dig her heels in justifying her duplicity, my anger softened into pity shaded with a dull sadness for her. She would likely return to Hollywood and continue to hustle and grind, use people and fight to get ahead, having learned absolutely nothing from this incredible place or the people who inhabited it. And realizing that she'd missed it all made me even more grateful that I hadn't.

"What did I expect from you?" I repeated back to her, almost incredulous at the audacity of the question. "I expected better, that's what. I expected that as a woman, you would have understood that tape changed the way people saw me and worse, the way I saw myself. And I would have *expected* for you not to have exploited that vulnerability."

"Hold on, I really don't think—"

"Yes, you do. You know exactly what you did, and maybe you'll never be sorry for it. But it doesn't matter now because through this experience, I've learned to stand on my own two feet, and the promise you made to me when we first met about how I could reclaim the narrative came to fruition not because of you, but in spite of you. So it looks like, on this one and only score, you were telling the truth—I *do* get to write my own ending."

Kate grabbed for her belongings and the handle of her bag before lifting her chin a bit higher. "Au revoir, Plum."

"Au revoir, Ms. Wembley."

And with that, Kate turned on her sky-high heels and teetered down the path, back off to La-La Land.

Chapter Forty-Two

The gentle sunshine warmed my face and shoulders as a light summer breeze wafted in the faint aroma of lavender, wild thyme, and ripe plums—the garrigue I'd come so fondly to associate with Provence. I inhaled deeply and hurried down the front steps of Château Mirabelle to meet the Vespa I spotted turning off the road. René climbed off the motorbike and set his helmet on its seat before ambling up the driveway to meet me.

Now that Jack and Claudine were 100 percent on board with the show's new direction, Tributary had signed off on a few more weeks of filming for the fully reimagined *Heart Restoration Project*. Though Elliott was less than pleased to be working alongside Bastien, the three of us had agreed to a reconciliation in the name of shooting material worthy of the show now built around our new star, Château Mirabelle.

Bastien accepted the fact that, though his heart was in the right place, his prowess with a hammer and nails (among many other construction skills) left much to be desired. He stepped aside as foreman, and we decided to call in the professionals to whip the house into better shape for the real renovation effort. Now that the house was *actually* the show's real focus, all the smoke and mirrors needed to be replaced with drywall and support beams, and the crew would have to work tirelessly to make as many improvements as they could with the limited time and budget we had left.

"Monsieur Laroque," I said, extending my hand, "thank you so much for agreeing to meet with me. I can certainly understand why you may have wanted to rid yourself of this project completely."

"Please, Mademoiselle Everly, call me René."

"Plum, then, please," I said, placing my hand to my chest, and smiled. "René, I'm truly sorry for how you were treated. Bastien never had the skills necessary for a renovation like this one, and we are all in agreement you should have been project manager from the start."

"Well it seems, if the rumors are true, that I was not the only one . . . how do you say . . . dans la merde?"

"Dans la merde?" I thought for a second. "Um . . . screwed?"

His eyes brightened, and he lofted a finger in the air. "Oui! Yes, screwed! Tous les deux." He gestured between the two of us with an enthusiastic wave, and then, as if running out of steam, he just sighed. René dug into his back pocket, pulled out an iconic pack of Marlboro Reds, and tapped one into his fingers. With the other hand he brandished a lighter, igniting the thin white end, and drew in a lazy drag before blowing it into the breeze. He offered me one, and when I shook my head to politely refuse, he tucked the lighter into the cigarette box and shoved it back in his pants. "Besides, ce qui est fait est fait," he said, waving his hand in the air.

"What is done . . . is done?" I translated.

The corners of his mouth lifted. "Très bien. It is a shame you are going back to Californie just when your French lessons are starting to really pay off."

"Actually, I'm not sure I am going back to Californie, I mean California, at least not right away. In fact, that's what I wanted to speak with you about—in addition to the apology, of course—I don't quite think 'what's done *is* done.' As you may have heard, the merde hit the fan when Jack and Claudine found out about Kate's twist for the show, but we managed to pitch a different spin on how we can deliver an even more compelling season, and we were hoping you could help us bring it across the finish line."

"I don't know if I quite understand." His forehead and lips both puckered in confusion. "What, uh, exactly do you need from me?"

"We were given another three weeks of budget to cover whatever we can finish of the restoration. Also, to finish gathering as much footage and conducting the rest of the interviews to piece together with the material we already have. As you can see"—I gestured to the lumber and materials still strewn around the front of the property—"we don't quite have a fully renovated château. So I guess I need you to give it to me straight. What are we working with? Are we days away from being able to finish this thing?"

Taking a minute to digest it all, he inhaled a long drag and blew it out in a forceful stream of smoke as he nodded. "Do you want the looking-at-life-through-rose-colored-glasses answer or the truth?"

I pounded my chest and raised my chin a little higher. "Go ahead, hit me with the truth. Who knows? It might actually be a welcome change."

He took one last drag, then started walking and talking like he was leading a tour through the Louvre, and I realized I was supposed to try to keep up. "The biggest lift was the foundation. Fortunately, the explosives that were detonated through the house did more superficial damage than structural, and we were able to repair all of it." He motioned upward. "As you know, there was quite a bit of mold in the upper level bedroom walls on the south side of the house where the roof was the most compromis. We have removed it, replacing all the Sheetrock and beams."

"And the roof itself?"

"The slate roof is brand new, and we managed to keep it as close to the original as possible down to the copper nails. It took some doing, but I was even able to procure enough zinc to re-create the ridge work. And finally the plumbing," he said, sucking in air. "Luckily most of the piping was still in decent shape. We replaced the kinked or broken pipes and introduced hot water into the kitchen and toilettes."

So far this all sounded pretty encouraging. Given how erratic the construction had been, I was astounded by how much of the renovation was actually completed. "Okay, so then what wasn't touched?"

He exhaled. "We started the process of rewiring the house but weren't able to finish. Since they had the production lights for filming, it was made lower on the priority list." René motioned for me to follow him inside to the entranceway. "None of the stairways are up to code. They all need to be widened and reinforced."

"That doesn't sound *so* bad."

He frowned. "I am not fini. There's no central heating or air. Right now the only heat source for le château is the fireplaces."

"That's okay, right? Adds to the charm. The ambience," I said optimistically.

He continued, "Most of the floors we haven't replaced need to be stripped and resealed, as does every single window and door in the house—ninety-two total to be exact."

"The château has almost a hundred doors and windows?!"

"Look, Ms. Everly, by most standards the house is restored or will be in a couple of more weeks when the crew is finished. It will be a château much like the ones that stood proudly in Provence at the turn of the century. But if you are asking me if it is now a modern dwelling with modern conveniences ready for a family to live in or guests to stay in comfortably, the answer is no. Achieving that would take a substantial investment."

"How much of an investment? Like ballpark?"

His eyes looked upward as he did the calculations in his head, and when he settled on a figure, he blew out a raspberry at the enormity of it. "*Pfft* . . . ballpark? Off the top of my head? I'd say around three to four million euros." Four million euros?! Jeez, it may as well have been a unicorn horn or a leprechaun's pot of gold—just as valuable and seemingly just as unlikely.

"Come, let's go back outside for un moment, I have one more thing I want to show you," he said.

I followed him to the back of the house overlooking the vineyard.

"I shared a drainage proposal with Mademoiselle Wembley, but she was not interested in any work related to the winery," René said.

"What kind of proposal?"

"A vineyard must be tiled before planting. Tiling allows excess water to flow to a drainage ditch and away from the vineyard. It is quite expensive, but also quite necessary, especially with the heavy rains we have been experiencing in Provence these last few years."

"What does something like that cost?"

"It is about four thousand euros an acre."

"Okay, that seems reasonable. How many acres is this vineyard?"

"Hmm, a little over sixty."

I did some quick calculations in my head. "So you're telling me it's about a quarter million euros to tile the vineyard?" That was like six times the amount of all my combined winnings from every reality competition I'd been on!

"With labor probably closer to three hundred thousand euros," he said, grabbing for my elbow when his answer almost bowled me over. "But I say all this to tell you, that this land—this terroir—is a worthy investment if you can find someone who can cultivate it back into a vineyard again. And for certain, it can be thriving and flowing and wonderful, but it will take some real money and quite a lot of hard work." René dropped his arms to his sides. "Plum, may I ask you a question? Do you really understand what you would be taking on if you decided to revive Château Mirabelle to her fullest potential?"

"Don't you mean that *we're* taking on?" I asked him with a hopeful smile and a curved brow.

"Oh? I'm sorry? I'm not sure I understand?"

"We. That *we* are taking on together . . . that is, if you will stay on and be project manager? I know deep down you love this house as much as I do. I know that's why you fought so hard to make sure Bastien did right by it."

"Plum, I do not think you can afford me."

"No, you're right. I can't afford you. But I'll figure something out. Château Mirabelle deserves the best, n'est pas?"

He surveyed the house with careful scrutiny, taking his time before answering, "Oui, yes, you may count me in."

"Merci," I exhaled gratefully.

"Good, and now that I am signed on, let's go remove all that vulgaire silver inlay," René exclaimed, marching off in the direction of the front door.

After René left, I found Elliott cozied up with his laptop on one of the sofas, bulbous headphones on top of his Kansas City Chiefs ball cap, in the grand salon. Perhaps hearing my footsteps or just sensing someone else in the room, he looked up from the screen.

"So," he asked, "what was René's verdict?"

"The house will be in really good shape for the show, but there's still a ton of work to be done for us to make her the heart of Maubec again. He's agreed to help, which is a pretty big win. It's still a huge undertaking, though." I slumped down on the couch beside him.

"Don't get ahead of yourself. One step at a time. We'll find a way," Elliott said, resting his hand on my leg as I snuggled into him.

I motioned toward his computer. "What's that you're working on?"

He sat upright. "It's the rough cut of all the footage we captured. Plum, your eye is spot-on. The best moments are the ones that you directed," he said, clicking the play button on the video. Suddenly, we were back in the Room of Murals at Camp des Milles with Hélène, the camera panning over the walls of art, zeroing in on the small details that humanized it. He zipped through more of the footage, stopping on certain scenes and exchanges to point out how my instinct enriched and enhanced each moment.

"It's really good, isn't it?" I said.

"It really is," he agreed, meeting my gaze.

"Remember on the carousel—"

"When you said you wanted to be me? How could I forget, it was the first time you said anything to me even slightly resembling a compliment," Elliott joked.

"I don't know if that was technically a compliment . . . ," I teased. "I'm pretty sure you just misheard me. But yes, when I said I wanted to do what you do—to be the one behind the camera instead of in front of it. I want to work on projects that matter and subjects I care about. I never felt more myself than I have here in Provence, and I want to find more stories to breathe new life into." I reached for his hand and nervously let the words spill out before I could stop myself, "And . . . and I want you and I to set off with our cameras and tell them . . . *together*."

He took a thoughtful half second before responding, a sweet smile gracing his face. "Where do I sign?"

Pushing his computer onto the cushions and out of the way, I leaped onto his lap and peppered his face with silly, sweet kisses—one to his cheek, his other cheek, his nose, his neck—each little smooch like the popping of champagne bubbles. He rolled me over, pinning me under him, and returned the playful affection, to the sound of my laughter. His eyes twinkled with mischief as he continued to press his lips over the exposed skin of my collarbone.

Elliott planted one last kiss before shifting back beside me and sighed. "As much as I would prefer to do *this* for the rest of our time in France, we should probably focus our attention on getting Château Mirabelle finished like you said."

"You don't happen to have a cool four million lying around, do you?"

He jokingly looked under the couch cushions and then patted down his pockets. "Sorry, other pants. What about you? You holdin' out on me, Everly?"

"Maybe? I mean, well, *I* certainly don't have that kind of dough. But I do know a few people who might. The thing is, I'm not sure if they'll go for it?"

Elliott passed me my phone from off the side table. "And I say, there's only one way to find out . . ."

Chapter Forty-Three

A few hours later and I hadn't made the call yet. I needed more time to practice my pitch so that my parents didn't think this was yet another one of my wild (and historically fleeting) ideas, but rather a solid investment with real potential for the future. Unfortunately, though, time was of the essence. With the finale airing in just a few weeks and the renovation budget practically tapped, I needed to find some more lifeblood for this project if Château Mirabelle was ever going to be truly restored back to its former glory. I held my phone tightly to my chest and looked at Elliott. "They're going to think I'm calling to ask for money."

From over his laptop, his blue eyes, bright with the illumination from the screen, lifted from the footage he was still editing. "Well, you kind of *are* calling to ask for money."

I shot him a look. "Not helping."

He lowered his MacBook screen and turned to me. "You have a solid business plan. Walk your parents through it exactly the way you just walked me through it. They'll see the potential in the château and the winery. It's all there. Really."

I took a deep breath and hit the dial button before I could change my mind. A few rings later, Dad answered.

"Plumkin, is that you?" he asked, clearing his throat. It was obvious I'd woken him up. "Everything okay? What time is it?"

"Here or there?"

"Both?"

"It's five p.m. here, so eight a.m. in California."

"Your mother must've let me sleep in," he said through a yawn. "What's going on? We haven't heard much from you these past few weeks, just a few texts here and there. How are things? Très bien, I hope," he chirped in a distinctively Californian accent.

"I'm . . . I'm actually pretty good, all things considered . . ."

Silence on the other end.

"Um . . . Dad? You still there?"

"'All things considered' *what*?" he urged. "I'm on the edge of my seat . . . or should I say, my bed. I was just waiting for you to continue. I wasn't sure if you were just embracing a dramatic pause or something . . . you just never know with you girls," he joked.

"Fair point, but not the case today. Actually, it's a bit of a long story, really. One that I was wondering . . . if you'd want to hear in person?"

Panic flooded his voice. "Oh God, are you in some sort of trouble?"

Scoffing, I sighed. "No, Dad, thankfully, not today. But I do have an idea—a business proposal—I wanted to run by you and Mom, and then maybe, if you think it to be worthwhile, I'll tell you the rest over a bottle of white . . . when you come to visit me here in France?" I lifted the end of my question to accentuate my request with an air of hope.

"Okay, you've got my attention. Let me get your mother on the phone."

Over the next forty-five minutes, I walked my parents through my plan. Once I was finished filming the new, more historically focused finale, Jack and Claudine (in payment for my emotional anguish and probably so I didn't sue the hell out of the studio) had promised to honor the agreement of letting me keep the deed to the estate once we wrapped. I'd also managed to negotiate that 2 percent of the residuals from *Heart Restoration Project*'s current airing season, all its streaming content, and any subsequent syndication would go toward keeping the property operational once it was up and running. But it might be months, possibly even years, before we saw any of that money.

The show's remaining restoration budget would address as many structural elements as possible, but as René pointed out, we'd barely be scratching the surface. The most obvious solution was to bring in my family as silent partners in the estate. They'd expand their B and B business portfolio into the European market, an idea they'd been aspiring to for years, and Château Mirabelle would become a full-service hotel with a fully operational winery my father would manage. It had the potential to be a win for all, if they agreed.

"So what do you think? If you don't want to be involved, I understand and will look for different investors, but one way or another, I am going to make this happen."

I'm not sure if he could sense the resolve in my voice, the sincerity of my ask, or the clarity of my conviction, but without a moment's hesitation, he said, "What do I think? I think we'll see you in France at the end of the month."

Almost four weeks later, the entire Everly family descended on the quiet out-of-the-way village of Maubec, France. It didn't take long for them to fall in love with the beautiful scenery, the warmth of the people, and most of all, Château Mirabelle. As they stepped onto the estate's cobblestone path, my father, ever the practical one, took in the impressive structure with a critical eye. He could see the potential, his excitement growing with every step.

I gave him a full tour of the house, starting in the fully rebuilt and refurbished wine cellars all the way up through the attics. A jaunt that should've taken about an hour took closer to three as Dad stopped to examine every piece of crown molding, every pane of stained glass, each elaborate fireplace, and, I swear, the framework on all ninety-two doors and windows.

"Dad, it's just another door," I said, dragging him from the library.

"Do you see that wainscoting? That's *not* just another door. That door is a thing of beauty."

"If you like that door, wait till you see the wood trellis out in the garden. Arches, lattice designs, carvings . . . the works," I teased. "C'mon, we've been inside all morning, let's take in some of that fresh Provençal air."

I guided my father, our arms linked, as we strolled leisurely through the expansive garden, passing beneath the magnificent trellis as promised, a weathered oak structure adorned with climbing roses and wisteria clusters, and then made our way to the vineyard.

"It's only been a few months away from home, and yet I feel like I have a lifetime to fill you in on," I said to Dad, linking my arm through his as we strolled through the narrow rows of grapevines.

"How about just the highlight reel then?"

"Elliott—who I can't wait for you to meet—edited the finale and sent it off just a few days ago, and apparently the test groups responded *even better* to this version than Kate's. The history angle, the town angle, the mystery of it all. They loved it. They loved it so much that the producers have already greenlit a second season. They want me and Elliott to visit some of the other châteaus that were part of the Dutch-Paris network and tell *their* stories. And I want to say yes, but first I need to know what you think about Château Mirabelle now that you've seen her? About my plan? Cause I won't abandon her. I will see this thing through."

Dad grinned from behind his hand as he rubbed the salt-and-pepper scruff on his cheek. He bent down to the ground, scooping a fistful of dirt into his hand. "Your friend René, he told me this land is still rich with minerals and ready to be a vineyard again. You know, I still haven't been able to produce a decent white in Ojai, but I think with the right vintner, we may just be able to do that here. What do I think? I think this place is every bit as magical as you described it, and . . ." He took a beat, as if a wave of emotion was making it difficult for him to speak. "And I think I've never seen my daughter so passionate and so self-assured about anything in her life." With his free hand he dabbed a bent knuckle into his tear duct, and then he said, "It's good to see you again, Plumkin. I knew you were still in there somewhere."

And all of a sudden, my dad looked like a much younger version of himself, and I leaped back in time to the days before *EVERLYday* became a hit, reminiscing about the girl I used to be—innocent and wide-eyed, brimming with dreams and unbridled optimism, wide open to a world of endless possibilities. A time before my TV persona assumed control of the wheel, racing me forward without even so much as a glance in the rearview mirror.

I fought back my own tears, turned to my dad, and asked, "So you'll do it? You'll invest in Château Mirabelle?"

"No," he replied, "but I *will* invest in Plum Everly."

To hear my father say those words after so many years of feeling like a failure and the black sheep of the Everly family was more gratifying and fulfilling than I could have even imagined. A lump of emotion formed in my chest, and I touched my fingers to it, relishing in the feeling. I spent so many years searching for myself—on television, in Rhys, in public opinion. Who would have ever thought I would finally find what I was looking for six thousand miles away in a sleepy small town in France.

As we stood there in the shadow of the cherished house that had stolen my heart, surrounded by the splendor of Provence and the towering mirabelle trees, I emerged from under their comforting shade, took a few steps forward, and allowed the sun's brilliant and golden light to wash over me.

Epilogue

I gladly welcomed the cooler temperatures October brought with it. And on one particularly temperate day, the breeze blew through the hills of Provence and through the open windows of Château Mirabelle, puffing the drapes gently with each easy gust.

I checked my watch again. Monsieur Grenouille and Madame Archambeau were by no means late for our housewarming but hadn't yet arrived. I also managed to convince Agnès, Pascal, and Odette to leave the inn in the very capable hands of Pascal's nephew for the afternoon and come meet my family and celebrate with us the *real* completion of Château Mirabelle. As my special guests for the day, theirs was the arrival I was most looking forward to.

Pear was bustling about in the kitchen putting the final touches on the platters of amuse-bouches she prepared from her latest bestselling cookbook, *Think Global, Eat EVERLYthing Local.* In the vineyard, Peach was finishing the tablescapes set upon large hand-carved wooden tables crafted from rustic white beech. But one of my favorite sights of all was watching my father strolling around the vineyard with René and Bastien, inspecting the vines and branches, intrigued by the nuances of the grapes and soil.

It seemed Château Mirabelle had brought us all together in more ways than one. Before my journey to France, I would have never in a million years believed my family would ever consider me to be an equal player on their team. But as we all bustled about, contributing our own little touches and individual talents, Château Mirabelle became a reflection of us all. And as if swept away by one of the breezy gusts, all the heartache for the years of judgment and hurt I'd felt as the outlier of my family disappeared, and instead, the frustration was replaced by fierce gratitude. I felt lucky to have them and, finally, their support. Maybe I'd had it all along, and just wasn't able to see it since I was so focused on being the one who didn't fit in. But we were sisters. We were family. And amid each one running their own multizillion-dollar company, they dropped everything to come to share their talents with me and Château Mirabelle, and for that, I couldn't be more grateful.

At last, I heard the engine of a car make its way up the driveway, and I hurried out to meet our guests. As they all climbed out, I stood on the steps of the grand entranceway and announced, "Bienvenue tout le monde. Je vous présente le Château Mirabelle," and then I offered an over-the-top gesture. And as if on cue, my sisters pulled the doors open from inside to reveal a spectacular view straight through the château to the salon lined in floor-to-ceiling windows, through which rolled the picturesque vineyards below. The sun streamed through the windows in wide, hazy beams, almost like a benediction.

My mom, ever(*ly*) the hostess, was eager to say hello to our guests and rushed to introduce herself. She unloaded Monsieur Grenouille's hands, full of pastry boxes tied with red ribbons, and set them down on the table. "Peach, can you get a tray for these?"

Madame Archambeau handed a lovely bouquet of sunflowers to Lemon, who said, "These are gorgeous. We'll put them into a vase to use as a centerpiece." And finally, Agnès, Pascal, and Odette offered up several bottles of wine, which Kiwi gratefully carried into the kitchen to be chilled for dinner.

They all continued inside, and I puffed out my chest proudly before I spoke. "Permettez-moi de vous de vous présenter les lieux, s'il vous plaît."

Pascal's eyes twinkled proudly. "Ma belle, look at you speaking perfect French. You have been my very best étudiante."

"To be fair, I think I was your only student," I joked.

He chuckled too. "Mais oui, but still. You should be très fière. You are not the same girl you were when you arrived, non?"

"I am proud, really. And thank you for saying that. Thank you all for everything." I spoke the words and, one at a time, I met the eyes of my new friends, trying to impress upon each of them the profound impact they had on me during my few short months in Provence.

Elliott stepped forward. "Actually, we have some great news to share with all of you. *Heart Restoration Project* has been such a big hit for Tributary that they greenlit a second season of the series to follow up on the role the Dutch-Paris network played in the Resistance across Europe. Plum and I will be leaving in a few weeks to start filming."

"We will miss you but, tu es un membre de notre famille, Prune. Pour toujours," Agnès said.

Mom elbowed me and whispered, "Prune? Did she just call you Prune?"

Tears welled in my eyes. Yes, we would be famille for always. I surveyed the foyer again, my family—both real and chosen—scattered around the space, and I was overcome with emotion. "Okay, okay, before I get myself all sappy, I want to show you the rest of the renovation! Venez, venez—on y va!"

I proceeded to show everyone all the nooks and crannies of the château, including the stunning eat-in kitchen with an adjacent dining area that looked out over the expansive landscape. The space was kept in the style true to the rustic provincial decor but was upgraded with state-of-the-art appliances disguised with adornments and cabinetry to maintain the illusion that they were all original fixtures and features.

Odette leaned against the kitchen island and said, "Plum, this is incredible. I'm truly speechless. After our conversation about Kate and the show and how the château was being left uninhabitable, I thought you would have cut your losses and run. I was so sure you'd try to sell it. When you told us you'd be staying in Maubec a bit longer to complete the renovations, I never could have imagined that this is what you had in mind. It's . . . it's parfait."

Monsieur Grenouille chimed in, "And after all the work you and Elliott put into learning about Château Mirabelle and its history, you should be proud to know that you have returned this landmark to the people of Maubec. It is no longer an eyesore, a difficult reminder of the past. It is reinvigorated, and bright, and represents all the things that Maubec can be once again. This château was never just a building, it's been a symbol for this town for as long as we can remember. After the war, it hurt too much for us to try to repair her. It felt like the wreckage was a necessary reminder of our pain and our history—all our family members and their sacrifice. And since the moment they blew it up, it's been withering away every day, taking with it the spirit of Maubec. But it's shiny, new, and most importantly, full of life. You did that. *You*, Plum. You gave us back our heart."

The tears were now freely falling, and I was unable to speak past the lump in my throat. Once I managed to swallow it down, I addressed everyone before me. "So we've prepared a delicious meal to share outside in the vineyard. Well, not so much *we*. Probably much to the delight of all of you, I left that task up to Pear, our resident kitchen wizard, to dazzle us with her cuisine, fresh from the château's gardens."

I led everyone through the flower-covered trellis; through the herb garden, fragrant with a mix of fresh mint, lavender, and basil; and out to the patio adorned with an elaborate tablescape of bright yellows and ocean blues. Tall glass vases filled with fresh lemons and sprigs of rosemary towered over the serving dishes piled high with charred vegetables, colorful sauces, and flaky fish fillets served over fluffy pearled couscous and white raisins. Between the spread of food, the eye-catching decor, and the breathtaking view, the scene looked like something straight out of a magazine spread. I considered for a moment drawing out my phone to snap a picture of the moment, but instead, I chose not to, simply taking it in, trying to hold on to every single morsel of its sweet perfection, just for me. My chest swelled with a sense of pride and gratitude when, from the corner of my eye, I saw my mom carrying out a tray of champagne flutes. I knew that was my cue.

Making their way up from the vineyards, Dad, René, and Bastien palled around as they ambled up the dusty path, Dad beaming like an excited child on Christmas. Flurries of excitement started to dance in my stomach, and I could barely contain myself for another minute. I waited for everyone to take their seats and took my place at the head of the long table. Mom, having set a flute next to everyone's place, made it around to hand me the last glass. I gave her a quick kiss on the cheek, which she returned with a wink, and then I faced the table to raise my champagne high. I realized my hands were shaking, half with nerves and half with excitement, almost feeling like I was back on the finale of *Love Lagoon* or *Celebrity Ballroom*, all the stakes finally laid bare. But this wasn't TV, this was reality. And damn if it didn't feel even better.

"When *Heart Restoration Project* finished airing, this château was in much better condition, but still not everything I'd hoped for, everything I knew it could be. There was still so much work to be done—the bones were back, but it still lacked all the things that make a home really come to life. After everything I'd learned about what happened here and everyone I'd met to whom this place meant something, I knew I had to finish what we started."

I moved around behind the chairs to step between my parents, who were beaming at me proudly, and placed my hand on my dad's shoulder, a gesture of gratitude for our collaboration and partnership. "I asked my family to invest in this property and help restore it to its full potential. You all know it had never been my plan to stay in Maubec. But after falling in love with the town and this house, apparently fate had an entirely different idea in mind." I couldn't help but flash a quick and meaningful glance at Elliott before continuing. "One that I am hoping Agnès and Pascal will want to be a part of."

Agnès and Pascal looked up from their plates as if caught by surprise to hear their names.

"After careful consideration, we've realized Château Mirabelle needs a *real* caretaker. Someone who can be here full time to oversee the hotel and winery. Someone who knows how to manage a property like this, knows the town and the people, and someone who loves all those things just as much as we do. I thought perhaps the two of you might want to live here and run it. Everything is brand new, so there wouldn't be much maintenance to worry about like at La Cigale Chantante. The truth is, I can't think of two better people to entrust this endeavor to."

It was clear that the Sauveterres were overcome with emotion, but none more so than Odette, who had her hand pressed to her chest and her eyes full of tears. She'd been ready and willing to sacrifice her own dreams to help keep her parents' struggling inn afloat, but now she wouldn't have to. She could return to Paris and resume her studies knowing her parents would be able to stay in Maubec with their friends to enjoy the life they loved, and most of all, they'd be "caretakers" of the château but not left to shoulder the burden alone. They'd have help and support to manage the property, while being able to step away from the day-to-day upkeep—something I knew that their sore backs and rickety knees very much appreciated.

I turned to look at Bastien. "I have one other proposition I'd like to make. Two generations ago, Sébastien Munier played a pivotal role in transforming Château Mirabelle into one of the most successful vineyards in Maubec. His treacherous actions are well documented, but few are aware of the price his grandson has had to pay for his sins." I shifted my eyes to gaze at Monsieur Grenouille. "Letting go of the past can be a formidable challenge, a lesson I have learned firsthand, but we must if we are going to have a better future."

A soft smile broke over Monsieur Grenouille's face as he nodded in understanding. "So, Bastien, will you agree to be the estate's vintner?" I asked.

"Is this a blague? A joke?"

"No, it's not a joke. Not even a little. I spoke with my father, and we need a master vintner, someone who knows this land and this terroir better than anyone. If you can bring the same passion and nuance to this vineyard's wine as you have with your own, well, Dad, you might finally get that award-winning white. We want to make this property and its vineyard the pride of Maubec once again. So, Bastien, what do you say?" I eyed him next to René, who gave him a spirited and congratulatory pat on the back.

Tears welled up in Bastien's eyes, and he struggled to form words. But his silence spoke volumes. Maybe now he'd finally be able to unburden himself of his family's legacy and create a brand-new one that was all his own.

"I know I'm leaving Château Mirabelle in fantastic hands"—I gestured to the end of the table where the Sauveterres and Bastien were still reeling with the news—"as I head off on this next adventure with Elliott." He tilted his flute to me and smiled. "So I guess there's nothing more to say except Bon—"

"Just a second, Plumkin," Dad interrupted, "if I may?"

I waved him on to continue, but he'd stepped away from the table for a moment to pull a large cardboard box from where it had sat out of sight.

With no room for it on the table, he placed the box down at my feet and stood before opening it. "Plum, we are so proud of you. This entire undertaking and what you have done with it . . . we know you have given it your whole heart. So your mom and I got to thinking, and, of course, we asked Elliott for some help, but we thought, after all Château Mirabelle has been through, it deserved to be renamed to celebrate its rebirth." He pulled out a stack of white linen napkins, the words *Château Adélaïse* embroidered in a soft lavender script. Below the name was the stitched outline of a proud and fearless lion, taken directly from their family crest. "Château Adélaïse," he announced with a flourish. "Has a nice ring to it, don't you think?"

Emotion swelled tight in my throat, and I swiped at a tear that had managed to squeak out. "I think . . . it is absolutely perfect."

"Then it's settled," Dad exclaimed, and lifted his champagne glass. "To Château Adélaïse!" he called.

To which everyone at the table enthusiastically raised their flutes and cried, "To Château Adélaïse!"

Later that night, after everyone had gone home and my family was relaxing inside, Elliott and I remained the only two people left in the vineyard. Snuggled under a blanket on a double-seated rocker overlooking the property, we soaked in one of our very last sunsets in Provence before we flew out to Geneva in a few days to start working on the "much-anticipated" second season of *Heart Restoration Project*. The back terrace of the winery featured tables made of wine barrels positioned throughout the space tucked under a canopy of string lights.

Elliott chuckled. "Kinda funny to have a winery with no wine . . . yet. Madame Archambeau barreled through most of what the Sauveterres brought for dinner."

I surveyed the acres of vineyard that sprawled far and wide and said, "Someday soon the wine here will be overflowing. But in the meantime . . ." I reached for a wine tote I'd set at my feet, slid one of the bottles from it, and held it up to Elliott. "Bastien brought us these from his private collection. He said that he was inspired by the mirabelle trees here at the château, and played around with the infusion of plum in this new blend. He said he thinks it's one of his best yet."

Elliott asked, "What was that thing Bastien said about the mirabelle when we first met him here?"

"If I remember right, he said something like, 'The mirabelle is a rare fruit that truly flourishes in this part of France,'" I answered, combing through my memory.

"Hmm." He turned and gazed lovingly into my eyes. "On this one and only score, I would say he is absolutely correct, ma mirabelle."

"Yes, ta mirabelle toujours. Your mirabelle always." I poured two glasses of the wine and held mine up to Elliott. "So what are we drinking to?"

He looked at me and then out at the orange sun melting lower and lower into the purple and pink clouds that floated on the horizon. The glow of the sunset warmed his smiling face, and he said, "To second chances and new beginnings."

"I'll drink to that," I said and took a long pull from my cup.

"Holy sweet Jesus," Elliott exclaimed and reeled back, staring at his wineglass in awe. "This is good, like *really* good. And you know I'm not a big fan of Bastien's. But seriously, this is phenomenal."

Elliott took another gulp and shook his head incredulously. Between each sip he would mutter some expletive of disbelief, but only after moaning with delight at its incredibly smooth and delicate taste.

"I can't wait to tell him you loved it," I said.

"Don't you even think about it! That guy needs a bigger head like I need a pair of stilettos," Elliott joked.

I chuckled and snuggled deeper into his chest. "So, Mr. Shaffer, are you ready for our next big adventure?"

He pressed his lips to the top of my head. "I have a feeling that every day with you is going to be a new adventure."

I turned my face up to his and pulled him down for a kiss. "We can only hope."

I kissed him again, running my hand up his cheek, and then rested my head on his shoulder, watching the golden sun set over Provence to the serene sound of singing cicadas.

ACKNOWLEDGMENTS

From Beth:

A heartfelt thank-you to my superhero husband, whose unwavering support and willingness to shoulder the load have allowed me the precious time to write. I couldn't do this without you, and I wouldn't want to. You are my rock. My "write or die," Danielle, who handled all this book's French (thank God!): I couldn't imagine being on this crazy ride with anyone else. And finally, as always, my beautiful Hadley Alexandra, ma mirabelle.

From Danielle:

It's always hard to adequately put my gratitude into sufficient enough words, but from the bottom of my heart, I want to thank my family and friends, near and far, who have been so supportive of me and this crazy journey. Writing and publishing really aren't easy to describe to those who aren't in it, but no matter how odd my path has seemed, they've been behind me every step. For those of you who have not only allowed me to be me but have celebrated my victories and picked me up from my many stumbles, I cannot thank you enough. To Mash and Haddie, my family away from home: Haddie Bean, thank you for sharing your mom with me and for all our *Nailed It!* binge-watches and makeover sessions! And to Mash: You have been a constant source of positivity and laughter. Thank you for welcoming me in as family, for your "small duffel" contributions, and for the Diet Coke and iced coffee you always keep stocked in the fridge for me—you truly are our glue. And to Beth—my other half: This whole thing has been such a wild ride. To consider how far we've come and how much we've been through since the minute you signed with FHP is a point of pride and true joy that I know, even though I can't describe, you understand. Of course you do, we share a brain! I wouldn't want to do this alone, but to be doing it with you has truly *made* the entire experience. Here's to hoping this is just the beginning.

From Both:

Thank you to Maria Gomez and Montlake for taking another chance on us. Angela James, our incredible developmental editor, for helping to whip this manuscript into shape! Finally, our agent, Jill Marsal, for believing in this book long before anyone else did and for pulling it—and us—out of the slush pile. And for our incredible readers and fans: Thank you for your excitement, enthusiasm, kind words, and shout-outs. You are why we write, and to know you are enjoying all the hard work we've put into our stories makes it all worthwhile. Follow us on social media and come say hello @merlinandmod, or visit our website, www.merlinandmod.com.

ABOUT THE AUTHORS

Beth Merlin earned her BA from the George Washington University and her juris doctor from New York Law School. A lifelong New Yorker, Beth loves anything Broadway, romantic comedies, and a good maxi dress. When she isn't writing, you can find her spending time with her husband, daughter, and two cavapoos, Sophie and Scarlett, at home or at their favorite vacation spot, Kiawah Island, South Carolina.

Danielle Modafferi, a high school English teacher and pun enthusiast, earned her MFA in writing popular fiction from Seton Hill University and, shortly after, founded Firefly Hill Press in 2016. By day, she helps her students discover the magic of language, and by night, she's a writer and publisher on a mission to unleash her creativity and help others do the same. Danielle loves making memories with friends and family, traveling to faraway (and some not-so-faraway) places, and snuggling with her two dogs, Jackson and Liam, who are also incidentally her biggest fans.